*For Julia, the angel looking
over my shoulder.*

....

*With thanks to Teri Ahlstrom, Joel Bezaire,
Neva Cheatwood, Jim deJonge, Jocelyn Pihlaja,
and John Sellers for their unwavering
support and invaluable assistance.*

PROLOGUE

To Your Holiness, the High Council of the Seraphim,

Greetings from your humble servant, Ederatz,
Cherub First Class,
Order of the Mundane Observation Corps

The first thing you'll notice about this report is that it's written in English. I have to apologize for that; after a few millennia on Earth I'm a little rusty in High Seraphic. Also, while the language of the angels is incontrovertibly more melodious than any earth-bound tongue, it lacks a number of words which are central to the telling of a story of such epic grandeur, such as *linoleum*, *ping-pong*, and *dickweed*.

I have abandoned the anapestic tetrameter form traditionally used for these reports, as it is surprisingly difficult to adapt to English. I got as far as:

> White balls bouncing in the house of the one
> And the corners of linoleum are peeling in the sun

I think this couplet has a certain epic feel to it, but on the downside it took me three weeks to write. In addition, I'm afraid this account has a bit more moral ambiguity than is really suited for the traditional form. I know, I'm supposed to clear up the gray areas and present things in black and white, but you'd be amazed at how complicated things have gotten here recently. In fact, it's hard to even know what bits to include in the story. Who's the main character? What's the point of the story? Could it be adapted into a TV movie? Your guess is as good as mine. Although it is true that HBO has expressed some interest.

Until now relations between Heaven and the Mundane Plane have been a one-way street. To us it was all about following the all-important Schedule of Plagues, Announcements, and Miracles. We made little adjustments here and there to keep history moving in the right direction, but we never actually got involved in what was going on. I'm sure you're familiar with the motto of the Mundane Observation Corps: *Eternally Objective.* I always took this motto very seriously. Many of my fellow cherubim tend, in fact, to be objective to the point of downright hostility.

Mercury was not, of course, an agent of the MOC. Mercury got his hands dirty on countless occasions. But in a way the motto applies even more to angels in his position. It was understood that whatever he did, he was expected above all not to *care.* I suppose you could see his actions as the logical consequence of that philosophy.

On the other hand, what do I know? You're the ones making the important decisions. I suppose you have agents trying to track down Mercury as you're reading this, and you probably have a pretty good idea of what you're going to do when—or if—you find him. Or maybe you're reading this with an open mind, hoping to find the answers to all the big questions. What was he trying to accomplish? On whose authority was he acting? Did he really build a snowman the height of a three-story building? And of course, what you need in order to answer those questions is a completely objective account of events.

Too bad I can't give you one.

As you know, the Mundane Observation Corps has access to a staggering amount of information; our agents are everywhere, recording anything of interest that happens on the Mundane Plane. This information is, however, useless unless it is framed in some kind of coherent narrative. In the past, the frame has been provided for us; the MOC has always been able to rely on the inexorable unfolding of the Divine Plan.

Like it or not, however, the events of this story have broken this frame. I've had to create my own frame, based on my own understanding of events. Your frame is sure to be different. I guess that's the one thing I'd like you to keep in mind as you read this. This report isn't just a book full of facts for you to absorb. As you read it, you're inevitably going to try to incorporate it into your own frame.

Good luck figuring it all out.

But of that day and hour knoweth no man, no, not the angels of heaven, but my Father only.

Matthew 24:36 (King James Version)

The results of this study indicate that the month of September of the year 1994 is to be the time for the end of history...Look, let's put it this way. My wife came to me and said we needed new linoleum in the kitchen. I told her that we should hold off on the effort and the expense of doing it until October or November of 1994.

The Reverend Harold Camping, in 1991

What if everything is an illusion and nothing exists? In that case, I definitely overpaid for my carpet.

Woody Allen

ONE

The Apocalypse has a way of fouling up one's plans. To its credit, humanity has done its best to anticipate the End of Days, but lacking any basis for a reliable timetable, they've jumped the gun on more than a few occasions. The Apocalypse's stubborn refusal to arrive on schedule has caused no end of trouble for the people who have volunteered to announce its arrival. Those waiting at the metaphorical arrival gate for the Four Horsemen of the Apocalypse are forced to eat a lot of metaphorical crow. And pay for a lot of metaphorical flooring.

As you'll recall from some of the early reports produced by our organization, Saint Clement I was one of the first to predict an imminent Apocalypse, around 90 AD. He went around for several years telling the masses that the end was near. The masses responded by making him into a boat anchor. Once he was out of the way, they were free to replace their old linoleum.

A Roman priest and theologian once used the dimensions of Noah's ark to predict that Christ would return in 500 AD. When 500 ended with a whimper rather than a bang, he was forced to admit it was time to retile his foyer.

Later Christian scholars argued that Christ would wait for the odometer to flip before returning in glory. Never mind that they were using the wrong year for Christ's birth; if it were up to them, there would have been a massive run on flooring materials at the beginning of the second millennium. The Great Linoleum Shortage of 1001 AD was forestalled only by the near universal inability to read a calendar.

Pope Innocent III was convinced that the Apocalypse would arrive on the 666th anniversary of the birth of Islam. The pope's regard for Mohammed notwithstanding, the mountain failed to arrive. He gave in and replaced the wood flooring in the Vatican with ceramic tile.

In 1669, the Old Believers in Russia barely avoided an expensive flooring upgrade by immolating themselves. This was before the days of zero-interest financing.

The Jehovah's Witnesses nearly single-handedly prompted the rationing of flooring materials at various points in the late nineteenth and twentieth centuries, with Apocalypses scheduled for 1891, 1914, 1915, 1918, 1920, 1925, 1941, 1975, and 1994.

After two thousand years of this, most people had grown a little jaded regarding the prospect of an imminent Armageddon. Predictions of The End became so common by the dawn of the third millennium that homeowners no longer thought twice about installing new flooring weeks or even days before a scheduled Apocalypse.

So it was not for lack of warning that Christine Temetri, an otherwise intelligent young woman who had recently purchased a nine-hundred-square-foot condo in Glendale, California, made the astoundingly ill-advised decision to have new linoleum installed in her breakfast nook only days before the Apocalypse was scheduled to start. Her decision was, if anything, the result of an overwhelming surfeit of warnings.

The latest of these warnings came from one Reverend Jonas Bitters, First Prophet of the Church of the Bridegroom. Jonas Bitters was a former recreational vehicle salesman who had, through a combination of spurious scriptural exegesis, excessive reliance on Google's automated Hebrew-to-English translation service, and mathematical errors that could have been caught by a bright third grader, happened upon a date for the End of Days that was within a hair of being accurate. When one considers that most eschatological timetables were off by decades—if not centuries or even millennia—Bitters was so close to the correct date that speculation has arisen in certain corners of Heaven as to whether he was somehow guided in his feverish stacking of errors by the Almighty Himself. Advocates of this theory point to the fact that if Bitters had not forgotten to carry the one in a certain equation, he would have been dead-on. Skeptics point out that if he had correctly counted the number of letters in YHWH, he would have been off by another eighty years.

The fact is that in cosmological terms, Jonas Bitters was about as close to dead-on as one could possibly hope for. Unfortunately for him, human beings tend not to think in cosmological terms— especially when those human beings have been standing on a plateau twenty miles outside of Elko, Nevada, for eight hours. Even Christine Temetri, who had the foresight to bring a lawn chair, a down jacket, a penlight, a book of expert-level crossword puzzles, and the lowest of expectations, was getting antsy about the amount of nothing that was happening. She did, however, have to give up some begrudging admiration for Jonas Bitters, whose enthusiasm remained undiminished in the wee morning hours.

The First Prophet stood some twenty yards from Christine, surveying the culmination of his life's work. Ten girls, ranging in age from thirteen to seventeen, stood before him, wearing only frilly polyester bridesmaid dresses of matching sea-foam green, shivering in the early morning desert cold. Each of them held an old-fashioned kerosene camping lamp.

On a plateau a few feet below the crest of the ridge stood maybe four dozen people, yawning and hugging themselves, trying to stay alert for the big event. The ten girls on the ridge, whose limbs were turning a shade of blue that clashed with the sea-foam polyester, had no such problem. Prophet Jonas had allowed them to wear jackets until four a.m., but as the promised event neared, he insisted that they be seen in all their wedding finery. As a result, the girls now possessed the sort of mental clarity that can only arise from a combination of certainty of one's divine purpose and impending hypothermia.

Carly, the oldest and most developed of the ten, began to jump up and down in an effort to stave off the cold, which had the effect of waking up most of the men in the audience. "Carly, stop that!" barked a dour woman at the front of the crowd, presumably Carly's mother. "Be dignified!"

Being dignified, unfortunately, was an option that was not available to the ten girls, who had the bad luck to be born to parents who were members of the Church of the Bridegroom. On the other hand, one could argue that at least three of them wouldn't exist if it weren't for the church, being as they were the biological daughters of Prophet Jonas—a fact unknown to anyone in the church except for Prophet Jonas, who had his suspicions about a couple of them. One positive consequence of Prophet Jonas's uncertainty in this matter was that despite the fact that he was an incorrigible philanderer, he had not as yet had sex with any of the girls. His self-control in this matter may also have been bolstered by the fact that he needed ten virgins from within the church to complete his Divine Mission, and thanks to his need to offer "counseling sessions" to any new female members of the church, there wasn't much of a margin of error.

Prophet Jonas checked his watch. It said 5:17 a.m. It was almost time. According to the *Angler's Almanac* (the only book that Prophet Jonas relied on outside of the King James Bible), the sun would rise precisely at 5:44 a.m. Even now, the first dim glow of morning was appearing in the east. In point of fact, he had expected the Bridegroom to arrive at midnight, as indicated in the Good Book, but he had been prepared for the contingency that the Guest of Honor might dawdle a bit longer in the Heavenly Foyer. Still, He would appear before dawn, that much was certain. Prophet Jonas cleared his throat and spoke.

"How y'all doin'?" he shouted at the crowd.

Murmurs of attempted cheerfulness arose from the crowd, whose members had expected the evening's festivities to climax more than five hours earlier. Most of them hadn't thought to bring folding chairs or breakfast.

"I said, 'HOW Y'ALL DOIN'!'" Prophet Jonas barked.[1]

Louder, but even less convincing, murmurs of attempted cheerfulness. Clearly those gathered in the predawn desert cold just wanted to go home. At this point it didn't much matter to them if home was on Jesus's spaceship or back in the trailer park in Carson City.

As for Christine Temetri, her lack of enthusiasm stemmed not from her disbelief, nor even from her disgust with a transparent,

---

1   Re-asking a question that is usually understood to be a rhetorical greeting in order to get a more enthusiastic response is a time-honored tradition among speakers who find themselves, through no fault of their own, addressing a bored, irritable group of spectators who would rather be home watching television.

philandering fundamentalist[2] nut job like Jonas Bitters. Her lack of enthusiasm was, rather, a result of boredom, pure and simple. Christine was bored because she knew what was going to happen at sunrise: the sun would come up. That's what always happened at sunrise. She had been through this routine a dozen times before, and never had anything remarkable happened at sunrise other than an eight-hundred-and-sixty-five-thousand-mile-wide ball of nuclear fusion coming into view above the horizon.

For Christine, 5:44 a.m. was (if the *Angler's Almanac* was to be believed, and she had no reason to doubt it) the time when she could pack up her lawn chair, throw it into the trunk of her rental car, and drive to Salt Lake City, where she would catch the 10:25 flight back to Los Angeles. Once back home, she would sleep for a few hours, then try to assemble her notes, such as they were, into a five-hundred-word article in time for the *Banner*'s deadline. Then, if the past few weeks' editions were any indication, the *Banner*'s owner and publisher, Harry Giddings, would trim the article down to a pithy caption below one of Christine's amateur shots of the girls in their bridesmaid dresses, something like:

Long wait anticlimactic for "ten virgins."

Well worth a plane ride from LA to Salt Lake City plus a four-hour drive to and from the middle of nowhere. Christine yawned, trying to remember that she should be happy that she at least had a job—and a job doing ostensibly what she wanted to do: write.

---

2   Although Christine thought of Jonas Bitters as a fundamentalist because of his rigid adherence to a literal interpretation of the Scriptures, technically his reliance on the *Angler's Almanac* as an additional source of revelation disqualified him from the fundamentalist club.

Before going to work for the *Banner*, Christine had been a marginally employed substitute English teacher with dreams of being a freelance writer. Unfortunately, no one seemed particularly interested in her ruminations on life in eastern Oregon—that is, until she took it upon herself to write a piece on an apocalyptic cult near her home. She had intended to expose the group as a front for polygamy and tax evasion, but she found the cultists so pathetic and deluded that she was unable even to feign journalistic objectivity.

What she had originally intended as a scathing exposé therefore turned into a facetiously deadpan news story, pretending to give the cult's pronouncements (number seven: women are forbidden to wear denim) serious consideration. She had submitted the story on a whim to the *Banner*, then a fledgling evangelical monthly. To her surprise, the *Banner's* staff loved the story and published it without alteration as a straight news piece. When the issue came out, her article proved to be so popular that the *Banner* decided to start a regular feature on fringe figures obsessed with the Apocalypse (cleverly named "End Notes"), and she was immediately asked for more. She rode a serendipitous wave of interest in the Apocalypse into a full-time job; nearly a year ago she had moved to Glendale, not far from the *Banner's* LA headquarters, but she had spent most of the last three years bouncing between interviews with ersatz prophets of varying degrees of sanity. During that time the *Banner* had become a semi-respectable news magazine, and she had developed an ambiguous but mutually beneficial relationship with the *Banner's* owner and publisher, Harry Giddings. *Time* might still not fear God, but it certainly feared the *Banner*.

So here she sat, at 5:19 in the morning, waiting for the sunrise or the Second Coming, whichever came first. As she was about to nod off in her lawn chair, she was startled by a sudden outburst from Prophet Jonas.

"FANTASTIC!" howled Jonas. "The time we have been waiting for is upon us!"

Intermittent clapping and the occasional cheer nearly drowned out the sound of the Ten Virgins' teeth chattering.

"The Bridegroom will be here any moment!" declared Prophet Jonas. "Are you ready?"

Muted cheers.

"I said, 'ARE YOU READY?'"

Muted cheers and some whistling.

"Brothers and sisters," said Jonas, more quietly, "allow me to read from the Sacred Texts." He opened a well-worn paperback to a page marked by a bookmark. "Elko, Nevada," he read solemnly. "Forty degrees, forty-nine minutes, fifty-seven seconds north; one hundred and fifteen degrees, forty-five minutes, forty-four seconds west. April twenty-ninth. Sunrise: five forty-four a.m."

"Brothers and sisters," he continued, winking almost imperceptibly at one of the more attractive sisters in the front row, "it is now five twenty a.m. We are assured by calculations based on the inerrant Word of God that the Bridegroom will arrive before dawn on this very day." He set the *Angler's Almanac* down on the makeshift podium that had been constructed at the last minute out of three fruit crates and picked up a heavier, leather-bound book, opening it to read:

"Then shall the kingdom of heaven be likened unto ten virgins, which took their lamps, and went forth to meet the bridegroom.

"And five of them were wise, and five were foolish.

"They that were foolish took their lamps, and took no oil with them:

"But the wise took oil in their vessels with their lamps.

"While the bridegroom tarried, they all slumbered and slept.

"At midnight the cry rang out: 'Here's the bridegroom! Come out to meet him!'

"Then all the virgins woke up and trimmed their lamps. The foolish ones said to the wise, 'Give us some of your oil; our lamps are going out.'

"'No,' they replied, 'there may not be enough for both us and you. Instead, go to those who sell oil and buy some for yourselves.'

"But while they were on their way to buy the oil, the bridegroom arrived. The virgins who were ready went in with him to the wedding banquet. And the door was shut.

"Later the others also came. 'Sir! Sir!' they said. 'Open the door for us!'

"But he replied, 'I tell you the truth, I don't know you.'

"Therefore keep watch, because you do not know the day or the hour."

Christine snorted involuntarily at Prophet Jonas's straight-faced delivery of the closing sentence, and then, sensing eyes upon her, she turned her attention back to finding a six-letter word for "banal."

Prophet Jonas, undeterred at her outburst, set down the Bible and exclaimed, "Behold, the Ten Virgins!"

The crowd clapped politely for the girls, who shivered and smiled weakly.

"Behold!" Jonas exclaimed again. "The Five Wise Virgins!"

The five girls farthest to the left reached down with their left hands and each picked up a one-gallon can of kerosene. Well, except for the girl in the middle, who had a milk jug that had been half-filled with kerosene. The middle Wise Virgin had absentmindedly left her can in Carson City and had to borrow a milk jug and half a gallon of kerosene from one of the other Wise Virgins—a violation of the spirit of the ceremony that did not go unnoticed by Prophet Jonas.

The crowd clapped for the Wise Virgins. "Go, Carly!" yelled Carly's mother through cupped hands, for no apparent reason.

"Behold!" Jonas hollered once more. "The Five Foolish Virgins!"

The five girls on the right looked at their feet, but finding no cans of kerosene there, pantomimed a sort of ditzy disappointment, holding out their free hands as if to say, "Whoops, I am such a Foolish Virgin, forgetting my oil. Whatever shall I do?"

Christine rolled her eyes and glanced at the display of her cell phone. It said 5:23. Twenty-one minutes until she could go home.

Second Prophet Noah Bitters, who was—not coincidentally—First Prophet Jonas's younger, better looking, but less charismatic brother, next led the crowd in quavering renditions of "Swing Low, Sweet Chariot" and (less appropriately) "Michael, Row Your Boat Ashore." Christine couldn't help but notice several of the Foolish Virgins jockeying for the Second Prophet's attention.

The songs gave way to an eerie silence. Prophet Jonas, trying to affect a look of confident expectation as he glanced at his watch, gave a brief, halting message, punctuated with pauses to allow for the sudden arrival of the Bridegroom. Finally, having run out of platitudes, he raised his eyes to the heavens and announced, "The wait is over!"

Christine checked her cell phone. It read 5:44 a.m. on the dot. In the east, the first rays of sun shot over the horizon. As more and more of the blazing disc became visible, it became clear that nothing else of note was going to happen.

Christine surveyed the members of the crowd, who were now shielding their eyes against the rising sun and looking expectantly at First Prophet Jonas Bitters. Prophet Jonas, a perplexed expression on his face, looked at the ten girls standing on the ridge just above him. The girls glanced nervously at each other, at Prophet Jonas, and at the crowd composed of their parents, relatives, and friends.

As surely as the great fiery ball itself, a troubling realization began to dawn on the assembled members of the Church of the Bridegroom. Something had gone wrong. But what? Could Prophet Jonas have been mistaken? No, that was inconceivable. Prophet Jonas was their wise and revered leader, infallibly led by the Spirit of God. If he was wrong, then everything they had worked for over the past eighteen years…it all meant nothing. No, it was impossible. There had to be another explanation.

As if in response to the collective prayer for some kind of alternate explanation, a shrill voice, apparently belonging to one of the Foolish Virgins, suddenly shrieked, "Carly's not a virgin!"

Gasps went up from the crowd. The other nine Virgins, Foolish and Wise alike, backed away from Carly in apparent horror.

"Carly!" Prophet Jonas croaked. "You've ruined us all!"

Carly, suddenly charged with short-circuiting the arrival of the Messiah, did the only thing she could do: she redirected the blame.

"Rachel's pregnant!" Carly shouted.

Rachel, a fifteen-year-old Foolish Virgin, shot daggers at Carly. "At least I didn't have an *abortion*," she hissed.

"That's a lie!" screamed a Wise Virgin, who realized too late that Rachel hadn't been talking about her.

The ten nominal virgins instantly devolved into a chaotic mass of screams, recriminations, and hair-pulling.

Prophet Jonas, who was secretly relieved to be able to replace his guilt and embarrassment with righteous anger, turned to face

11

the crowd. "You wicked, wicked people!" he hissed. "I ask for ten virgins, and you give to me ten harlots! Ten painted sluts, not fit to be temple whores in Sodom itself! Ten brazen strumpets, hawking their wares in the streets of Babylon! Ten—"

"That's enough," interjected Second Prophet Noah Bitters, who had to admit that he was impressed with the number of synonyms for *prostitute* his brother knew. "There's no need to censure these girls any further. I'm sure their embarrassment is more than enough—"

Prophet Jonas shot an accusatory glare at his brother. "Did you know...?" he asked.

Noah Bitters looked shocked. "Did I know? What kind of question is that? I'm your brother, Jonas!" None of these responses, of course, actually answered the question.

"I love you, Noah!" called one of the younger Foolish Virgins from the ridge.

Noah smiled weakly at his brother, whose face went red with rage. Prophet Jonas looked, Christine thought, like a cartoon character who was about to shoot steam from his ears. With Jonas momentarily paralyzed by anger, Noah sprinted off into the desert. A split second later, his brother followed, howling decidedly non-Biblical curses after him.

The members of the congregation muttered to each other. A few of the ostensible virgins' parents marched up the ridge to retrieve their respective daughters. Others simply got in their cars and left. A few lay flat on the ground, pummeling the desert sand with their fists and weeping.

Christine packed up her folding chair, threw it in the trunk of her rented Corolla, and checked her cell phone once more. It was 5:46 a.m. Plenty of time to get to the Salt Lake City airport for the 10:25 flight to Los Angeles.

TWO

William Miller, a nineteenth-century Baptist preacher, predicted that Jesus Christ would return sometime between March 21, 1843, and March 21, 1844. When March 21, 1844, passed without incident, Miller revised his calculations and adopted a new date: April 18, 1844. Like the previous date, April 18 passed without Christ's return. Miller publicly confessed his error but maintained that "the day of the Lord is near, even at the door."

In August 1844 at a camp meeting in Exeter, New Hampshire, one of Miller's followers, Samuel S. Snow, presented his own interpretation: that Christ would return on October 22, 1844. By this time, Miller inexplicably had thousands of followers who were eager recipients of Snow's message.

The sun rose on the morning of October 22 like any other day, and October 22 passed without incident. This nonevent was dubbed by historians the "Great Disappointment."

There had been many disappointments prior to this one, and there have been many more since, but never has there been another Great Disappointment. Even the Great War was demoted to World War I after a second, even bigger war just two decades later, but the Great Disappointment remains a nonevent without sequel, even after a century and a half. *The Godfather III* notwithstanding, that's a big disappointment.

If you were lucky enough to be a journalist covering this nonevent, you could legitimately claim to have been a witness to history. You could regale your grandchildren with stories of the time you had seen nothing happen on a truly mammoth scale. Christine Temetri, however, had the ill fortune to be born over a hundred years too late to cover the Great Disappointment, and as a result had been cursed to cover a series of Mild Disappointments that didn't even really warrant the capital letters. There's something to be said for covering spectacular failures; that was, in fact, what most journalists did most of the time. Covering an endless series of Mild Disappointments, on the other hand, was just demoralizing.

It wasn't that Christine disbelieved in the Apocalypse. She had always sort of believed in it as a concept, the idea that the human race would eventually have to account for its many sins—war, hatred, Michael Bay films—but she couldn't remember a time when she had thought of it as an actual historical *event*.

At some point she must have thought of it as a definite, temporal occurrence, thanks to her Lutheran parents, just as at some point she had believed that Adam and Eve were real live people. But as she had gotten older, the extreme ends of the Bible had begun to fray in her mind. She did her best to hold onto the middle, but Genesis and Revelation were too remote from her own experience to connect to anything concrete. In college she had once read about the Heisenberg Uncertainty Principle, and despite the fact that she tended to think of physics as occupying a realm of eclectic trivia that was fundamentally divorced from daily reality—like the rules of tennis or the intricacies of the Electoral College—the idea of certain truths being inherently unknowable resonated with her. These days she tended to think of herself as a Heisenbergian Christian: she believed in the broad outlines of Christianity, but she was unable to pinpoint the specifics of her creed. She was OK with the wave; it was the particles that tended to escape her.

As she drove east across the barren landscape toward Salt Lake City, the latest Mild Disappointment continued to assault her in the form of the blazing sun burning globs of red-hot lava in her field of vision, and it was difficult not to take the harassment personally. "What are you mad at *me* for?" Christine grumbled at the unreasoning sun. "I'm on *your* side." But the sun shines on the just and the unjust alike, and Christine's unwavering faith that the fiery orb would rise that morning was no protection against its blinding rays.

Intentionally driving into a dazzling sunrise was, Christine mused humorlessly, a pretty decent metaphor for how her career as a reporter was going. There was no longer any pretending that her job consisted of anything other than intentionally ignoring the blindingly obvious. Every few weeks she would jet off to some remote yet strangely familiar locale where she would be subjected to a predictable combination of questionable Biblical interpretation, scapegoating of some group or other for the word's travails (most often homosexuals or Muslims, but occasionally Jews or Catholics and, in one case, the infield of the Los Angeles Dodgers), and "continental breakfasts" that seemed to hail from the lost Eighth Continent of Stale Muffins and Under-ripe Cantaloupes. And as the *Banner's* representative, she was expected to act "professional" and take it all seriously, even the obviously inedible melon shavings. She was a jaded veteran being asked to play the wild-eyed amateur ("Gosh, the world is ending *tomorrow*? Well, now I feel a little silly about limiting myself to a single muffin at the motel this morning, heh heh"), and she became a little more jaded with each unremarkable sunrise.

These days she couldn't even justify her job on the basis of the entertainment value she provided to the *Banner*'s readers; it was clear that even the most assiduous apocalyptic clock-watchers were getting a little bored with the repetitive nature of her columns. What Harry's motivations were in continuing to assign these stories she couldn't imagine.

As the sun mercifully crept higher in the sky, Christine glanced in the rental car's rearview mirror to get an idea of how badly her appearance had been tarnished by the sleepless night in the desert. Human females are conditioned to base their sense of spiritual well-being on their physical appearance; it was to Christine's credit that she merely hoped that she looked better than she felt. Still, it was ill-advised for her to be checking her appearance in the rearview mirror, and not only for the usual reason that it's a bad idea to use a vital safety feature of a fifteen-hundred-pound, gasoline-powered steel machine for making sure one's eyes aren't noticeably puffy. It was an especially bad idea in this case because people who looked at Christine's face tended to stare at it for a few seconds longer than was appropriate under the circumstances, whatever those circumstances were. Christine herself was not immune to the effect, even when her circumstances required regular scrutiny of her surroundings to ensure that she was still on the appropriate side of the highway.

People found themselves staring at Christine's face for the simple reason that they could not figure out how such an odd combination of features could be arranged in such a pleasing configuration. Her nose was too long and pointed, her eyes were too narrow and far apart, and the lines from the sides of her nose to the corners of her mouth were too pronounced. Her hair was not quite dark enough to be seductively exotic, nor curly enough to suggest carnal desires bubbling unseen under her overly placid demeanor and slightly uneven complexion.

Despite this, she managed to be strikingly beautiful, in the sort of way that made the beholder believe that he or she was the only person on earth capable of recognizing her beauty underneath those overly aggressive features. Even now, flying obliviously across the desolate landscape of eastern Nevada, she found herself transfixed by her appearance and wondering just what the deal with her face was.

As she was about to veer off the unrelentingly straight highway, her cell phone rang on the seat next to her, and she tore her eyes from the mirror, taking a moment to recalibrate the Corolla's course before picking up the phone. The display read, "Harry."

Christine sighed. Her boss, Harry Giddings, had the irritating habit of sending her across the country on these wild-goose chases and then forgetting where she was and wondering why he hadn't seen her around the office for a few days. Best-case scenario, he had yet another crackpot in mind for her to interview, and it was urgent that she get on the next plane back to Los Angeles—as if maybe she had intended to lollygag around the Salt Lake City airport for a few hours, just for giggles. She tossed the phone back on the passenger's seat. Harry would just have to wait. She had some things to say to him, but not over a cell phone while she was a thousand miles away. He wouldn't be happy about her dodging his call, but he'd get over it. Harry being unhappy wasn't the end of the world.

THREE

Supernatural intrusions upon the Mundane Plane are quite a bit more frequent than most of the plane's residents imagine. Unfortunately for those—like Christine Temetri—who are looking for such occurrences, these intrusions tend to happen in precisely the places that people aren't looking. This is mostly because extraplanar agents generally take great care not to be noticed, but also to some extent because human beings have an uncanny knack for looking in exactly the wrong places.

So it was that while Christine was in the middle of nowhere waiting for the no-show Bridegroom, evidence of a reality beyond the Mundane manifested itself in her condominium in Glendale. The supernatural impinged on Mundane reality in the form of a demon breaking into her condo and making a grilled cheese sandwich.

Had she been home, Christine could have told the demon to avoid using the sandwich grill, as her now-deceased cat had chewed through the insulation of the cord. She had a mind to fix it—the cord, not the cat, which was decidedly beyond patching up with electrical tape—but as usual, she had left the task for a more opportune time, having understandably failed to anticipate that her apartment would be invaded by a being from another plane with a hankering for grilled cheese.

But the demon had taken great care to ensure that Christine, the only person who knew the dangers of the frayed cord, was not at home at the time of the sandwich-making, and therefore she was not around to warn him, nor even to ask him why he was in her kitchen making a grilled cheese sandwich in the first place.

It occurs to me that I may have made it sound as if the demon broke into Christine's condo specifically in order to make a grilled cheese sandwich, which is not at all the case. He broke in with the singular goal of vandalizing her condo;[3] the sandwich-making was what is commonly known as a "crime of opportunity."

Here is what happened:

Once he was satisfied that Christine would be out for some time, the demon, who went by the name Nisroc, used a very small amount of interplanar energy to line up the tumblers in the lock on Christine's front door. He then thought better of this, having considered the fact that vandals tended not to be expert lock pickers. It would make a much more convincing crime scene if the door had been forced open. So, having relocked the door, Nisroc backed up a few feet into the hall and then rammed his shoulder into the door.

This was a surprisingly effective maneuver; unfortunately, the effect was primarily to cause a great deal of pain to radiate from Nisroc's shoulder to the rest of his wiry, five-foot-two frame. Nisroc then miraculously re-unlocked the door, rationalizing that there must be at least one vandal out there who was also a disgruntled former locksmith.

---

3   If you don't know why a demon would want to vandalize Christine's apartment, well, I hate to be the one to tell you this, but you're a bit out of the loop in Heavenly intrigue. You probably should start attending some meetings. The good news is that it makes a better story if you don't know at this point.

Nisroc walked into the apartment and began systematically tossing items—candle holders, paperback books, Bed, Bath & Beyond coupons—from shelves and end tables onto the floor. He had never vandalized anything before, but he figured that disrupting the condo's organizational system was a good start. He realized, though, after getting rather far along in this task, that Christine's condo *had* no organizational system. In fact, it seemed to him that he had rather improved things by clearing several shelves and end tables of random detritus.

This was a demoralizing setback to Nisroc, who didn't particularly want to be vandalizing a condo in Glendale in the first place. He had recently converted to demonhood after a long and reasonably successful career as a courier angel, and he had protested that the commission of petty crimes was beneath him. His new superiors had insisted, however, that he prove himself with a simple task before advancing to higher functions. And now he was in danger of screwing it up.

Trying to remember which items he had just put on the floor, Nisroc began to pick up objects from the floor and place them on the shelves and end tables. When it seemed like there was too much stuff on the shelves, he would move a few items back to the floor. He realized, however, that he was subconsciously aiming for a more-or-less even distribution of items, which was a sort of order. What he wanted was complete chaos, but his angelic sense of order insisted on asserting itself, despite his worst intentions. Nisroc cursed to himself. Enough of this nonsense, he thought. Time to get to the main event.

He regarded Christine's breakfast nook, which consisted of a small table and two chairs resting on low-nap tan carpet. Nisroc shook his head. Who puts carpet in a breakfast nook? He told himself he'd be doing the owner a favor by ruining the carpet.

Probably even improving the resale value, not that anybody was buying condos in Glendale these days.

Right, ruining the carpet. How does one go about ruining carpet? A can of spray paint would come in handy, but Nisroc hadn't thought to bring any. He meticulously ransacked the kitchen, looking for something capable of causing permanent damage to the carpet. In the fridge, behind a block of cheddar cheese and a Tupperware container of something blue and fuzzy, he found a ketchup bottle. Bingo.

He carried the ketchup bottle to the breakfast nook and popped open the lid. Time to do some serious damage, he thought. But there was only about half a bottle of ketchup, and he wanted to make it count. He didn't want to just make random blotches of ketchup. It should be something meaningful, something offensive. Something that would make the owner really want to get rid of the carpet. A satanic symbol, he thought. Yes, that's it.

Unfortunately, Nisroc didn't know any satanic symbols. That is, he knew the official logo that Lucifer's marketing people had come up with—a vertical ellipse with horns protruding from it, encircled by a horizontal ellipse—but that logo never really took off and was rarely used anymore because people tended to confuse it with the Toyota emblem.

As a result, demons working on Earth who wanted to leave a satanic calling card were left with the symbols that had been devised by humans, such as goat heads, pentagrams, and the evil eye. As a new transfer, however, Nisroc hadn't yet attended Lucifer's seminar on Branding for the New Millennium, and was thus starting from scratch.

He had heard that an upside-down cross was sometimes used, so he started with that, carefully drawing perpendicular ketchup lines on the carpet. He was rather satisfied with the result until he realized that he had drawn it upside down from the perspective of someone in the kitchen—when viewed from the front door, it was a normally oriented cross. Nisroc cursed again. He didn't have much ketchup left. Now what?

Nisroc started to feel hungry. Angels technically have no need to eat, but Nisroc, like many agents of Heaven who have spent altogether too much time on the Mundane Plane, had developed some bad habits. One of these habits was eating when he was nervous. He eyed Christine's sandwich grill and remembered the block of cheddar in the fridge. A grilled cheese sandwich might be just the thing to calm his nerves.

He had to plug the grill in to make it work; someone, it seemed, had carelessly left it unplugged. As he set about making a grilled cheese sandwich with the defective sandwich grill, it occurred to him that the cross could rather easily be made into a swastika, which he vaguely remembered was the emblem of some very evil group of people, like the Nazis or ABBA.

Munching on his sandwich, Nisroc lengthened the shorter legs of the cross and then drew new lines extending them at right angles to the left. Perfect! Or...bloody hell, did the swastika spin to the right or the left? Jiminy Crickets, this was turning out to be a huge pain in the ass. It spun right, didn't it? Yes, he thought it did. And anyway, the carpet's owner would still want to replace it, even if the swastika were facing the wrong way, wouldn't they? And what the hell was that smell?

Nisroc gasped as he turned to face the kitchen. Flames were licking up the curtains beside the kitchen window. Now what? Pangs of guilt and fear struck his heart. Had Heaven found him out? Was this the fire of divine retribution? As he watched it slowly begin to tickle the cabinets, he reflected that if Heaven were punishing him, they were taking their sweet time about it.

No, this was not the terrifying Fire of Divine Justice; it was the less frightening but still dangerous Fire of Defective Kitchen Appliances. Still, it would behoove him to leave quickly. He had to assume that if the possibly mis-oriented swastika didn't do the trick, the fire certainly would.

Nisroc finished off his sandwich and left.

FOUR

There is never a good time to find out that your condo has been vandalized and nearly burned down by a demon, but immediately after Mild Disappointment Number Eighteen is a particularly bad time.

The first indication Christine had that something was wrong was the smashed doorframe: someone had forced their way into her condo. Christine pushed open the door and walked inside. The condo smelled like burnt plastic, and one wall of the kitchen was badly scorched. A backwards swastika, drawn in what looked like blood, graced the floor of her breakfast nook.

"Damn it," Christine sighed, feeling completely defeated. "*Now* what?"

There was a note on the kitchen table from the fire department apologizing for smashing her doorframe. Below this was a disclaimer that indicated that the fire department was not responsible for any damage done to the property caused by their efforts to put out the fire. Below this someone had scrawled "Sorry!" as an apology for the disclaimer. Below this was a section labeled "Cause of Fire." The box for "defective electrical appliance" was checked. Below this, written in very small print, was a notice that she would most likely be receiving an invoice for the cost of the fire department's services. The sandwich grill, now a blackened mass of warped metal and charred plastic, its cord snipped off, sat sheepishly next to the note.

Having satisfied herself that nothing had been stolen and that the damage was limited to the scorching of her cabinets and defacing of her carpet, Christine collapsed into one of the chairs that had been moved aside to make room for the ketchup drawing and regarded the inverted symbol. She noticed an empty ketchup bottle that appeared to have been precisely placed in the corner of the breakfast nook with studied carelessness. So, she thought, at least it's not blood. Bloody waste of ketchup though.

She wondered who might have wanted to do this to her condo. Presumably a member of one of the cults she had covered over the past three years, someone who wasn't happy with the coverage they had gotten. She racked her brain trying to think of which group might be using a backwards swastika as a calling card, but she came up with nothing. Maybe it was just bored kids or a disgruntled neighbor who had found out that she was a sixteenth Jewish on her mother's side. But the note said that the fire department had forced the door open, which meant that it had been locked when they showed up. So…someone who had a key to her condo? That made no sense either. And what was up with the sandwich grill fire? Had the vandals intentionally seized upon the damaged appliance to create a fire? Or had they gotten hungry partway through their vandalizing? That seemed like a stunning lack of commitment even for your typical street hoodlums.

She called the police to report the crime, making the mistake of referring to the ketchup drawing as an "inverted swastika."

"A swastika?" asked the young woman who had answered the phone, suddenly very concerned.

"Well, it's *inverted*," said Christine. "Backwards."

"Oh, it's a *backwards* swastika?" said the woman, a bit let down.

"Yes," said Christine. She went on, determined to regain some momentum. "They used nearly a whole bottle of ketchup. It's all over my breakfast nook."

"But it's not an actual swastika."

"No," Christine admitted.

"So this wasn't a hate crime."

"A *hate* crime?"

"A crime committed against you because of your ethnic, religious, or gender identity. A hate crime."

"How would I know that?" Christine asked. "How could I know the emotional state of whoever did this? I don't even know who did it."

"Ma'am, what I'm saying," the woman said impatiently, "is that you have no reason to believe that this vandalism was an act of hate directed against you because of your ethnic background, religious affiliation, or sexual orientation."

"Well," replied Christine, "I've got a pretty good idea they didn't care for my carpet."

There was a pause as the woman took in this new information. "Carpet?" she asked. "I thought you said the vandalism was on the floor of your breakfast nook."

"That's right."

"Ma'am, are you saying that you have *carpet* in your *breakfast nook*?"

Sure, thought Christine. Blame the victim. The carpet was asking to have ketchup spilled on it, right?

"Look," said Christine. "I didn't put in the carpet. It was there when I bought the place. I was going to replace it eventually..."

"You were going to replace the carpet?"

Damn it, thought Christine. "*Eventually*," she said. "Are you going to send someone out?"

"Because someone walked into your unlocked condo…"

"It was locked," Christine said.

"…squirted ketchup on your carpet, and made themselves a sandwich?"

"Nearly burning down my condo."

"With your own defective appliance. Ma'am, you're going to have to come down to the station and fill out a report."

"A report, right," sighed Christine. "I'll get right on that." She hung up.

What was the point of filling out a report? If the police couldn't be bothered to even visit the scene of the crime, it seemed highly unlikely that they would put much effort into locating the vandals. Failing the perpetrators doing their part by also showing up at the police station to fill out a report, the odds of them being apprehended seemed small. Presumably the insurance company would require her to report the incident before reimbursing her, but she wondered if it was even worth it to file a claim. Her experience with making insurance claims was that the expense of the repair was generally about $1.46 more than her deductible—and that three months later her premium would go up by thirty-eight dollars.

She made a call to a locksmith, who promised to be out within the next two hours, and then started to clean up her apartment. I say that she *started* to clean up because about five minutes into the project she realized that she rather liked the vandals' creative use of the condo's space, and she decided to leave things more or less as they were. Whoever the vandals were, they possessed, in addition to a facility with locks, a rather sublime aesthetic sensibility. She imagined a gang of white supremacist interior decorators who, frustrated with their clients' bourgeois tastes, had turned to a life of vandalism and illicit sandwich-making.

As she was mulling this, there was a knock on the door. The door, not being what it used to be, swung wide open to reveal a great grayish-skinned hulking man standing in the hallway. He was wearing a navy blue jumpsuit with a nametag that read "Don."

Now the thing about jumpsuits is that they are specifically designed to subdue and emasculate their wearers. A jumpsuit is not something that a street punk throws on before going on a crime spree. No one wears a jumpsuit unless they've been instructed to by someone wearing a tie.[4] Ordinarily, if Christine had seen this man in her doorway mere minutes after discovering that her condo had been broken into and vandalized, she would have been terrified. But as it was, a split second of fear gave way to a subconscious thought process that amounted to "Oh, he's wearing a jumpsuit. Thank God."

"Hello," said the great gray man in a gruff voice. "I'm Don, from Don's Discount Flooring. I'm looking for the Frobischer residence. I've got an address here, but it got all smudged." He held a wrinkled sheet of paper in his hand.

"Oh," said Christine. "Ah, Mrs. Frobischer is—was—across the hall, in 1609."

"Was?" asked Don. "She moved?"

"Uh, no," said Christine. "She died. Last Thursday. Slipped and fell in the shower."

"Shit," mumbled Don, staring blankly at the paper. "Pardon my French. I guess she won't want her linoleum installed then."

---

4   Or by someone else wearing a jumpsuit, who has been instructed to do so by someone wearing a tie, and so on.

"I'd say that's a safe bet," said Christine. "I would hope that wherever she is, she's beyond concerns about linoleum."

"Uh," Don grunted in assent. "I was supposed to install it on Thursday, but I had a conflict with another job. If I'da done her installation instead of that one…"

"I know what you mean," said Christine. "I almost went over to borrow a cup of skim milk that afternoon. I keep thinking…"

"…I'da done the installation and got stuck with the bill. Good thing I canceled."

"Er," said Christine. "Yes, I suppose from that angle…"

"Sometimes things just work out, you know?" said Don. "Gives you goose bumps."

Christine smiled weakly. It didn't look like Don had goose bumps. Don didn't strike her as the sort of person who knew how to get goose bumps. Just his mention of the phrase *goose bumps* gave her, well, goose bumps.

"Speaking of which," said Don, "what happened to your floor?"

"Oh, uh…" Christine began. "Someone broke in…that is, came in and—"

"Can I take a look?"

Sensing a shiver coming on, Christine shrugged her shoulders to conceal it. This was taken by the hulking Don as a gesture of assent, and he walked past her into the condo.

"Is that a swastika?" he asked.

"Technically, no," said Christine. "I'm calling it an *akitsaws*."

Don stared at her.

"It's an ancient Celtic symbol that means, 'I have a learning disability.'"

Don's brow furrowed. "You do?"

"No," said Christine. "I was saying…anyway, it's ketchup. I was thinking I'd pour a bottle of club soda on it and see if that helps."

"Naw," said Don. "You'll never get that out."

"Oh well," said Christine, hoping to wrap things up. Don was giving her the creeps, jumpsuit notwithstanding.

"This looks like the same layout as Mrs. Frobischer's condo," he said.

"Yeah, I suppose it is," said Christine. "Anyway, I should probably…"

"I've got the exact amount of linoleum you need for this space in my van. I'd give you a great deal, since I'm already here and the linoleum is already cut to size. Fifty percent off installation."

"I doubt Mrs. Frobisher and I have the same taste in flooring," said Christine.

"It's a very nice pattern," said Don, pushing her to the verge of goose bumps again. "Very universal. It's a welcoming sort of pattern. Let me just go get it from the van. You'll see what I mean." He walked to the door.

Christine tried to object but couldn't come up with the words. Don returned a few minutes later with a roll of what she had to admit was perfectly nice breakfast nook flooring. Better than her carpet certainly, even without the ketchup stains. Don was right: it was a very welcoming pattern. He offered to install it for four hundred dollars—far less than her deductible.

What the hell, Christine thought. That's one problem out of the way, with minimal expense and effort. She had the man's name if anything went wrong: Don, from Don's Discount Flooring. And after all, he was wearing a jumpsuit.

FIVE

Harry Giddings sat in his office on the fifth and top floor of the *Banner*'s headquarters and fretted. Harry had spent his life preparing, and now that he had done everything he could think of to prepare, he wasn't sure what to do. He would have paced, but he had noticed that pacing tended to have a disquieting effect on the *Banner*'s staff, who could see his movements at the bottom of the horizontal shutters covering the plate glass windows on either side of his office door. He could have lowered the shutters all the way, but that would have tipped off the staff that he was pacing. So he fretted quietly in his office, unaware that what the staff feared most was the idea of Harry Giddings fretting quietly in his office.

Harry Giddings was a man of convictions—formidable, impregnable, inspirational, and often contradictory convictions. Harry believed so many ridiculous and unjustified notions that the sheer weight of probability dictated that at least a few of them would end up being true. Thus it was that Harry's belief that he would play a pivotal role in the impending Apocalypse was misguided, completely absurd, and entirely accurate.

The Apocalypse was not, for Harry, a matter of faith or conjecture but rather a certain, if somewhat imprecisely defined, event. It was, in his mind, somewhat like an earthquake or a surprise visit from one's in-laws: something for which one could never be fully prepared but which was destined to occur sooner or later. Harry knew with certainty that the Apocalypse would occur during his lifetime and that he would play some significant part in it.

Harry couldn't be fully blamed for believing this bit of silliness because, after all, he had been informed of it by an angel. He couldn't be entirely let off the hook either, though, because the angel in question was himself not only out of the loop but transparently drunk and not a little deranged.

More on that later.

Harry's belief that he was guided by the voices of angels that only he could hear was, surprisingly, one of the least unreasonable of his many absurd beliefs. For example, he also believed that God created photosynthesis before He created the sun and that all of the world's animals had once taken a Mediterranean cruise together. Having convinced oneself of those unlikely propositions, accepting the notion that one is hearing the voices of angels is pretty much a cakewalk.[5]

Fortunately, most of these beliefs were so far removed from the day-to-day operations of a Christian media empire that Harry managed to become far more rich and successful, by any reasonable standard, than almost any of his (ostensibly more rational) critics. It seemed that at the end of the day, what mattered wasn't whether one believed, for example, that the Creator of the

---

5   People of a "scientific" bent have been known to ridicule those, like Harry, who believe unlikely notions such as the idea that the Universe was created in six days and that the first human being was formed by God breathing into a lump of clay. It should be noted that the latest scientific theories entail that (1) all of the matter in the Universe was once compressed into an area smaller than the point of a pin; and (2) life came about when a chance collision of molecules accidentally lined up *three million nucleic acids* in exactly the right order to form a self-replicating protein.

Universe had once stopped the Earth from revolving around the Sun in order to skew the odds in a skirmish between two Bronze Age tribes, but whether one had had the foresight to short-sell WorldCom in May of 2002. Materialists scoffed at Harry's worldview while secretly coveting his portfolio.

Harry was always in the right place at the right time. He foresaw the Internet bubble, the housing bubble, the renewable fuels bubble—even the hydrogen bubble, which was virtually impossible to see even when one knew it was there. How much of Harry's success was due to angelic guidance and how much was due to his own instincts or just dumb luck is impossible to say. What we do know is that through a series of shrewd acquisitions, well-timed expansions, and tax loophole exploits so convoluted that they bordered on poetic, Harry Giddings built the most powerful Christian media empire on Earth. He owned radio stations, television stations, publishing companies, newspapers, and recording studios, along with fourteen donut shops and a surprisingly large factory in Vietnam that made those little plastic things that they use to tie off loaves of bread.

The true reach of Harry's empire was unknown even to the angels of the Mundane Observation Corps, as it was as much a legal fiction as an actual corporation, comprised mostly of dizzyingly complex licensing agreements, syndication arrangements, shell companies, and small stakes in a variety of other similarly Byzantine corporations. Our accountants found one particular branch of Harry's empire that served only to obfuscate the activities of the other branches. This branch was so good at what it did, however, that it eventually succeeded in becoming completely ignorant of what the other branches were actually doing, and at last inspection existed as a completely independent entity, busily hiding the details of what it was doing from itself.

There wasn't necessarily any malice in any of these activities; Harry, for his part, did his best to run a reasonably respectable business. Shell companies, plausible deniability, and intentional obfuscation were merely a routine part of business in the twenty-first century. Such defense mechanisms helped forestall audits, hostile takeovers, and intelligent questions from shareholders, all at a cost of only a few hundred million dollars in lost productivity per year. Like the monarch butterfly, which has evolved a body chemistry that causes it to taste like burnt Styrofoam to predators, Harry's empire was a thing to behold—but you wouldn't want to take a bite out of it.

The jewel in Harry's crown was the *Banner*, which was within spitting distance of being the most popular news magazine in the world. News magazines were admittedly a bit old-school by the twenty-first century, but an old-fashioned weekly publication made from actual dead trees lent his enterprise some much-needed respectability. An organization that could afford to lose as much money as the *Banner* did week after week was a force to be reckoned with.

The *Banner* also helped keep Harry focused on his ultimate mission—to usher in the Apocalypse. Unlike the other elements of his empire, which he had mostly acquired and then either built upon their untapped potential or looted them for all they were worth, the *Banner* was Harry's baby. He had built the *Banner* from nothing—deliberately passing over several magazines on the verge of bankruptcy that he could have picked up for pennies on the dollar—because he wanted its focus to be pure: when the Apocalypse occurred, the *Banner* would announce it first.

That wasn't his stated intent, of course. One had to maintain appearances. The mission statement of the *Banner* was to be the best news magazine in the world. So he had assembled a vast network of reporters—in LA; New York; Washington, DC; London; Tokyo—all with the ostensible purpose of providing the most timely, accurate, and insightful news coverage possible. But the Big One, the one story he was really waiting for, was still out there. And he was going to get it.

Christine Temetri had, through her own blind initiative, become an integral part of the plan. Harry, preoccupied with powers and principalities, hadn't initially thought to cover the fringe elements—the crazy cultists who kept popping up and predicting The End. But when Christine sent in her first story, he realized that the *Banner*'s readers would eat it up. And hell, didn't John the Baptist himself start out as a lunatic eating locusts and ranting about the arrival of the Messiah? Maybe one of these commune-dwelling crackpots had the inside track. Harry certainly wasn't about to miss out on the big story just because it came from a disreputable source. And now more than ever, he needed all of his eyes open. If what he had been able to glean from the angelic voices was true, then The End was very close indeed. And this business in the Middle East with the Israelis and the Syrians, didn't it seem to point to a dispensational acceleration? Sure, there had been a lot of abortive skirmishes in the Middle East in recent years, but this one seemed like it had some legs. And yet, his next move remained unclear—and so he fretted.

Harry's fretting was, however, cut short when he heard the voice of the *Banner*'s news editor, Troy Van Dellen, somewhere in the cubicle maze outside Harry's office.

"Hello, gorgeous!" said Troy's lilting voice.

That kind of labored flirtation could only mean one thing: Christine was back from…Wisconsin, or wherever she had been. Harry had some vague idea that Christine had been somewhere remote and insignificant—Michigan? Minnesota?—following up on another crackpot lead. Harry rarely got involved in the dispensing of assignments; although his fondness for Christine afforded her more direct access than his other reporters, he ordinarily allowed Troy to manage Christine. Troy Van Dellen was a perky blond Baylor graduate who had started three years earlier as copy editor and worked his way into his current position through a combination of shrewd political maneuvering and unparalleled journalistic instincts. It was said of Troy Van Dellen—not to his face—that the only story he couldn't sniff out was that of his own sexual orientation. Or maybe he did realize it and was merely adhering to the *Banner*'s unofficial "don't ask, don't tell" policy.

Harry opened his door to see Christine trying desperately to disengage herself from conversation with Troy. Christine had never gotten along with Troy; it seemed to Harry—who was admittedly not the best judge of other people's emotions—that she was frightened by his intensity, resentful of his age, and, perhaps, jealous of his hair. Harry generally tried to at least make a show of discouraging Christine's attempts to make an end run around Troy to get to him, but today he wasn't in the mood.

"Christine," Harry said authoritatively. "I need to see you in my office."

Troy, evidently assuming that Christine was in trouble, gave a smirk and sauntered away. Christine trudged down the corridor to Harry's office, walking right past him and collapsing with a *whoomf!* onto Harry's leather couch.

"Did Lexus not seed fans to light Mike Hondo," Harry heard Christine say.

Harry didn't know what this meant and didn't feel particularly like asking for clarification. Whatever nonsense was on Christine's mind, Harry had more pressing concerns.

"How was Nebraska?" he asked, trying to steer her onto the desired path.

"Did you hear what I said?" Christine asked tersely. "Dyslexic Nazis vandalized my condo."

"Oh!" exclaimed Harry. "I thought you said..." He trailed off as he realized that he had most likely misheard her again.

"What?" Christine asked.

"Sorry?"

"You thought I said what?"

"Oh, nothing," Harry said. "I just misheard you the first time. Anyway, I'm sorry to hear about...that." He hoped he was supposed to be sorry to hear whatever he was supposed to have heard. It seemed like that was what she was angling for. "So, when did you get back?"

"Yesterday. I walk down the hall to my condo, exhausted from this idiocy in the desert with that creep Jonas Bitters, and somebody has smashed—"

"Bitters! Wow, I forgot all about that. I guess the Bridegroom didn't arrive as expected. Sorry you had to fly out to Utah to—"

"Nevada."

"Yeah, Nevada, to do that story..."

"I'm not doing the story, Harry."

"No problem," said Harry, who was a bit relieved not to have to tell Christine that they had no room in the upcoming issue for the Bitters piece. "I've got something better for you anyway. Have you heard of this wacko in Berkeley, Galileo Mercury?"

"Gosh, a wacko in Berkeley," Christine replied. "How exciting. Tell me more."

"So...you're not interested."

"Harry, I'm not doing this anymore."

"Doing what?"

"The Apocalypse circuit. I can't take it any longer."

"Really?" Harry said. "I thought you enjoyed doing these stories."

"Why would you think that?"

"Didn't you say something at the Christmas party about how much you enjoyed talking to all these eccentric, charismatic figures?"

"Yeah, that sounds like me," said Christine dryly. "Except instead of 'eccentric, charismatic figures,' I said 'narcissistic sociopaths.' And then I did this." She pointed her index finger at her temple, firing an imaginary pistol. "I can see how you would misinterpret that."

Now that Harry thought about it, he did remember Christine doing that. This sort of misunderstanding was one of the reasons Harry tried not to get involved in the day-to-day management of people. He had the prevalent weakness among dominant human males of assuming that everything was just peachy with their subordinates until one of them did something really drastic to get their leader's attention, like keeling over dead. If he had realized how dissatisfied Christine was with these assignments, he'd have found someone else to cover them. But this wasn't the best time to be hunting for a replacement.

"I think you might like this Mercury guy," Harry said. "He's not your typical Doomsday cult leader."

"So," Christine asked, "he's not a narcissistic sociopath?"

"Er…" Harry had to admit that he couldn't make that guarantee. In fact, from the little he knew about Mercury, he had to assume that he *was* a narcissistic sociopath. Being a narcissistic sociopath was, after all, the major qualification for being on his list of interview candidates for Christine.

"Look, Harry, I'm sure this Galileo Mercury—the name alone inspires confidence, by the way—is one of the new breed of enlightened Doomsday cult leaders. But I'm just not interested. The Armageddon thing is getting old. Hell, even our readers are getting bored. You're not even running half my stories anymore."

"Christine, trust me. This is important stuff. We may not run a story on every End Times cult out there, but it's important to have someone there, in case…"

"In case what?"

Harry changed course. "OK, fine," he said, getting up and walking to the door. He yanked the door open and yelled, "Troy! Get in here."

Troy strode in, looking puzzled but still hopeful that Christine was in trouble. Harry closed the door behind him and once again took his seat.

"What do we have for Christine other than these Apocalypse characters?" he asked Troy.

"I thought she was going to be interviewing that Galileo person," said Troy, peering skeptically at Christine.

"He'll have to wait," said Harry, trying to sound like he was making a sacrifice on Christine's behalf. In reality, the Mercurians—as they were being called—had just popped up on his radar that morning and thus far hadn't done anything particularly newsworthy. It would probably be premature to send Christine to Berkeley at this point.

"Well," said Troy, "I suppose she could interview Katie Midford."

"Katie Midford," repeated Harry. "You mean the waitress who wrote those satanic children's books?"

"Young adult fantasy, yes," said Troy. "She wrote the Charlie Nyx series."

"Ugh," said Christine, who was vaguely familiar with Midford's books. Her objection to them wasn't so much that they were satanic as that they were childish and trite. At least, that was the impression she had gotten from skimming one of the book jackets and a review in the *Times*. If she were perfectly honest with herself, she would have admitted that she was not a little resentful of Midford's success. While Christine was struggling to survive as a journalist, a talentless hack like Katie Midford was making millions from fabricated garbage about troglodytes and vampires. The only thing worse in her mind than the Charlie Nyx mania that was sweeping the nation was the anti–Charlie Nyx movement that was being spurred on by Christian publications like the *Banner*.

"Isn't that whole thing sort of played out by now?" she asked hopefully. "I mean, she's on what, book five of the series? I would think that by now the lines are pretty well drawn between the pimply, socially inept dorks in favor of the books and the humorless, self-righteous dorks who are against them. Did a prominent dork switch sides or something?"

"I take it," said Troy, "that you haven't heard about Midford's latest marketing gimmick."

Christine flashed Troy a look that managed to convey both impatience with Troy's roundabout way of making a point and preemptive disdain at whatever that point might turn out to be.

"Get this," said Troy. Troy was the only person Christine knew who began sentences with a dramatic use of the phrase "Get this." He went on, after a suitably dramatic pause, "Midford's marketing people held a contest to select the *Antichrist*."

"Oh for Pete's sake," muttered Christine. "And now we're going to send a reporter to Katie Midford's house and ask her absurd questions about whether she really was once a high priestess in a voodoo cult, and how she responds to allegations that she wrote the original manuscripts of the Charlie Nyx books with the blood of an infant." She turned to Harry. "You realize they're manipulating you, right? They *like* it when you demonize them. It helps them sell more books. And movie tickets, and action figures, and God knows what else."

"Be that as it may, Christine," replied Harry, "it's still a story. We're obligated to report on it. And she's right here in LA. No need to get on a plane for once."

"I won't do it," said Christine, shaking her head obstinately. "Besides the fact that it's a completely manufactured story with no intrinsic value, I meant it when I said no more Apocalypse stuff. Armageddon, the Four Horsemen, the Antichrist…I don't want anything to do with any of it."

"This is what's happening in the world," said Harry. "You can't pick and choose what news stories—"

"No, *I* can't, but *you* can," said Christine. "And you *have*, for the past three years. For some reason you've decided that all I'm good for is interviewing these apocalyptic nutcases, and if that's the case, then I need to find another line of work. Or start my own cult, maybe. After all, I know all the pitfalls. For crying out loud, Harry, just give me a real story."

Harry regarded her sternly. After a moment, he turned to Troy. "What about the olive branch thing?" he asked.

"What?" yelped Troy. "No, she can't…she's never…"

"What olive branch thing?" asked Christine.

"I thought we were sending Maria on that," said Troy. "She's supposed to be flying out of Afghanistan any day now…"

"She's still hemmed in by that damned warlord blocking the road to Kabul," said Harry. "The earliest she'd be able to get to Tel Aviv would be Friday. If things continue to escalate, that may be too late."

Troy's brow furrowed. "Still, I think we're better off taking that chance. Maria has experience with this sort of thing. Or we could send..." Troy trailed off, unable to come up with an alternative.

"What sort of thing?" asked Christine, becoming frustrated. But neither man answered.

A recent spate of violence across the globe had strained the *Banner's* admittedly limited resources. Despite his belief in an imminent Apocalypse, Harry had taken his time in staffing the *Banner's* overseas bureaus, stressing—as he said—quality over quantity. He was particularly concerned with the quality of the Middle East bureau, to the degree that it currently consisted of precisely one high-quality individual—who was now over a thousand miles away from the scene of the violence in Israel, covering an insurgency in Afghanistan. The Afghanistan correspondent was in Somalia, filling in for another reporter, who had been pulled to South Africa.

"There's no one else," said Harry. "And you have to admit, Christine has earned this. She's been writing about the end of the world for three years now. Maybe it's time we send her there."

"Send me where?" demanded Christine. "Dammit, what are you two talking about?"

"Israel, Christine," Harry answered. "There's been an incident in the West Bank, and things are starting to get messy over there. Messier than usual. Most likely it will blow over by the time you get there, but there's also a chance that things could really get out of hand."

"Messy how?" asked Christine, knowing that there was only one kind of messy that was likely to get Harry's interest.

"Fighting," said Troy. "Between the Israelis and the Syrians. Maybe the Iranians, too."

"You mean," Christine said, "like an actual war?"

"Yeah, Christine," said Harry. "Like an actual war. Don't worry, we'll be pulling Maria out of Afghanistan if the fighting drags on, but I want to get someone on the ground as soon as possible to get a sense of what's going on over there."

"I don't…" started Christine. "That is, I'm thrilled to have the opportunity, but I wouldn't even know where to begin…"

"Don't worry," said Harry. "Thanks to the *Banner*'s history of support for Israel, we've got some pretty good connections over there. General David Isaakson, for one."

Christine nodded weakly. She was certainly no expert on the Middle East, but she knew that name. *Everybody* knew that name.

"You…want me to interview…" she began.

"Yes, Christine. I want you to interview the guy they're calling the Architect of the Apocalypse. I hope you'll forgive this violation of your new policy."

She nodded again.

"Troy," said Harry, "finish briefing Christine and then get her on the first flight to Tel Aviv."

SIX

On the Mundane Plane, as you know, every name has an origin. Before Armageddon was an event, it was a place, like Kent State or Altamont. Unlike Kent State or Altamont, Armageddon was an event almost as soon as it was a place, and it continued to be that event over and over, until everybody knew the event and almost nobody remembered the place.

The mountain of Megiddo—sometimes called Har-Mageddon, or Armageddon for short—has been the site of a lot of really big disagreements throughout human history. This is a rather surprising fact, as on first glance there wouldn't appear to be anything near Megiddo worth disagreeing *about*. Megiddo is devoid of nearly everything that commonly causes violent disagreements among people, such as petroleum deposits, waterfront property, and soccer matches.

In actuality, the disagreements generally occurred elsewhere—often hundreds or even thousands of miles away—but no matter how vehemently the involved parties disagreed about whatever it was they were disagreeing about, they somehow always managed to agree to duke it out at Megiddo. The Battle of Megiddo is sort of the Superbowl of geopolitical conflicts—not so much a single event as a recurring contest featuring the two strongest teams of the current season.

The Battle of Megiddo was first fought in the fifteenth century BC between the armies of the Egyptian pharaoh Thutmose III and a large Canaanite coalition led by the rulers of the city-states of Megiddo and Kadesh.

The Battle of Megiddo was next fought in 609 BC, between Egypt and the Kingdom of Judah.

The Battle of Megiddo was again fought in 1918 between Allied troops led by General Edmund Allenby and the Ottoman army.

The Battle of Megiddo was about to be fought again.

Armageddon, the place, was scheduled to become Armageddon, the event, one last time, just days from the date of Christine's linoleum installation. Christine had no way of knowing this, of course. She was, however, starting to feel very uneasy about her linoleum, for reasons she couldn't quite pinpoint.

So this is it, Christine thought. *Armageddon.*

She looked around, trying to take in the spectacle. I should get a T-shirt, she thought. She supposed they offered a nice selection in the gift shop—maybe something along the lines of "I was at Armageddon, and all I have to show for it is this lousy T-shirt."

Below the terrace, the sheer walls of the Jezreel Valley fell away. It was midmorning, but much of the valley was still in shadow. Christine tried to picture massive armies clashing in the ultimate battle for the fate of the world below. Unfortunately, Christine didn't have much of an attention span, and her thoughts drifted back to her linoleum. It had been less than a day, and already she was having trouble picturing the pattern in her mind. She wondered if that was normal.

What am I even doing here? she wondered. I'm not qualified for this. I should be teaching high school English, not covering a war in the Middle East. I should be in the land of predicates and infinitives, not Predator missiles and *intifadas*. True, she had agitated for a "real assignment," and they didn't get much more real than this. But she had envisioned a happy medium between First Prophet Jonas Bitters and General David Isaakson of the Israeli Defense Force. Maybe a public official embroiled in some sort of sleazy sex scandal or, conversely, a porn star running for office.

She had brushed up on the details of the situation on the plane ride over. This particular crisis had begun with the deaths of several Palestinian teenagers at the hands of Israeli soldiers in the West Bank. Harry's disclaimers notwithstanding, the story had not blown over while she was in transit to Tel Aviv. In fact, it had done whatever the opposite of blowing over was.

So here Christine stood, on the brink of Armageddon, thinking about needless carnage and her linoleum. The Olive Branch War, they were calling it. Well, except for the BBC, which insisted, as a matter of principle, on calling it the "so-called Olive Branch War." She wondered what the point of it all was. She wondered why it was necessary for so many to suffer and die. She wondered if she would still like the pattern when she got home. She wondered why, five thousand miles away from her condo in Glendale, she couldn't get her brain off her floor. Linoleum, she thought. That's a funny word. Linoleum. Li-no-lee-um. Linoleumlinoleumlinoleum.

Precisely at ten a.m., she was met by a clean-cut man in a khaki uniform who showed her some credentials that could have been purchased from a vending machine for all she knew, and informed her that he was to escort her to the general. She was helped into the back of a Lincoln Navigator, blindfolded, and then driven for nearly an hour along a circuitous route that seemed to be designed to hit every pothole in the Middle East. Finally, having reached the "undisclosed location" that was playing host to General Isaakson, she was led out of the vehicle and escorted inside some kind of building. Only then was the blindfold removed.

The building was an unremarkable concrete block house. In place of ordinary home furnishings there were the hastily assembled trappings of an Israeli military headquarters: folding chairs, tables, laptops, and telephones all tethered by a chaotic mass of wires that fed into a conduit running through the wall to a generator humming in the next room. Elite armed guards stood watch on the front porch. Israeli soldiers patrolled the alleyway outside. In the distance were the sounds of explosions and men shouting.

At a folding table before her, engrossed in paperwork, was a stout, gray-haired man. Christine recognized him from pictures as General David Isaakson, but he seemed smaller and less threatening than she expected. A cigarette dangled from the corner of his mouth.

"Do you ever get the feeling," said Isaakson, looking up from the papers, "that you're being manipulated by forces beyond your understanding?"

The question unnerved Christine. Of course she had felt that way. In fact, it had never really occurred to her that there was any other way to feel. What was more disturbing was that this man, General David Isaakson, was arguably one of the most powerful men on earth.

"No," she said. "Have you?"

"Not until about three weeks ago," said General Isaakson.

Even before the start of the Olive Branch War, thought Christine. "Why, what happened…?"

"I apologize," said the general, shoving his chair back and snapping to his feet. "I'm being rude. My name is David Isaakson. You must be the reporter from the *Banner.*"

"Christine Temetri," said Christine, shaking the general's hand.

"Please, have a seat," said the general. He gestured to another chair across the table.

Christine sat down, and the general took his seat.

"So," said the general. "So how is Harry Giddings?"

Christine involuntarily clenched her teeth and then forced a smile in an effort to counteract this display of pique, catching a glimpse of the unflattering result in a metallic briefcase on the general's desk. She looked, she thought, like an otter whose head had been crushed with a mallet.

It wasn't that she didn't like Harry. She didn't, but it wasn't that. Mostly she just disliked being asked about him, in the way that famous people's children dislike being asked about their parents. Christine's usual tactic was to turn the question around on the questioner. This, in fact, was her method of dealing with most questions, which is one of the reasons she wasn't a very good substitute English teacher.

Christine had learned years ago, as most journalists do, that the main drawback to asking so many questions was that questions tended to provoke answers. After all, it is difficult for a journalist to formulate a coherent narrative when subjects keep providing information that is, by and large, irrelevant to the point one is trying to make.

The question that came out of her mouth was not one she had rehearsed on the plane ride over.

"How well do you know Mr. Giddings?" she asked.

"We met at that conference in Norway a while back. We've had occasional contact since." The general added, after a moment, "He seems very sincere in his love for the land of Israel."

Christine frowned. "It doesn't bother you that Harry's interest in Israel stems from his belief that Israel is destined to play a pivotal role in the Christian Apocalypse?"

The general shrugged. "I'm a soldier, not an ideologue. I take allies wherever I find them." He went on, "It's quite a vote of confidence that Harry sent you here to cover this story. I must admit that I'm not familiar with your work. Have you been to the Middle East before?"

"Er," said Christine. "Not exactly. In college, I came very close…"

"How close?" said the general, taking a drag on his cigarette.

"Portugal."

"I see," said the general, clearly unamused.

Christine felt a sudden tickling of sweat down her left side. The initial pleasantries having concluded, the interview was going badly. The general waited stolidly, his stone gray eyes seeming to stare through her. Christine was used to feeling morally and intellectually superior to her subjects, but Isaakson made her feel silly and insignificant. She wished very much she hadn't said that thing about Portugal. Had she offended him? Forget it, she told herself. Just press on. Make your next question count.

"I understand," she said, "that Israel is often referred to as the Portugal of the Middle East."

The general, his face still expressionless, said nothing.

A bead of sweat trickled down her right side as well. She shivered involuntarily and then tried to hide it by coughing. The dusty air caught in her throat, and she broke into an authentic coughing fit. Good lord, what am I doing? Christine thought. *Get a hold of yourself.*

When she finally recovered, she said, "To tell you the truth, General, I really don't know why Mr. Giddings sent me here."

"But you have covered a war before?"

"In a sense," said Christine.

"What sense?"

"Well, in the sense that a three-day takeover of a Circle K by seventeen inbred mountain people calling themselves the Army of Heaven can be considered a war."

Christine's thoughts drifted to a kid she knew growing up named Steve. Steve was both mentally slow and exceptionally large for his age—a combination that frequently resulted in people looking at him the way General Isaakson was looking at Christine now.

"The fact is," Christine said, "I'm out of my league on this assignment. Normally I do what we call 'fluff' pieces. I mean, our readers don't consider them fluff pieces because, well, they're mostly a little insane, but between you and me I haven't done much serious news. You remember that guy who claimed his dog was channeling Nostradamus? I covered that. Oh, and I broke the story about the Toltec prophecy that said the world would end on August thirty-first of last year. I probably would have gotten a Pulitzer for that one if the awards had been given out before Labor Day."

"No matter," said Isaakson. "You must be sure to make it to Jerusalem."

Christine was somewhat heartened by the fact that Isaakson didn't seem ready to dismiss her entirely despite her performance. She could only guess that he appreciated her honesty.

"I would certainly like to," she said, "but I'm not sure how much longer I'll be here. I expect to be replaced by the first string in a day or two."

The general smiled wryly. He was either warming to Christine or had at least decided to find her amusing. He looked about the dim room at the hastily assembled trappings of the Israeli force's headquarters. Isaakson seemed pleased at the humble appearance of the nerve center guiding this arm of his nation's massive incursion into Syria.

"It's a shame," he said.

"What is?"

"That you won't be here for a few days longer."

"Why?"

The general took another drag on his cigarette. Christine noted that the pack, lying on the table next to the case, was labeled *Lucky Strike*. "You're going to miss the end of the war."

Christine was skeptical. "The end of the war? I'm certainly no military expert, but everybody seems to think you're hopelessly bogged down in Imtan…"

"We're keeping three divisions of Syrian troops occupied in Imtan."

"And how many divisions have you deployed there?"

"Three."

"Ah. Forgive me for questioning your military genius. Remind me of the strategic importance of Imtan again?"

"It has no intrinsic value as a strategic target."

"Then why are you attacking it?"

"A better question would be, 'Why are they defending it?'"

"If I had to guess," Christine said flatly, "I'd say it was because you are attacking it."

The general's lips pursed in mild irritation.

"A valid reason, but not a sufficient explanation in itself," the general said. "If the target had no strategic importance, one would expect the enemy to put up little resistance."

"So," Christine began, "you're attacking Imtan..."

"Because the Syrians are defending it. Precisely. Also..." The general paused, his stony façade failing to conceal his eagerness to tell more.

General Isaakson was nearly seventy, but he looked twenty years younger. This, Christine reasoned, was God's way of compensating him for the fact that he was brutally ugly and had looked to be on the verge of middle age since his bar mitzvah. He had been born with a full head of bristly white hair matted by amniotic fluid and meconium—an aspect which he seemed to have taken pains to maintain over the years as he had bounded up the ranks of the Israeli military. He looked the same in every picture Christine had seen of him. The hideous scar running from his left temple to his upper lip, which she had at first taken for a war injury, was present even in his school pictures. During the course of her hurried background work on him, she had learned that it was the result of an accident that occurred at the age of ten, when he was helping his father build a horse barn just outside of Bethlehem. He had fallen from a ladder and his face had caught on an exposed nail. Tetanus nearly killed him, and the scar healed irregularly so that although it had faded over the years, even today it looked like a river that had flooded its banks. This event, along with a series of other carpentry-related mishaps, ultimately prompted David Benjamin Isaakson to swear off construction and pursue a career as an officer in the IDF.

War had been as kind to him as his civilian upbringing had been cruel. It seemed that every skirmish took a little more of the edge off Isaakson's disconcerting visage, and he had been known to joke that he would start to look for a wife only after Armageddon had rendered him passably handsome. As a recently promoted *Aluf* in the Israeli army in the early part of the twenty-first century, his involvement in the big showdown was looking like a safe bet.

"What?" Christine said impatiently. "There's something about Imtan that the public isn't aware of?"

"Oh, I shouldn't go into detail," Isaakson said. "But off the record...we have intelligence that indicates that Imtan may be of particular importance."

"You seem to be getting a lot of bad intelligence lately."

"Some bad, some good."

"That Palestinian school? Was that good or bad?"

"Hmm. Taken in isolation, that was a disaster. But you have to understand, there is more to the picture..."

"I saw the part of the picture with the forty-eight dead children. It would take a lot of puppies and rainbows in the rest of the picture to balance that out."

"*Christine*," Isaakson said quietly. It was the first time he had used her first name. "Christine, I like you. You have a good soul. That is why I'm telling you this, not because you're a reporter, or because you work for Harry Giddings. I feel that you need to know, because I believe in what I'm doing here, and I want you to be able to say, after I'm gone, that I was a brave man who believed in what he was doing. Understand?"

"I do," said Christine, but she suspected that this display had very little to do with his concern for her opinion and very much to do with the fact that she worked for Harry Giddings. Perhaps she was being cynical, but the idea that this battle-hardened general was suddenly opening up to her of his own accord was difficult to swallow.

"We've been getting a lot of intelligence lately," the general said. "I can't tell you the source, but this intelligence, these tips, they seem to come in threes."

"Three tips at a time," Christine repeated, impatient with the game. "About what? Enemy positions? Munitions locations? Getting red wine out of cashmere?"

"Various tactical considerations," Isaakson said. "The thing is, one of the tips is inevitably wrong. As a result of this sort of misinformation—and I'm not necessarily saying this is what happened—we might end up bombing a school full of children or..."

"Attacking a strategically irrelevant city in southern Syria."

"Hypothetically, although Imtan may yet prove to have some importance," Isaakson said. "In any case, we have no choice because two of the three tips are always correct, and their value outweighs the cost of pursuing the other one."

"'Outweighs'? To whom? Because I think you'd be surprised at the screwed up priorities of Palestinian schoolchildren."

The general's eyes closed. Christine couldn't be certain, but it seemed as if he was struggling to maintain his stolid demeanor. When his eyes opened, they were cold and distant. Was this also part of the performance? "That," he said, "was undeniably a tragedy. I regret having to...I regret doing that. In fact, it's primarily because of that...miscalculation that I have..."

There was another blast, closer than the previous one. Louder shouts this time. Christine could almost make out what the men were saying.

"Are we safe here?" Christine asked.

The general waved his hand vaguely. "These rockets," he said dismissively. "Like children's toys. They go up in the air and fall onto a street, or a house, or a park. The odds of them hitting anything of importance…"

"Less than one in three?"

"Much less."

"It helps when your definition of 'important' doesn't include houses, streets, or parks."

"Relax, Christine. We're safe here. God is on our side."

"Oh, good," Christine said, trying to strike an even chord between sardonic and relieved. She couldn't tell if he was being facetious—a fact that unnerved her almost as much as the nearing explosions.

There was a hissing that became a roar.

A puzzled look came over the general's face. It was the closest thing to fear that Christine had seen him express. "Get down," he said calmly, but he did not move except to grab the metallic case and grip it tightly to his chest.

She obeyed without thinking, diving under the cheap table.

The flash was visible even through closed eyes. Then everything went dark.

She regained consciousness seconds or minutes later. She could see little through the cloud of dust and heard only a sound like a constant rushing wind. It was nearly dark despite the late afternoon sun, and she dimly surmised that the building was still largely intact. The smell of burnt masonry filled her nostrils and tickled her throat.

She became aware of someone coughing nearby, trying to speak. It was the general. "Here!" he gasped. "Take this." He was thrusting the case toward her. Blood streamed across the surface of the case and onto her jacket.

"What…what is it?" she stammered.

"Check it with your baggage," he said raspily. "If they ask, tell them it's a laptop computer."

"But what is it?"

Barely visible through the haze, the general appeared to be smiling. "A laptop computer," he said.

Of course it was. Silly.

"Take it…" he said almost inaudibly, "to Mercury."

The general crumpled into a lump next to her.

Christine lay under the table, covered with dust, her head pounding. She seemed to be otherwise unhurt.

Mercury? she thought. Like, the *planet*? That didn't make much sense. On the other hand, he couldn't possibly mean…no. He couldn't mean *that* Mercury. Christine filed away the request for later processing.

She got slowly to her knees, hitting her head on the underside of the folding table.

"Dammit!" she growled.

As if it had been awaiting her command, the roof collapsed. Timbers split and came crashing down on the table, followed by a shower of tiles and a cascade of bricks. The general was buried under the avalanche.

"Oh God," Christine whispered.

Impossibly, the table held. Had the beams just happened to fall in such a way as to leave the table intact? she wondered. The odds…

Still, it wouldn't matter. The walls had largely collapsed as well, turning the table's recess into a sarcophagus. If someone came along to dig her out, the shifting weight would most likely buckle the table's thin legs. She imagined she could hear, over the ringing in her ears, the table groaning as it tried to hold the weight of the building. An attempt to call for help resulted in her hacking up dust and gasping for air. She covered her face with her T-shirt but was unable to stop before she had coughed her throat raw. Well, she thought, I probably won't try that again for a spell.

She considered tapping on the nearest table leg with a chunk of brick in the hopes that someone might hear the sound, but she couldn't bring herself to do it, fearing that the slightest touch would bring the roof crashing down upon her.

Christine had always expected her death to be ironic. Prior to taking refuge from an avalanche of cinder blocks under a folding table on the Israeli/Syrian border, she had often imagined being nibbled to death by rabid squirrels while on the way to a PETA rally, or having a massive coronary while playing Hearts in the cardiac ward of Our Lady of the Sacred Heart hospital on Valentine's Day. She vaguely suspected that the only reason she was still alive now was that the Universe was waiting to finish her off until it had come up with a better punch line.

She didn't pretend to know much about the Universe, but one thing she knew was that it had a pretty good sense of humor. She was also pretty certain that she was something of a favorite target for the Universe's new material. Death by folding table was a decent gag, she thought, but not really worthy of the Universe. Better than slipping to one's death on a banana peel, but not by much. She definitely preferred some of the Universe's earlier work.

She tried to distance herself from her circumstances and imagine how funny it would be to a far-off observer—perhaps an elderly gentleman in Akron, Ohio, fifty years from now—if she were to tap on the table leg in hopes of drawing attention to her plight, only to cause the table to collapse, delivering a load of three thousand pounds of bricks crashing down upon a plucky brunette with green eyes and $180 in unpaid parking tickets in Glendale. Still not really Universe material, she thought. But then, maybe she just didn't get it.

The air was becoming muggy, but the dust refused to settle, and between the lack of oxygen and the increasing pain in her head, she was finding it more and more difficult to make sense of the Universe's setup. It was difficult to remember, in fact, whether she wanted her situation to be funny or not, and who the gentleman in Akron was, and why he wasn't helping her out with this whole deal rather than just sitting there staring at her and wondering if maybe there wasn't something better on pay-per-view.

While all of these semi-coherent notions bobbed about her head, she noticed movement through cracks in the rubble. It was a person, clawing toward her, clearing the rubble, it seemed, with his or her bare hands. Blindingly bright light streamed through the dusty air. The figure was a silhouette in reverse, sunlight streaming through its elegant frame.

Strange, she thought, her impeccable sense of direction still functioning even as she slipped back into unconsciousness, the sun isn't ordinarily to the north.

SEVEN

We angels tend to derive a sense of meaning from our place in the Heavenly bureaucracy. Mortals, who come into the world devoid of that sort of explicit guidance, are not so fortunate. As a result, many of them spend a good deal of time and energy looking for some sort of meaning in their existence.

With humans as with angels, *meaning* is generally assumed to be synonymous with *order*, as if one could imbue one's life with meaning by discovering some secret plan that governs one's existence. People inclined toward this sort of thinking often claim not to believe in coincidences. What they actually mean, however, is that they believe in a principle often referred to as *synchronicity*—the idea that events which appear to be causally independent are, in fact, connected in some deeper way.

Only one man of note has gone on record as literally disbelieving in coincidences. That man was St. Culain the Indifferent, who taught that no two events ever occurred at precisely the same time. St. Culain also theorized that time was divided into discrete particles called chrotons, which were roughly the duration of three ten-thousandths of the span of one of the pope's sneezes.

This latter embellishment was thought to be a concession to the Church, which had threatened to immolate Culain for the heretical assertion that the Father, Son, and Holy Spirit rotated shifts as God.[6]

Culain was dismissed by his contemporaries, and he one-upped them by refusing to acknowledge their existence. His lifetime saw the disintegration of the last bastions of the Roman Empire, the rise of the papacy, and the birth of Islam, none of which particularly impressed Culain. He died in 646 AD when he choked on a chunk of salted pork while ruminating on Zeno's paradox. His grave marker bears the inscription *Panton in suus vicis*, or "Everything in its time."

Culain's ideas garnered renewed appreciation by the inventors of early mechanical computing machines, and on December 31, 1899, he was canonized as the result of a software glitch at the Vatican.

Christine Temetri had never heard of St. Culain the Indifferent, but she was about to experience the sort of absurdly unlikely string of events that he would have appreciated. Observe:

Christine awoke in what appeared to be a hospital bed. The clock on the nightstand next to the bed said 5:36 p.m. The oversized gown she was wearing read, "Property of Tel Aviv Medical Center." An oxygen mask was strapped to her face.

She pulled off the mask, brushing a cloud of dust from her hair in the process. Her throat was dry and scratchy and her eyes

---

6   A lesser known but related teaching of St. Culain is that the principle of cause and effect is an illusion. Culain argued that Event C could not cause Event E unless the end of Event C and the start of Event E were adjacent in time. But this would mean that there could be no time in between C and E, giving C no time in which to cause E. Further, if time wasn't made up of indivisible elements like chrotons, then each event could be split into an infinite number of smaller events, each with an infinitely small duration. Since C and E each had an infinitely small duration, and there was no time in between them, the length of time from the beginning of C to the end of E was infinitely small. As this was true of all Cs and Es, the entire chain of all events that had ever occurred and would ever occur would take an infinitely small amount of time. This would result in everything happening at once, which was clearly not the case, particularly during the mind-numbingly dull Dark Ages.

burned, but other than a few minor scratches and bruises, she seemed to be uninjured.

Her escape from the collapsed house was the sort of event that even secular journalists tended to describe as "miraculous." Christine, having a firmer grasp on the precise meaning of that word than most secular journalists, however, reserved judgment. She had to admit, though, that she was amazed to be alive.

Isaakson, she had to assume, was not so lucky. He must be dead, crushed to death under the weight of broken cinder blocks and timbers. She wasn't sure how to feel about this. It was, of course, horrific to see another human being die like that. On the other hand, that sort of death wasn't entirely unexpected for someone in Isaakson's position. He had been, she supposed, one of the good guys—to the extent that there were any good guys in this sort of conflict—but how many deaths had he himself caused? Would his death, in fact, save lives? Or would it cause the Israelis to retaliate brutally, escalating the conflict even further? She wished she understood the politics of the situation better. Fights over land and national sovereignty she could understand, but the players in this war seemed to be acting out a script that had been handed down to them, without sufficient direction, from prior generations. And then there were people like Harry, who seemed to be pulling strings from somewhere offstage.

The war itself had been an exercise in fateful escalation, each side reacting predictably to the real or perceived offenses of the other. It began when a group of Palestinian teenagers, reacting to a recent crackdown on demonstrations in the West Bank, had started pelting Israeli soldiers with rocks. A lucky shot knocked a soldier unconscious, and in a desperate attempt to rescue their fallen comrade, the Israelis opened fire, killing several of the teens. One of the Palestinians, a ten-year-old boy, had been carrying a makeshift cane—or a sword, depending on the source—fashioned from a branch of a nearby tree, which happened to be of the species *Olea europaea*. This imparted the otherwise inconsequential skirmish with symbolic significance and led to a series of escalations resulting ultimately in the outbreak of the Olive Branch War.

As she pondered these things, a nurse opened the door to her room.

"Oh, good, you're awake," said the nurse, a solidly built, matronly-looking woman. "I was starting to get concerned." Her English was good, although it slouched uncomfortably toward Yiddish.

"I think I'm all right," said Christine. "Just a little banged up. And of course, I inhaled a lot of—"

"We're running out of rooms," clarified the nurse. "There's a war going on, you know."

Christine wasn't sure what to make of this. Was she being accused of deliberately occupying a room that could have been given to someone more deserving? "Yes," she responded flatly. "I was in it."

"Mmm," said the nurse. "If you could clear out by six, that would be very helpful."

"Really," insisted Christine, feeling that she wasn't getting due consideration for the ordeal she had just been through. "The house I was in was hit by a rocket. I was with…" It occurred to her that it was probably inadvisable to say more. Her meeting with Isaakson was supposed to have been a secret.

"So you were spelunking in a house then?" asked the woman.

"Spelunking?" said Christine. "Why would you…?"

"This was pinned to your jacket," the nurse said, handing Christine a crumpled piece of paper. It read, in neatly handwritten block letters:

SPELUNKING ACCIDENT

"We had to look up 'spelunking,'" explained the nurse. "We thought it might be something, you know, *kinky*."

Christine stared at the note uncomprehendingly. "Hang on," she said. "You mean you just *found* me here? You didn't see anyone drop me off?"

The nurse shook her head. "The admissions nurse just looked up and there you were in the waiting room, with SPELUNKING ACCIDENT pinned to your shirt. There didn't seem to be anything particularly wrong with you, but we couldn't wake you up. Figured you were just tired from a hard night of spelunking. So we cleaned you up a bit and gave you some oxygen. Anyways, like I said, it would be helpful if you could check out at the front desk before six."

The nurse continued to stand there, smiling disingenuously at Christine, as if she expected her to clear out that very second.

Christine smiled back. "It's not six o'clock yet," she said, and picked up the remote control for the television.

The nurse sighed disgustedly and trudged off.

Christine turned on the television, flipping through the channels to find some kind of report on what had happened with Isaakson. Every four or five clicks she would land on a news report of some kind, but the top story of the day seemed to be the release of the latest book in the Charlie Nyx series. She couldn't fathom what would prompt scores of people to dress up as wizards and goblins and camp outside a bookstore for three days for a silly children's fantasy book, but there they were, in London, New York, even places like Minneapolis, where one would think people had more sense. It was surreal that mere miles from the epicenter of the war, people were more concerned with a fictional teen warlock than with the mounting toll of the fighting. And just when she thought the reports had exhausted everything that could possibly be said about a book which no one had yet read, there were the obligatory shots of religious fanatics protesting the book's release—in Nashville, Houston, even places like Denver, where one would think people would have more sense.

Christine alternated between flipping rapidly through the channels in an attempt to land by chance on an actual report on the war, and waiting out the fluff on a given channel in the hopes that eventually they would have no choice but to report some actual news. The results of both strategies proved disappointing.

Eventually she settled for a channel that showed a young Frenchman in a flack jacket standing among some sort of ruins and yammering mellifluously into a microphone about something that one could only assume was happening just over his right shoulder. He was not at all unpleasant to watch. He reminded Christine of a younger, French-er Peter Gabriel. Unfortunately, Christine was disappointed to find that she could understand virtually nothing of what the flack-jacketed, Peter Gabriel-esque man was saying.

She had no good reason to think she might understand him; her misguided hope rested on the scant French she had learned during the single semester she spent as a French major in college. She had gotten two-thirds of the way through French 101 before despairing of pronouncing French vowels correctly and deciding that if she ever traveled to France, she could just as well be mocked for not speaking the language as for speaking the language through her nose. She had abruptly switched her major to English and, as a result, could only be certain that the young, French Peter Gabriel was not hailing a taxi or ordering foie gras.

As if the torrent of vowels and soft consonants pouring from the reporter's mouth weren't enough for Christine to decipher, French words also began to scroll across the bottom of the screen. Every third word was familiar to her, but she didn't have time to piece them together before they scrolled off the screen. It was like being in the reception line at a college roommate's wedding. She gathered, after several feverish minutes of deduction, that there was some sort of war going on.

What she did *not* see or hear was any reference to the death of General Isaakson. If the clock on the nightstand was to be believed, she had been out for over four hours. Long enough for the news media to have found out about Isaakson. Even the *French* news media.

Had Isaakson made it out alive? That seemed very unlikely. She had seen him crushed under a massive pile of concrete. At the very least, he was very badly injured. Something like that would have made the news.

The sound of her cell phone's ring broke the melodious stream of meaningless syllables emanating from the television. Christine found it in her purse beside the bed. The display read, "Harry."

She pressed a button and grunted into the phone.

"Christine?" said Harry. "Are you OK? I got a call from a hospital in Tel Aviv. Who is that with you?"

"Nobody. French reporter on TV."

"You speak French? What's he saying?"

"*Je ne sais quoi,*" Christine said, pressing MUTE on the remote control. The reporter, whom Christine had begun to think of as *Pierre Gabrielle*, continued to motion energetically over his shoulder, as if he were juggling. Christine wondered if the MUTE button on French remote controls was labeled MIME.

"So you're OK?" asked Harry.

"Considering that I recently inhaled about half a house, yes," said Christine.

"They told me what happened," Harry said. More quietly, he added, "Isaakson's people."

"So Isaakson is d—"

"Shh!" Harry whispered. "They're keeping it under wraps for now. At least until they've assessed the damage. They don't want to embolden the Syrians."

"But we're going to report it," said Christine, trying to avoid making her statement into a question. "We *have* to report it."

"We will," said Harry. "Soon. The Israelis just need a chance to get a handle on things. This sort of event can act as a catalyst, provoking more violence. We need to make sure—"

"Harry," Christine interjected, sensing once again that there was something Harry wasn't telling her. "What is this about? We don't work for the Israelis. We're a news magazine. If I'm going to risk my life getting the last interview…" She was seized by a sudden coughing fit.

"Don't worry, Christine," Harry said once the coughing had subsided a bit. "The Israelis have asked for a couple of days. We can still make next week's deadline. It might leak to the news channels before then, but we'll be the only print magazine with the story. Fax your notes over, and I'll have Maria start on it right away."

"My notes," rasped Christine, who was starting to realize what a terrible reporter she actually was. "Right."

"You do have notes?" asked Harry. "From your interview with Isaakson?"

"Well, I have a pretty good opening line."

"Which is?"

Christine cleared her throat as if preparing to read from her notes. "Holy shit," she pretended to read. "It's a fucking *rocket*."

"Christine," said Harry flatly.

"Of course," continued Christine, "we'll have to tidy it a bit for general consumption."

"Fine," said Harry. "Don't worry about it. We don't need much more than a headline anyway. Something terse, like 'Sudden Death on the Syrian Border.' But not that, of course. Something more tasteful."

"How about 'General Mayhem on the Syrian Border?'" Christine offered.

Harry, choosing not to acknowledge her suggestion, went on, "We'll do some generic pictures of devastation and work up a retrospective on Isaakson. We can do a first-person essay about what it was like to be with him in his last moments. What was it like, by the way?"

"Frankly," said Christine, "it was surreal. He had this…" She trailed off, having caught sight of a silvery briefcase resting innocuously in the corner of the room. What the hell? She dropped the phone and got out of bed, trying to ignore the sudden rush of blood and pain to her head. Having seized the case, she made her way back to the bed.

"Christine?" the phone said.

She picked it up, cradling it with her shoulder. She tried to open the case, but it was locked. "Oh, I was just saying…"

A combination lock stared back at her. The case said, "SO?"

Christine found it strange that the case was challenging her in this manner. In her experience, briefcases weren't ordinarily so sassy.

"I was just saying," Christine continued absently, "that I'm not sure Isaakson gave me anything I can use."

She blinked at the case. Now it said, "Five oh seven." The combination lock's tumblers had been left on those digits. The case looked like titanium. She would need some kind of explosive—or a lot of patience—to get it open. She had neither.

"Well, think about your angle on the story during the flight back," said Harry. "You can fly back tomorrow, right? I'd like to have you in town so we can talk about the story. Also, I was hoping you'd be able to make it to the Covenant Holders conference in Anaheim. I'm doing the keynote address, remember."

"Keynote," repeated Christine absently, still staring at the silvery case. She didn't know why Harry kept reminding her about that damn Covenant Holders event. Sure, it would be nice to attend in support of Harry, but there was something unsettling about being in a stadium packed with tens of thousands of fundamentalists. Besides, how much support could one man possibly need?

Christine's attention was drawn to something that had appeared on the television. The French news channel had segued from the war to what they were presenting—if the whimsical graphics of the Four Horsemen of the Apocalypse were any indication—as a bit of the lighter side of the news. The screen then showed a blurry photograph of a man who looked vaguely familiar. Underneath the picture, amid a cloud of incomprehensible French, were three words Christine recognized: *Berkeley*, *Apocalypse*, and *Mercurians*.

More indecipherable words appeared on the screen, followed by a date: *le sept mai*. The seventh of May. Something about that date seemed familiar. The French news channel cut to the image of a mushroom cloud, and then to a group of blow-dried

Frenchmen in a news studio chuckling good-naturedly. God, I hate the French, thought Christine.

"So?" Harry asked. "Can you fly back tomorrow?"

"I think so," said Christine. "Hey, about that Mercury character, do you still want me to check him out?"

"Don't worry about it," Harry said. "Like you said, I'm sure he's just another Apocalypse nut. There's no time to get a story for this week's issue anymore anyway. And I understand that if Mercury is to be believed, the world is going to end on May seventh, so next week is out."

A chill shot down Christine's spine.

Le sept mai. The seventh of May: 5/07.

She looked at the briefcase again. It said, "SO?"

Was it possible, she wondered, that Isaakson had meant the Mercury who ran an apocalyptic cult in Berkeley? That these two men were somehow connected? It was hard to imagine that they both even existed in the same Universe.

"That was a joke, Christine," Harry said.

"Hmm," said Christine. "What if I fly into SFO instead of LAX? Look into the Mercurians a little and then head home?"

"Well," said Harry, "it's fine with me, if you really want to. But I thought you weren't going to do any more of these Apocalypse stories."

"Trust me," said Christine. "This is the last one."

EIGHT

Christine's trip back to the States was uneventful. After once again experiencing the wild-eyed joy of Heathrow International, she popped three Demerol left over from a tooth extraction and boarded her flight to San Francisco, wondering, not for the first time, why prescription narcotics were so much more readily dispensed for minor surgery than for bouts of being tossed halfway across the globe in a giant steel tube. With the help of the opiate fairies, Christine slept soundly through a movie she vaguely recalled as *Charlie Nyx and the Unlimited Effects Budget*, and thanks to the giant steel tube making a good show of outracing Earth's rotation, she was on the ground a scant six hours after she left. She spent the next fourteen hours dozing in the Villagio Inn of San Mateo, a cheap hotel that she dreamt had been constructed under a pile of rubble shored up by a massive Formica folding table.

At present she was guiding a Toyota Camry across the Bay Bridge toward Berkeley. Troy had provided the address of the Mercurian cult and some basic information about Galileo Mercury, and she was trying to focus on what questions she might ask him. Unfortunately, her mind currently resembled a Hollywood cocktail party, with a roomful of third-rate notions all simultaneously vying to be the center of attention. There was the titanium case that she was supposed to bring to another planet, that damned teenage warlock Charlie Nyx, the constant nagging sensation that something wasn't right with her linoleum...not to mention, slumped right in the middle of the festivities, the corpse of David Isaakson, architect of the Olive Branch War.

Christine had, at present, no other plan than to show up at the front door. She certainly had no intention of handing over the case to Mercury, at least not until she knew what it was and whether he was even the right Mercury—a possibility that seemed less and less likely the more she thought about it. She probably shouldn't even have taken the case on the plane, but she hadn't known what else to do with it. A palpable wave of relief had flowed over her when it passed innocuously through airport security. For now it would remain in the Camry's trunk.

Berkeley struck Christine as an interesting place, bustling with pedestrians who evidently thought they had better things to do than get out of the way of a smallish Japanese car. Ninety percent of them looked to be younger than twenty-five, and the other ten percent were either homeless people or university professors, the former being distinguishable from the latter by their elegantly crafted cardboard signs assuring her that "ANYTHING WILL HELP." She theorized that the professors were either too proud to carry such signs or too poor to afford cardboard.

She felt almost entirely recovered from her ordeal, although she was popping lozenges like an echinacea addict in an effort to keep her low-grade cough from erupting into a grand mal–like fit of involuntary muscular contraction. As she neared the address, she checked her appearance in the rearview mirror. Other than a few nearly healed nicks and scratches, she thought she looked almost respectable.

She managed to tear herself away from the mirror in time to avoid running down a woman who was either a physics professor or a bag lady, and she found herself smack in front of 507 Olive Avenue. By a miracle on par with her rescue from the folding table sarcophagus, she found a parking space just off Telegraph. Flush with this success and the relief of having avoided killing any homeless and/or tenure-track pedestrians, she got out of the car and walked the fifty yards to the front door of the Mercurian headquarters.

The house was an odd choice for the headquarters of a cult, apocalyptic or otherwise. Christine had never seen a cult head-quartered in a Victorian mansion. Cults, particularly those of the "the end is near" variety, tended to prefer more modern—and less permanent-seeming—structures. A building like this had a way of hinting that you weren't the first batch of wing nuts it had housed, and you wouldn't be the last.

She was met at the door by a young woman who had an oddly tired and pallid look that made Christine think that maybe she wasn't getting enough artificial coloring in her food. Her skin was pale and grayish, her hair was mousy and grayish, and her teeth were yellowish and grayish. This, thought Christine, is why God invented sunlight. And whitening strips.

"I'm Ariel," said the woman, in a voice that seemed to be wandering through her larynx on its way to somewhere else. "I can take you to him."

Christine balked, having expected somewhat more resistance, but then she darted after the waifish girl, who seemed likely to disappear into thin air. They meandered through the massive house, past several other Ariels and their male counterparts. Other than sporting the blandly cheerful look of individuals who had surrendered their critical thinking ability in order to mindlessly follow an authority figure, they looked like ordinary college students. On second thought, Christine noted, they looked exactly like ordinary college students.

They came to a cheery room that had probably been intended as a sort of study. It would have been difficult for anyone to study in it at present, for a number of reasons. First, the room was unfurnished except for a single, overly large plywood table. Second, the table was being unrelentingly harassed by a small plastic ball. Third, and most importantly, the sound of the ball bouncing off plywood was so loud that it made one feel like a kernel of popcorn in a tin kettle, listening to its brothers explode.

"Hwaaaaaah!" exclaimed the lanky man on the left side of the table. It was unclear whether it was a cry of victory or exasperation—or merely exultation in the simple joys of ping-pong.

The man was tall, maybe six foot four. He had the physique of a cyclist and the hands of a harpsichordist, thought Christine. He could just as well have been a long-distance runner and concert pianist, but a journalist of Christine's stature was conditioned to avoid such clichés. His features were pronounced and aquiline. Deep-set green eyes peered mischievously out from under his prominent brow. His hair was—there was no other word to describe it—silver. Were it not for the absurd hair, Christine would have put him at about twenty-five.

"Hwaaaaaah!" he shouted again as he executed a particularly unremarkable shot.

The lanky man's opponent was a pudgy young Asian man wearing a blue and yellow Cal Berkeley sweatshirt, who parried every shot effortlessly. He appeared simultaneously amused and frightened, like someone who had learned how to juggle chainsaws but hadn't yet learned how to stop.

"I'm looking for Galileo Mercury," Christine said.

"Hwaaaaaah!" the tall man exclaimed again, slicing his paddle sideways to connect with the ball. The ball shot off the paddle in the direction of his opponent but then arced wildly toward Christine. She threw up her hand, catching it an inch from her nose.

"English!" the tall man said.

The Asian man looked relieved. He quietly put down his paddle and began to slink away.

"I'm from Glendale," corrected Christine.

The tall man shook his head. "English. I'm learning how to put English on the ball. Galileo here is teaching me."

The Asian man stood there, blinking dumbly at Christine, a pained expression on his face.

Christine turned to the shorter man, who was now halfway out the doorway.

"You're Galileo Mercury?"

The Asian man sighed in resignation.

"Not what you expected, eh?" said the tall man. "I thought journalists were supposed to be objective. No preconceptions, that sort of thing. Is there some law that a Chinese dude can't be named Galileo?"

Christine sputtered uncertainly. "Er…" she started.

The tall man dropped his paddle on the table and approached her, holding out his hand.

"I'm Mercury," he said. "But you have to admit, it would be pretty funny if Galileo Mercury was a Chinese dude. Toby, get us some beers, would you?"

The Asian man, evidently named Toby, left. He had the distinct look of a recent parolee.

"Toby's a good kid," Mercury said. "Not really the cultist type, to be honest. Let's sit in the drawing room."

He led her to a medium-sized room populated with a variety of mismatched and oversized easy chairs. He thumped into a massive floral thing, and she took a seat in a Naugahyde monstrosity across from him.

"I'm Christine Temetri," she began. "With the *Banner.*"

"I know," Mercury said. "I've been reading your stuff. Really phenomenal stuff. Hysterical, really."

"It's not really supposed to be…"

"I know," he said. "That's what makes it so funny."

Christine decided to start over. "Most cult leaders don't acknowledge that they are running a cult," she said.

"Don't they?" Mercury asked.

Christine waited for him to say more. In her experience men of his sort needed very little prompting to launch into a soliloquy or diatribe.

Mercury glanced about, seeming to be searching for the right words. Finally he spoke.

"What do you think is keeping Toby?" he said.

"Well," Christine said, "I haven't known Toby that long. He seems like the kind of guy who would be capable of getting a couple of beers, but I'm basing that assumption mostly on his aptitude at ping-pong."

Mercury nodded, seeming satisfied with this assessment. "Anyway, where were we?"

"Your full name, it's Galileo Mercury?"

"Full name," Mercury said thoughtfully. "You mean like on my driver's license?"

"Well, yes."

Mercury nodded. "No," he said.

"No, it's not Galileo Mercury?"

"No, it's not on my driver's license."

"What is on your driver's license?"

"There's really no telling," Mercury said. "I don't have one."

"You don't drive?"

"Well that's a bit of a leap, isn't it? I never said I didn't drive. I said I didn't have a license. And technically that's not true. I have a de facto license."

"A de facto license."

"Right. So far, no one has prevented me from driving. I've been de facto permitted to drive. The limitation of a de facto license, of course, is that I can't tell you what name is on it. Also, I have to rely on Toby to buy my beer. Speaking of which, if that guy could serve a Sierra Nevada half as well as he can serve a ping-pong ball..."

Toby entered, bearing two green bottles.

"Ah, Toby!" Mercury said, taking the bottles and handing one to Christine. "I was just talking about what an excellent server you are. Do me a favor and run to the 7-Eleven for me. We're out of Rice Krispies. And get some of those marshmallow Peeps, if they have them. Have you ever made Rice Krispy bars with marshmallow Peeps, Christine?"

"I'm afraid not," Christine said, setting the beer down next to her chair.

"Ooh, you'll love it. They're like regular Rice Krispies bars, but with this sugary glaze on them. Also, it's fun to watch the little chicks melt in the pan. *Peep! Peep!* Stick around, this is going to be crazy."

Toby nodded and left again.

Christine tried again. "So your full name..."

"Mercury. Just Mercury. I use *Galileo* because people insist that you need two names these days. I suppose it's meant to prevent confusion. They give you two names to differentiate you from everyone else who has two names. Anyway, it's got a ring to it."

"But your given name..."

"I used to go by Ophiel, but people seem to have an easier time with Mercury. My given name is nearly impossible to pronounce," he said. "Cherubic doesn't transliterate well into English."

"Cherubic? Like the little angels with the rosy cheeks?"

"Exactly, Christine. Put that in your article. Maybe if you take a picture of me taking a leak in the garden you can get your article published in *Better Homes and Gardens*, too."

"So...you're saying *you* are a cherub?"

"I am."

"And you were sent down from heaven for some divine purpose, I suppose."

"More or less."

"And that purpose is...?"

"I honestly couldn't tell you. I missed that meeting."

"But you're assembling a group of followers here..."

"Followers? Freeloaders, is more like it. I let them stay here in exchange for, you know, favors."

"What kind of favors?"

"Well, theoretically things like escorting Snap, Crackle, and Pop home from the 7-Eleven," said Mercury. "But I have yet to see how that particular project pans out."

"So this isn't a cult?"

"Oh, I suppose it is," Mercury said, waving his hand vaguely. "I haven't put that much thought into it."

"But you teach them things. Indoctrinate them in the faith, as it were."

"I tell them a few stories now and then. They like hearing about the football games between the Seraphim and the Cherubim.

I mean *real* football, by the way, not the pansy kind where you can't use your hands. Now there's a rivalry! I think the Cherubim have a real shot this year. Oh, and the end of the world stuff. They can't get enough of that. Although I have to say, I'm not sure they're really paying attention. This generation, you know, they don't know how to live for the moment."

"Live for the moment?" asked Christine skeptically.

Mercury nodded, downing the last of his beer. He looked sadly at the empty bottle. "That's it," he said. "No more. Pity."

Here we go, thought Christine. Here comes the Doomsday spiel. She forced herself to ask the obligatory question, like someone peeling open a long-forgotten Tupperware container lurking in the back of the fridge. "So," she said, "the world is ending?"

"Of course," replied Mercury, without hesitation. "But you know that. Surely someone in your position has seen the signs. Wars and rumors of wars, famines, plagues, widespread use of steroids in Major League Baseball…and you've heard about the Antichrist, of course."

"The Antichrist?"

"Yeah, you know, the Charlie Nyx thing." Mercury was now attempting to balance the beer bottle upside down on his palm, without much success.

Christine sighed, convinced that she had hit a new low in a career that was littered with some pretty impressive lows. Even that flaky cad Jonas Bitters had the good sense not to hinge his eschatological pronouncements on a fictional adolescent warlock.

"I must be the only person on Earth who doesn't give a shit about Charlie Nyx," Christine muttered. "Between the books and the movies and these ridiculous publicity stunts…"

"It is a strange way to pick the Antichrist," Mercury admitted.

Christine raised an eyebrow at him. "You do realize that it's just a stunt, right? They picked some guy at random and called him the Antichrist. It's just a stupid, sick joke."

"Sick, yes. Stupid? That remains to be seen. I'm betting Lucifer has something up his sleeve. Picking that dickweed Karl Grissom to be—"

"Karl?" said Christine dubiously. "The Antichrist's name is Karl?"

"Yeah, some dumb schmuck in Lodi. South of Sacramento, I think."

"Lodi? You mean like in the song?"

"What song?" asked Mercury.

"You know," said Christine. "The Credence Clearwater Revival song."

"'Proud Mary'?" offered Mercury.

"No, the other one."

"'Bad Moon Rising'?"

"No."

"'Born on the Bayou'?"

"'*Lodi*,'" said Christine coldly.

"Right," said Mercury. "South of Sacramento. There's a song about it." The beer bottle fell from Mercury's palm and rolled under Christine's chair. Mercury looked like he was trying to decide whether it was worth going after it, based on the limited entertainment value the bottle had provided him so far.

Christine pressed on. "So tell me, Mr. Mercury, what is your role in all of this?"

"I thought I covered that," Mercury said. "I missed the meeting. Maybe I'm supposed to…hold a sign or something? You've seen the greeting cards."

"Uh huh. So what are you doing here?"

"Well, right now I'm savoring a slight buzz and anticipating another mark in the win column against Toby."

Christine gritted her teeth.

"Well, Mr. Mercury," she said, "it's been a pleasure. I'd love to stick around, but I've got lunch with a leprechaun. I understand he has some information regarding the whereabouts of a certain pot of gold."

"Leprechaun," considered Mercury. "Nice. Mythical creature. You do believe in angels, of course?"

"Mr. Mercury…"

"Just Mercury."

"I seem to have made a mistake. I just got back from an assignment in Israel, and someone mentioned the name 'Mercury.' For some reason, I assumed they meant you, but clearly I was mistaken."

Mercury nodded. "Wow," he said. "There's simply no reason for your face to be as attractive as it is. It's like six different faces that have been welded together."

Christine sighed again, regretting ever having listened to Pierre Gabrielle and the magic briefcase. What the hell was she thinking? There was no way General Isaakson had meant *this* Mercury.

"Hey," said Mercury, "would you like to see a card trick?"

"I'm sorry?"

"A card trick. Here."

Mercury produced a deck of cards from his pocket. The backs of the cards were adorned by pairs of cherubim riding bicycles.

"Examine the deck."

"Mercury, please. I don't have time for card tricks."

"Trust me, card tricks are about all you have time for at this point. Examine the deck."

"OK, one fast trick and I'm leaving."

"I bet you say that to all the cult leaders."

"Funny. The deck looks fine."

"Pick a card. Don't show me."

Christine rolled her eyes. She picked a card. Seven of hearts.

"OK, now put the card back and shuffle the deck." He handed her the deck and closed his eyes while she shuffled.

"Hand me the deck," he said.

She did.

"Now look in your back pocket," he said with a wry smile.

Christine was dubious. "There's no way…" she began as she reached into the back pocket of her slacks. Her fingers touched the smooth edge of something that felt suspiciously like a playing card. She pulled it out and looked down.

"Is that your card?" Mercury said knowingly.

"No," Christine said flatly.

It was the ace of spades.

"No?" Mercury asked. He seemed genuinely surprised.

Christine said, "That was fun. Maybe you should stick with ping-pong."

Mercury turned the card over, examining every detail. When the card continued to stubbornly refuse to admit to being the seven of hearts, he proceeded to examine the rest of the deck. The look on his face reminded her of General Isaakson just before the rocket struck. After a moment of brow-furrowing, he fanned the cards, turning them so she could see.

Every card was the ace of spades.

"Ah," Christine said. "Toby must have gone to a lot of 7-Elevens to get you fifty-two of those."

Mercury dropped the cards. Black aces scattered everywhere.

"This isn't good," he said. "We need to go."

"We?" Christine asked.

"Go!" he said more firmly, pointing to the exit. "Now!"

She followed dumbly as he raced out the front door and into the street. He crossed at an angle, darting through the traffic. Car horns blared. Christine followed tentatively, dimly wondering why she was leaving a perfectly amicable Victorian mansion to follow its clearly insane occupant into a busy street.

"What?" she growled as she caught up to him on the sidewalk on the far side of Telegraph. Mercury had stopped and turned to face the direction he had come. At first she thought he was waiting for her, but his eyes were fixed on the house.

"What the hell are we...?"

"Not Hell," said Mercury. "Heaven. Watch."

Christine tried to follow Mercury's gaze. "I don't..."

There was a blinding flash of light. Before her eyes clamped shut, she thought she saw something like a pillar of fire, some twenty feet in diameter, shooting straight down out of the clouds. When she opened her eyes a second later, the entire house was engulfed in flames. Anyone inside must have been incinerated instantly.

"Those people..." she started.

Mercury sighed, shaking his head. "Friggin' cultists," he said. "They never learn."

NINE

The Antichrist, meanwhile, was having a bad day. He had only this morning been dethroned as the reigning *BattleCraft* champion of Server 7, and now his mother was getting on his case again.

"Karl?" she said in that particularly annoying tone that she used when she spoke. Thankfully, his mother lacked both the motivation and the stamina to climb the steep, carpeted steps to his dusty brown room in the dusty brown attic of her dusty brown house in a dusty brown neighborhood in the middle of the dusty brown part of Northern California. Unfortunately, that hadn't stopped her from screeching incessantly upstairs at Karl for most of the past thirty-seven years.

Ninety-six percent of the people who had met Karl's mother had, at one time or other, described her as "unpleasant." The remaining four percent, who were somewhat more perceptive, tended to describe her as "unpleasant and a little *off*." In fact, Karl's mother was—unbeknownst to anyone—a medical curiosity: she had been born without an appendix, in place of which was a second gall bladder.

"Karl!"

"*What?*" he howled back. "*Jeez*, Ma. I'm getting dressed!"

"You've been getting dressed for twenty minutes. You're going to be late!"

"Myah-myah-myah-myah-MYAH-myah!"

"Karl, are you mocking me?!"

"No, Ma."

"You'd better not! Now get down here!"

"This shit is hard to get on, Ma! Give me a second."

"Don't you curse at me, young man!"

Karl let out a torrent of profanity.

"Karl!"

Karl Grissom was a thirty-seven-year-old film school dropout and part-time pizza delivery guy who was still acclimating to his role as the Antichrist. If it were up to him, he'd have stuck with just the pizza delivery gig, but his ma wouldn't have it. "A great opportunity," she called it. And it was, for *her*: an opportunity for her to get her hair styled and her toenails painted and her eyebrows plucked. Her eyebrows had been so sparse and uneven that the poor stylist had ended up removing them completely in a futile effort to produce something like a definitive line. Ma had been outraged at first, but she took it as an opportunity to have new eyebrows tattooed just above the originals, so that her face now ironically seemed to be expressing the exact horrified surprise felt by anyone who was unfortunate enough to meet her.

Karl hated his mother, which was one thing he had in common with everyone else, whom he also hated, but not as much as he hated his mother. He hated her first of all because every day for the past nineteen years she had nagged him to stop playing with his "toys" and do the laundry, despite the fact that not once in his life had he ever *done* the laundry. He couldn't fathom why she still thought he might someday break down and wash his own clothes. He certainly never gave her any reason to believe that he would. Ten years ago this week, in fact, he had stopped picking up his underwear from the bathroom floor in an attempt to convince her that her nagging was causing him to regress developmentally, but this tactic had had no noticeable effect on her behavior. He was still planning his next escalation in their little power struggle.

Karl had become the Antichrist quite by chance, at least as far as any human being knew.[7] It was very important for legal reasons that his selection appear random. For this purpose, Karl had been a good choice, because anyone looking at him could only assume that he had come into the position through sheer, unadulterated luck.

Like most thirty-seven-year-olds who lived in their mother's attic, Karl was a fan of teen warlock Charlie Nyx.

The Charlie Nyx books were extremely popular with those who had read them and extremely unpopular with those who had not. Despite their understandable lack of familiarity with the finer points, it was, surprisingly, the latter group that was able to discern that the true mission of Charlie Nyx was not to defend the great city of Anaheim from troglodytes, nor even to generate truckloads of money for Katie Midford, but rather to promote the diabolical interests of Lucifer himself.

---

7   The identity of the Antichrist is, of course, less important than the fact that there *is* an Antichrist. No one cares much what the Antichrist says or does, but they feel better knowing he's around. In this way, he is much like the pope or the United Nations.

It is probably not entirely coincidental that both the pope and the United Nations have often been accused of *being* the Antichrist. Other individuals and organizations have also made the short list, of course. Nero was an early favorite, and dictators like Napoleon and Hitler were strong contenders. Even the affable U.S. president Ronald Wilson Reagan—who had the distinction of having six letters in each of his three names—was named as a potential Antichrist. Later, the name of vaunted Israeli general David Isaakson also tended to crop up among people who discussed such things.

Yet, on some level, most people seemed to sense that someone like Hitler was a little too obvious a choice. Once you make it clear that your intention is global conquest, the mystery is gone and people start to look for someone with less pedestrian aims. Start talking about a Brotherhood of Man or a New World Order, though, and ears perk up.

People also seem to intuitively understand that Antichrist is really more of a figurehead position. They expect the Antichrist to make ominous pronouncements that can be disassembled and slotted into a prefabricated eschatological framework, not impose martial law or orchestrate mass killings. It is safe to say, however, that nobody expected the Antichrist to look quite like Karl Grissom.

Everybody figured the Antichrist promotion was a joke, of course. Even the Mundane Observation Corps didn't take it particularly seriously. The applicants were more interested in money or fame than being conscientious servants of the Evil One. The only ones who took the gimmick seriously were the anti–Charlie Nyx activists. And Lucifer, it turns out.

Karl Grissom was not, by most accounts, the ideal Antichrist. Christian fundamentalists would have preferred someone a little more threatening, and the publisher of the Charlie Nyx books would have preferred someone with substantially less neck stubble. For his part, Karl would have preferred someone else to have been selected as well, because he felt that he had better things to do.

Karl would bristle at the suggestion, occasionally made by neighbors and his mother's canasta circle, that he was just an unmotivated loser living in his mother's attic. Karl had ambitions. Karl was a *musician*.

This claim would have surprised everyone who had ever met Karl (including his mother), as Karl didn't play any instruments, had never learned to read music, and didn't own any albums. He did, however, have a library of 26,923 illegally downloaded songs on his computer, and he had thus far incorporated samples from 327 of them into an epic rock opera he was writing entitled *Shakkara the Dragonslayer*. He had been working on it for seventeen years, although his first real breakthrough hadn't occurred until the release of Flat Pack's dance remix of "Sweet Child o' Mine."

All of this Antichrist stuff was, in Karl's opinion, a big distraction from his art. He was getting very close to calling it quits with the whole business. If it weren't for the free publicity, he'd never have agreed in the first place. His mother was thrilled with the money he had won, but Karl never paid much attention to financial matters. He had never wanted to *win* the contest; he had been hoping to be one of the runners-up who got ten grand and an autographed copy of the latest Charlie Nyx book.

Karl finally got the costume on, except for the helmet, and plodded downstairs to the kitchen, where his mother waited.

"People are counting on you, Karl."

"Whatever," Karl said. Like his mother gave a crap about other people. All she cared about was maintaining the steady stream of checks that Karl signed over to her. He got in his mother's Saturn and drove to the Charlie's Grill in Lodi, where the fans of Charlie Nyx waited impatiently for the Antichrist to appear.

TEN

"Natural gas explosion."

"Excuse me?"

"That's what they'll blame it on. The authorities."

Christine tried to sigh, but it came out as a series of short huffs. Her knuckles were white on the steering wheel. They were on the highway, heading east. She was vaguely aware that she was going the wrong direction; she would need to head south at her first opportunity to get on a highway that would take her back to Los Angeles. She wasn't sure what she'd do when she got back to Southern California; some small part of her was trying to pretend that she could leave all of this insanity behind her in Berkeley. That illusion would be easier to entertain, of course, if the cherubic lunatic weren't sitting next to her, fiddling with the radio. Mercury had simply gotten into the car, without even bothering to ask for permission. She had been too shaken to make an issue of it.

"You have no idea how much divine retribution is blamed on natural gas explosions," Mercury was saying. "It's criminal, really. Natural gas is quite safe, generally speaking."

"Natural gas explosion..." Christine mumbled, trying to airbrush the image in her mind until that caption fit. But every time she replayed the scene, the fire always started out *above* the house.

"Should have gotten a Mundanity Enhancement Field. A pillar of fire won't work in an MEF. Disrupts the interplanar energy channels. Of course, my card tricks wouldn't work either." He sighed. "The interplanar energy channels are a harsh mistress." He finally took his hand off the radio's tuner knob, having settled on Dishwalla's "Counting Blue Cars." "Ooh, I love this song," he said.

"You...blew up...that house..." sputtered Christine. It was a series of unconnected thoughts that had somehow come out as a sentence.

"*I* blew it up? Hardly. I don't have the authority to call down a Class Three pillar of fire, even if I wanted to. Which, of course, I didn't. My ping-pong table was in there."

"But you knew..."

"The card trick was the tip-off. Ace of spades. Somebody's idea of a joke."

"So the house blew up because you screwed up a card trick?"

"No, the card trick got screwed up because the house was going to be blown up. You see, I can't perform miracles without—"

"Dammit," Christine spat.

"Something wrong?"

"I don't even know where I'm going. We should have stayed there. The police..."

"...are going to be looking for someone to blame," Mercury said. "Are you familiar with Walter Chatton?"

"No," replied Christine, impatiently. "Should I be?"

"Walter Chatton devised a theory which states that when you're trying to explain something, you should be prepared to keep adding to your explanation until whatever it is that you set out to explain is fully explained."

"Fascinating."

"The idea never really caught on."

"Hard to imagine why," Christine said irritably. "Wilbur Cheetham was clearly a misunderstood genius."

"Actually, it's a rather unhelpful theory, particularly for people who are paid poorly to explain a virtually unlimited number of nearly inexplicable incidents. It was the best response Walter Chatton could come up with to another principle of limited usefulness, called Occam's Razor. You know that one, I suppose?"

Christine was tiring of the lecture. "Something about not trusting an Italian woman who shaves more than twice a day?"

"Occam's Razor states that—"

"I know, I know. The simplest explanation is the best."

"More or less. It might be better summarized as 'Don't needlessly complicate an explanation.' You know who loves Occam's Razor?"

"Kittens?" offered Christine, who was trying to focus on more pressing matters than a rivalry between medieval theologians.

"The police. The authorities. Right now, the simplest explanation is a natural gas explosion. The police aren't going to trouble themselves to satisfy Walter Chatton. They're going to go from point A, unexploded house, to point C, exploded house, and they're going to pencil in 'B, natural gas explosion,' between them. Unless, that is, you and I show up uninvited at point B with a look on our faces that says, 'Something far more troubling than a natural gas explosion.' Understand?"

Christine hated to admit that this person, this clearly insane person listening to catchy early 1990s pop songs in the passenger seat of her rented Camry, was making sense. But of course, he was. What *would* she tell the police? A pillar of fire descended from the heavens as divine retribution for a bungled card trick?

"So you screwed up a card trick, and now someone is trying to—"

"I executed the card trick flawlessly," countered Mercury. "For a journalist, you're not much of a listener. The card trick was foiled by an interloper. I didn't figure a card trick would show up on Heaven's radar, but somebody must have gotten a trace on me. Two somebodies, in fact. Not just anybody can authorize a Class Three pillar of fire, so that was presumably the work of my superiors. The people I work for aren't known for issuing warnings, though, so the card thing must have been someone else trying to get my attention. It's a good thing they did, too, or we'd never have gotten out of the house in time. Lucky, huh?"

Christine took her eyes off the road to direct a pained glance in his direction.

Mercury began again. "You see, I can't perform miracles without—"

"Oh, good lord," Christine said. "I can't believe I'm listening to this. You're telling me that the card trick was a *miracle*?"

"What, you don't believe in miracles?"

"I don't believe that card tricks are miracles."

"Well, most aren't. Neither are most escapes from collapsed buildings."

"You—how did you know about that?"

"Unauthorized miracles of that sort make it on the news."

"The news? They haven't even released the fact that General Isaakson…"

"Dead, I know," said Mercury. "Possibly another minor miracle."

"You're happy he's dead?"

"Happy? What does that have to do with anything?"

"You said it was a 'minor miracle' he was dead."

"I said 'possibly.' That was one lucky rocket strike, otherwise. Or unlucky, if you're General Isaakson."

"Or someone else in the house."

"Well, to be fair," Mercury mused, "that's the second house in three days that's blown up around you. You might consider the fate of the people who've been unfortunate enough to be in your vicinity." Having evidently lost interest in the conversation, Mercury lapsed into singing along with the radio.

We...count...only blue cars...

It was true that up to this point, Christine hadn't thought of it in quite that way. It was as if two sides of her brain had been arguing about how to process the input it had received over the past two days.

"What a run of bad luck I've had," said Side One.

"Ah, but how about all those people being killed? That was quite tragic, wasn't it?" said Side Two.

We have...MA-ny questions...like children often do...

"Yes, but look at me. I've nearly been killed in two separate, highly unlikely explosions, and now my body is quite badly scraped up," Side One responded.

"True, true. Terrible about the killings though, isn't it?" Side Two replied.

"Indeed it is," acknowledged Side One. "And ordinarily I'd be rather torn up about it, but at the moment I'm somewhat preoccupied by my own ill fortune."

...all your thoughts on God, cuz I'd really like to meet Her...

But what had promised to be an amicable disagreement was now in danger of gelling into an unfavorably one-sided perception of the events. It was dawning on her that the deaths of

General Isaakson, Ariel, and however many others had one thing in common: her. The logical conclusion was that she was somehow the proximate cause of the explosions. Was someone trying to kill her? Was the Universe itself out to get her? If so, why? Hadn't she done what the Universe wanted, following its cryptic signals to Mercury? The Universe, she was beginning to think, was something of a jerk.

There was no other explanation. Someone Up There was trying to kill her. The rocket strike could be explained as bad luck, but pillars of fire from the heavens didn't just happen. On the other hand, if the Universe wanted her dead, presumably there were more effective—not to mention subtle—ways of bringing that about. So…if someone or some*thing* had it in for her, they were far from omnipotent, but they did seem to have access to information about her whereabouts. Did they find out from Harry? Or did they find out the same way that Mercury had?

…tell me am I very far…

"What news?" Christine asked.

Am I very far now…

"Where did you hear about me and General Isaakson? You said that you heard it on the news. But they haven't…"

Ami VE-ry farnow…

"Mercury."

Oooowamiveryfarnow…

"MERCURY!"

"What?"

"Shut *up!* For Pete's sake. If this is what angelic choirs are like, remind me to take some cotton balls into heaven with me. Because I swear to God, if I have to hear the angelic host belting out Sheryl Crow songs…"

"No danger of that," said Mercury.

"Thank God. Wait, are you saying…"

"Angel Band."

"Huh?"

"You asked where I heard about you and General Isaakson. Angel Band."

"Angel Band? Did you just say 'A*ngel Band*'? How much time do you spend coming up with this stuff? Because honestly, it's starting to sound like you're making it up as you go along. If you're going to be delusional, at least put some effort into it."

"Hey, you asked."

"So do you have a special Angel Band radio? Maybe a secret decoder ring?"

"Angels can hear things on what you might call a 'subplanar frequency.' Transmission of information by way of the manipulation of interplanar energy fluctuations."

"Don't suppose you'd be willing to demonstrate?"

"Better not. If they're looking for me, they'll latch on to me the second I tune in."

"Of course," said Christine. "We don't want *them* to find you."

"So," said Mercury, "where are we going?"

"I have to go see the Antichrist," Christine said, in a misguided attempt to put Mercury off balance. She was trying to think of a way to find out if he knew anything about the briefcase without tipping him off. Her rapidly fading hope that he might actually be *the* Mercury was the only reason she hadn't kicked him out of the car five minutes outside Berkeley.

"Oh jeez," said Mercury. "Seriously? The *Antichrist?*" He said it as if she had announced she was going to a Nickelback concert.

"What do you have against the Antichrist?"

"He's an ass, Christine. A real dickweed."

"Well," said Christine, "he is the *Antichrist*…"

"Hey, we all have our jobs to do. That's no excuse for being a dickweed."

"You know," replied Christine coolly, "I didn't ask you to come along. This is my job. I'm a reporter. What do you do? Play ping-pong and eat Rice Krispies bars?"

"Trust me, Christine, if you knew what my job was, you'd be happy that I spend my time playing ping-pong."

"I thought you didn't even know what you were supposed to be doing. You missed that meeting, remember?"

"I have a general idea. SPAM."

"You're supposed to be sending spam?"

"Schedule of Plagues, Announcements, and Miracles. SPAM. It gives the angels their assignments."

"Oh, of course," said Christine. "*That* SPAM. I suppose they send updates over…"

"Angel Band, right."

Christine sighed heavily. "Anyway, you convinced me that this guy in Lodi, Kevin…"

"Karl. The Antichrist's name is Karl."

"Yeah, you convinced me that this Karl is the honest-to-goodness Antichrist, and I'm going to Lodi to ask him some questions about his plans. For example, does he plan to rule with an iron fist? Or does he prefer a more lightweight carbon fiber fist?"

"I think you're going to be disappointed," replied Mercury.

"Why? Is it because he only has five heads? Because between you and me, six-headed Antichrists are overrated."

"Nah, he's not very interesting," said Mercury. "Just, you know, a typical dickweed. If it weren't for that contest…"

"Right, the contest Lucifer used to pick the best Antichrist," said Christine dryly.

"You're not a big Charlie Nyx fan, are you?"

"I'm indifferent to Charlie Nyx. Mostly, I'm just so sick of hearing about him that I change the channel whenever I hear the name. They're children's books, for Pete's sake. I couldn't even avoid him on the trip back to the States. That damn movie with the magic and the trolls and the warlocks..."

"Personally, I love the books," said Mercury with apparent enthusiasm. "The way Katie Midford paints the subterranean realm underneath Anaheim Stadium, I feel like I've been there."

For some reason, this comment unsettled Christine. "You do realize that there aren't really monsters living under Anaheim Stadium?"

"Please, Christine," said Mercury. "I'm not crazy."

"Right, I forgot. You're a perfectly sane ping-pong-playing cherub."

"Why the hell would you want to interview that wanker? You know who you should interview? Me."

"What do you know that anybody would care about?"

"Well, I know that the Antichrist is a big wanker, for starters."

"Yeah, I got that. You're not a fan. So what do you know about David Isaakson?"

"The Israeli general?" said Mercury. "Not much. He's been a PAI for some time. Like yourself."

"PAI?"

"Person of Apocalyptic Interest."

"Really. I suppose you're a Person of Apoplectic Interest as well?"

"I'm an angel, Christine. That doesn't even make any sense. Your friend Karl the Antichrist has recently become a PAI though."

"Of course."

"It's all connected, all of these events. It's going to get weirder. There are no such things as coincidences."

"Really?"

"No, not really. Of course there are coincidences. I was trying to sound deep."

Christine glared. "You're not a very convincing angel," she said.

"That's pretty much what the other angels tell me," Mercury agreed.

"So in your mind," said Christine, "Charlie Nyx, the Olive Branch War, and Karl the Antichrist are all related somehow."

"Not in my mind. I'd keep them all separate if I could, but it's too late for that. Clock's ticking, you know. I have to say, Karl as the Antichrist was an unexpected casting choice. Wish I was in on *that* meeting."

"I thought he was chosen randomly. In a contest."

"Random! God doesn't play dice with the Universe, Christine."

"I don't blame Him. The Universe cheats."

"The contest was a façade. Lucifer handpicked this guy. God knows why."

Christine's curiosity about the extent of Mercury's delusion got the better of her. "So the author of the books, Katie Midford, she's an agent of Satan?"

"Not sure about Katie Midford. She may just be a prawn."

"A pawn."

"No, a prawn. You know, a little fish."

"Prawns aren't fish," said Christine irritably. "They're shrimp. I think you mean 'pawn.' Like the little pieces in chess that get sacrificed for the queen."

"I thought those were prawns."

"They're *pawns*. Prawns are shellfish."

"Yeah, that's her all right. A greedy little prawn."

Christine resisted the urge to scream. "Walnut Creek," said a sign.

"How about I drop you off in Walnut Creek?" she said, trying to make it sound like an attractive option.

"Why, what's in Walnut Creek?"

"Cherub convention," Christine said. It was worth a shot.

"Really?" Mercury actually sounded excited. "American Cherub Society or North American Council of Cherubim?"

"Uh…the second one."

"Ha! There is no North American Council of Cherubim! They merged with the International Cherub Association in 1994!"

"Seriously?"

"No, not seriously. Wow, are you gullible. So when were you going to tell me about the briefcase in the trunk?"

ELEVEN

The Antichrist was clearly out of his element.

All that was really expected of him was to cut the ceremonial ribbon in front of the newest Charlie's Grill, but he was having difficulty with the giant ceremonial scissors. Finally, he bit into an edge with his teeth and tore the ribbon the rest of the way. Red-faced and drenched with sweat in the hundred-degree heat, he muttered an obscenity and stomped off.

The crowd cheered this display of mildly satanic behavior.

"The Antichrist, Karl Grissom!" shouted a diminutive man who had presumably been standing next to Karl the entire time.

The crowd clapped politely for the Antichrist and the man they assumed was the Antichrist's dwarf henchman, but was, in fact, the director of marketing for Charlie's Grill, Inc. The dwarf henchman marketing director proceeded to hand out free cheeseburgers while the Antichrist made his way to the parking lot. A local high school marching band began to play a jazzed-up version of the Charlie Nyx movie theme.

Behind a line of police tape, in the parking lot of the Burger Giant next door, a group of several dozen protesters held signs with slogans like "Pray for Karl Grissom" and "Karl Grissom GO

TO HELL." Despite their lack of both logical consistency and complimentary cheeseburgers, they were a spirited group.

Having fulfilled his contractual obligations as Antichrist, Karl plodded through the crowd toward his mother's Saturn. This whole business was getting a little old. He had half a mind just to call it quits. And at this point he didn't even know about the man with a high-powered rifle who was lying in wait on the roof of the Burger Giant across the street.

The man's name was Danny Pilvers, and he was a would-be assassin.

Would-be assassins are often virtually indistinguishable from actual assassins, the one vital difference being that the former are, generally speaking, far less dangerous. If anyone had seen Danny on the roof with his rifle, they would have assumed that he was an actual assassin. Even Danny himself thought he was an assassin.

Danny was wearing army camouflage and had his crosshairs trained on Karl Grissom, the Antichrist. As Danny was on the opposite side of the roof from the crowd and was making a point of being very still, no one seemed to have noticed him.

Danny's hands shook, not because he was afraid, but because he was angry. He was angry with Karl the Antichrist. He was angry with Katie Midford and her dwarf henchmen. He was angry with Charlie Nyx, despite the fact that Charlie Nyx was only a twelve-year-old boy, and a fictional one at that. Danny was angry at all of these people because he believed that they made a tapestry of religion. Hadn't the angels told him so?

The angels had not, in fact, told him so. What they had said was "travesty." In fact, they had repeated it several times. "A travesty," they said. "A *travesty* of religion." Finally they had given up, satisfied that Danny understood the gist of what they were saying.

Despite having served three tours in Afghanistan, the only civilian employment Danny could find was as a fry cook at Burger Giant—an injustice made no less severe in Danny's mind by the fact that his highest ranking position in the military was also that of fry cook. Danny was, in summary, a very angry person with a high-powered rifle and a fifth-grade education. It had taken very little in the way of supernatural guidance to get him to direct both his anger and his rifle at Karl Grissom, the Antichrist.

Danny took a deep breath, trying to steady his hands. "A tapestry of religion," he muttered, and flicked off the gun's safety.

Across the street, Karl Grissom fumbled with his keys.

TWELVE

Preternaturally dexterous fingers spun the tumblers.

6...6...6.

Click.

"I should have known," Christine said.

The case opened to reveal what appeared to be an ordinary notebook computer.

"Ask and it shall be opened," Mercury said.

"Isn't it 'knock and it shall be opened'?"

"Whatever. I opened it, didn't I?"

"So what does five oh seven mean?"

"Five oh seven?"

"The date the Apocalypse is supposed to start. That was the number the lock was set to before."

"Ah," Mercury said. "Synchronicity. Don't read too much into it. It tends to happen when there is a spike of activity in the SPAM. You'll likely see more of it as things progress."

"Things?"

"The End Times. Armageddon. The Second Coming. The seams are starting to show."

"So this is...really happening?"

They were sitting at a park bench at a rest area off Highway 4, just west of Sacramento. In light of Mercury's inexplicable knowledge of the attaché case in her trunk and General Isaakson's death, Christine was finding herself entertaining some truly absurd notions regarding all that had transpired recently.

"Like clockwork," Mercury said. "They're following the SPAM to the letter. Guess they didn't need me after all. Although I bet they're freaking out about Isaakson's missing briefcase by now."

"And you're really…"

"An angel, yes. Wanna see another card trick?"

"No!"

"Easy. Man, you're jumpy."

"Jumpy? This is the end of the world you're talking about!"

"I know," Mercury said. "Blows, doesn't it?"

"Can't you do something to stop it?"

"Not likely. Somebody's obviously got a transplanar energy trace on me. You saw what happened with my card trick. Imagine what would happen if I really started to interfere with things."

"So you're just going to let this happen?"

"Who do you think I am, Christine? I'm a friggin' *cherub*. Do you know where I rank in the angel hierarchy? Cherubim are the bottom of the angel food chain. Hell, if we were any lower, we'd be…"

"What?"

"It's not important. Trust me, there's nothing I can do. It's not personal; I like this place. I'd rather not see it end. That's the main reason I'm not helping out with the…"

"The *main* reason? You kinda sorta like Earth, so you're not going to help out with blowing it all to hell? What other reasons do you have?"

"Well…I don't know if you've noticed, but I'm not really a team player."

"Oh for…remind me to thank you for your lack of participation when the moon falls out of the sky. So what is this damn thing anyway?"

Mercury tapped the power switch, and the computer began to boot up.

"This," he said, with a flourish, "is one of the Four Attaché Cases of the Apocalypse."

"One of the four…isn't that supposed to be *horsemen* of the Apocalypse?"

"You have to understand that these things are allegorical. They didn't have laptop computers when John had his vision on Patmos."

"And the closest thing he could come up with was *horsemen*? That's not even *close*. How about…I don't know…magic boxes of the Apocalypse?"

"Oh, yeah, because 'the Four Magic Boxes of the Apocalypse' sounds really ominous."

"It's just the first thing I thought of. I'm sure he could have—"

"Watch out!" Mercury cried. "Here come the Four Magic Boxes of the Apocalypse!"

A nearby family moved to a more distant picnic bench.

"Fine," said Christine. "So this is one of the Four Attaché Cases of the Apocalypse. What do they do?"

"Depends which one it is. This happens to be the Attaché Case of War. See?"

He held the case so she could see the black insignia of a sword-bearing horseman. Christine recalled wondering about the symbol when the case was on Isaakson's table. Mercury set it back down. The screen now showed what looked like a satellite image of the globe.

"Got it. So what do we have to do, teach this thing tic-tac-toe so that it will understand the futility of war?"

"Not that simple, I'm afraid. The case isn't much use to us. But in the right hands…"

"Like General Isaakson's."

"Right. Potentially very useful. It's basically an intelligence device. Watch."

Mercury brushed his finger across the screen. The globe spun obediently. He tapped it and it stopped moving. He tapped it twice, in the vicinity of the Middle East. The screen zoomed in on the area west of the Mediterranean. He double-tapped it two more times, until the screen showed the border of Israel and Syria. She noticed that near the border on both sides were clusters of red dots.

"What are those?" she asked.

"Violence," Mercury said. "More precisely, violent intentions. The Attaché Case of War is patched into an extraplanar system that monitors violent thoughts occurring anywhere on Earth. Red patches are generally battlefields or gatherings of terrorists. Or soldiers."

"So this is how the Israelis knew where to hit. How they were able to move so quickly into Syria."

"Correct."

"But the Palestinian school…Isaakson said something about getting bad information. One-third of the 'tips' were wrong, he said."

"Yeah, that's the rub with the Attaché Cases of the Apocalypse. They're rigged to give you inaccurate information. Only two-thirds of those dots are actually centers of violence. The others could be…"

"Schools. Libraries. Mosques."

"Anything," Mercury said. "Generally something that looks like it could be a legitimate target."

"Why two-thirds?"

"That seems to be the maximum acceptable threshold. If it were less accurate, the political backlash would be too great. But using the case in conjunction with conventional intelligence, the Israelis could be certain of being right often enough to outweigh the costs."

The phrase echoed in Christine's brain. *Outweigh the costs...*

"Also, there is some significance to the fraction *two-thirds.*"

"And that is...?"

"In the Bible, perfection is represented by the number seven. Imperfection is represented by the number six. The decimal representation of two-thirds is point six repeating."

"So the number goes on forever," said Christine.

"Yeah," replied Mercury. "Always falling just a little bit short."

"So the number of the beast isn't six six six..."

"Technically, no. It's point six repeating."

"But...why?"

"Why what?"

"Why give the Israelis a faulty intelligence tool?"

"In a word," said Mercury, "mayhem."

"Mayhem?"

"I'm only guessing, but I think the idea is to provoke the Israelis into escalating the violence in the Middle East. Give them a weapon that promises to shift the fundamentals of the conflict in their favor, but at the cost of additional, entirely pointless violence."

"Violence that will inevitably provoke a response from the other side."

"Right," said Mercury. "Humans are nothing if not predictable."

"Why did General Isaakson want you to have the case?"

"He said that?"

"His last words were, 'Take it to Mercury.'"

"Well," said Mercury. "That could mean anything."

"He was holding the case when he said it."

"OK, but maybe he meant another Mercury."

"That's what I thought at first," said Christine. "I actually thought he meant the planet."

"The planet?"

"You do realize you share your name with a planet?"

"Don't remind me. Smallest planet in the solar system," said Mercury. "After everything I did for the Romans. That's gratitude for you."

"Mercury isn't the smallest…wait, you're saying the planet is *named after you*?"

"You know any other Mercurys?"

"Well, there's the god…"

Mercury grinned.

"You're not a god," said Christine.

"No," admitted Mercury, "but you'd be amazed at the impression you can make with a few miracles and a funny hat."

"How old *are* you?"

"Let's just say that I could tell you some stories about Tarquin the Proud that would make your hair curl."

"I have no idea what that means. And you haven't answered my question. Why did General Isaakson want you to have it? How does he even know you?"

"I may have…sort of…given it to him."

"What? Why? I thought you said you hardly knew anything about him."

Mercury shrugged. "I don't. It was my job. Besides, I thought it might be a good thing, you know, helping the Israelis get rid of the terrorists and suicide bombers. I didn't know the whole thing with the olive branch was going to happen. I hadn't really thought it through at that point."

"You didn't know it was one of the Four Attaché Cases of the Apocalypse?"

"Why would I? I thought they were supposed to be *horsemen*."

"So who told you to do this?"

"My boss, a seraph named Uzziel. He assured me it was in the SPAM."

"And was it?"

"Honestly, I'm not sure," said Mercury. "The SPAM is ridiculously long and hard to interpret. Nobody knows who wrote it, and it's written in High Seraphic, a language hardly anybody speaks anymore. I understand it has something like fifty different words for snow."

"You're thinking of the Eskimos."

Mercury snorted. "I think I would know if the SPAM was written by Eskimos. The point is that sometimes we just have to take it for granted that the higher-ups know what they're doing. So I did what I was told. But when I found out about the plans for the Apocalypse, I went AWOL."

Christine thought for a moment. "How did you know I had the case?"

"Lucky guess. I knew you were with Isaakson when he died. And I'm one of the few—angels or humans—who knew he had the case. I figured he must have mentioned me, which is why you showed up at the house."

"That girl, Ariel—she seemed to be expecting me."

"She was, in a sense," replied Mercury. "I gave her a list of the PAIs, along with pictures when I had them. I figured it was only a matter of time before one of them showed up. Synchronicity, you know. The illusion of free will is straining under the weight of determinism."

"The what is doing what under what?"

"Certain things have to happen for the Apocalypse to take place. They're going to happen, no matter what you and I do. We can go with the flow, or we can fight it, but the river is going where it's going. All we're doing is splashing around in the stream."

"So then...what's the point, if nothing you do is going to make any difference in the long run?"

Mercury shrugged. "Splashing is more fun."

Christine's eyes fell to the scattered red dots on the screen. "May I try?"

"Sure."

"How do I get it to..."

Mercury tapped a globe icon in the corner, and the blue-green image of Earth appeared again.

Christine spun the globe until the western coast of North America was visible. She tapped until the Bay Area filled the screen. Dots of red appeared here and there, seeming to spiral out from an epicenter in Oakland. She zoomed to their approximate location. No state boundaries or other markings were present; she had to go purely by the topography and the masses of red dots marking congested areas.

"Allow me," said Mercury. He deftly navigated the terrain until Highway 4 was visible—not a red line marking the highway, but what looked like the actual highway. His finger zipped along the highway until he found a pathetic patch of green amid the desert-like landscape. *Tap-tap*, and a little brown building was visible. *Tap-tap*, picnic tables. *Tap-tap*.

"Holy crap, that's *us*," said Christine.

"That's about as close as it'll go," Mercury said. He looked up and waved.

A tiny figure on the screen, barely recognizable as Mercury, waved up at Christine.

"Now slap me," he said.

"OK," she said, and slapped him across the face.

"Ow! What the hell?"

"You said to slap you."

"Yeah, but normal people hesitate a little."

"Sorry. I don't really like you."

"Clearly. OK, now watch the screen, and *then* slap me."

"OK."

She drew her hand back to slap him again, then looked at the screen. Next to the figure of Mercury was a smaller figure cloaked in a bright red aura.

"See that? Violent intentions. You don't even need to actually slap me for the…"

She slapped him again.

A flash of red lit up the screen.

"Ow!"

"Sorry, I wanted to see what would happen."

"Glad to be able to satisfy your curiosity," Mercury said, rubbing his reddened cheek.

"Also, I wanted to slap you again."

"Yeah, I got that."

"So in this instance at least, the case was accurate."

"Yes," Mercury said. "It will reflect any violent intentions. It also gives a lot of false positives, however. So it's pretty accurate if you know what to look for, but if you just scan an area for violent intentions, you'll get a lot of bogus info."

He tapped a spyglass icon, and then double-tapped the screen several times, causing the view to zoom out. He then drew a circle on the screen with his finger and tapped a button bearing a sword icon. An hourglass appeared for a second, and then the screen zoomed in on an area south of Sacramento.

"Hmmm," said Mercury. "Maybe something happening in Lodi." He zoomed in further until a bright red pinpoint appeared on the screen. He zoomed in on the red point until a brightly glowing red figure was visible in the center of the screen. The figure appeared to be climbing onto the roof of a small building. A few yards away was another building, over which waved a flag bearing the familiar logo of Charlie's Grill.

"Lodi?" Christine asked. "You mean…?"

"Yeah, like the song."

"You said what's-his-name, Keith, the Antichrist, was in Lodi. Is that him?" She pointed at the red dot.

"Hard to say," said Mercury. "I know he shows up at Charlie's Grill openings sometimes. But as far as I know, these sort of celebrity appearances generally don't involve the celebrity climbing onto the roof of the building next door."

"So who…?"

On the screen, it appeared that a crowd was assembling in the parking lot. The figure now glowed so brightly that his or her features were obscured.

"Wow," said Mercury.

"What? Who is it?"

"That, if the case is to be believed," said Mercury, "is one very angry individual."

THIRTEEN

A common belief on the Mundane Plane is that the lack of free will is what separates angels from human beings. This, of course, is rubbish. Given that the Almighty has preordained all things, free will is necessarily an illusion. As illusions go, however, it's an extremely convincing one, and we angels are just as subject to it as humans are. The difference is that humans, being mortal, don't have an eternity to make up for their mistakes, and therefore they take the illusion much more seriously.

One of the consequences of the hold this illusion has on human beings is the disproportionate amount of their limited time that human beings spend trying to figure out just how much freedom they don't have and what, if anything, they can do about it.

Two schools of thought have emerged on the issue.

The determinist argues that in a Universe governed by the principle of cause and effect, every event must have a cause. Further, if every event has a cause, then there is no such thing as "freedom"—every event is determined by the prior succession of events. The actions of human beings are not immune to this rule: everything a person does must have been determined by prior causes. Free will, then, is an illusion. Everything human beings have ever done—and will ever do—has been determined for eternity.

The advocate of free will blames the determinist for excusing all sorts of crimes, from child abuse to mass murder. After all, if everything we do is determined for us, then there can be no such thing as guilt or responsibility.

The determinist responds, "Well, what are you blaming *me* for? I didn't make the rules. Don't shoot the messenger and all that."

The free will advocate replies, "Why *shouldn't* I shoot the messenger? After all, if I do, it won't be my fault. It may simply have been determined from the beginning of time that I was going to shoot you."

Eventually the determinist concedes that perhaps the best option is for everyone to pretend that we have free will, since we don't really seem to have any choice in the matter, and he rather likes not being shot at.

The free will advocate begrudgingly accepts this compromise but insists that he is being magnanimous and was in no way obligated to do so.[8]

---

8   More recently, the free will advocate has been attempting to find ways to bolster his position by enlisting the help of quantum physics, which seems to indicate that the principle of cause and effect breaks down at the subatomic level. In fact, if the quantum physicists are to be believed, the entire Universe rests on top of a creamy layer of utter randomness.

The determinist points out that replacing causality with a roll of the dice doesn't really help the free will advocate's position much. It just means that when the serial killer turns out to have had a perfectly comfortable middle-class upbringing, he now has the option of blaming a run of bad luck for that unfortunate incident with the hatchet.

The determinist also points out that the randomness occurs at such a low level that it's unlikely to have much of an effect on anything of importance. For example, when you flip a coin, there are literally trillions of quantum events that go into determining whether the coin comes up heads or tails. It's as if every time you flipped a coin, you set into motion a trillion subatomic coin-flippers who each flip a coin and then report back to your coin with the results.

Ping! goes the coin. *Ping!* go a trillion subatomic coins.

"Well?" says the first coin. "What'll it be?"

"OK," say the trillion subatomic coin-flippers. "Forty-nine point nine nine nine nine eight four five one zero three five point nine nine percent of us say heads, and fifty point zero zero zero zero one five four eight nine nine six five five percent of us say tails. Phil, as usual, says to land on your edge and balance there. So it's basically fifty/fifty."

The first coin says, "Great. You guys are a big help, as always," and ends up on heads because it has a lot more important things to consider other than quantum phenomena that nobody gives a crap about.

Neither school of thought is in the end entirely satisfying to those who hope to find some shred of meaning in their existence, which is why many mortals—particularly those of a religious bent—tend to believe in a sort of fragile balance of free will and determinism. That is, they believe in a certain amount of freedom, but not so much as to cause the Divine Plan to go off the rails. They believe, in essence, that people are so many subatomic coin-flippers.

In the end, there isn't much practical difference between the two positions, which explains how most people on the Mundane Plane are able to believe, to some degree, in both of them simultaneously.

One such person was Danny Pilvers, who had been predestined from the beginning of time to be a would-be assassin. Danny Pilvers took very seriously indeed the illusion that he was making choices of his own free will. He had, he believed, made up his own mind to assassinate Karl Grissom, the Antichrist, while simultaneously believing that assassinating Karl Grissom was his inexorable destiny.

As fate would have it, he managed to be wrong on both counts.

Christine didn't know, of course, that Danny Pilvers was a would-be assassin. To Christine, who was just pulling into the parking lot some fifty feet away, he looked very much like an actual assassin. The fact that no one else noticed Danny was a testament to how still he was able to be, as well as how preoccupied the spectators were, because his green camouflage clashed badly with the brick-red tile roof of the Burger Giant.

Christine gunned the accelerator.

"Get down!" she shouted. But the Camry's windows were up, and the Charlie Nyx theme was reaching a crescendo. Even the roar of the engine was drowned out by crashing of cymbals.

Karl Grissom stood next to his car, fumbling with his keys. He was wearing a black polyester Antichrist costume which, despite having been custom-made for him, appeared to be at least three sizes too small. On his head was a football helmet—sans faceguard—that had been spray-painted black and had two large goat horns glued to it. What with the goat-head helmet and metal-studded black leather gauntlets, Karl was having a hell of a time with his keychain.

Most people would consider what happened over the next three seconds to be a highly unlikely set of coincidences. In fact, it was a highly unlikely string of events occurring in rapid succession, topped off with two minor miracles.

First, the Charlie Nyx theme ended, and the polarized crowd erupted in polite applause and hisses, respectively, depending on which side of the cheeseburger demarcation ribbon they were on.

Danny Pilvers took a deep breath.

Karl Grissom removed the goat helmet and placed it on the roof of the Saturn.

The director of marketing for Charlie's Grill said, "Let's have one more round of applause for the Antichrist. Give it up for Karl Grissom!"

Everyone looked toward Karl, who was now completely hidden from the crowd by the Saturn and the goat-head helmet.

Karl dropped his keys and bent over to pick them up.

Danny Pilvers, who had trained the sight of his rifle precisely between the goat horns, squeezed the trigger.

A bullet traveled from the barrel of the rifle toward the area that Karl's head had occupied roughly four tenths of a second earlier. The bullet punched a finger-sized hole through the front of the helmet.

The same bullet then punched a similar hole through the back of the helmet.

The bullet, having thoroughly enjoyed this hole-punching business, proceeded to punch holes in the windows of four nearby cars, finally coming to rest on page 328 of a dog-eared copy of *Gravity's Rainbow*, which is 186 pages farther than anyone else had ever gotten.

The helmet flew off the Saturn, caromed off a Dodge Caravan with two shattered windows, and smacked Karl Grissom in the forehead, knocking him unconscious.

Gasps of horror, excitement, and/or glee escaped from the crowd.

Christine's Camry slammed to a halt in front of Karl's Saturn. She threw the door open and yelled, "Get in!"

Karl did not get in because, having been struck on the head by a football helmet 2.8 seconds earlier, he was still unconscious.

Danny Pilvers, whose view of the Antichrist had been obscured by a rented Camry, decided to redirect his anger to a more accessible target. He set his sights on the plucky brunette behind the wheel and squeezed the trigger again.

At this point, Minor Miracle Number One occurred: the bullet discharged by Danny Pilvers's rifle decided, halfway between Danny and Christine, that it didn't share the hole-punching affinity of its comrade. It decided, in fact, to stop in midair, reverse course, and jump right back down the barrel of Danny Pilvers's gun. It did this with enough enthusiasm to throw Danny Pilvers off balance, causing him to roll off the tiled roof of the Burger Giant, bounce off the limb of a nearby shade tree, and break his collarbone on the value menu next to the drive-through.

Immediately thereafter, Minor Miracle Number Two occurred: the left rear door of the Camry opened by itself. Karl Grissom's limp mass rose three feet off the ground and floated into the Camry, coming to rest gently on the backseat. The door closed itself.

Christine, half expecting a pillar of fire to descend at any moment and void her insurance, turned and stared dumbly at Mercury.

"This would be a good time to leave," Mercury said.

She nodded and threw the car into reverse, peeling dramatically out of the parking lot. Screams and shouts from the bewildered bystanders followed them.

"Well," said Mercury. "That's going to get us some attention."

FOURTEEN

"I don't get it," Christine said. "Why does this stuff keep happening? Is this part of some kind of plot?"

She was having a hard time processing the sheer number of explosions, killings, and near killings she had experienced over the past few days. There didn't seem to be any rhyme or reason to it. Was this what she had to look forward to for the rest of her life, however long that would be? Just a series of random explosions? Where was the Universe *going* with this? She was beginning to feel like a character in one of Katie Midford's juvenile novels, in which—she had heard—every chapter ended with an explosion to keep the reader's interest.

They were back on the freeway, now headed south on I-5. Karl lay moaning and holding his head in the backseat. Mercury had looked him over and determined that he hadn't been seriously injured. Christine had to trust that angels knew about such things. Karl's house wasn't far; Mercury had rattled off the address—apparently from memory—in response to Christine's rhetorical hand-wringing about what to do with Karl. She figured she'd drop Karl off at home and then continue to her home in Southern California.

Mercury was in the passenger's seat, fiddling with the controls of the Attaché Case of War. "Man, things are heating up in Syria," he said.

"Well?" Christine demanded.

"Well what?"

"Is there a point to all this, or is it just the Universe toying with me again?"

"Hmmm," said Mercury, "I did mention something about the Apocalypse."

"And what was that back there? I mean, am I wrong or did Karl *float* into the backseat of my rental car?"

"Minor miracle," said Mercury. "All cherubim can do them. Assuming there's no interference, that is. I'm surprised they let me get away with two of them. Maybe they didn't have time to trace me after the first one."

"Two miracles?"

"Yeah, the first was more impressive, really. That second bullet was headed straight for—"

"And what are you *doing* here, anyway? If you didn't want to be involved in the Apocalypse, why are you hanging out with me and Karl the Antichrist, playing with your magic box?"

"The Apocalypse isn't like jury duty, Christine. I can't just opt out because I don't feel like playing."

"So you're just along for the ride?"

"Something like that. You're a fun person to hang out with. Besides, if you're going to risk your neck to do something stupid like save Dickweed here from assassination, I feel obligated to keep you from getting yourself killed."

"Hey," said Karl from the backseat. "What the hell?"

"None of this makes any sense to me," Christine said.

"Did you expect it to?" Mercury asked.

"It's just…" Christine said. "I pictured the Apocalypse being more…"

"Organized?"

"Well, yes. Isn't there supposed to be a more structured time-table? Rivers of blood, that sort of thing? I mean, what does this guy Karl have to do with anything?"

Karl sat up, still rubbing his head. "Did you hit me with your car? I think I've got whiplash. It hurts like a mother—"

"He's the Antichrist," explained Mercury. "Can't have an Apocalypse without an Antichrist. That would be like *The King and I* without Yul Brynner."

"Yul Brynner died in 1985."

"And it hasn't been the same since, has it?"

"OK, but this guy is clearly not the actual Antichrist. Look at him."

Karl was a heavyset, balding man in his late thirties, with pasty skin and a dull look in his eyes. He had the look of someone who spent most of his time playing video games in his mother's attic, probably because he did, in fact, spend most of his time playing video games in his mother's attic.

"What are you, retarded?" said Karl. "Everybody knows I'm the Antichrist. And guess what, now the Antichrist is going to sue you for hitting him with your stupid car and then kidnapping me—I mean him. Who are you people anyway?"

"She's a reporter," said Mercury. "She's doing a story on you."

Christine started, "No, we're taking you—"

"And what happened back there? I don't even remember…"

"You passed out back at Charlie's Grill," said Mercury. "Must have been the heat."

"Where's my friggin' helmet? I only have six of those, you know." He was peering at Christine in the rearview mirror. "Your face is kind of weird."

"We're taking you home, Karl," Christine said.

"For the interview," said Mercury. "We're going to interview you at home."

Christine turned to Mercury. "Why are you doing this?"

"You are a reporter, right? Karl here is a big story. Even bigger now that someone has tried to kill him."

Christine muttered, "Why would anyone want to kill *him*?"

"Kill who?" asked Karl.

"'*Kill who?*'" repeated Christine incredulously. "Don't you know what—"

"Charlie Nyx," interjected Mercury. "There's a plot to kill Charlie Nyx."

"Well, duh," said Karl. "The Circle of Seven was exposed at the end of *Charlie Nyx and the Flaming Cup*. The Urlocks wanted to kill Charlie so that—"

"Shhhh!" Mercury said. "Christine hasn't read *The Flaming Cup* yet. Don't spoil it for her."

"You haven't read…have you read *any* of the Charlie Nyx books?"

"She's a journalist. Not much of a reader."

"That's me," said Christine. "If it weren't for my duties chauffeuring the Antichrist to and from assassination attempts, I'd never lift my knuckles off the ground at all."

"So she's a reporter," said Karl. "Who are you?"

"Well," Christine began, "he's an angel…"

"Agent," Mercury said. "She means agent. I'm here to talk to you about doing a cameo in the next Charlie Nyx movie. Name's Mercury."

"Mercury? Is that Jewish or something?"

"Yes, exactly," Mercury said. "I'm a six-foot-four Jew with silver hair. Just like Jesus."

"What about my car?" said Karl. "You can't just leave my car at Charlie's Grill."

"Why don't you get some sleep, Karl," said Mercury. "You probably have a concussion from that knock on your head."

Christine said, with some concern, "Aren't you supposed to keep someone awake if they..."

But Karl was already snoring in the backseat.

"Don't worry," said Mercury. "He doesn't have a concussion. Probably. Anyway, that was just a mild sleep suggestion. Perfectly safe."

"Another minor miracle?"

"It may surprise you to find that many people find me very persuasive. I don't resort to using miracles for every little mundane thing."

"Just momentous tasks like card tricks."

"That was a demonstration. Special circumstances."

"Like wanting to impress me?"

"Why, did it work?"

Christine decided to change the subject. "Do you know as much about Karl as you do about me?"

"More. Not to denigrate your importance, but he *is* the Antichrist."

"So you're saying that he really is *the* Antichrist? Not just the winner of some stupid contest, the *actual Antichrist*?"

"That's the intel I have," Mercury said. "He wasn't exactly what I expected either."

"Then who was that trying to shoot him?"

"Not sure," said Mercury. "That wasn't in the SPAM."

"The Schedule of..."

"Plagues, Announcements, and Miracles."

"But why would it be? I wouldn't think that shootings by crazed gunmen would make it onto that kind of schedule."

"No, you're right. In fact, individual mortals don't play much of a role in the Apocalypse. Your role is primarily to panic, start wars, and die from pestilence. Those are activities normally done in large groups. When an individual person does something truly unexpected, there is usually some unauthorized supernatural intervention involved."

"So," she said to Mercury, "you're saying that we have no say in our own Apocalypse? The whole thing has been scheduled for us, and we don't even get to play?"

"Pretty much. But that's basically your whole history in a nutshell. We give you a certain amount of freedom, but when things go too badly off course, the SPAM kicks in. Cherubim like me make adjustments and get things moving in the right direction again."

"So what happens when someone like Lee Harvey back there goes off his meds?"

"Precautions are taken to keep things like that from happening."

"Very effective, I see. So why did you save Karl?"

"Oh, you know. It seemed unsportsmanlike. I still think he's a dickweed."

At this point, three things happened at almost—but not quite—exactly the same time.

First, Christine noticed a blue light flashing in her rearview mirror. Two cops on motorcycles. Probably CHP, she thought.

Second, she passed a sign reading, "Lodi Next 3 Exits."

Third, Christine realized that Creedence Clearwater Revival's "Lodi" was playing on the radio.

"Dammit!" Christine spat.

Just about a year ago, I set out on the road...

"What?" said Mercury.

"Police," said Christine.

Seekin' my fame and fortune, lookin' for a pot of gold...

"I think this is Lynyrd Skynyrd," said Mercury.

"CCR," said Christine. "It's synchronicity."

Things got bad, and things got worse, I guess you know the tune...

"Synchronicity?" said Mercury, glancing in the rearview mirror. "OK, now *that's* the police."

"It's CCR. Creedence Clearwater Revival."

"Creedence Clearwater Revival is pulling us over on motorcycles? Damn, this is a weird town."

Oh lord, stuck in Lodi again.

"What do I do?"

"Well, if they were cops I'd pull over. But I don't know what the protocol is for being pulled over by John Fogerty."

"What, no miracles up your sleeve for this one?"

"Every miracle I perform is one more chance for you to be playing ping-pong with Ariel for eternity. So what do you say we take our chances with Ponch and John here."

Christine grumbled and pulled over. The cops stopped about twenty feet back. One remained on his bike, while the other walked up to Mercury's side of the car. Mercury rolled down the window.

"Nice bike," Mercury said. "I was going to get one, but my wife here says they lower your sperm count. We're trying to have another baby," he added, glancing lovingly at Karl, still sound asleep in the back.

"Step out of the car, please," said the cop. He was muscular and tall—almost as tall as Mercury. An angular jaw jutted out from beneath his visor.

"Something wrong, officer?" asked Christine.

"Please just step out of the car, sir," said the cop. His hand was on his holster.

"OK," Mercury said. "But I am *not* going to squeal like a pig, no matter how nicely you ask."

Mercury got out and stood in front of the cop.

"Turn around."

"You have to buy me dinner first."

"Turn *around*," the cop said, more angrily this time. His thumb flicked the snap of the holster.

"OK, OK, no need for that. Can I see some ID, though?"

The cop looked sternly at Mercury for a moment, then started to laugh. He reached into his belt and pulled out a small piece of charred paper. He held it up for Mercury to see.

It was the ace of spades.

The cop flicked the card at Mercury. It twirled and landed at his feet, facedown. A pair of bicycle-riding cherubim adorned the back.

"Striking resemblance, isn't it?" the cop said. He holstered his gun and removed his helmet. The man could have been Mercury's brother.

"Gamaliel," said Mercury coldly. "I suppose that's Izbazel back there."

The cop on the bike smiled and waved.

"They're cherubim," said Mercury to Christine.

"Oh, thank God," said Christine, stepping out of the car. "We thought you were going to arrest us for kidnapping, or being involved in the assassination attempt. You have no idea how relieved—"

"That was pretty stupid, using the Attaché Case of War," Gamaliel said. "You made it very easy to find you. Good thing we started intercepting the signals after the pillar of fire destroyed your house. That was impressive, by the way. You've evidently made someone very angry."

"Evidently," said Mercury.

"You know what we want, Mercury."

"Well," said Mercury, "if you're anything like me, a Styx reunion tour is pretty high on the list."

"Give him to me."

Mercury started, "I'm sure I don't—"

"The Antichrist, Mercury. Hand him over."

"Hang on," said Christine. "We just saved this guy's ass. What exactly are you planning on—"

Gamaliel pulled his gun. "Obviously," he said flatly, "we're going to kill him."

FIFTEEN

It was a testament to Mercury's persuasiveness that he was able to convince Gamaliel and Izbazel to sit down over a cup of coffee like civilized beings and work out what was to be done with Karl the Antichrist. It was a testament to Karl's incessant whining that they ended up at another Charlie's Grill, just three miles down the highway from the last one, watching him scarf down three cheeseburgers.

"So you see," Izbazel was saying, "we're the good guys here."

"How do you figure?" Christine asked.

"No Antichrist, no Apocalypse. Having an Apocalypse without the Antichrist is like…help me out here, Gamaliel."

Gamaliel started, "It's like…"

"*The King and I* without Yul Brynner," Mercury said.

Izbazel's brow furrowed. "Hasn't Yul Brynner been dead since like…"

"Nineteen eighty-five," Christine said. "I tried to tell him. So you want to kill—"

"*Eliminate* a key component of the Apocalypse, yes," said Izbazel.

Karl looked long and hard at Izbazel and then said, "Are you gonna eat those fries? Did you know that I can eat here for free? You guys have to pay, though."

"He *is* a dickweed," muttered Mercury.

Christine said, "You can't just kill—"

"Eliminate," said Izbazel. "And why not? Save millions of lives by eliminating one annoying little..."

"Dickweed," said Mercury. "Can we settle on 'dickweed'?"

Karl interjected, "Who did you say you guys were again?"

Izbazel spoke up. "We're from the production company. We want to give you a cameo in the next Charlie Nyx movie."

"How much?" Karl said, his mouth full of fries.

"I'm sorry?" Izbazel said.

"How much do I get? I don't do this stuff for free, you know. Why didn't you guys get more ketchup? Nobody ever gets enough ketchup."

"Don't worry, Karl," said Izbazel. "You'll be taken care of."

Christine had a bad feeling about Izbazel. He was smaller than Mercury and Gamaliel, and he had a grating voice and a nervous, fidgety way about him. He reminded Christine of the sort of door-to-door salesman who had a way of hinting not very subtly that if nobody bought the remarkable cleaning products he was selling, he might have to return to his career of stealing electronics from the homes in the neighborhood.

She was less certain what to make of Gamaliel. He was brawny and handsome, and had the easygoing way of the high school football star who hadn't yet learned that his ability to throw a perfect touchdown pass was in no way going to translate into anything remotely useful in the real world. He seemed likable enough, but there was something about him she didn't quite trust either. Part of what troubled her was that while Izbazel seemed to be the one calling the shots, she couldn't see Gamaliel falling for his sales pitch.

"How many of you are there?" asked Mercury.

Gamaliel smiled, revealing rows of perfectly formed, brilliantly white teeth. "Enough to throw a wrench into the SPAM."

"Is that movie lingo?" asked Karl. "You know what I've always wondered? What's a 'grip'? And what's the difference between a 'grip' and a 'key grip'?"

"On whose authority are you acting?" Mercury asked.

Gamaliel glanced at Izbazel, who remained stony faced. Gamaliel shrugged. "Best not to say at this point."

Christine said, "So you guys are what are known as..."

"Fallen angels, yes," said Gamaliel. "Although I'm not certain the paperwork has gone through." He glanced at Izbazel, who shrugged.

Izbazel added, "We prefer the term 'free spirits,' of course. 'Fallen' makes it sound like we're just clumsy. I mean, it's not like we tripped or something. 'Hello, what's this? Someone needs to do something about that little rise in the floor there.' It takes some chutzpah to declare your independence from the Heavenly bureaucracy."

Gamaliel continued, "Anyway, we'll definitely be designated as Fallen if we don't check in soon. As will your pal here, by the way. You might as well join us, Merc. You're going on the list either way."

"I'm waiting to see how the first-round draft picks go before I pick a team," said Mercury.

"In any case," Gamaliel explained to Christine, "being a fallen angel isn't as ominous as it sounds. It's like when you got labeled 'impertinent' in fourth grade."

Christine's jaw dropped. "How the hell...?"

"PAI," said Mercury. "It's all in the dossier."

"Holy hell," said Christine. "How did *I* get sucked into all this?"

"Not really sure," said Gamaliel. "The PAI designations are made at a pretty high level. Above our pay grade, as it were."

Christine shook her head. "So let me get this straight: God tells you it's time for the Apocalypse, and you decide to take it upon yourself to stop it?"

"Well," said Gamaliel. "First of all, it's not like God held a press conference for all the angels. There's quite a layer of bureaucracy between us and God."

"But...you've *seen* Him?"

"Oh, of course I've *seen* Him. Old guy, long flowing beard. Uncanny resemblance to Charlton Heston."

"You're making fun of me, aren't you?" said Christine.

"Do you even believe in God, Christine?" asked Gamaliel.

"To be honest, I'm not entirely sure."

"Well then, I'm not entirely certain I've seen Him," said Gamaliel. "Fair enough?"

"But how can you not be certain whether you've seen God? Either you have or you haven't."

"I would agree," said Gamaliel. "Either I have or I haven't."

"So...which is it?"

"Not sure. How would I know?"

"What do you mean?"

"I mean, God isn't a koala bear."

"I'm sorry?"

Gamaliel said, "It's not like I can go down to the God exhibit at the Heaven Zoo and snap pictures of God munching on eucalyptus leaves and say to myself, 'Yep, that's God all right, because it says so right there on the plaque.' You mortals think that once you step outside the Mundane, everything is crystal clear. It's true that some things become clearer, but whole new levels of ambiguity open up as well."

"So…angels are just as confused as human beings are?"

"Confused? Well, I suppose so. But we are confused on a higher level, and about more important things."

"OK, but the SPAM, it presumably comes down from God Himself?"

"Presumably," said Gamaliel.

"So is it God who's behind this Apocalypse? Or Lucifer?"

"Both," answered Izbazel. "The events of the Apocalypse are governed by a legal document called the Apocalypse Accord. God isn't a direct signatory, of course. He doesn't get involved at that level. The Accord was hammered out over several thousand years by various representatives of Heaven and Hell. And things are complicated by the fact that Lucifer isn't the only demon with pretensions to world domination. There's Beelzebub, for example. And Tiamat. A lot of us were actually betting on Tiamat to be the predominant demonic power. Lucifer was something of a dark horse. Hey, Mercury, didn't you used to hang out with Tiamat back in the day?"

Mercury shrugged. If Christine didn't know better, she'd have said he was embarrassed. "I was on her staff for a bit in the third millennium BC. I was on the ziggurat."

"You were on what?" said Gamaliel.

"The ziggurat. Step pyramid. Everybody was building pyramids back then."

"Oh yeah," said Gamaliel. "The global pyramid race. What was that all about anyway?"

"Beats me," said Mercury. "It was just the thing to do at the time. Nobody really put much thought into why. Pyramids were like the parachute pants of the third millennium BC. The Egyptians schooled us all, of course."

"Well, they did have Osiris on their team at the time."

"Yeah," said Mercury. "Hard to compete with that. I tried to tell Tiamat to go in a different direction. I thought domes were the way to go. But she wouldn't listen. She just wanted to keep building taller and taller ziggurats. Well, you know how *that* turned out."

"The *point* is," interjected Izbazel irritably, "nobody fully understands the entire plan. The angels are all just acting on orders, doing their part to bring about the Apocalypse because that's what we've been told to do. My feeling is that if God wants the Apocalypse to happen, He's not going to let me stop it."

"So you're *testing* Him?" Christine asked incredulously. "You're going to try to stop the Apocalypse and see if God lets you?"

Izbazel said, "Let's just say that I'm tired of having my life dictated by some stupid, arbitrary schedule that I don't even understand. Angels have better things to do than…anyway, it's stupid and I'm sick of it."

Christine said, "So the guy with the rifle, that was your doing?"

Gamaliel shrugged. "Danny Pilvers is an unstable individual. We may have whispered in his ear a bit. Angels can be very persuasive."

"We try not to get involved directly in Mundane events," said Izbazel. "We work through human agents when we can. But your little stunt back there prevented the…adjustment we were trying to make. So now we need to finish the job and get out of here before somebody traces us and we get hit with a Class Three."

"Just so we're clear then," Christine said, "none of you cares a whit about millions of people dying from plagues, famine, and war. Mercury just wants to hang out like an apocalyptic tourist, and you guys want to kill an innocent person to thumb your nose at the angelic bureaucracy. Is that about right?"

"Our motives are irrelevant," Izbazel said. "The point is that we're trying to stop the Apocalypse. You have to admit that's a worthwhile cause. And it certainly justifies eliminating an individual who has contributed absolutely nothing to the greater good."

"What it comes down to," Christine said, "is that you want to kill an innocent person to prove a point. You don't even know that killing him will stop the Apocalypse. You're just guessing."

"I gotta pee," said Karl. "Move it."

Karl was seated in the middle of the semicircular booth, flanked by Gamaliel and Izbazel. Christine and Mercury were on the outside. Christine and Gamaliel stood up to let Karl out.

"It's not that simple, Christine," Gamaliel said. "We've been working on the Mundane Plane for most of the past seven thousand years, and after a while you realize the futility of trying to—"

"Hey, Karl's on TV!" exclaimed Mercury.

A TV hanging from the ceiling in the corner was tuned to a news channel. On the screen were shaky images from someone's camcorder, taken at the event in Lodi earlier that day. The ticker on the bottom of the screen read, "'Antichrist' Karl Grissom shot in the head...location of body unknown..."

The video showed Karl walking to his car, and then it cut to a shot of the helmet being struck by a bullet and dropping out of sight. Then a white Camry pulled in between the camera and Karl. The rear door on the opposite side of the car opened, there was some blurry movement, and then the car screeched away.

There were shots of Karl's deserted Saturn, surrounded by police tape.

"Holy crap," said Mercury. "They think he's dead."

"That'll make this even easier," said Izbazel. "So what do you say, Mercury? You're not going to cause trouble for us, are you?"

"Never should have done that card trick," Mercury muttered to himself. He looked at Izbazel. "I'd prefer to stay out of it altogether."

"Then stay out of it," said Izbazel. "Stay here and finish your coffee. Do whatever it is you do. We'll take Karl off your hands."

"He *is* a dickweed," said Mercury thoughtfully. "This isn't going to come back to me, is it?" He was absentmindedly smearing ketchup around his plate with the long edge of a french fry.

"We never even saw you," said Gamaliel.

Izbazel nodded. "This doesn't concern you, Merc. You just got caught in the middle of it. You're not supposed to have anything to do with the Antichrist in the first place. You didn't want to be involved in the Apocalypse, and I can respect that. So *stay uninvolved.*"

Gamaliel said, "We're not asking you to do anything. Just stay out of our way, and don't make trouble for us later on. We didn't see you, and you didn't see us. The Antichrist got shot in that parking lot, and then somebody dumped his body in a ravine in the foothills."

"Hmmm," said Mercury. "Here's the thing. There are different levels of noninvolvement." He now had a fry in each hand, pushing ketchup around his plate.

Gamaliel looked puzzled. "I don't follow you."

"You see," Mercury went on, "I'm involved now, whether I like it or not. So anything that I do at this point is going to have repercussions."

"Sure," said Gamaliel. "But what do you mean by 'different levels of noninvolvement'?"

Mercury said, "Well, for example, there's the level where I let you take Karl and give him the hole in his head he so desperately needs. That's one possibility."

"Uh huh," said Gamaliel.

"And then…" Mercury started. "Hey, look! I made a ketchup angel!" He seemed genuinely surprised.

The two fallen angels looked down at Mercury's plate. He had indeed made a ketchup angel.

"Have either of you ever made a snow angel?" Mercury asked. They shook their heads.

"Funny, isn't it? We spend hundreds of years down here and never bother to make anything, even for fun. It's such a human trait, wanting to make a mark on your surroundings."

"Vanity," said Izbazel. "Nothing lasts forever."

"True," said Mercury. "But I think I'd like to leave a mark before it's over. I want to make a snow angel. Or…no, a snowman! I'll make a snowman!"

"Folly," said Izbazel. "Talk about something impermanent. Besides, where are you going to find snow this time of year?"

Gamaliel was still examining the ketchup angel. "It looks a little like Bamrud," he said, cocking his head.

"Bamrud?" Mercury said.

"You remember. Cherub, worked for the MOC until the Middle Ages."

"Oh yeah! Wasn't there some kind of scandal…?"

"They caught him skewing plague statistics. Trying to beat the spread, you know."

"That's right! What's old Bammy up to these—"

"Please!" Izbazel interjected. "Can we get back to the matter at hand? Mercury, all we need from you is an assurance that you won't interfere with our plan to eliminate the Antichrist."

"Oh, right," Mercury said. "As I was saying, there are different levels of noninvolvement. On one level, I let you take Karl and have your way with him. Another..." Mercury sat back and smiled broadly. "Another is that I sit here talking to you about that first level, not to mention ketchup angels, just long enough for Christine to get Karl back on the interstate. That's another possibility."

Izbazel stood up. A white Camry peeled out of the parking lot.

"Damn you, Mercury! I told you to stay out of this!"

"I am," said Mercury. "Completely uninvolved. You guys want cheesecake?"

"Let's go," barked Izbazel. He started for the door, Gamaliel following. "We'll catch them on the bikes."

"I wouldn't do that if I were you," Mercury said.

Izbazel stopped and turned, fuming. "*More noninvolvement, Mercury?*"

"If you guys leave, I won't have anybody to talk to. I was thinking of calling Uzziel."

Izbazel growled, "What's Uzziel going to do? He doesn't have the authority to—"

"Forget it," Gamaliel said. "He's got us."

"How's that?" Izbazel asked.

"Angel Band. They'll trace it right here. They'll be on us in seconds. Of course," Gamaliel said, looking sideways at Mercury, "they'll get him, too."

"Yeah, they'll get me," Mercury said. "But where am I going to hide when this place is gone anyway? They were always going to get me. Now or a few weeks from now, what's the difference?"

Izbazel was furious. "So you're going to let the Antichrist live? You're just going to let it happen. The Apocalypse, Mercury. The end of your precious world."

Mercury shrugged. "None of my business," he said. "Have a seat, boys. It's just the three of us, stuck in Lodi again."

Gamaliel sighed. "I always hated the Allman Brothers."

SIXTEEN

There were thirty-eight Charlie's Grills on I-5 in between Yreka, California, and Los Angeles, spaced so that on a road trip from one end of the state to another one could eat breakfast, lunch, and dinner—not to mention brunch, linner, and several other meals to be named later—from a completely standardized menu of entrees that ranged in quality from passable to mediocre.

This proliferation of family restaurants was not, despite the protestations of anti-sprawl advocates and concerned cardiologists, part of any kind of diabolical plan. This isn't to say that there was no plan, or that there weren't demonic entities involved in its inception, but the actual marketing strategy and franchise agreements were no more intrinsically satanic than was the norm for the hospitality industry. Charlie's Grill was evil only to the extent that it concealed the unremarkable character of its food with a façade constructed of faux brick walls and artificially weathered signs promoting no-longer-existent brands of soda and/or motor oil with slogans like "The smoothest yet!" That is to say, it was about as evil as Applebee's.

Charlie's Grill was, pure and simple, a moneymaking operation for Lucifer, who had long ago come to terms with the fact that while spreading depravity and ruination was his true calling, it didn't always pay the bills. Lucifer was a true believer in the adage that no one ever went broke overestimating the number of times a day that Americans can pull over for cheeseburgers. It wasn't an exciting or particularly sinister way of making money, but it did make possible all sorts of other costly but worthwhile diabolical schemes, so Lucifer expanded the operation at every opportunity.

Thus it was not really all that surprising that precisely as Izbazel and Gamaliel sat fuming at Mercury in the Charlie's Grill on the outskirts of Lodi, another fallen angel was just finishing up a grilled cheese sandwich in a Charlie's Grill just north of Los Angeles. The angel's name was Nisroc.

Nisroc, as I believe I've established, had a habit of eating grilled cheese sandwiches when he was nervous. He was in the process of developing another bad habit, that of rebelling against the Divine Plan—although to be fair, this was at present more of a vague inclination that was in danger of gelling into habit than a full-blown habit, per se.

Nisroc pulled out of the parking lot in his green 1987 Chevrolet El Camino, sipping an extra large Diet Dr Pepper. He had no particular reason for choosing diet soda, but drinking unpalatable low-calorie beverages eased his guilt somewhat at indulging gustatory cravings that had no basis in his angelic biology. He turned north on I-5, traveled for 6.2 miles, and then, slavishly following the GPS unit he had been given, made an abrupt right turn into the middle of nowhere.

He drove due east—or as close to due east as the terrain would let him—for another 1.8 miles, kicking up so much dust that, even with his superhuman vision, he could hardly see to avoid the rocks and occasional specimen of brillo-pad-like vegetation. Meanwhile, the GPS was imploring him to please make a U-turn at the earliest opportunity, because it did not at all like where this was going. Nisroc didn't particularly like where it was going either, but he was pretty sure he no longer had much of a choice. At last the El Camino coasted to a stop as near as he could get to the coordinates he had been given. Taking a deep breath, Nisroc grabbed a silvery briefcase from the passenger seat and got out.

Spying the horizon, he saw that he was not alone. A big white refrigerated truck—the sort used to deliver frozen fish to restaurants—sat perched on a plateau about two hundred yards away. Next to it stood a lone figure. Nisroc walked toward him.

They met atop the plateau, Nisroc and another angel, who introduced himself as Ramiel. Nisroc knew the name—Ramiel had recently been classified as Fallen. Nisroc wondered how long it would take for his own paperwork to go through. His superiors had undoubtedly noticed his disappearance by now.

"So this is it," said Ramiel, taking the case from Nisroc. The case was plain except for a small insignia of a skull.

"The one and only," said Nisroc, feeling less certain than ever of his decision.

"Do they know it's missing?" Ramiel asked.

Nisroc shrugged. "I've been out of contact for a few days. They've probably classified me as AWOL by now. I imagine finding the case is going to be a fairly high priority."

Ramiel smiled. "Don't worry," he said. "We'll put this baby to good use."

Ramiel carried the case to a flat area of ground that had been marked with orange spray paint and set it down. He dialed the combination 6-6-6 and popped open the case. The device's screen came to life, displaying an hourglass while it readied itself.

Nisroc considered leaving but suspected that this course of action would be taken as cowardice. No, now that he had come this far, he would have to see it through.

"Let's see what this baby can do," said Ramiel. Nisroc got the feeling that Ramiel was the sort who used the word *baby* to refer to inanimate objects a lot. He sighed.

Nisroc was at this moment supposed to be on the other side of the globe, in southern Asia. He was supposed to have delivered the Attaché Case of Death to an Australian relief agency working in Kashmir, but he didn't understand the reasoning behind this decision, and his requests for justification went unanswered.

When an agent of Lucifer approached him, offering him anything he wanted in exchange for the case, he had initially said no. He was not one to be swayed by material things—although the eternal membership in Lucifer's exclusive golf club and resort on the Infernal Plane was sorely tempting. What finally pushed him to Lucifer's side was that while Heaven only offered unsatisfactory bureaucratic answers to Nisroc's questions, Hell had at least explained to him what they planned on doing with the case. He would have preferred that their plan be something other than reducing Earth to an uninhabitable ash heap, but at least they were up front about their motivations. One had to respect that.

He still had mixed feelings about the whole business, but he supposed it was too late to ask Heaven for a do-over at this point. He had heard that the Almighty was infinitely merciful, but the bureaucracy was eternally unforgiving—and it was the latter that signed his paychecks.

"Mind helping me with the corpses?" said Ramiel.

Nisroc grunted assent. He imagined that as one of the Fallen, he would be subjected to questions like that more often.

They walked to the refrigerated truck and opened the back. The truck was parked facing up a slope, and as the doors swung open, a pile of corpses tumbled out onto the dusty ground. There must have been a baker's dozen of them, in an assortment of shapes and colors.

"Robbed the city morgue last night," said Ramiel. "You'd be amazed how many people LA goes through in a day."

Having been to LA, Nisroc was not at all amazed. He nodded, feeling a bit squeamish. "I don't suppose we could just—"

"No miracles," said Ramiel. "Can't take a chance on somebody picking up our signature. We've got to move them by hand."

"Won't Heaven pick up the signature of the case anyway when we use it?"

"They might," said Ramiel. "Although I understand these cases have a surprisingly small energy footprint. But yeah, we've got to do this fast. Five minutes and we're out of here."

"OK," said Nisroc. "Which one first?"

"Doesn't matter," said Ramiel. "Let's drag them all over and line them up. Hopefully we've got enough."

They dragged the corpses to a spot near the case, lining them up side by side.

Ramiel opened a panel inside the Attaché Case of Death, pulling out a pair of what looked like defibrillation paddles. They were connected to the case by thick coils of wire.

"Ready to see this baby in action?" asked Ramiel.

Nisroc smiled weakly.

"Grab that shovel," Ramiel commanded.

"What do I need a shovel for?"

"What do you think? These guys are going to be popping up like gophers. I need you to whack them as soon as they wake up."

"What? We're going to kill them again?"

"Kill, stun, whatever. I just don't want them wandering around and asking stupid questions while I'm trying to work. We don't have time for that."

"It seems unsportsmanlike," said Nisroc, observing the row of corpses piteously. "Cruel, even."

"Look, they're already dead, OK? They're *supposed* to be dead. You can't do anything to them that's worse than what's already happened."

"But doesn't bringing someone back to life give you some responsibility for them? It's like adopting a puppy. You can't just whack the puppy with a shovel when you're done with it."

"Why not?"

"Because you can't! It's just not done!"

"Whatever," said Ramiel. "Just grab the shovel."

"Fine," grunted Nisroc. He had to admit that having the undead wandering around was not going to make things any easier. This was no time to be developing scruples. If they were going to do this, it had to be done right.

Ramiel flipped a switch on the case, took hold of the paddles, and knelt over the first corpse, a bloated drowning victim in her late twenties. The case hummed ominously.

"Clear!" yelled Ramiel, pressing the paddles onto the woman's chest. A surge of interplanar energy surged through her body, causing it to jerk wildly. As the case channeled mysterious energies, its inner workings moved on a logic of their own, dictated by the numerical constant $0.666\ldots$

The Attaché Case of Death is so named because it allows the user to exercise power over death itself. A device that can *cause* death is, of course, hardly revolutionary. Humankind has been perfecting such devices—from the flint-tipped spear to the triple bacon sausage burger that had briefly graced the menu of

Charlie's Grill—for thousands of years. The remarkable thing about the Attaché Case of Death is that by channeling supernatural energies in a precise way, it can actually *reverse* death.

The power of the case is nearly unlimited, but like its brothers, the Attaché Case of Death was built with an intentional design flaw. Every use of the case is a roll of the dice. Two-thirds of the time it will work exactly as hoped, bringing the subject back to life. There is always a 33.3 repeating percent chance, however, there will be what can mildly be described as "side effects." Sometimes these side effects include freak lightning storms or flash floods. Sometimes they include spontaneous combustion. And sometimes they are something altogether unexpected.

The Attaché Case of Death is not without logic, however, and it tends to take advantage of naturally occurring phenomena to maximize damage while minimizing the amount of energy it uses. If used in a wooded area, it might cause a forest fire. If used on a boat, it might cause a hurricane. If used at a precisely determined spot directly on top of the San Andreas Fault, it might cause an earthquake.

Which is exactly what Ramiel, minion of Lucifer, was hoping for when he reanimated the late Isabella Gonzalez, age twenty-eight, of Venice Beach.

"Dios mio!" screamed Isabella, sitting bolt upright. She was wearing a lacy white dress.

"I'm really very sorry about this," pleaded Nisroc, and smacked Isabella on the head with the shovel. She fell limply back to the ground.

Ramiel sat quietly for a moment, his ears straining for any sound.

"Nothing," he said. "Next!"

They moved to the next corpse, a heavyset older gentleman.

"Clear!" yelled Ramiel.

"Where…is this heaven?" gasped the old man, his eyes blinking in the desert sun.

"I'm sorry," said Nisroc, and smacked him with the shovel.

Still nothing happened. They moved to the next corpse, a middle-aged woman.

"Clear!" yelled Ramiel.

The woman let out a terrified scream.

"Really, I'm *very* sorry," said Nisroc, and smacked her with the shovel.

Still nothing.

"Clear!" yelled Ramiel.

"Oh my God what—"

"Sorry!"

Twang!

This went on three more times before the El Camino spontaneously exploded, showering them with bits of trim and pieces of its engine.

"I'll be needing a ride," said Nisroc.

Ramiel nodded. "We're running out of time," he said. "They may already have pinpointed our location. We've got to get out of here. Clear!"

"Holy sh—"

Twang!

"Sorry," said Nisroc. Then, to Ramiel: "I don't think this is going to…"

The earth began to shake.

"Thank God," said Ramiel, forgetting himself.

Nisroc grunted agreement. He was glad to be done with the shovel-smacking business.

"Let's just hope that does it," said Ramiel. "Otherwise we'll have to come back with more corpses in a few hours and fire this baby up again."

"So we're not going to load these back into the truck?" said Nisroc, motioning to the corpses. He couldn't fully hide his relief.

"No time. We gotta split."

They hopped in the truck and sped off through the desert.

Not long after, Isabella Gonzalez awoke in the desert north of Los Angeles with seaweed in her mouth and one hell of a headache, surrounded by corpses. This was not how she had expected her honeymoon to end.

On the other hand, having just married the second Sedgwick in the personal injury law firm of Sedgwick, Sedgwick and Golaska, it probably couldn't have been expected to end much better. The best that could have been expected was a long and uneventful marriage with a second-tier Sedgwick, a prospect that she now realized—thanks to her brush with death and a smack on the head with a shovel—did not interest her in the least.

Isabella was a paralegal in the firm of Sedgwick, Sedgwick and Golaska, having been hired for her intimate knowledge of personal injury law, her attention to detail, and her fantastic breasts. Isabella was used to her breasts factoring into all of her interpersonal relationships; she was, in fact, thrilled when she learned that they were only two of four qualifications taken into account by the hiring committee at Sedgwick, Sedgwick and Golaska. Sadly, she could not be so certain about the motivations behind the marriage proposal of the second Sedgwick.

She had accepted the proposal, she realized now, mainly at the urging of her family, who were concerned for her long-term financial prospects, very much enjoyed the use of the second Sedgwick's pool and hot tub, and wanted her to marry while her breasts could still command top dollar. There was no denying that breasts like hers were a ticking time bomb; the effects of age and gravity could only be deferred for so long. So she had married the second Sedgwick to get them off her back (her family, not the breasts, which remained firmly attached to her front), but now that she was miles away from him, she felt as if a great weight had been lifted from her shoulders.

The weight returned when she sat upright, but it was a good kind of weight—the kind of weight that meant that she was finally on her own, finally responsible for her own fate. For the first time in her life, she was free.

Getting to her feet, she regarded her surroundings. Where was she? Somewhere in the desert outside of Los Angeles, she guessed. Tire tracks led down to what looked like a highway in the distance. Lying on either side of her were half a dozen corpses.

Who were these people? she wondered. Other wedding reception attendees who had drunk too much and fallen over the side of the *Aztec Princess*? It seemed unlikely. She didn't recognize any of them, and none of them were wearing formal attire. Also, three of them had bullet holes in their foreheads.

She gave up trying to make sense of the situation. Whatever had happened to these people, it was clear that her life had been spared. It didn't matter why or by whom. She had been given a second chance. That's all that mattered.

She would walk to the road, hitchhike into town…and then what? Change her name, get a job as a waitress? It didn't matter. Things would work out. She was young and alive, and she still had a good three, maybe three and a half years to secure her future before her breasts gave out. She was free.

Isabella Gonzalez took a deep breath and smiled, her head held high. She strode boldly toward the highway—toward her limitless future.

She got three steps before she was engulfed in a pillar of fire.

SEVENTEEN

"You'll be sorry you did this," said Izbazel.

Mercury shrugged. "I doubt it," he replied. "You overestimate my capacity for introspection."

"You've had your fun," Izbazel chided. "You've done your part to make sure this pointless war goes on as planned. We'll never catch up to the Antichrist. Now hand over the case."

"I think I'll hold on to it for a while," said Mercury. "I like the pretty pictures it makes."

"I suppose you're going to hand it over to Uzziel, like a good angel? Get back into Heaven's good graces?"

Mercury shrugged again.

"You're an angel," Izbazel said. "You can't just sit out the Apocalypse."

"I'm a contentious objector."

"You mean conscientious."

"No, there's nothing conscientious about it. I'm just objecting, for the sake of objecting. I'm a highly contentious objector."

"You have to pick a side," Gamaliel said.

"Why?" asked Mercury. "You didn't."

"Of course we did," replied Gamaliel. "There really are only two sides: pro-Apocalypse and anti-Apocalypse. You know this whole thing is a charade. The two supposedly opposing sides have been hammering out the details of this 'war' for millennia. The real opposition—the only real choice—is to try to stop this senseless carnage."

"Senseless carnage, right," Mercury repeated. "So who are you working for?"

"Sorry?" said Gamaliel.

"Come on, guys. You didn't hatch this little revolt on your own."

Gamaliel said, "I assure you, we're acting autonomously."

"No, you're not."

"How would you know?"

"First of all," Mercury said, "there are two of you."

"Right," said Gamaliel. "We're working autonomously together."

"And how many other autonomous angels are on the team?"

Gamaliel started, "That's none of your—"

"OK, Merc, listen," said Izbazel. "There are a few others. You know I can't give you names at this point. But we've got several high-placed angels…"

"Higher than you, I take it?" said Mercury.

Izbazel sat back and smiled. "If you really want to know, hand over the case. I might even put in a good word for you. Maybe find you a place on the team."

Mercury cocked his head thoughtfully. "A place on the team, eh? What positions are still open, now that you two have filled the moron and backup moron spots?"

"Dammit, Mercury!" Izbazel growled. "You think you're so high and mighty, staying above the fray and all. You know what you are? You're a coward, not to mention a fool. You think your wisecracks are going to help you when all Hell breaks loose on this plane? You're going to be wishing you had picked a side. At least we'll go down with a fight. You're going to get rolled over like…an ant."

"An ant?" Mercury said, frowning. "You almost had me when I thought you were going to say 'turtle.' I wouldn't want to get rolled over if I were a turtle. But an *ant…*"

"Fine," said Izbazel. "Let's agree to disagree and go our separate ways. But, Mercury, you're going to have a hard time claiming neutrality if they catch you holding on to that case. If the Apocalypse does happen and Heaven wins, like everybody expects, you're going to be in some serious trouble. But if you hand the case over to us, then you can't be charged with anything more serious than being AWOL. In fact, you could argue that you tried to do your part by saving the Antichrist from us. The case is no use to you. Just hand it over, and we'll walk away."

"What do you even need the case for?" asked Mercury. "All it does is pinpoint centers of violence. How does that help you?"

"Just trying to make sure it doesn't fall into the wrong hands," said Gamaliel.

"I have an idea," said Mercury.

"Yes?" said Izbazel.

"You wanna see a magic trick?"

"Come on, Mercury," said Gamaliel. "You know what happened the last time you tried a card trick."

"No, not a card trick," said Mercury. "A real magic trick. Watch." Mercury picked up a spoon from the table and held it up, gently pinching the neck with his thumb and forefinger.

"Seriously, Mercury," said Izbazel. "No more 'magic.' They have a bead on you. We'll be lucky if it's only a Class Three this time. They'll probably blast this whole town just to make sure you don't get away."

Mercury squinted and began to slowly caress the spoon with his thumb.

"Come on, Mercury," said Gamaliel. "You may be a little crazy, but you're not suicidal."

Mercury stared at the spoon, deep in concentration.

Izbazel pleaded, "Merc, think of all the people in this restaurant. All the people in this town. You want to get them all killed over a stupid magic trick?"

Conversations ceased at other tables as all of the diners turned their eyes to Mercury.

"Merc," said Izbazel.

Mercury's eyes closed. His hand began to move rhythmically back and forth.

"Merc, come on."

Sweat beaded on Mercury's forehead. His breathing deepened.

"Mercury, dammit! Stop!" Izbazel was near panic.

The head of the spoon began to move, ever so slightly, at odds with the handle.

"Mercury, you lunatic, Stop it!"

The head of the spoon bent forward.

There was a collective gasp from the restaurant's patrons.

Izbazel and Gamaliel both leapt to their feet. They ran to the door, flung it open, hopped on their motorcycles, and screeched away.

The head of the spoon sagged and wilted, then fell to the table. Mercury held only the handle. He picked up the fallen piece and held both pieces up, one in each palm.

The restaurant erupted into applause.

A small boy who had been sitting nearby walked up to the table.

"How…did you…do that?" he gasped.

Mercury smiled. "Trick spoon." He snapped the pieces together and handed them to the boy.

The boy stared at the spoon in his hand. "How do I…?"

"You'll figure it out," said Mercury. "Anybody can do it. Just remember, the real trick is in the presentation."

Mercury paid the bill and left.

EIGHTEEN

The Antichrist had spent the night on Christine's couch. As if she hadn't been through enough, she had heard on the drive down that a minor earthquake, centered just north of Los Angeles, had hit the area. Fortunately, it had apparently done little damage. She was so exhausted from the drive and the day's events that she fell asleep with her clothes on as soon as she had satisfied herself that her linoleum was no worse for wear.

Christine had leveled with Karl, explaining what had happened in Lodi. Well, she had *almost* leveled with him. She had to tell him that she was a Secret Service agent to get him back in the car, and she had kept up the ruse so that he'd let her take him to meet Harry.

She wasn't entirely certain why she was taking him to meet Harry; it just seemed like the thing to do. Until now, Harry's tendency to commingle the spiritual with the temporal had always made her a little uncomfortable, but now that the two had collided in the unlikely form of Karl Grissom, she found herself envying Harry's way of looking at things. If anyone would know what to do about Karl, it would be Harry.

She had told Karl that Harry was the director of a covert branch of the Secret Service based in Los Angeles that was charged with protecting Drew Barrymore and the Antichrist. Karl was the kind of person who would readily accept an absurd story if it were filled out with enough bizarre and arbitrary details.

The next morning they met Harry in his office at the headquarters of the *Banner*. Despite her ambivalence toward Harry, she was relieved to be in the company of a more-or-less normal, sane individual.

Harry was, inexplicably, completely taken with Karl.

"So you weren't wearing the helmet? On the video, it looks like…"

"I guess I ducked," said Karl. "Yeah, I have pretty fast reflexes."

"He bent over to pick up his keys," Christine said. "The bullet missed him completely."

Harry closed his eyes and spoke aloud. "'And I saw one of his heads as it were wounded to death; and his deadly wound was healed: and all the world wondered after the beast.'"

"Is that from a book?" asked Karl.

"Revelation thirteen verse three," said Harry.

"That's pretty cool, I guess," said Karl. "I know almost all the lyrics to R.E.M's 'The End of the World as We Know It.'"

Christine started, "*Everyone* knows almost all the—"

"That's great, Karl," said Harry. "You obviously have a lot of potential."

"So did you get him yet?" Karl asked.

Harry said, "Whom?"

"The guy who tried to shoot me, of course. Did you catch him or what?"

"Er," Harry said.

"Harry isn't at liberty to discuss such matters," Christine said. She added, for good measure, "National security."

Harry gave Christine a puzzled look. Christine found her attention drawn to an interesting tuft of carpet. She wondered how her linoleum was holding up.

"Karl, would you like a soda?" asked Harry. He held out a dollar. "There's a machine in the lobby, on the first floor."

"About friggin' time," said Karl. "I'm practically dying of thirst." He stomped out of the room.

"Sorry," said Christine. "I had to tell him you were Secret Service to get him down here."

Harry nodded, as if he had figured it was something like that. He sat down behind his desk and motioned for Christine to take a seat in one of the chairs opposite him. In the middle of Harry's desk, next to his flat panel monitor, was a beautiful, leatherbound King James Bible.

Christine proceeded to tell Harry an edited version of the previous day's events. She left out Mercury and the pillar of fire. In her version, Gamaliel and Izbazel were a couple of anti–Charlie Nyx fanatics who had threatened Karl in Lodi.

"I'm not really sure what to do with him," Christine concluded. "Should we take him to the police?"

"I'd like to do a story on him," said Harry. "Have you interviewed him yet?"

"Uh," Christine began. "Does listening to someone talk about Charlie Nyx until you start to consider the merits of swerving into oncoming traffic count as an interview?"

"He's a person of…he's an important person," said Harry.

"No," said Christine. "He's a…." Only one word came to mind. "He's a what?"

"A…dickweed," said Christine.

"That's not really for us to say," admonished Harry. "A lot of people think that this Antichrist contest is the final straw in the mockery of religion. I'd like to hear what Karl has to say about that."

"Honestly, Harry, I don't think he's put a lot of thought into it. And frankly, Karl is only a story because people like us are saying he's a story. You do realize that the Charlie Nyx marketing people are using you, right? The more we whine about their stupid pseudo-satanic marketing gimmicks, the more books they sell."

"Pseudo-satanic?" said Harry. "That's an interesting distinction. 'He who is not with me is against me.' Matthew twelve verse thirty. On what side of that line are your pseudo-Satanists?"

Christine was getting fed up with Harry's deliberate obtuseness. "Harry, please. You can't honestly believe you understand what's going on here well enough to report on it. What if you're only seeing a very small part of the picture? What if there are..." She struggled to convey the baffling complexity of the situation without referring to motorcycle-riding cherubim, magical briefcases, or pillars of fire. "What if there are forces beyond your understanding at work here? What if you're just a prawn, er, *pawn*, being manipulated on a chessboard?"

"Then I have a responsibility to report what I see from my square on the board."

"OK, but you also have a responsibility to not pretend that you can see the entire board."

"I'm not following you, Christine. Where are you going with this?"

"Look," said Christine, grabbing the Bible from Harry's desk. She flipped it open to near the end and began to read:

"And I saw the woman drunken with the blood of the saints, and with the blood of the martyrs of Jesus: and when I saw her, I wondered with great admiration. And here is the mind which hath wisdom. The seven heads are seven mountains, on which the woman sitteth. And there are seven kings: five are fallen, and one is, and the other is not yet come; and when he cometh, he must continue a short space. And the beast that was, and is not, even he is the eighth, and is of the seven, and goeth into perdition. And the ten horns which thou saw are ten kings, which have received no kingdom as yet; but receive power as kings one hour with the beast. And he saith unto me, The waters which thou sawest, where the whore sitteth, are peoples, and multitudes, and nations, and tongues. And the woman which thou sawest is that great city, which reigneth over the kings of the earth."

She closed the book. "Are you going to tell me, Harry, that you understand all of that?"

"Revelation seventeen," said Harry. "That passage refers to the Whore of Babylon, who appears at the very end of the tribulations. Many scholars think that she signifies Rome, although during the Middle Ages it was commonly thought that—"

"The fact is," said Christine, wagging the Bible at Harry, "you have no idea who or what the Whore of Babylon is. It's all conjecture. So while you waste your time looking for the Whore of Babylon in the current events section of the paper as if it were some kind of diabolical version of *Where's Waldo*, real events are occurring that people need to know about. I mean, I hear there's a war going on somewhere."

"We'll cover that, too," said Harry. "It's all…"

"Connected?"

"I was going to say 'important.' All of this stuff—the situation in the Middle East, Karl, the thing with the corn in South Africa…"

"The corn in South Africa?"

"Oh, the AP just reported it. There's some kind of mutant strain of corn that's taking over South Africa. We've got Dave looking into it."

"Mutant corn? Are we talking about twelve-foot stalks of corn walking down Main Street or what?"

"Nothing that dramatic. A biotech company down there has been doing some testing of biogenetically altered, pesticide-tolerant corn. Evidently some of it got away from them, and they're having a hard time getting it under control."

Christine was dubious. "Doesn't corn move kind of…slowly? It sounds like they're not trying very hard."

"I don't know the details, but I guess a lot of people are concerned. They were counting on this new strain of corn to ease poverty in sub-Saharan Africa, but now it looks like this corn might actually wipe out a lot of other crops. Crazy stuff."

"Yeah," said Christine. That *was* weird.

"And then there's this thing with the morgues. Have you heard? Somebody broke into a morgue downtown yesterday and stole a dozen corpses. Then this morning they broke into another morgue and stole ten more. Explain *that* to me."

"Easy," said Christine. "Somebody underestimated the number of corpses they needed."

"The point is," said Harry, "there's a lot of crazy stuff going on in the world, and the public needs a sane voice to explain it to them."

For a moment Christine didn't follow him. "Oh!" she eventually said. "You mean *us*."

"The *Banner*, Christine. We have a responsibility to report all of these events as part of a coherent narrative that people can understand."

"But that's my point," sighed Christine. "You don't know the whole story, so the only way you can come up with a narrative is to *make one up*."

"We've been given the narrative. God tells us of His unfolding plan for creation."

"And you feel that you understand this plan?"

"God has given us His blueprint for history. We just need to open our eyes and ears."

"So you believe with one hundred percent certainty that we're headed toward Armageddon?"

"We've always been headed toward Armageddon. It's just a question of proximity. Look, we're not going to go on the record as saying, yes, this is the beginning of the Apocalypse, but I certainly do think it's our responsibility to point out how our current situation mirrors the teachings about the End Times found in the Bible."

"Fine," said Christine. "Let's say you're right. Let's say—hypothetically speaking—that we really are in the End Times. In that case, hypothetically, what would our position be?"

"Position? I don't follow you. We're a news magazine. We don't take positions; we report the news."

"But clearly we do take positions. I mean, this is a Christian publication. So we take the Christian position. Or at least *a* Christian position."

"Of course," said Harry. "But that's like saying we take the position of truth over falsity. It goes without saying that we are on the side of truth. *Time* and *Newsweek* claim to be on the side of truth, too, of course, but they have a different understanding of truth. A deficient one, in my opinion. Any conception of truth that leaves out God—or makes God only a contingent possibility—is inherently deficient. There is no truth apart from God."

It was rare for Harry to go off on such an abstract tangent, and it was throwing Christine off her train of thought. "I guess what I mean," she said, "is...are we pro-Apocalypse or anti-Apocalypse?"

Harry laughed. "You might as well ask whether we're pro-earthquake or anti-earthquake."

"OK," said Christine. "Are we pro-earthquake or anti-earthquake?"

"What difference does it make?"

"It makes a difference," said Christine. "If you could stop an earthquake, would you?"

"Of course, but that's a ridiculous…"

"What if we could stop the Apocalypse?"

"You can't stop the Apocalypse. It's part of God's plan."

"But what if you could? I mean, you and I have our differences in how we interpret 'God's plan,' but you know that I appreciate the way our staff covers natural disasters. Even when that meteor hit the Bellagio last year, we never even mentioned the possibility that it was some sort of divine retribution. Which is, of course, more than I can say for a lot of religious media outlets…"

"What's your point, Christine?"

"When an earthquake or a hurricane hits, we treat it as a tragedy—in other words, as something that should not have happened. An objectively bad thing that we would have prevented if we could have. I mean, maybe it's God's will that thirty-three thousand people died in an earthquake in Pakistan last year, but we don't cover it like, 'Sorry, folks, God's will, you know. Better luck next time.' We may acknowledge that it's part of God's plan, but we also acknowledge that sometimes God's plan *sucks*. So how is the Apocalypse different? I mean, if we can see it coming, shouldn't we try to stop it?"

"You're talking about the Second Coming, Christine. Christ returning in glory. It's not a bad thing."

"Right, but evidently Christ can't return until the earth has been turned into a molten slag heap, which kind of blows. I just don't get why the Prince of Peace has such a destruction fetish. Can't He just swing by in glory some sunny Tuesday after lunch?"

"Careful, Christine. Remember that the tribulations of the End Times are the result of man's sin. It isn't Christ who desires destruction."

"Exactly! He doesn't want it, we don't want it. Po-tay-to, po-tah-to, let's call the whole thing off."

The Antichrist returned, bearing a Dr Pepper. "The selection of snacks in your vending machine sucks. Did you say something about potato chips?"

"No," Christine said. "We were talking about—"

"Stopping earthquakes," said Harry.

"That's stupid," said Karl. "You can't stop earthquakes."

"Precisely," said Harry. "They just…"

Karl pulled the tab on the can. There was a pop and a hiss.

"…happen," finished Harry.

The floor shook beneath their feet.

Christine clutched the edge of Harry's massive oak desk with her right hand as the room shook. Harry's oversized Bible was still in her left. "Oh no," she said, sounding more like a mother scolding a habitually misbehaving child than someone afraid for her life. She was starting to get fed up with almost dying in a freak disaster.

Karl was standing in the middle of the room, arms spread and feet splayed, like someone trying to balance on top of a seesaw. Harry was in the process of trying to crawl under his desk.

The *Banner*'s offices were on the fifth—and top—floor of the building, so the vibrations of the earthquake were alternately softened and magnified as they worked their way up the structure. While the bottom of the building jerked and rumbled, the top swayed and snapped like the boughs of a willow tree. Ceiling tiles fell and walls groaned. Harry's computer crashed to the floor. It went on, and on, and on.

"I'm going to be sick," said Karl, still holding the can of Dr Pepper, which was now spewing its contents on the floor.

Christine felt the same. *Just fall down already*, she thought to the building. Her goals in life had been reduced to keeping her breakfast down until she was crushed by falling concrete.

Just when it seemed that the building couldn't possibly take any more, an interplanar portal opened in the floor, right in the middle of the room.

Christine didn't *know* it was an interplanar portal, of course. It was roughly circular, about three feet in diameter, and comprised of a strange interlocking pattern of glowing lines. It looked as if someone were shining a spotlight covered with a cardboard cutout pattern onto the floor. It looked so much like that, in fact, that the three of them momentarily looked at the ceiling. Their eyes found nothing to explain the illuminated pattern on the carpet.

"Oh man," cried Karl. "This is it. I'm dead."

"Don't be stupid, Karl. You're not dead," shouted Christine, sounding more certain than she felt. But she realized somehow that she knew what the thing was.

"It's a doorway," she said. "Some kind of portal. I think someone is trying to help us get out of here."

"A doorway?" said Karl. "To where? Hell?"

"No!" shouted Harry, peering out from under his desk. "My work isn't done yet! Go away!"

"Does it matter?" said Christine. "We're dead if we stay here."

"Screw this," said Karl as he stepped into the circle. His frame shimmered for a moment and then was gone.

The room pitched violently. A fluorescent light fell to the floor with a crash. Massive cracks snaked along the walls.

"Harry!" yelled Christine. "This may be our only chance!"

"No!" cried Harry again. "I have to see it through! I'm not ready to die!"

"You're going to die if you stay here," shouted Christine. "We don't know what's on the other side of that thing. Maybe God is offering you a way out so you can finish your work."

A plate glass window shattered.

"You have to go through, Harry!"

"No! You do it!"

"I will, but I'm not leaving you here! I'll be right behind you."

Harry tentatively got to his feet, gripping the edge of the desk. "I'm…scared," he said.

"Of course you're scared, Harry. But you have to do this. It's our only chance."

Harry crept toward the portal. One hand still held firmly to the desk. "But…I don't know what's on the other side," he murmured.

Christine let go of the desk and grabbed the Bible with both hands. She lifted it in the air and brought it down hard on Harry's white-knuckled hand. Harry screeched in pain, letting go of the desk.

"It's called 'faith,' Harry," growled Christine. "Look into it."

She shoved Harry with all her might toward the portal. He stumbled into it and disappeared. As the ceiling fell down around her, Christine dove after them.

NINETEEN

Christine, Harry, and Karl found themselves in an altogether strange and yet uncannily familiar place.

"Are we in Hell?" asked Karl fearfully.

"Close," said Harry, who was still visibly shaken but doing his best to regain his composure. "It looks like…"

"An airport terminal," finished Christine.

It did indeed resemble the concourse of a medium-sized airport. There were gates, waiting areas, and throngs of tired-looking individuals lugging baggage from one place to another. There were even shops with whimsical logos in a strange alphabet, places that presumably sold snow globes and baseball caps at entirely unjustifiable prices. Only one thing was missing.

"There are no planes," said Harry. "There are gates, but no planes. People seem to be arriving out of nowhere."

Then he noticed something like a hummingbird zipping towards them down the concourse. As it got closer, he realized that it was much bigger—and creepier—than a hummingbird. It was a small, fleshy pink man in what looked like a cloth diaper, with wings sprouting from his back.

"Taking in the view?" asked the winged creature.

"Sorry?" said Harry.

"Tell me," said the creature, "on the pathetic plane you came from, do the natives customarily wear each other as hats?"

"Er, no," said Harry.

"Then I suggest you move," it said. "You're standing on the portal. No telling when the next group will arrive."

They looked down to see a complex pattern etched into what looked like a fifteen-foot square sheet of marble.

"Yes," said the creature. "Take it all in. Why should you do what I tell you to do? It's not like I've been working here for eight thousand years or anything."

They shuffled sheepishly to the waiting area.

"Can you tell us where we are?" Christine asked.

"Certainly," said the creature. "First, though, I should like to give you a bit of advice."

"Er, OK," said Christine.

"To maintain freshness," the creature said, "keep mushrooms in a paper bag in the refrigerator."

"I've heard that," said Karl.

"Oh," said the creature sardonically. "Then I suppose it *must* be true. If *you've* heard it. It's not like I've been working this job for nine thousand years or anything."

"You said—" Harry started.

"Who *are* you?" Christine said. "*What* are you? You look like a cherub...I mean, what I thought cherubs—"

"Cheru*bim*!" snapped the creature. "And I'll tell you who I am."

"OK," said Christine.

"First, though," it said, "a bit of advice."

"Fine."

"To unstick a stubborn zipper, try rubbing a pencil over it several times."

"Why are you telling us these things?" Christine asked, bewildered. "Are we likely to find stubborn zippers and mushrooms here?"

"Why am I telling you these things?" the creature asked incredulously. "What kind of silly question is that? Is this your first time in a planeport? You realize that if you keep asking questions like that, it's going to cost you."

"We don't have any money," said Christine. "I mean, I've got a few dollars, but I don't even know what—"

"Money!" the creature scoffed. "I work for tips!"

"I'm sorry," said Christine. "As I was going to say, I don't even know what kind of money—"

"Not money!" the creature spat. "*Tips.* I work for tips. You know, how to get red wine out of cashmere. That sort of thing."

Christine frowned. "I don't know how to get red wine out of cashmere."

"Not yet you don't," said the creature. "But if you keep asking silly questions, you will."

"Hold on," said Harry. "You mean that you will help us in exchange for us listening to *your* tips?"

"Wouldn't you like to know?" said the creature.

"Yes," said Christine. "We would."

"Fine. Then I will tell you. First, however, a bit of advice."

"Wait," said Christine. "You still owe us one. You gave us two tips but you still haven't told us your name."

"My name," it said, "is Perpetiel. Perp for short."

"OK, Perp," said Harry. "Where are we?"

"You really don't know?" asked Perp.

"Do people normally ask you questions they know the answer to?" said Christine impatiently.

"Do you really want to know?" said Perp.

"No!" growled Christine. "I mean, that last one was a rhetorical question. But we do want to know where we are, even if it means you have to tell us how to get red wine out of cashmere."

"Oh, I'm not going to tell you that."

"Why not?"

"Because now you're curious about it. I'm not going to waste my advice answering questions you want to know the answer to. That's not how it works. By the way, you should always send a thank-you note after a job interview."

"I couldn't care less about getting red wine out of cashmere," Christine lied. "Just tell us where we are."

"As you wish," said Perp. "If you don't want a cat to jump in your lap, avoid making eye contact with it."

"Really?" asked Karl.

"No, Karl," said Christine. "I'm pretty sure that one is wrong."

"Who cares?" said Harry. "Now he's got to tell us where we are."

"This," said Perp, motioning around him, "is a planeport."

"It looks like an airport," said Christine. "Except that there are no planes. The one thing that it is missing, in fact, are planes. Why would you call it a planeport?"

"In blackjack," Perp said, "if the dealer has an upcard of five, don't take any new cards because the dealer will probably bust. It's called a planeport because it allows you to travel from one plane to another. That thing you were standing on was an interplanar portal. But surely you knew that. You had to step on one to get here."

"We didn't have much choice," said Christine. "We were about to die in an earthquake. The 'portal,' as you call it, just appeared in front of us."

"Really?" asked Perp. "That's actually…rather interesting. You don't know who might have opened an emergency portal for you? Do you know any important angels?"

Christine and Harry both looked at the floor, making non-committal noises.

"Well," said Perp. "In any case, it appears you've been summoned. Follow me."

"Summoned?" said Harry. "By whom?"

"How would I know?" said Perp. "Nothing on my schedule for today, but you know how seraphim are. They think nothing of an unscheduled summoning. You can figure that a properly riveted joint will have three-fourths of the strength of the pieces it joins together."

Perp turned and flew back down the concourse the way he had come. The three of them had no choice but to follow.

They walked for what seemed like miles through the planeport, while Perp prattled on about how to thaw a frozen car door lock, calculate the height of a building using only a thermometer, and make mock hollandaise sauce.

Perp, it turned out, was a sort of combination skycap and escort, who tended to bewildered travelers such as themselves—although he took pains to note that he had never met a group quite so bewildered as they. There were other porter angels escorting other travelers, but none who looked like Perp. Amid advice on the best wine to serve with chicken and how to find the fastest ferry across the river Styx, Perp explained to them that he was a very "traditional cherub." Evidently angels could, to some degree, choose their own physical appearances, and several hundred years ago it had been fashionable to appear as a nearly naked infant with birdlike wings. Currently the style was to look more like an adult human male, but Perp was never much for jumping on the fashion bandwagon. "In another five hundred years," he said, "the infant look will come back around. *Then* who'll be the trendsetter?"

Presumably most of the "people" they passed were, in fact, angels of some sort. From what they could gather from Perp's occasional pertinent comments, the three of them were the only actual human beings in the planeport, and perhaps the only human beings who had ever been to the planeport.

Perp suddenly turned down a narrow hallway, leading them to an unremarkable conference room. It was the sort of depressing little meeting room that had no windows except for a panel of glass that served only to make one nostalgic for the corridor one had just left. At the head of a long faux-mahogany table sat a tall, angular man who, although he superficially resembled the other angels Christine had met, had a softer, tired look about him. He was wearing a suit that made him look a bit like a used car salesman.

"Have a seat," said the man.

The three of them sat. Perp buzzed quietly back down the hall.

"What the hell is going on?" Christine demanded.

"That's what I'm hoping to determine," said the angel.

"And you are?" asked Harry.

"My name is Uzziel. I'm a seraph."

Uzziel, thought Christine. I know that name. He's...Mercury's boss?

"So...are we dead?" said Karl.

"No," said Uzziel. "But you almost were. If I hadn't opened that temporary portal in Harry's office, you would be. So, explain yourselves."

The three of them sat dumbly for a moment, staring at Uzziel.

"Er, what?" said Harry.

"That earthquake wasn't on the Schedule. Clearly someone is up to something."

"Clearly," said Harry. "But as you just mentioned, the earthquake nearly killed us, so presumably that someone isn't us. Unless you're suggesting that the three of us were attempting suicide by earthquake."

"Well," said Uzziel, obviously rethinking things. "Well, it *is* your fault."

"My fault?" said Harry. "How on earth could it be *my* fault?"

"Not just yours," Uzziel said. "The fault is all of yours."

"Well, sure," Harry said. "Original sin and all that. In a sense, I suppose we're all to blame…"

"No," said Uzziel impatiently. "The fault. It's yours."

"I as much as admitted that," replied Harry, starting to get annoyed. "I'll concede that humanity in general is to blame for the evil in the world. But if you're suggesting that the three of us are somehow specifically—"

"Not the three of you," said Uzziel, impatiently. He made a broad, sweeping gesture with his hands. "*All* of yours. The fault. It belongs to you. All of you. Earth."

"I think he means…" said Christine.

"I know what he means. He's trying to blame us for the damned earthquake. Listen, pal," Harry said, stabbing his finger at Uzziel, "you're the angel. You're supposed to know what's going on with the earthquakes and Apoc…that is, the other stuff that's going on."

Christine's eyes narrowed toward Harry. "What did you just say?"

"Nothing," said Harry. "I was just saying that angels shouldn't expect us to know about earthquakes when they're the ones in control of everything." He turned to Uzziel. "You are in control, correct?"

"Well, yes," said Uzziel, suddenly on the defensive. "Don't misunderstand me. A little wrinkle like an assassination attempt or an unplanned earthquake isn't going to derail things. I'm merely attempting to pin down a few X factors so that there aren't any further surprises. I believe you're all aware that plans for the Apocalypse are well under way..."

Karl said, "The plans for *what?* I thought I was just supposed to be in a movie."

"Er," said Uzziel. He turned to Christine. "He doesn't know?"

Christine shrugged.

"OK, so," said Uzziel. "Karl, you understand that you are the Antichrist, correct?"

"Duh," said Karl.

"I'm not sure you understand, Karl," said Uzziel. "We're not just talking about some silly contest anymore. You're the *actual Antichrist.*"

Karl stared blankly at the angel.

"Ah, OK, then," said Uzziel.

"It's part of his charm," explained Christine.

"Hmmm, right," said Uzziel. "And Christine and Harry, you understand that you have been designated as Persons of Apocalyptic Interest?"

Christine couldn't muster the effort to feign ignorance. She and Harry both grumbled something vaguely affirmative, and then each of them examined the other suspiciously, as if to say, "And you were planning to tell me this *when?*"

"So here's the deal," Uzziel continued. "A lot of work has gone into planning this. I mean, thousands of years of negotiations between our people and Lucifer's people."

"People?" asked Christine.

"Sorry, it's a generic term for sentient beings. When I say 'people,' I generally mean angels, although of course humans are occasionally involved."

Christine and Harry nodded understandingly. Karl looked like he wanted to ask a question but couldn't decide what the question was.

"As I was saying, a lot of work has gone into designing the Attaché Cases of the Apocalypse, getting them to the appropriate people..."

"Selecting the appropriate Antichrist..." added Christine.

"Er, yes," said Uzziel. "That's not my department, of course. Not to mention centuries of groundwork, setting up the situation in the Middle East, funding the right biotech companies...you get the idea. And now somebody's trying to foul it all up. Killing off General Isaakson, trying to assassinate the Antichrist, stealing the Attaché Case of War..."

Christine wanted to weigh in, but she couldn't decide whose side she was on. She was, in fact, having trouble figuring out what sides there were to choose from. She found herself looking around for a menu.

"Have you seen the case, Christine?" Uzziel asked. "Does Mercury have it?"

So he knows Mercury's off the reservation, thought Christine. What about the other two, Gamaliel and Izbazel? How do they figure into this?

"Mercury?" asked Harry. "The cult leader in Berkeley? When did you...?"

"Our intelligence indicates you met Mercury shortly before... the natural gas explosion."

Christine snorted. "Natural gas explosion! You sent a pillar of fire to incinerate the house!" Christine was only guessing. She had no idea who was responsible for the pillar, but this joker seemed like a good bet. "A *Class Three* pillar of fire," she continued, jabbing her finger at Uzziel. "What, a Class Two wouldn't have gotten the job done? That's just sloppy, if you ask me."

Uzziel sighed. "Mercury was a problem," he said. "He had access to some sensitive information about the Apocalypse, and he could have caused some trouble for us if he decided to. We were watching the interplanar energy channels for his signature. It was decided that if anything came up, we'd torch him."

"And everybody around him."

"We suspected you were with Mercury," said Uzziel, "and that you had the Attaché Case of War. Collateral damage is sometimes unavoidable. You were another X-factor, another unknown that could throw off our calculations. And we couldn't let the case fall into the wrong hands."

"Right," said Christine. "No telling what could happen if it got into the hands of someone really dangerous. The next thing you know, there'd be rivers of blood, stars falling from the sky…"

"We're not about chaos or violence for no reason," explained Uzziel. "That is, that's not the *plan*. I'm sure the other side has differing ideas. These things have to be orchestrated in a very precise way. Otherwise, the Apocalypse would degenerate into pointless mayhem."

"Well, that would clearly be a problem," observed Christine acerbically.

"Enough explanations," Uzziel said. "Does Mercury have the case?"

"I…don't know," said Christine. "I haven't seen him since Berkeley…"

"Hello?" said Karl. "Don't you remember leaving him with the movie guys in Lodi? The ones that you said were going to—"

"Karl's not quite himself," interjected Christine. "He got hit on the head when that lunatic tried to kill him in Lodi."

"What movie guys, Karl?" asked Uzziel.

"There were these two guys on motorcycles. At first I thought they were cops, but it turned out they wanted to put me in the next Charlie Nyx movie. We went to Charlie's Grill in Lodi, because I can eat there for free, and they were talking about movies and stuff and then I had to go to the bathroom and that's when Christine said she was Secret Service and we had to leave and I didn't get to pee until Stockton."

"Did you get their names, Karl?"

"Uhhhh…one of them was Izzy, right, Christine?"

Christine sighed. No point in resisting anymore. She wasn't even sure whom she was protecting, or from what. "Izbazel and Gamaliel."

Christine thought she saw the angel turn even more pale.

"What did they want?" asked Uzziel.

"I told you," said Karl. "They were going to put me in a movie."

"They wanted to kill Karl," said Christine. "They said, 'No Antichrist, no Apocalypse.' They were trying to get Mercury to hand him over without a struggle. That's when I grabbed Karl and left."

Karl stared dumbly at Christine.

"So," said Uzziel, "we've got another faction in play. Someone trying to stop the Apocalypse at all costs."

Harry scoffed, "You can't *stop* the Apocalypse. It's God's will."

Everyone's eyes rolled. Even Karl's.

"I'll put together a team to find Mercury and the other angels and retrieve the case," Uzziel said. "We'll have to open a portal to Lodi. These emergency portals are killing me. I'm so over budget on this thing as it is, Michael's going to have my head. So," Uzziel said, "you really don't know anything about the earthquake?"

"You mean other than the fact that it almost killed us and probably leveled my building?" Harry said. "No."

"So you don't have…it?"

"Have, um, what?" asked Harry.

"Why," said Uzziel, "the Attaché Case of Death, of course."

"The Attaché Case of Death can cause earthquakes?" Christine asked, dumbfounded.

"Among other things," said Uzziel. "It's the most powerful of the four. If it's fallen into the hands of the renegades…"

"Yeah, it'll totally mess up your whole Apocalypse," said Christine. "We get it."

"Not only that," said Uzziel. "This faction threatens the balance between the forces of good and the forces of evil. Lucifer might use this as an opportunity to…"

Christine and Harry looked quizzically at Uzziel.

He continued, "But I'm getting ahead of myself. We're still in damage control mode for now. Assuming we can pick up our three renegade cherubim and recover the Case of War, we should be able to get back on track. If we watch the channels for the signature of the Attaché Case of Death, we should be able to pick it up the next time they use it. If we can recover the Case of War, we should be able to pull off the Apocalypse even without the Case of Death. We'll be a little over budget, but we'll get it done. We all want the same thing here, right?"

Harry nodded. Christine snorted. Karl started, "I'm not sure I…"

"Right," said Uzziel. "OK, Harry and Karl, I'll take you to a portal that you can use to get back to Los Angeles. Christine, you stay here." He pulled what appeared to be a small silver bell from his pocket, shook it three times, and then, despite the fact that it made no discernable sound, slipped it back into his pocket.

"Wait," Christine said. "What am I supposed to do here?"

"Nothing," answered Uzziel. "You're going to wait out the Apocalypse here. I've summoned Perp to come back and keep you comfortable. Just don't be stingy with the tips."

Christine got to her feet, openmouthed, trying to decide whether she was going to protest and, if so, what she was going to protest about.

"Listen, Christine," Uzziel said as he ushered Harry and Karl to the door. "There are two reasons for someone to be designated as a Person of Apocalyptic Interest. There are people who have a clearly prescribed mission, such as Harry Giddings, General Isaakson, or—and I can only assume here—Karl Grissom. Then there are the wildcard PAIs—the people that a representative from either side has identified as a potential troublemaker. People who have the potential to derail the plan. People like you."

"People like *me*?" Christine protested. "What did *I* do?"

"It's nothing you've done…that I know of. But you're an unknown quantity. Too risky to leave you down there. Anyway, it will be over before you know it."

"Why can't I just go home? I never wanted to be involved in any of this anyway. I don't even understand half of what's going on. How would I interfere with it?"

"You're a little too close to the action to be an unknown quantity. We've been watching you, of course. The Apocalypse Division has its agents, and then there's the MOC, but we're spread a little thin and we have to wait for the MOC's reports to be approved by the Observation Committee…"

"Does it matter at all to you," Christine said, "that I have no freaking clue what you're talking about?"

"Angel politics," said Uzziel. "Forget it. Hopefully none of it will matter by the time I get back."

Perp opened the door and buzzed back into the room. "You rang?"

Uzziel said to him, "I need you to take care of this one for a little while."

"Of course," said Perp. "You can substitute olive oil for butter in most recipes."

"If you have more questions," said Uzziel to Christine, "Perp here can help you out."

Uzziel escorted Harry and Karl out of the room and closed the door, leaving her alone in the interplanar limbo with Perpetiel.

TWENTY

"Do you suppose it was a trick?" asked Gamaliel.

Izbazel glared at him.

"Some kind of trick spoon? What kind of angel carries a trick spoon?"

"Forget it," said Izbazel.

After ditching their motorcycles and changing into civilian clothes, Izbazel and Gamaliel had checked into a depressing motel in East LA. With the Covenant Holders conference going on, it was the closest vacancy they could find to Anaheim Stadium. The motel was called the "Aloha," presumably because for any sane traveler pulling into this place, hello would also be good-bye. There was no evidence beyond the name of any kind of Hawaiian theme—unless the toilets in Hawaii made a horrific screeching sound that resembled a hippopotamus gasping for air through a saxophone. The two angels sat on the edge of the lone double bed in the room, plotting their next move.

Izbazel prided himself on being a particularly clever angel, and he didn't like the idea of being outsmarted by an interloping amateur like Mercury. Nor did he like the idea of Gamaliel knowing he had been outsmarted by Mercury. Gamaliel's involvement in the angelic rebellion was an important element of Izbazel's plan, and his involvement depended on his confidence in Izbazel. Gamaliel was a rather malleable angel, if you knew which buttons to push, but it hadn't been easy to get him to go along with a plan to assassinate the Antichrist. And if he started to get the feeling that Izbazel didn't know what he was doing…

Izbazel didn't need Gamaliel in order to execute the plan, certainly. But his involvement lent their project a certain legitimacy. No one would be particularly surprised to see Izbazel rebelling against Heaven—in fact, they might even figure out who he was really working for. But Gamaliel…it was hard to see him as an agent of Lucifer. It wouldn't be at all difficult to convince the authorities that Gamaliel was only pretending to be rebelling, and that he was, in fact, working undercover on orders from someone higher up in the angelic bureaucracy. And that's exactly what Izbazel was counting on.

"So, what now?" asked Gamaliel.

"Nothing has changed," replied Izbazel. "Things have progressed far enough in the Middle East that the Case of War is no longer necessary. We've ensured that the gaze of Heaven is fixed on the Olive Branch War."

"What about Karl?"

"It would have been nice to have disposed of the Antichrist," admitted Izbazel. "But in a way, it's better to let things progress a bit first. If we wait until Karl has been formally denounced, then there's no wiggle room for either side. They can't try to pull a designated hitter on us."

"A what?"

"A designated hitter," said Izbazel a bit condescendingly. "You don't follow Mundane baseball?"

"Not much of a sports fan," said Gamaliel.

"In the American League, you can designate an alternate hitter if your pitcher can't hit the ball."

"Isn't the idea of baseball that everybody on the team has to hit? It seems like that rule kind of goes against the spirit of the game."

"One of Lucifer's more ingenious ideas," Izbazel mused in a thoughtful tone.

"To be sure," conceded Gamaliel.

"The point is, we don't want to kill Karl only to have Heaven claim that he wasn't really the Antichrist after all. Once he's been formally denounced, there will be no legal recourse. Both sides will have to admit that the Antichrist has been taken out of the game. Lucifer will cry foul, and the whole business will be tied up in the courts for the next five thousand years."

"No Antichrist, no Apocalypse."

"Exactly."

"And we're certain he will be formally denounced at the Covenant Holders conference tonight?"

"Absolutely," said Izbazel. "Christine will take him to Harry, and Harry has been led to believe that his whole life has been leading up to this. He won't let us down."

"It's helpful that these people are so predictable," said Gamaliel. "It takes a lot of the guesswork out of these sorts of schemes."

"Quite," Izbazel said. "That's the great thing about these Covenant Holders. You publish a book with the right words in it, and they'll burn it. Call somebody the Antichrist, and they'll denounce him. They're well trained."

"What I don't get," said Gamaliel, "is what's in it for them. I don't understand what makes someone want to accept what amounts to a prepackaged belief system. Wouldn't the sane thing be to evaluate every part of any belief system, in case there were mistakes in it somewhere?"

"Ah, but that would lead to anarchy," chided Izbazel. "You can't have every adherent of a religion picking and choosing from among the different elements of the religion, as if it were some sort of buffet."

This answer seemed to puzzle Gamaliel. He said, "But there must be something like a thousand different religions on this plane. Don't you already have to pick a religion? I mean, using your buffet illustration, hasn't a person already had to choose which restaurant to go to before they even get to the buffet? What sense does it make to force everybody at a particular restaurant to order the same thing when they can just go to a different restaurant? You're letting them make one big decision but denying them a bunch of little ones. It makes no sense."

"What you're failing to understand," said Izbazel, taking the tone of a patient teacher imparting wisdom to an eager but slightly dim pupil, "is that people find it comforting not to have to make all those little decisions. Sometimes it's easier to pretend that all the little decisions have been made, so one doesn't have to worry about them. We angels don't fully appreciate the complexity of living on the Mundane Plane. The number of choices that a person has to make in a typical day can be overwhelming."

"But these people," Gamaliel replied, "these Covenant Holders, they keep talking about growing spiritually. How can you 'grow spiritually' when you refuse to grapple with any of these little questions? Aren't the little questions the ones that really matter in the end? The big questions don't matter if you get all the little ones wrong."

"It's not that they don't grapple with them," said Izbazel. "It's just that they have all the answers given to them in advance. Their version of grappling is to keep asking themselves the questions over and over until they get what they've been told are the right answers."

"That sounds to me more like conditioning than growing."

"True," admitted Izbazel, "which is what makes them so useful to us. But don't be too hard on them. Angels often act the same way. We assume that the higher-ups have thought through the ramifications of the SPAM. We assume that we're part of a system that ultimately makes sense to Michael, or God, or *someone*. All the little details may not make sense to us, but we go along with it anyway."

"But *we* have a responsibility," said Gamaliel. "We're soldiers in a conflict that is much greater than us. If every individual soldier were to question his role in the conflict, you'd have…"

"Anarchy," said Izbazel. "Soldiers refusing to follow orders for the sake of following orders. A military-style organization becomes impossible to maintain. War itself ultimately becomes impossible."

Izbazel went on, "Look, don't you think that humans feel the same way about their role in the Universe? They have to believe that they have a responsibility to a higher power, or their lives mean nothing. So they give up some of their free will, telling themselves that at least some of the questions have already been answered and some of the decisions have already been made. Life becomes livable, at the expense of a little freedom. Humans and angels are no different in this respect."

"But we…" said Gamaliel. "We're different, you and I."

"Certainly," said Izbazel. "We're doing the right thing, despite the fact that we're going against what we've been told is right."

"I suppose," said Gamaliel. "But for some reason it still doesn't *feel* right."

"Such feelings are the result of the conditioning you mentioned earlier. We've been trained to feel bad when we break from the SPAM."

"Maybe," said Gamaliel. "Sometimes I have the nagging sense that it's more than that."

"Listen, Gamaliel," said Izbazel. "I used to feel the same way. But now I *know* what we're doing is right. You'll get to that point too. For now, I just need you to trust me. This is going to work out. Do you trust me?"

"Yes," said Gamaliel. "I do."

"Good," said Izbazel. "Now I have some business to attend to. You wait here."

"What kind of business?"

"Nothing you need to concern yourself with, Gamaliel. It's better if you're not privy to all the little details. Plausible deniability, you know."

Gamaliel nodded. "Yeah, OK."

"We'll meet back here at four. That should give us plenty of time to get to the stadium and kill Karl after Harry denounces him."

"OK," said Gamaliel. He didn't look happy that Izbazel was leaving to attend to some secret business, but he was resigned to his limited role in the scheme. Poor sap, thought Izbazel. He has no idea what he's mixed up in.

"See you at four," said Izbazel, walking out the door.

It was a good thing Gamaliel was so malleable, thought Izbazel. With incompetents like Ramiel and Nisroc on the team, Izbazel ended up having to micromanage everything. Somehow the two of them had managed to burn through nearly two dozen corpses and cause two earthquakes, yet they still hadn't gotten the channel reconfiguration right. Izbazel wasn't going to let them screw it up this time. If the reconfiguration wasn't done by the time Karl was killed, Heaven might have a chance to figure out what Lucifer was really up to before he could put his plan into action. And Lucifer would blame Izbazel.

"Bloody incompetents," muttered Izbazel as he miraculously popped the locks of a Nissan Pathfinder in the motel's parking lot. He jump-started the vehicle and got on the northbound freeway, heading for the desert north of Los Angeles.

Back at the motel, Gamaliel was breathing a sigh of relief that that pedantic twit Izbazel was finally gone. He found it excruciating to listen to Izbazel wax philosophical when it was clear that Izbazel didn't even fully understand the mission that Lucifer had entrusted to him. It was all Gamaliel could do to play the dutiful lackey while trying to keep Izbazel from irreparably screwing up Lucifer's plan.

Lucifer's weakness, Gamaliel had concluded, was his pathological need to be demonstrably superior to anyone around him—a trait that precluded him from hiring underlings who were more than marginally competent. Izbazel was the epitome of this sort of minion, a sycophant untainted by conscience or even critical thinking. Izbazel was so intent on pleasing Lucifer that he had jumped the gun, so to speak, with that psychopath Danny Pilvers, trying to get Karl killed before he was even officially denounced. That would have been disastrous for Lucifer; Gamaliel had been on the verge of intervening when Christine and Mercury showed up at Charlie's Grill. Now, thanks to Mercury, Lucifer's scheme could proceed as planned. Up to a point, anyway. Gamaliel had his own reasons for wanting to subvert Lucifer's plan, but the time had not yet come for that.

For now, he had to do his best to keep events proceeding as Lucifer expected—and this required more work than Izbazel realized. Gamaliel made a brief encoded call over Angel Band, requesting two temporary portals. He needed to get to the plane-port to make a quick trip across the Atlantic and back again before Izbazel returned. He had some last-minute details to take care of.

TWENTY-ONE

With some difficulty, Christine managed to convince Perpetiel to give her a tour of the planeport. Despite the obvious differences, it really was about as interesting as a midsized airline hub. In place of lettered signs with the names of destinations on them, the gates were marked with exotic symbols that represented each of the different planes. The same symbol was repeated in more intricate fashion in the portal itself. There were no ordinary windows or doors; the planeport seemed to exist in a sort of self-contained space outside of any of the planes to which it connected. Harried interplanar travelers tramped down the concourse, vanishing into thin air as they reached their respective portals.

Most impressive were the security guards, great hulking winged angels who carried flaming swords. Christine was almost disappointed not to actually have the chance to see them in action; mostly they were standing around at various checkpoints, patting down travelers and examining their luggage for God knows what. The guards' mighty blades smoldered harmlessly in jeweled scabbards hanging from their belts.

While she and Perp walked, Christine managed to squeeze some answers out of Perp to her more pressing questions about the Apocalypse, in exchange for first listening to long stretches of advice of dubious value.

"If you're going to keep me here while my world is destroyed," Christine said, "the least you could do is explain to me a little more clearly what the hell is going on. Like, who is Uzziel, in the scheme of things?"

"Fine," Perp sighed. "When ants travel in a straight line, expect rain. When they scatter, expect fair weather. Uzziel works for the Apocalypse Bureau. He's what you'd call middle management. His boss—well, he has several bosses, but his main boss—is one of seven Assistant Directors of the Apocalypse, who report to the Undersecretary for the Apocalypse, who reports to the Secretary for Apocalyptic Affairs, Michael, whom you've probably heard of."

"You mean, *the* Michael?"

"Correct. Archangel. Important guy."

"Wow. OK."

"Then there's the Mundane Observation Corps. Completely separate entity, with entirely different concerns. They report—ultimately—to the Observation Committee, which answers to the Seraphic Senate. The MOC has far more in the way of intelligence resources than the Apocalypse Bureau does. They observe virtually everything that happens on the Mundane—that is, on Earth. On a lightweight bicycle, the tires should last two to three thousand miles. If they last longer, they're too heavy. Unfortunately, the raw data is not available to the Apocalypse Bureau, for various reasons having to do with interplanar security, checks and balances, that sort of thing. There were concerns that if the Bureau had direct access to MOC intelligence, there would be…abuses. In fact, much of the current separation of functionality goes back to the Vesuvius Scandal, when agents of the Bureau misinterpreted data from the MOC that seemed to indicate—"

"Good lord," said Christine. "I mean, this is fascinating and all, but is there any way we can stay in the current century?"

"Hmph," said Perp. "There's no biological difference between a puma, a cougar, and a mountain lion."

"Thanks for clearing that up," said Christine. "Now if you could—"

"So the MOC observes everything, but the Bureau usually doesn't get the data until a few days or even weeks later. And they often only get summaries and have to fight to get the really sensitive information declassified. It's a constant battle between the two organizations."

"And how do you know all this?"

"Me? I'm under Transport and Communications. We hear everything. Well, not the most sensitive information, but generally the T&C angels are the best informed. If the cats aren't sleeping on the radiators, turn down the heat. As I understand it, the Bureau has been trying to keep tabs on you, but it's been rather difficult. And right now, they can't risk losing track of you."

"I suppose you know who it was that rescued me from the rubble of that house in Syria then?"

"Hmm, no. I don't think anything of that sort was in the SPAM. In fact, that whole bit with Isaakson was unplanned. Presumably the renegades were responsible for Isaakson's death, but I've got no information regarding your rescue."

"So," said Christine. "Here I sit, in the waiting room of the Apocalypse."

"Precisely. You have no idea how much planning has gone into this. Can you imagine what it's like trying to get the angel hierarchy and the demon hierarchy to agree on anything? The angels alone are bad enough. You've heard the joke about the three seraphim, right?"

"No."

"Ah, well, I think the joke is 'What has eighteen wings and nineteen opinions?' But I've kind of ruined it. In any case, a lot of people would be very upset if things went sour now."

"But, presumably, some people would like very much to see the Apocalypse fail," Christine said.

"I suppose," admitted Perp.

"That's what all this is about, isn't it? That's why I'm here. Because somebody is trying to throw a wrench in the works?"

"True. And between you and me, I wouldn't be surprised if Lucifer is trying to gain some kind of unfair advantage through all of these unplanned events."

"Well," said Christine, "he is *Satan*, right? Treachery would seem to go with the territory."

"I imagine so. Even grizzly bears won't attack groups of four or more people."

A thought nagged at Christine. "You said that Uzziel's boss is the archangel Michael?"

"His boss's boss's boss, yes."

"And he reports directly to…?"

"Erm, well, that's where things get complicated. Above the archangels is another tier of beings. There's no word for them in English. The word in Seraphic means something like 'Eternals.' The Eternals are, essentially, to the angels what angels are to humans. I've never seen one, of course, but I'm assured that they are quite real."

"And above the Eternals…?"

"Erm," said Perp. "*Above* the Eternals. Not sure about that. There may be another tier above them."

"And above that tier…"

"Well, there's no point in speculating. Let's just say that we all have a place in the Divine Order."

"But for all you know, it could be turtles all the way up."

"I'm sorry?"

"Forget it. Human expression. The point is, you never stopped to think that maybe the Universe is just an endless hierarchy of bureaucrats, all doing what they've been told, without any understanding of *why*? Or worse yet, maybe Michael and his pals are just *pretending* to be getting orders from On High?"

Perp stared blankly at her. He began again, "You see, Uzziel works for one of seven Assistant Directors of the Apocalypse, who report to—"

"Yeah, I got it," said Christine. "So you're saying that Heaven's bureaucrats and Hell's bureaucrats negotiated a plan for the Apocalypse, and now you think Lucifer is double-crossing you?"

"Well, that's a rather simplistic...basically, yes."

"What do you think they're after?"

"Oh, the usual, I suspect. Power, control, et cetera."

"Right, but specifically, what are they trying to do?"

"Hmmm," said Perp. "Hmmm. Ahhhh. Hmmm."

"You're completely incapable of thinking treacherously, aren't you?"

"Hey, I'm the one who told you I thought Lucifer was up to no good."

"Yeah, congrats on that. Everybody else seems to think that Lucifer is such a straight shooter. Way to see through the façade."

A hurt look swept over Perp's fleshy face. "It's not easy, you know, working with angels all day and then trying to deal with the minions of Lucifer. People are more likely to remember you if you always wear the same outfit."

"Exactly!" said Christine. "I mean, not about the outfit thing. That's ridiculous. But you need someone like me to help you figure this stuff out. Someone who is used to dealing with... What's that?"

Christine's gaze had drifted to a portal that looked eerily familiar.

"That?" Perp said. "Just another portal."

"Where does it go?"

"Oh, nowhere you'd be interested in."

"Really," said Christine flatly. She had seen this particular pattern before. There was no mistaking it. It was, she mused ruefully, a very welcoming pattern.

"Tell me," said Christine, standing in front of the portal, her eyes transfixed, "how do these portals work exactly? Could I just draw one of these patterns on the ground and open a portal to anywhere I want?"

"Certainly not," said Perp. "There is a very precise method for creating the pattern. Also, on most planes there are only a handful of geographic locations where the transplanar energy channels converge in such a way as to make a portal possible. And you can only travel between adjacent planes."

"So what planes are adjacent to Earth?"

"Erm," said Perp. "It doesn't really work like that. You understand that terms like 'adjacent' and 'planes' are really metaphors. We're not talking about 'planes' as in two-dimensional figures, like sheets of paper. It might be more helpful to think of a plane as a sheet of paper that is rolled up as cylinder and then stretched out like a garden hose. And then, ah, tied up with several thousand other hoses, crushed flat again, crumpled up like a tissue, and then had holes punched in it at various places. And then the holes are filled with, oh, say macaroni."

"Yes," said Christine. "That's very helpful."

"The point is that the whole thing might seem rather arbitrary to a mortal being such as yourself. For example, Earth only has a single feasible portal location at present."

"Is it in Glendale, by any chance?" Christine asked.

"Glendale? Never heard of it. No, it's in a place called Megiddo. As I understand it, there are two adjacent planes with portals to Megiddo. One is from a plane within the Heavenly sphere of interest, and the other is from some godforsaken place under Lucifer's control."

"So there's a portal between the Middle East and Hell?"

Perp shot Christine a pained look. "Well, first of all, there's no plane called 'Hell.' Hell is the absence of God, and there is no plane where God is completely absent. Conversely, Heaven is the presence of God."

"So…whatever plane God is on, that's Heaven?"

"Erm, in a manner of speaking."

"So," Christine mused, "Heaven is like God's Air Force One."

"Excuse me?"

"Never mind. Wait, if Megiddo is the only place you can open a portal on Earth, then how did Uzziel open a portal to Harry's office in LA?"

"Oh, temporary portals are another thing entirely. They're very expensive, and they only last a few minutes. Also, you can only use them to get to an interplanar hub, like this planeport. When boiling eggs, add a pinch of salt to keep the shells from cracking."

"So there's no reason anyone would create a portal in my condominium in Glendale?"

"Not unless they planned to move the building to Megiddo at some point. Or reconfigure the interplanar energy channels. The former being the simpler option, by far."

"Hmmm," said Christine, regarding the familiar pattern of the portal with interest.

"You don't just reconfigure the channels. You'd need some kind of massive—"

"Oh my!" Christine suddenly exclaimed, pointing at something over the cherub's shoulder. "Is that Joseph Smith?"

Perp turned, a sour expression on his face. "I wasn't informed of any...hey, wait!"

But it was too late. Christine had disappeared through the portal.

"Duplicitous race," muttered Perp.

TWENTY-TWO

Harry's affinity for Christine was threatening to spoil what would otherwise be a moment of unmitigated triumph. His feelings of exhilaration at the imminent realization of his destiny were intermingled with guilt about getting her mixed up in this whole sordid business. Of course, in a sense everyone was mixed up in it—it was, after all, the Apocalypse—but he had rather hoped to keep things on a professional level. His unplanned and prolonged proximity to Karl wasn't helping his state of mind either.

"This blows," said Karl. "That dude coulda at least called us a cab or something. And I'm freaking starved. We need to get a pizza. You should call for a pizza."

"My house is just a few blocks up," said Harry. "You're welcome to whatever food I've got."

He and Karl had been unceremoniously transported to a cul-de-sac in Harry's Pasadena neighborhood and were now trudging toward his house. Harry hoped to change his clothes and take a shower before the conference, and he had high hopes that Karl would shower as well. The smell emanating from Karl's sweaty body was the only thing distracting him from Karl's incessant whining.

"You should call for a pizza. It could, like, be there by the time we get there."

"Uh huh," said Harry.

"Is there a Charlie's Grill around here? I can eat there for free."

"No."

"Are you sure? I think I've been here before. Let's go that way."

"Karl, this is my neighborhood. I *live* here. There's no Charlie's Grill around here."

"What a stupid place to live."

"Yeah," Harry replied. "I really wasn't thinking when I bought a house in a residential neighborhood."

As Karl's recitation of grievances dulled to a nearly indecipherable, monotonous hum, Harry's thoughts drifted back to Christine. What was it about her? He had, he assured himself with some success, no romantic interest in her. He was a happily married man. In any case, he was married, and he was perfectly OK with how that situation had turned out. His wife supported him in his career, although she wasn't privy to the details of his visions. She was under the impression that God spoke to him in the sort of vague but reassuring way that allows one to achieve great things without being clinically insane.

Harry, for his part, allowed those around him to believe he was somehow privy to some sort of ineffable spiritual knowledge while steadfastly denying that God ever spoke to him—a statement that was accurate if somewhat misleading. In point of fact, it was the angels, not God himself, who spoke. And they did not speak *to* him so much as *around* him. He seemed to be receiving random snippets of conversations and images, as if he were an AM radio tuned to the same frequency as the cell phones of commuters whizzing past on a nearby freeway. It was a frustrating way to receive information, tending to be comprised of snippets such as:

"...the inexorable fate of the Universe to be..."

or

"...decree the immediate and total destruction of every..."

This had been going on for his entire life; it had, in fact, been a bit of a shock to realize in his youth that not everyone on Earth was subjected to the occasional incoherent snippet of a conversation about incomprehensible matters being held by mysterious and invisible beings.

Most of these beings seemed to have no idea that he could hear them, which tended to undermine the hypothesis that Harry had been chosen to be some sort of modern-day prophet. Prophets were generally thought to be recipients of intentional communication from On High, not accidental receptors of the occasional errant angelic missive. Harry chose to believe, however, that God had allowed him to eavesdrop on these communications for reasons of His own.

He was aided in this belief by two individuals. The first was his devoutly religious mother, who had been convinced since before Harry was even born that he was destined to be a great prophet. It was never quite clear to Harry why she believed this, but he did his best to play his part, as this conviction seemed to provide his mother a good deal of pleasure.

The other individual was an entity that Harry referred to—or would have referred to, if he ever spoke of such things—as "The Messenger." The Messenger, it seemed, spoke directly to Harry. Or, in any case, didn't seem to be talking to anyone else and seemed to have a vague understanding that Harry could hear him. And Harry could hear him, all right. Loud and clear. Many times, in fact, Harry had wished that the Messenger's semi-coherent ramblings didn't come through quite so clearly. The Messenger was a real downer.

The Messenger didn't provide much in the way of new information, but he provided a sort of framework in which to place the snippets that Harry received. Through these fragments, filtered through the morose assessments of the Messenger and colored to some extent by the impassioned religiosity of his mother, Harry managed to get an overall sense of how the Apocalypse was going to go down. It was his knowledge of these imminent events that had propelled him to build his media empire. He wanted to be ready to proclaim The End when it came.

Harry had always been cognizant of the danger of becoming so wrapped up in the business of empire building that he would miss out on his true calling, to be the harbinger of the Apocalypse. He was, however, unprepared for the distraction caused by his feelings for Christine. It's the Apocalypse, he kept telling himself. What does one person matter in the scheme of things?

But he couldn't shake the feeling, as he trudged along the quiet streets of Pasadena toward his destiny, that Christine's fate was somehow linked to the fate of the world itself.

TWENTY-THREE

Christine stood in the middle of what appeared to be the lobby of an office building. There were four doors, one in each wall. She was standing on a shimmering circular pattern of light. Next to the portal was the sort of dull, abstract sculpture that inspires office building workers to think dull, abstract office building thoughts.

This was not at all what Christine was expecting. This was not, after all, her condo in Glendale.

Was she wrong, then, about the pattern she had seen at the planeport? No, it couldn't be. She would know that pattern anywhere; she had seen Don from Don's Discount Flooring install that very pattern in her breakfast nook only a few days ago.

She stepped off the portal and regarded it studiously. Strangely, the pattern didn't match that of the portal she had stepped through in the planeport. She had seen this pattern before as well, though: it matched the one that had appeared mysteriously in Harry's office.

Presumably if she were to step back onto the portal, she would be transported back to the planeport. So that explained why the pattern on this one matched the one she had seen in Harry's office. They both had the same destination: the planeport.

Wheels turned slowly in her head. If portals with the same pattern went to the same place, then she was wrong about the portal she had seen at the planeport. It matched her linoleum—there was no question about that. But the pattern matched not because the portal in the planeport went to her condo, but because they both had the same destination: here.

"So," she said to herself, "someone has built a portal between my condo and this place, whatever this place is." But this portal wasn't it, because this one went to the planeport. That meant that somewhere near here there was another portal that would take her to her condo.

This comforting thought quickly gave way to a troubling realization. Someone had installed the linoleum portal for a reason. That meant someone intended to use the portal to travel from here to her condo, or from her condo to here. Why? And where was *here* anyway?

Suddenly a small man in a slightly iridescent blue suit burst through one of the doors. "Come then," he said in a hurried tone. "No time to waste. We need you on the floor, ay-sap!"

Christine opened her mouth only to find she had nothing whatever to say, so she closed it again.

The man clutched her wrist and dragged her back through the door through which he had arrived. Christine went along, not knowing what else to do.

"You'll start small," the man said. "Cheating on biology exams, that sort of thing. It's a lousy job, but everybody has to start somewhere. Come on, let's go."

Christine followed the man helplessly as he led her through several doors and then through a maze of cubicles populated with pale, desperate-looking people staring blearily at computer screens and speaking into headset microphones. She tried to make out what they were saying, but their voices blended into a senseless buzz about her. There were no windows or doors that seemed to go anywhere other than more cubicle space. Christine got the sickening feeling that this entire plane was nothing but one gigantic cubicle farm.

"Excuse me," Christine shouted at the man's back. "I'm not sure I'm who you're expecting. I was just looking for…"

But he clearly wasn't listening, and Christine was out of breath from half-sprinting after him. They turned left, then right, then left again, negotiating an apparently random course through the cubicle labyrinth. By the time Christine decided she had had enough, she was hopelessly lost. Perhaps she could ask one of the desperate souls in one of the cubicles she was passing for help, but they didn't look terribly helpful.

The man stopped so abruptly that Christine nearly ran into him.

"Here is your cube," he announced. "Number 21482."

It was a dreary, barren little space, adorned only with a headset, an old-fashioned monochrome monitor, and a well-worn keyboard. There was a beep, and a block of text appeared on the monitor. The characters were completely foreign to Christine.

"Go ahead," instructed the man. "Make the call."

"What?" Christine asked.

"Just follow the script," he said. "Twenty-six-year-old woman on the verge of stealing a blouse. She's already told the attendant that she has five items, when in fact she has six. All she needs to do is tuck it into her purse. Put the damn headset on!"

"I'm sorry," Christine said. "I think there's been a misunderstanding. I went through that portal thinking that…"

The monitor beeped again, and another line of text appeared.

"Oh, good grief," the man said. "Well, we've lost her. She put the blouse back. I hope this isn't indicative of your capabilities.

The agency said you had six hundred years of experience in corrupting mortals."

"Look," said Christine. "I wasn't sent by any agency. I'm not interested in doing this, whatever this is. I'm just trying to find the portal that will take me home."

The man's face paled, which was saying something because it was pretty pale to start out with. He glanced about nervously.

"What did you say?"

"I'm looking for a portal."

He eyed her suspiciously. "A portal to where?"

"To Earth. That is, the Mundane Plane. Glendale, California, to be specific."

A look of complicit understanding came over the man's face.

"I apologize," the man said. "I didn't know you were one of *them*. I was told your people weren't going to start arriving until later in the day."

"Yes, well," Christine said, trying to decide if this new misunderstanding was preferable to the last. "Yes, well, they sent me ahead, you know, to check things out."

"Of course, of course," the man said, suddenly very accommodating. "We were expecting a new recruit in Petty Corruption, so I assumed..."

"Yes, well," Christine said again, trying to strike an air of impatient disdain. "So I suppose you'll be taking me to..."

"Right!" said the man. "You'll want to see the munitions, of course. And the portal. Oh my, I've forgotten to introduce myself. I'm Nybbas. I manage the Floor."

"The Floor?" Christine asked.

"The Corruption Floor," said Nybbas. "We generally just refer to it as the Floor. This is where the magic happens. Most of the corruption in the Universe starts right here. A few choice words whispered in the right ear at the right time…we've been at it for nearly ten thousand years. As you can see, we've gone high-tech over the past few years."

Nybbas smiled broadly, surveying the endless expanse of demons clacking away in the green glow of their decidedly low-tech twelve-inch monitors.

"But we've never seen anything as exciting as *this*, of course. Who would have imagined that…" His voice grew hushed. "That Lucifer would use *this* place as his base of operations for the Apocalypse. Speaking of which, let's get you over to see Malphas. You'll want to make certain that the munitions are ready, I'm sure."

"Oh," said Christine. "Ah, yes. The munitions."

"That's what I thought," said Nybbas. "Right this way."

And with that, he was off again.

"What did you say your name was?" he shouted over his shoulder.

"I'm Chris…" she started, then realized that *Christine* was probably a very unlikely name for a demon. "…pix," she finished.

Nybbas stopped suddenly again and turned to peer at Christine. "Did you say *Crispix*?"

"Er," Christine said, wishing she had eaten something more ominous-sounding for breakfast. "Yes, Crispix. I'm a demon."

"Not *the* Crispix?"

"Er, yes. The very same."

"Well, then this truly is an honor. It makes perfect sense that Lucifer would send someone of your rank, of course. I see you've dropped the horns. And the flaming sword."

"Yes," said Christine. "I'm trying to keep a lower profile these days. It's hard to stay incognito when you're carrying around a flaming sword."

"Tell me about it," said Nybbas. And he turned and led Christine back through the cubicle maze.

They walked for what must have been close to a mile through a series of hallways punctuated by massive, low-ceilinged cubicle farms lit by oppressive, flickering fluorescent lights.

"Quite the operation you have here," observed Christine.

"Nine hundred thousand Corruption Representatives," said Nybbas proudly. "The result of an eight-hundred-year job re-training program. Most of these CRs were performing unskilled demonic activity only a few centuries ago," he said, gesturing broadly. "And now look at them!"

Christine glanced about at the fearful, pasty-faced creatures populating the cubicles all around her.

"You there!" said Nybbas, stopping in front of a fleshy, pallid-skinned demon. "What did you do before you started working here?"

The man glanced painfully up at Christine. "Routine possession. I once caused a villager to bite the head off a live rat. They burned him at the stake. Horrifically painful. And yet, still better than..."

"You see?" said Nybbas. "There are thousands of success stories just like that one. But enough of my bragging. No time to waste."

Eventually he led Christine to a massive steel door which, after Nybbas had punched a combination into a keypad, opened to reveal a spacious, dimly lit warehouse. He led her past steel shelves piled high with dusty crates and boxes until they reached a cluttered desk in the midst of the capacious room. Seated at the desk, with his back to Nybbas and Christine, was a heavyset man in gray overalls. Christine thought there was something vaguely familiar about him.

"Malphas?" said Nybbas gingerly. "There is someone here to see you."

The gray mountain of a man that was Malphas turned to face them, a surly look upon his face. "You!" he said as his eyes met Christine's.

Christine knew him instantly, even without the jumpsuit.

"Don?" she said. "Aren't you...Don, from Don's Discount Flooring?"

TWENTY-FOUR

"You should call for a pizza," Karl said again. "I'm friggin' starved."

"Uh huh," said Harry. They were now only a few blocks from his house, and Harry's patience with Karl was wearing thin.

"So what's this thing we have to go to? Some kind of convention? Do I have to sign autographs? I hate signing autographs."

"It's a Covenant Holders conference. You've heard of the Covenant Holders?"

"What's a cunniventoder?"

"Covenant. Holder. It's a Christian group."

"Like Stryper?"

"Who?"

"Stryper. You know, to hell with the devil. Those guys were queer."

"It's a group of people with shared beliefs who come from all over the country to meet together. There are speakers and events."

"Do they wear Spandex?"

"*Spandex*? No."

"Sounds lame."

"Yes, Karl, I'm sure it would."

"What's that supposed to mean?"

"Nothing."

"No, what did you mean? You say stuff like that, and it sounds all nice, but your lip does this thing where you think you're better than me."

"My lip is doing no such thing."

"See? You're mouth is all, 'My lip is da da da whatever,' but your lips are like, 'I'm better than Karl.'"

"Karl, can we not talk for the rest of the way? I'm getting a headache."

"No, screw you and your cover letter holders. I don't have to put up with this crap. I'm the Antichrist, and I'm going home. To Lodi." Karl took a sharp turn to the left and marched off.

"Karl."

"Shut up."

"Karl, that's the wrong direction."

"Is not."

"Karl, you're walking northeast. If you keep going, you'll hit Las Vegas."

"Then I'll go to Las Vegas."

"It's two hundred miles away, Karl. Across the Mojave Desert."

"Then I'll go there."

"Karl, come on. Come back. I'm sorry if I did a lip thing at you. I won't do it again."

Karl turned. "I can't see very well from here, but I bet you're doing the lip thing right now."

"I'm not, Karl. Come here and see."

"Why should I?"

"Karl, have you ever heard the term *destiny*?"

"Maybe," answered Karl.

"Your destiny," explained Harry, "is what you were meant to do. Everyone has a destiny. My destiny is to proclaim the

Apocalypse. I believe that your destiny is to come with me to this conference."

"Why?"

"Why what?"

"Why do you think that's my density?"

"Destiny, Karl. It's a long story, but I believe that there are powers beyond this world, and I believe that those powers have chosen to communicate some important things to me. They have told me that it is my destiny to be the herald—the guy who announces the Apocalypse. And they have told me that you are part of that destiny."

"OK, but what if I don't believe in your powers?"

"That's OK, Karl. I don't expect you to. I just need you to trust me that this is the right thing to do. This is the way things are supposed to be."

"Hunh," said Karl.

"I'll even get you a pizza. I can order it with my cell phone. We should have enough time to eat before we have to leave for the conference."

"OK," Karl said grudgingly.

"Excellent," Harry said. "Things are going perfectly according to plan."

"It's cool that you're so sure of everything," Karl said. "It seems like I'm pretty much always kind of confused."

"It's called 'moral clarity,' Karl. It's a gift."

"Cool," said Karl, nodding his head slowly in admiration. "Can I have it?"

"It's not really mine to give, Karl."

"But can I learn it from you?"

"Well, I suppose you could, but we don't really have time for—"

"Afterwards, then. After the culvert rollers thing."

"Yes, well, I'll certainly see what I can do about that. Destiny may have other plans."

"What do you mean?" Karl demanded. "Just teach me it. I'm not going unless you teach me it. The mortal clarity."

"Karl, it's not something you can just teach someone. It takes years of—"

"I've got time," said Karl. "I don't have to work because of the Antichrist thing. I could spend every day with you, learning mortal clarity."

"Karl, my moral clarity goes along with my faith. You understand? My religion. You can't have moral clarity unless you have faith."

"So I have to change religion?"

"No," said Harry. Then, thinking better of it, he said, "Yes, actually. You need to change religion."

"OK," replied Karl obligingly.

"Karl, you can't just change your religion, just like that. This is a serious decision. It's a life-changing event."

"OK."

"Can we just put this discussion off until after the conference?"

Karl didn't look happy, but at last he said, "Yeah, I guess."

"Thank God," said Harry quietly. "I take your sentiments seriously, Karl, I really do. It's just that there's a lot going on right now, and I'm not sure this is the best time to—"

"What's the name of it?"

"The name of what?"

"Our religion."

It was all Harry could do to keep control of his lip. "Christianity. Christianity is *my* religion. *I* am a Christian."

"Cool," said Karl. "Me too."

"No, you're not! You're not a Christian, Karl. You haven't con-verted. Not yet. You can be a Christian tomorrow if you still want to. Just not today, OK? Today you still have to be the Antichrist."

"Fine," said Karl glumly. "Are you going to order pizza or what?"

TWENTY-FIVE

"I go by many names," said Malphas to Christine, ominously.

"One of which," said Christine, "is evidently 'Don of Don's Discount Flooring.'"

"You two have met?" asked Nybbas.

"We have," said Christine, realizing that her only chance of surviving this encounter was to stick to her bluff. "I'm Crispix. Lucifer sent me to make sure everything is in place for the invasion."

"Crispix," said Malphas, eyeing her suspiciously. "I am surprised that His Luminescence did not inform me of your involvement in this matter. When we last met, you were highly convincing as a mortal who hadn't a clue what we were actually installing in your condominium."

"A necessary ruse," said Christine. "The Luminous One needed independent verification that everything was being done according to his specifications."

"Hm," grunted Malphas. "And now you've come to check up on us again?"

"It's in all of our interests to ensure that everything goes smoothly with the invasion," said Christine. "Wouldn't you agree?"

Malphas grunted reluctant agreement. "So I suppose you'll want to see the munitions?"

"You suppose correctly," said Christine. "Let's see them. It. Let's see the munitions."

Malphas led the two of them to a vault tucked into the corner of the warehouse. He spun a combination on the door and then yanked open the massive steel door. Flicking on a light switch, he beckoned them inside.

"Here they are," said Malphas. "Six hundred sixty-six of them. Each powerful enough to level a small city." He picked one of the billiard ball–sized items from its place on the shelf and handed it to Christine.

Christine turned it over in her hand, trying to appear nonchalant. It was heavy, but it easily fit in the palm of her hand. It looked like a glass apple.

"Yes," she said thoughtfully. "These will do…I suppose."

"You've seen an anti-bomb before, of course?"

"Of course," said Christine.

"It's Heavenly technology. We've got more destructive weapons, but we were told to use these. I suppose they want there to be some confusion as to who is responsible for the attacks. Although it seems to me that everyone's going to figure it out pretty quickly."

"You're going to send these through the portal?"

"That is the plan. The brigade will be arriving in a few hours. As soon as we get the word, we'll activate the portal and send them through."

"To Glendale."

"Right."

"You need six hundred and sixty-six of these to blow up Glendale?"

Malphas looked quizzically at her. "Of course not. They'll be dispersed as widely as possible before detonating. Each recruit has a designated checkpoint. Surely your people informed you of all this?"

"Yes, yes," said Christine. "Just making sure that you're clear on all the details. I'd like to see the portal now, if that's all right. That is, take me to the portal."

"I'll need that back," said Malphas.

"Right," said Christine, handing the glass apple back to him. He replaced it in its padded slot on a shelf in the vault.

After shutting the vault behind them, Malphas led them to a small closet off the warehouse. In the middle of the floor, a roughly circular geometric pattern was etched into the floor. Christine had never seen this particular variation, but she assumed that it was the symbol for the portal in her condo.

"It's a bit out of the way," said Malphas, "but our calculations indicate that this is the optimal location for the portal. Or will be, anyway. After the reconfiguration is complete."

"The reconfiguration," repeated Christine. "Yes. How is the, ah, reconfiguration progressing?"

"It's a tricky business," said Malphas. "But our people are confident that one more quake will do it. In fact, Ramiel just reported in. We're hoping for another one any minute now. If it works, we should see…"

As he spoke, the portal began to glitter around its edges.

"There!" exclaimed Nybbas. "They did it!"

"Excellent," said Malphas. "Now as soon as Izbazel gets his lazy ass over here, we'll know for sure."

"Izbazel is coming here?" Christine said weakly, the bravado suddenly draining out of her voice.

"He was supposed to be here already. This whole plan rests on his shoulders. If he doesn't take out the Antichrist... But first things first. We're not even certain the portal works yet. Izbazel is supposed to be the first one through."

"Can't we test it before Izbazel gets here?" Christine asked.

"We could," said Malphas, "but we've been forbidden to do so. Lucifer wants Izbazel to be the first one through."

"Yes, well," said Christine, realizing that her only chance to get out of here alive—much less stop this diabolical plot—was to go through the portal before Izbazel showed up. Once he arrived and recognized her, it was all over.

"Yes, well, there has been a change of plans," Christine found herself saying. "His Luminosity wants me to go through first."

Malphas frowned. "It's not like Lucifer to change his mind at the last minute like this. I'll need to run it down through channels."

"No can do," said Christine. "There's a...that is, Lucifer suspects that there's a mole in the organization. Somewhere up the, er, down the channels. I mean, somewhere in the chain of command. A traitor. Quisling. A fifth column, if you will. Someone feeding information to the other side. That's why I'm here. Had to, you know, circumvent the channels."

"This is highly irregular," said Malphas. "You're expecting me to believe that Lucifer is deliberately keeping his subordinates in the dark?"

"Would it be the first time?" asked Christine.

"And now he sends you, Crispix, a demon who was still on bad terms with His Luminescence the last I heard."

"Lucifer needed someone from outside of his organization," said Christine. "Can't you see it was the only way to be sure?"

"Not to mention," said Nybbas, "that we haven't actually verified your identity. You could be any shape-shifting demon, for all we know. Why, you could be an angel."

"Or human," said Malphas.

"Human!" chortled Christine, feeling sick to her stomach. "Tell me, do you get many humans down here? Besides, how do you explain that I was the one who contracted you to do the portal installation? Lucifer sent me because he knew you would recognize me as someone else who was in on the plot."

"Hmm," said Malphas.

"Were any other demons aware of what you were doing in that condo in Glendale?"

"No," admitted Malphas.

"You were under orders from Lucifer himself. There is no way I would know about that—no way that I could have shown up here—unless Lucifer himself told me about it. Unless," she added sardonically, "you allow for an absolutely absurd set of coincidences."

"Well," Nybbas noted thoughtfully, "we could always test to see if she's human."

"We don't have time for that," snapped Christine.

"It's a simple test," offered Nybbas helpfully. "We just chop your head off and then stick it back on. If it reattaches, then you're not human. I have a relatively sharp scythe around here somewhere."

"Look," said Christine. "What is it that you think I'm going to do once I go through that portal? Warn the Los Angeles police to be on the lookout for six hundred sixty-six demons armed with glass apples? In any case, I've got my orders, and I'm going through. You do what you have to do."

Christine closed her eyes and took two steps forward, expecting a giant leathery hand to yank her back. But the hand didn't come. The next thing she knew, she was standing on the linoleum in her condo.

Home.

For a moment she imagined that the whole thing was some kind of dream or hallucination. But even here the evidence of world-shaking events was visible: books lay scattered on the floor where they had fallen from the shelves, several windows were broken, and a massive crack ran from floor to ceiling of one wall. Los Angeles as a whole must be reeling in the wake of the earthquakes.

So. What now? She half-expected Malphas to materialize before her eyes, ready to yank her back to that demonic place. They were probably checking her story right now. It might take seconds or minutes for them to realize that it was all nonsense, and then they'd send somebody through to get her. And that would be it. The end, for her and for the entire world.

What if she were to tear out her linoleum? That would presumably destroy the portal. How hard could it be to tear out linoleum? All she would need was some kind of...

It occurred to her that she had no idea how to remove linoleum. Maybe peel up one of the corners with a screwdriver? She had a screwdriver somewhere, but she vaguely remembered it was the kind with a cross for a tip, not the flat kind. It had a name, something biblical. Peter? Paul?

Damn it, there was no time for this. She noticed an award she had received from the Evangelical Society of Journalists lying on the carpet near the edge of the linoleum, where it had presumably fallen during one of the earthquakes. She had won the award for one of her first assignments, back when she still thought she might be doing the world some good by reporting on apocalyptic cults. It was sort of flower shaped, with a marble base and a glass body that came to a sharp point at the top. She had always thought it was supposed to be a flame, but it occurred to her now that it looked a little like a bird. A pigeon, maybe. Didn't she read once that a pigeon was essentially the same thing as a dove? Or was that cougars and mountain lions?

She grabbed the flower-bird-flame thing and carried it to the center of her linoleum, roughly where she had appeared. Kneeling on the floor, she raised the ambiguous award above her head and brought the point down as hard as she could. *BAM!*

The impact shot through her hands and arms. It was like striking concrete.

Inspecting the point of impact, she saw only a tiny divot in the surface of the linoleum, and even that was springing back into shape. After a few seconds there was no evidence of any damage.

She tried again, even harder this time. Once again, the floor refused to budge more than a millimeter, and the brunt of the impact shot through her body. She felt it in her toes.

The third time the award shattered, and a shard nearly sliced open Christine's wrist. Still no damage to her floor was evident.

Christine cursed herself for acquiescing to the installation of Mrs. Frobischer's linoleum in her condo. Poor Mrs. Frobischer; Lucifer's minions had probably killed her to set up this whole linoleum ruse. She had to admit, though, that she was impressed with the linoleum's durability. She would recommend Don's Discount Flooring to anyone who didn't mind the occasional demonic intrusion on their breakfast nook.

She toyed with the idea of leaving the gas open on the oven and hoping for an explosion—after all, it had been hours since the last time she had nearly died in an explosion—but she suspected that such a plan would result in the incineration of the entire building while leaving her linoleum intact. Besides, she remembered hearing that natural gas was actually quite safe, generally speaking. She would need to rig something to create a spark, something on a timer maybe. She wished that she had watched more movies where this sort of thing was done. She tended to watch a lot of movies featuring Hugh Grant. Had Hugh Grant ever needed to explode a condominium? She thought not.

This was not, she thought ruefully, a job for an English major from Eugene, Oregon, who didn't know a router bit from a Philips screwdriver. Philips! That was it!

It occurred to her that her stove was electric.

She needed to get out of the condo. She needed to find Mercury.

Mercury.

He was her only hope. The world's only hope. He was, ironically, the only one whom she could trust, because he was the only one acting on motivations that she could comprehend. Selfishness she could understand. The abstract impetuses of angels and demons were beyond her. There were no good guys in this story, as far as she could tell. There were only the bad and the incompetent. The closest thing to a good guy was, she grimly realized, Mercury.

She had no idea where he was or whether he would even want to help her. But if she could convince a pair of demons that she was sent by Lucifer himself to check up on them, maybe she could convince Mercury that it was in his interest to help her put an end to this idiocy. The thought did occur to her that maybe there was nothing Mercury could do, even if he wanted to, but she shoved it back into the far recesses of her mind. One impossible task at a time.

TWENTY-SIX

There is a good deal of confusion among angels about how the Mundane Plane got its name. A common misconception is that the name arose from the fact that the plane is, to the typical extraplanar visitor, almost unfathomably dull. The relative dullness of the Mundane Plane is, however, only a symptom of a more profound difference, and it is that difference that gave rise to the name.

To best understand this difference, one should consider the fact that over the past few centuries on the Mundane Plane, an overwhelming movement has arisen to describe everything that happens there in what is known as "scientific terms." This movement is perplexing to angels, as we are used to dealing with a Universe that is arbitrary, unpredictable, and completely beyond comprehension.

Most occupants of the Mundane Plane labor blissfully under the illusion that the Universe operates according to certain definite and inexorable rules. It is thought that one needs only to ascertain these rules through scientific experimentation, after which one can insist that the Universe continue to act according to these rules from that point on. When the Universe opts not to follow a rule that it has been given, the scientists assume that the rule is inadequate, not that the Universe is misbehaving.

The situation is rather like that of parents who observe their son doing his homework diligently every night at seven o'clock and decide on this basis to enact a rule that their son *should* do his homework every night at seven o'clock. When, on the following three nights, the son does, in fact, do his homework every night at seven o'clock, the parents congratulate themselves for their excellent parenting and are perhaps invited to speak at a parenting conference in Belgium.

Then, on the fourth night, the son decides to watch cartoons at seven o'clock. The parents, thinking themselves powerless to control their son's behavior, modify their rule to allow their son to watch cartoons on Thursdays. If he takes the weekend off, they append their rule with a Weekend Exception. If he starts taking days off apparently at random, they suspend the rule until some PhD candidate in Indiana informs them that their son's homework schedule correlates with the cycle of the moon, or possibly the programming schedule of the Cartoon Network. The PhD candidate is probably wrong, but it makes the parents feel better, and the PhD candidate gets his dissertation published in the *Connecticut Journal of Juvenile Homework Studies*, so everybody is happy.

This goes on until the rules used for predicting the son's homework schedule get so unwieldy that they are thrown out in favor of a far simpler explanation that has fewer holes—for example, that the son is simply trying to drive his parents crazy. This is what is known as a paradigm shift.

The amazing thing about this method is that it *works*, at least on the Mundane Plane. The Universe, generally an ornery and capricious beast, has for some unfathomable reason allowed itself to be domesticated on the Mundane Plane. For the most part, within the confines of the Mundane Plane, the Universe actually acts in a predictable fashion. Thus it is that Mundane scientists can gradually eke out an understanding of the laws by which their plane operates.

What these scientists don't realize is that the laws which they so painstakingly formulated are themselves completely arbitrary and do not apply to most of the Universe. Most of the Universe doesn't give a damn about things like entropy or the conservation of energy. On planes other than the Mundane, the shortest distance between two points might involve a jaunt through an abandoned tire factory, and an object at rest tends to stay at rest until it finds something more interesting to do. Principles that are thought to be ironclad laws on the Mundane Plane are more like general suggestions to the rest of the Universe.

In fact, even on the Mundane Plane the Universe is not completely housebroken. Occasionally, even the Mundane Plane experiences violations of its supposedly inviolable physical laws. These violations are referred to as *miracles*, and they are the result of a being—usually, though not always, an angel—manipulating supernatural energy that flows through invisible tunnels that perforate every plane. These tunnels are commonly referred to as interplanar energy channels.

Mundane science does not permit the existence of miracles because Mundane science has never even been able to establish the existence of the interplanar energy channels—an oversight that would be rather embarrassing if anyone on the Mundane Plane had any way of knowing about it. But as science won't admit the existence of anything that hasn't been scientifically proven, it can't ever be held responsible for missing anything. In this way, science is like a judge who is in charge of recusing himself from a case where he feels that he has a conflict of interest.

Anyone familiar with the mysterious workings of the interplanar energy channels, then, would not have been surprised that not a single scientist[9] could be found among the dozens of people who had gathered to see a six-foot-four man with silver hair building a gigantic snowman in a freak snowfall just south of Bakersfield.

Snow angels, it turned out, were not all they were cracked up to be, but Mercury had higher hopes for his snowman. So far it was twelve feet tall, and that was only the bottom sphere. Mercury had started rolling it by hand but was pretty well exhausted by the time it was four feet in diameter. At that point, the snowball began miraculously to roll itself. The snowfall itself was, of course, a minor miracle as well. Nearly three feet of snow had fallen in giant, heavy flakes over the past two hours in a roughly circular area about a hundred yards across.

This was, to Mercury's knowledge, the first time an angel had personally created anything on the Mundane Plane. The fact that it was in the most ephemeral medium was of no account; he didn't really expect to finish it. He was surprised, in fact, that his casual manipulation of extraplanar energy hadn't already brought the angelic cavalry raining down on him.

Mercury paused a moment in his task and looked skyward. The snow continued to fall, impossibly thick, and the heavens gave no sign of wanting to obliterate him with a pillar of fire. He shrugged and continued to work. Around him, at what they presumably thought was a safe distance, a ring of onlookers stood openmouthed, agape at the freak snowfall and the absurdly large snowball rolling itself in circles along the ground.

"Enjoying yourself?" asked a woman's voice.

---

9   Television meteorologists don't count.

Mercury turned to see who it was. Her features were nearly obscured by the thick blanket of flakes drifting down, but there was no mistaking that face.

"Christine!" he yelped, with an enthusiasm that surprised him.

"The world's going to hell, and you're making snowballs?" Christine said.

"Snow *man*," corrected Mercury. "He's not really ready for prime time yet. How'd you find me?"

"I just started driving north from LA. When I heard about a freak snowstorm outside of Bakersfield, I figured you were involved. You're cheating, you know."

"How do you figure?"

"You're supposed to roll them by hand. It's no fun if you use magic."

"Miracles."

"Whatever." "So it turns out that my linoleum installer is in league with Satan."

"Most are," said Mercury. "And don't get me started on the masons."

"Seriously," said Christine. "He's a demon named Malphas. You know him?"

"Doesn't ring a bell," said Mercury.

"Anyway, he's evidently installed a portal from my condo to a place called the Floor. They're planning to send six hundred sixty-six demons with bombs through it. They're trying to destroy the world."

"Impossible," said Mercury. "First, the transplanar energy channels aren't right in Glendale. You'd need some kind of massive..."

"Earthquake. Or quakes. To reconfigure the energy channels."

"Yeah, and to *cause* an earthquake you'd need..."

"The Attaché Case of Death, which they apparently have."

"Really? Wow. That's...still, there would be no point. Lucifer can't just go off the reservation and send a horde of demons through a portal with...did you say *bombs*?"

"I think they called them 'anti-bombs,' whatever that means."

Mercury whistled long and low.

"What? What are anti-bombs?"

"Very short-lived portals. When triggered, they open a rift to an empty plane. The rift creates a massive vacuum, sucking everything around it into the other plane. An implosion rather than an explosion. Hence *anti*-bomb. I didn't realize Lucifer had access to them. But as I was saying, Lucifer can't just send his minions through a portal to wreak havoc whenever he wants. There are very clear rules for the Apocalypse. The final battle takes place at Megiddo. That's why it's called Armageddon."

While they talked, a group of young boys, having overcome their initial fear of the giant self-rolling snowball, were now playing in the snow nearby. They quickly tired of trying to build a snow fort, the destructive whims of the giant snowball making such an endeavor precarious, and they agreed instead to have a snowball fight. The boys split into two groups, which headed for opposite ends of the snowfield.

Christine, irritated with Mercury's skepticism, said, "Do you think I'm making this all up? Don—that is, Malphas—gave me the whole rundown. They're not going through the Megiddo portal. They're going through Glendale. Through *my* condo. A surprise attack."

"But that's suicide," Mercury replied. "The interplanar authorities would never allow it. There's a complex system of checks and balances that prevents things like this from happening. If there weren't, Lucifer would have blown this place up long ago."

The two groups of boys had sent out their advance teams with a supply of snowballs and were now gingerly testing each other's defenses. Christine noticed, in the middle of the escalating fray, one little boy who seemed to have been left out of the negotiations. He sat midway between the two groups, pathetically building something unrecognizable out of snow.

"Oh, and Izbazel is on Lucifer's team after all," Christine said. "They said something about needing to eliminate Karl. But that doesn't make any sense; the Antichrist is supposed to be on their side."

"A Buckminster Fuller fan, I see," said Mercury to the small boy laboring alone in the snow.

"Huh?" the boy grunted.

"He's the wizard of the dome."

The boy looked confused. He had the kind of openmouthed, squinty-eyed face that always looked a little confused but which really only took its proper shape when it was seized by full-on bewilderment. It was in full bloom now. "It's a casshole," he said, as if Mercury must be blind not to recognize a casshole when he saw one. The boy's nose, having evidently noticed the snow, began to drip big globs of snot, as little boys' noses are required to do under such circumstances.

"And a fine casshole it is," said Mercury. "None of those pesky vertical walls or turrets to defend. Anyone attacking that casshole would ride their horses right up one side and down the other looking for a way in. Genius."

The boy, having given up trying to understand anything Mercury was saying, slapped another shapeless glob of snow onto the sloped side of his castle.

As the snowball fight escalated, Mercury and Christine stepped back to avoid the crossfire. Christine noticed, though, that the two sides had evidently agreed to leave the snotty little castle-builder alone. The war raged, but the boys were careful to make a wide berth around him.

"Izbazel working for Lucifer," said Mercury. "I figured as much."

Christine said, "If Izbazel is working for Lucifer, why would he want to kill Karl? Karl is on their side. I mean, he's the Antichrist, right?"

"Well," said Mercury, "ostensibly Karl is on their side. But between you and me, I have a hard time seeing what he brings to the table exactly. He's a liability, if anything."

"An astute observation. What's your point?"

"Well, let's suppose for a moment that if the Antichrist were eliminated by a third party, a supposedly renegade faction of angels..."

"Yes? Then what?"

"Well, conceivably Lucifer could cry foul. He could argue that the renegades were actually taking orders from Heaven. I suppose the plan would be for Izbazel to kill Karl and then turn himself in, claiming that he was acting on orders from Michael."

"Slow down. Lucifer has Izbazel kill Karl, but blames it on Heaven?"

"Right. I mean, that's the obvious assumption, right? One of Hell's agents gets killed, you'd assume that Heaven is to blame. But Heaven can't just kill Karl. Not yet. It's a violation of the Apocalypse Accord."

A sudden shout from one of the snowball fighters rang out. "Hey! You hit Timmy!"

The snotty castle builder, who was evidently named Timmy, had the remnants of a snowball sliding down his face and neck. His mouth was open wider than before, in the kind of rictus grimace that portended a crying jag for the ages.

"Did not! It was Tyler!"

"It was not, you liar. I saw you!"

As Timmy let loose a horrific scream, soldiers on both sides of the snowball conflict indignantly accused the other side of having whacked poor bewildered Timmy with a snowball. Yelling gave way to a vigorous volley of snowballs.

"So," Christine said, trying to remain focused on the larger issue, "Lucifer blames Heaven for breaking the terms of the Apocalypse Accord by killing Karl. How does that help him?"

"It gives him…" Mercury started struggling to be heard over the fracas and Timmy's injured howls. "It gives him an excuse to withdraw from the Accord. As you know, Lucifer got the bad end of that deal. Following the Accord to the letter, Lucifer is bound to be defeated. It's all there in black and white. But if he accuses Heaven of cheating and then pulls out of the Accord… all the terms of the Accord, which were hammered out over centuries by Heaven and Hell, are voided. Everything is thrown into disarray. Then, while Heaven is off balance, Lucifer launches a surprise attack, supposedly in retaliation against Heaven's violation of the Accord. If you're right, and there's now a portal between Glendale and one of the planes under Lucifer's control…"

"Trust me, I just traveled through it myself a few hours ago."

"Then Lucifer now has the means to launch a surprise attack on the Mundane Plane and a legal excuse to do it. Michael's forces would be mobilized at Megiddo, waiting for the hordes of demons to show up. But they never show up because they're busy smuggling anti-bombs into Glendale. Wow. This could be…wow."

As the snowball fight grew more rancorous, Christine's eyes followed a young, blond-haired boy who found himself only an arm's length from an enemy combatant—a boy who appeared to have at least two years and five inches on him. The smaller boy, having just thrown his last snowball, was empty-handed, while the larger boy held a snowball in each hand. The larger boy grinned and pulled back his right arm to pelt his little blond adversary.

Christine watched as the face of the younger boy telegraphed a complex and fateful series of thoughts—all in the instant it took the older boy to aim his snowball.

The first thought that occurred to the younger boy was, "Gosh, I wish *I* had a snowball. But I don't, and if I reach down to make one, I'll get smacked in the head and probably have snow stuffed down the back of my shirt."

The boy's second thought was along the lines of, "Of course, it wouldn't *have* to be a snowball. Anything that would smack my opponent in the head hard enough for me to get away would do."

This thought was quickly followed up with, "Do I have anything like that? Something like a snowball, but maybe a little harder. Something that would work well at close range. Like a rock. But not a rock, because I don't want to crack his skull open and be grounded for a week. Something in between the hardness of a snowball and the hardness of a rock. Maybe something hard on the inside, but wrapped in something soft."

Finally, it occurred to the boy that he did indeed have something like that with him. Two of them, in fact. One on the end of each wrist. Bone wrapped in skin. Perfect!

The younger boy's fist popped out at lightning speed, smacking the older boy in the nose. A look of shock came over the older boy's face. He dropped his snowballs and clutched his face as it began to bleed.

The younger boy, realizing that he had transformed the character of the battle from snowball fight to something else entirely, turned and ran. The older boy, forgetting about the blood pouring from his nostrils, pursued him with newfound rage. All around Mercury and Christine, boys were now pummeling each other mercilessly with their fists.

"So," Christine said, finding it ever more difficult to concentrate, "this could be really bad. If Lucifer gets away with killing Karl."

"Yes, well," said Mercury thoughtfully. "On the upside, Armageddon is averted."

"And the downside…"

"Something far worse happens."

"So you believe me?"

"The pieces do fit together," admitted Mercury.

Two boys, their faces bloody and their limbs intertwined, rolled in between them.

"And you'll help me stop it?"

"*Stop* it? How on earth do you expect to stop it? And what's the point? If Lucifer fails, the Apocalypse will go on as planned. Either way, this plane is screwed."

"I know," said Christine. "But—oh for crying out loud." She scooped up a handful of snow and shoved it down the back of the top boy's pants. The boy, a pudgy and unpleasant-looking specimen, howled and jumped up.

"Hey!" he yelped. "What's your problem?" He and the other boy, sensing the presence of a common enemy, bent over to scrape up snow to make snowballs.

"A little help, Mercury?" said Christine.

Mercury shrugged. He knelt to make a snowball and hurled it at the pudgy boy. It missed by a good two feet.

Both boys began to laugh. "Nice throw," said Pudgy.

"I was kind of hoping," said Christine, "that you would…"

The snowball boomeranged in midair, coming back to smack Pudgy in the back of the head.

"Hey!" yelled Pudgy, turning around. Snow slid down his neck and back. Then, to the boy's horror, the chunks of snow lifted off his body and began to float in the air in front of him. The remnants of the snowball reassembled themselves before his eyes. Pudgy ran, with the snowball in pursuit. The other boy, having witnessed these events, ran off as well. Three more miraculous snowballs, and the area was deserted except for Christine, Mercury, and Timmy. A group of spectators remained on the perimeter of the snow field, but even they had shrunk back. Timmy, who seemed to barely notice the miraculous happenings about him, was happy to be able to get back to his amorphous glob of snow. "This is gunna be the bestest casshole ever," he murmured.

Mercury nodded. "You have a gift for cassholes," he said.

"We've got to stop him," Christine said.

A puzzled look crept across Mercury's face. "It's just a casshole, Christine. Try not to take everything so seriously."

"*Lucifer*," said Christine through gritted teeth. "We can't let him kill Karl."

"Oh," said Mercury. "Right." His brow furrowed. "But as I said, even if we could stop him, all that would mean is that the Apocalypse would go on as originally planned. Is that what you want?"

"No," admitted Christine. "But it seems to me that if Lucifer is betting all his chips on this double-cross with the Antichrist, then he's probably unprepared for the real thing. So if we can stop this plot, or expose it, then he'll be forced to go through with the Apocalypse as originally planned, and he'll get his ass kicked."

"He was always going to get his ass kicked. That was the agreement."

Something about this troubled Christine. "OK, this is the part I don't get," she said. "This Apocalypse Accord. It's a sort of contract between Heaven and Hell, right?"

"Right."

"And it was negotiated between the best minds among the angels and the best minds of the demons."

"Oh, no," said Mercury. "Where did you get that idea? It was negotiated by *lawyers.*"

"All right, but presumably these lawyers, the lawyers on each side, had the best interests of their respective sides in mind."

"Yeah, right. I mean, what?" said Mercury, his attention on Timmy's featureless castle. "Sorry, I'm getting bored."

"My question is, why would Lucifer negotiate a contract that ensures he will lose?"

"Ah," said Mercury. "You're assuming the Apocalypse Accord is a treaty negotiated by equals. The fact is, though, it's more like a plea bargain. You don't get away with rebelling against Heaven. I mean, not long term. It's like those cop shows where they film the bad guy running away from the cops in a stolen car. He's one guy in an old Corolla hatchback, being chased by eighteen cops with automatic weapons in turbo-charged Crown Vics, but he just keeps running."

"OK, I get it. Lucifer's delusional."

"I mean, the cops have radios. All they have to do is call the cops in the next town."

"Yeah, all right. So he negotiates a deal, trying to make the best of—"

"And then they put those nail strips down and blow all his tires, sparks are flying from his wheels, but he still keeps running. He doesn't have a snowball's chance in hell of getting away, but he just keeps running. It's madness."

"Yeah, I understand. You're saying that—"

"And then you realize that you're watching the whole thing from a helicopter. A *helicopter*, Christine. You can't outrun a helicopter in a beat-up Corolla with four flat tires."

"Mercury, I got it. Lucifer has no choice but to—"

"Still, you have to hand it to him," said Mercury thoughtfully.

"What?"

"It makes for good television. Now, what were we talking about?"

"The Apocalypse Accord. You were saying that—"

"Right, so Lucifer's got to make the best of a bad situation. He negotiates the best deal he can, which is a bloody battle for this plane. He's going to lose, he knows that, but he's going to create some carnage on the way down."

"And how does that work exactly?" asked Christine.

"How does what work?"

"I mean, this battle, it's supposed to happen at Megiddo, right? That's where the portal is. So what's supposed to happen, exactly? Angels and demons pour through the portal and start beating the crap out of each other?"

"Not exactly. The fighting is done mainly by your people. Humans, I mean. The angels and demons are just auxiliary support. And of course, the actual battle at Megiddo is just part of it. There are signs and wonders, disasters and plagues, et cetera.

That's about as much as I can tell you. Like I said, I've missed a few meetings."

"But things turn out OK in the end though, right? The good guys win."

"Yeah, I suppose. But if Lucifer is planning on pulling out of the Accord, there's no telling what might happen."

"That's why we have to stop him. If we can stop his attack through the Glendale portal, then he'll have no choice but to go back to plan A. He'll have to send his demons through at Megiddo instead. They'll be disorganized, and Michael will be ready for him. Maybe with that kind of advantage, the good guys can wipe out Lucifer while minimizing the carnage."

"You're pinning a lot on the hope that Michael isn't itching to lay down some serious destruction, regardless of what Lucifer does."

"Yeah," admitted Christine. "I guess I'm still hoping that the good guys will end up being good guys. In any case, I can't help but feel like all this is happening for a reason. That I was meant to overhear this plan so that I can stop it."

"So you think that Michael has already figured out Lucifer's double-cross?"

"I don't know," said Christine. "Maybe somebody above Michael. Or somebody above somebody above Michael. I can't comprehend all the politics, but I can't shake the idea that somebody somewhere has to ultimately be in charge. And if somebody is in charge, then I can't believe that he or she or it has entrusted the fate of the world to some arbitrary bureaucracy. Life can't be all about deciphering puzzles and playing one side against another. Ultimately, you just have to do what you feel is right."

An unexpected voice intruded upon their conversation.

"*Yes,*" said the voice, from the edge of the snowstorm. "Let's all decide for ourselves what is right or wrong. What do we need the Divine Plan for? Perhaps we were meant to disregard our orders and spend our last remaining moments building snowmen."

The figure drew closer. It was Uzziel.

"So you found us," said Mercury.

"You don't make it very difficult," said Uzziel. "A snowstorm in Bakersfield is something of a red flag."

"I'm surprised it took you so long," said Mercury.

"My first inclination," said Uzziel, "was to hit you with a Class Four, but I have to admit you piqued my curiosity with the snowstorm. I thought maybe you were up to something. I should have known you were just entertaining yourself. It's what you're best at. And you, Christine. I believe I made it very clear that you were to remain…"

"Listen, Uzziel," said Christine. "I know you have your orders, but there are things happening here that you don't understand. I overheard a demon named Malphas…"

"Malphas!" spat Uzziel. "Figures that you'd have gotten mixed up with that troublemaker. I need to take you both into custody before you complicate things even further."

"We're not 'mixed up' with Malphas," said Christine. "I accidentally transported myself to a place called the Floor, where he and a guy by the name of Nybbas were plotting to send a horde of demons through a portal in my condo tonight."

"Nonsense," said Uzziel. "The Apocalypse Accord clearly states that Megiddo will be the beachhead for the demonic onslaught. In any case, it would be impossible to create a portal anywhere else, except from the planeport. And I'd like to see Lucifer try to smuggle a horde of armed demons through the planeport. Now I've had enough of your freewheeling nonsense. There are dates that have to be met, plans that need to be seen through. Enough!"

And as he spoke, a pillar of fire shot through the clouds, striking the massive snowball. It exploded into great sloppy globs of snow and water. The flakes stopped falling, and the snow on the ground suddenly began melting away. As Timmy's castle too began to melt, he once again began to sob uncontrollably.

A circular area of the ground in front of Uzziel began to glow in a strange, intricate pattern.

"All aboard," said Uzziel. It was not a request.

Mercury, Christine, and Uzziel filed onto the portal, disappearing into thin air. Timmy, long trails of snot hanging from his nose, sat alone in the mud.

TWENTY-SEVEN

The Apocalypse Accord is a long and mind-numbingly detailed document, hashed out by seraphic lawyers over the course of several thousand years to cover every conceivable aspect of the Apocalypse. Regarding the Antichrist it reads, in part:

The Antichrist is to be the official representative of Lucifer on Earth. The Antichrist must be a human being of Semitic descent (at least one-sixteenth on the father's side), and is to be selected by Lucifer (or his designated representatives) a minimum of forty days prior to the commencement of Phase One of the Apocalypse. Once selected, the Antichrist's name must be submitted to the Seraphic Senate for approval. Upon having his or her name submitted to the Senate, the Antichrist comes under legal protection of the Senate's Committee on Persons of Apocalyptic Interest, and may not be physically harmed or coerced in any way by any parties to this agreement. (See "When Are Agents of Heaven Permitted to Attempt to Kill the Antichrist?" in Appendix L.) The Senate then has seven days to ratify or veto the selection. If the candidate is vetoed, the Senate must also provide a written rationale for their veto. (For a detailed list of Antichrist qualifications, see Appendix F: "So You Think You've Got a Candidate for the Position of Antichrist?") If the Senate does not veto or ratify the candidate's selection within seven days, the candidate's selection is assumed to be ratified by default. Once a candidate is ratified, the Side of Heaven has forty days to publicly denounce the candidate as the Antichrist and an agent of Lucifer. Failure to adequately denounce the candidate within forty days of his or her ratification will cause the Hosts of Heaven to be held In Breach of this Accord, and to be ascribed penalties as detailed in Appendix H ("Denunciation: Why It Matters"). Once the candidate is denounced, he or she shall be considered to be the Antichrist and will be accorded various Powers and Principalities. (See "Legal and Tax Ramifications of Being Classified as the Antichrist" in Appendix P.)

The entire document is some seven hundred pages long and is the work of nearly three hundred angelic lawyers, nearly half of whom work on a plane known as the Courts of the Most High. The Courts of the Most High are the crown jewel of the Heavenly bureaucracy, employing a bewildering quantity and variety of civil servants all commissioned with the same task: to prevent anything from happening in the Universe that has not gone through the appropriate channels and had the requisite paperwork signed off by the appropriate authorities, at least one of whom is always at lunch. No actual productive work is done in the Courts of the Most High, but the staff of the Courts have the proud distinction of having prevented more work from being done on more planes than any other entity outside the United States Congress.

As Christine and Mercury had gotten it into their heads to Do Something, it was inevitable that they would wind up in the Courts of the Most High. Doing Something was frowned on by the Courts, at least if one did not have the appropriate licenses and certifications. The only hope for someone planning to Do Something who ran afoul of the Courts was a phenomenon known as the Bureaucratic Inertia Paradox.

The Bureaucratic Inertia Paradox occurs when one arm of the bureaucracy charged with preventing someone from Doing Something cannot prevent that thing without running afoul of another arm of the bureaucracy. Getting around this other arm of the bureaucracy requires the first arm to Do Something, which it is constitutionally incapable of doing. The bureaucracy is therefore faced with an impossible choice: either (1) let someone Do Something, or (2) Do Something to prevent someone from Doing Something. Either way, Something happens, which the bureaucracy cannot tolerate. The machinery of the bureaucracy grinds to a halt, spewing forth a noxious cloud of smoke, and is unable to function again until the foreign object—in this case, the party attempting to Do Something—is removed. Observe:

After a brief stopover at the planeport, Christine and Mercury found themselves in a massive, glittering metropolis that seemed to be nestled in a bank of clouds. Angels darted to and fro over their heads. Uzziel was leading them down a path that appeared to be paved with gold bricks. Two humorless cherubim bearing flaming swords followed behind.

"Is this...Heaven?" Christine whispered to Mercury.

"Yes," said Mercury. "Er, no. That is, this plane is part of the Heavenly sphere of influence. It's known as the Courts of the Most High. This is where most of the business of Heaven gets done. Or is prevented from being done, rather."

"Uzziel told me that Heaven is where God is."

"Well, yes, technically that's true. On the other hand, God is not limited by time and space and therefore is everywhere. Or nowhere. The point is, calling Heaven the presence of God is like defining the Universe as the place where all the stuff is."

"Huh?"

"It's not a very useful definition, practically speaking. If you're an angel on the side of Good, you've got to draw a line somewhere, so you know where *we* end and *they* begin."

"So Heaven and Hell are just arbitrary, meaningless terms," said Christine.

"I wouldn't go quite *that* far..."

"But you said yourself that you angels define Heaven and Hell using criteria that have nothing to do with the actual meaning of the terms."

"True," admitted Mercury. "We've essentially redefined the terms to make them more useful."

"But you can't *do* that. You can't take a word, strip it of its meaning, smuggle in some other meaning, and then keep using the word as if nothing had happened. It's like North Korea calling itself the Democratic People's Republic of Korea."

"What's wrong with the 'Democratic People's Republic of Korea'?"

"Other than the fact that the only accurate word in that name is 'Korea'?"

"What about 'of'?" said Mercury. "I think 'of' is OK."

"Quiet!" snapped Uzziel. "We're entering the court."

"What are we doing here?" Christine whispered. "What's going to happen to us?"

"Uzziel's taking us to his bosses," Mercury said. "Some of his bosses, anyway. One of the panels he reports to. Uzziel has a lot of bosses. He actually has a whole staff of people dedicated to keeping track of who his bosses are."

"Are we in trouble?" asked Christine.

"Well, I don't think we're getting medals," replied Mercury. "Are we, Uzziel?"

Uzziel shot him a murderous look.

"No medals," whispered Mercury.

Uzziel led them into a building that would have been unremarkable had it not been plated with gold and encrusted with rubies. They made their way through a maze of marble hallways, eventually ending up in a semicircular room with a definite judicial feel to it. At the front of the room, facing the three of them, sat seven angels wearing white robes. They did not look pleased.

"Behold!" exclaimed Uzziel. "The Arbitration Panel of the Subcommittee for Adjudication of Matters of Alleged Violations of the Apocalypse Accord, the honorable seraph Cravutius presiding!"

He turned to the seven angels. "Your Holinesses, I present to you the renegade cherub Ophiel, aka Mercury, and his accomplice Christine Temetri. These two have been the ones causing all of the trouble of late."

"All of the trouble!" exclaimed Mercury. "That's overstating it a bit. Sure, we were tangentially involved in *some* of the trouble…"

"Silence!" proclaimed the seraph in the middle of the table, who was evidently named Cravutius. He wore a crimson sash that Christine assumed was meant to indicate his position as the head of the court. Either that or he was the only angel who hadn't gotten the "no sashes" memo.

The crimson-sashed angel went on. "You are in serious trouble, Ophiel. You had better start offering some explanations for your behavior if you expect any leniency at all. Now what exactly is your involvement with the renegade faction?"

"What renegade faction?" asked Mercury.

Uzziel hissed, "Playing dumb isn't going to help you, Mercury. I suggest you tell them everything you know."

"We know Izbazel and Gamaliel are involved," said another seraph. "We also know that you have not had close ties with either of them in the past. If you tell us everything, we may be disposed to believe that you are not directly involved in the rebellion."

"Izbazel and Gamaliel are idiots," Mercury said. "I would never have anything to do with those two."

"That's a good start," said Cravutius. "Now what can you tell me about the renegades?"

"Renegade," said Mercury.

"Excuse me?"

"As far as I can tell," Mercury said, "there is only one renegade angel."

"Only one? Are you saying that Gamaliel is not in on the plot? That Izbazel is somehow using him for his own ends? Because we have some reason to believe…"

"No," said Mercury. "I mean neither of them is a renegade. They're both just following orders."

"I can say with certainty that they are not," said Cravutius. "We have assurances from representatives of Michael himself that his ministry is not running any covert operations involving either of them."

"You misunderstand me," said Mercury. "I didn't say whose orders they are following."

"Careful, Mercury," warned the other angel who had spoken up. "If you are making accusations, you had better be able to back them up."

Mercury shrugged. "I'm making no accusations. You asked me about the renegades, and I'm telling you that as far as I can tell, every angel I know is just following orders. Every angel, that is, but one. He's your renegade."

"And that angel would be…?"

"Well, me, of course," said Mercury. "I mean, 'I.' That angel would be I. That's right, isn't it?" He turned to Christine.

"I think so," said Christine. "The question is whether *I* is the subject or the direct object in that sentence. I believe that the consensus is that the correct statement would be 'That angel is I.' To be more precise, if you assume that 'would be' is a linking verb, you would use the—"

"Are you being coy with this court?" seethed Cravutius.

"Not at all," said Mercury. "I should be the subject of this inquiry. Or the direct object. Whichever. I'm your renegade."

"Meaning what?" demanded Cravutius.

"Meaning," said Mercury, "that all of the angels I have encountered are following somebody's orders. All except for me. I'm acting autonomously. Ergo, I'm your renegade."

"You," hissed Cravutius, "are a *joke*. A laughingstock among angels. Do you realize that?"

"Well," said Mercury, "my philosophy has always been that if you can make one person laugh, you're already doing better than John Calvin."

"You don't even rise to the level of a renegade," said the other vocal angel. "You're just a spoiled child, doing his best to make the adults angry."

"Wow," said Christine. Suddenly all eyes were on her.

"I mean, you're totally right," she said to the angel who had spoken last. "He *is* like a spoiled child."

"So you disapprove of his behavior," said the center angel.

"To the contrary," said Christine. "I finally understand why he's such a pain in the ass. You self-righteous baboons are enough to make Job rethink his allegiances."

"See?" said Mercury to Christine. "It's not just me, right?"

"You DARE?!" growled Cravutius. "Speak to me in this manner again, and I will—"

"You'll *what*?" snapped Christine. "What are you going to do to me that trumps the *Apocalypse* that you're planning for my planet? You've played that card already, Clarence."

"'Clarence'?" asked Mercury.

Christine shrugged apologetically. "He's the angel from *It's a Wonderful Life*. I was trying to think of a more insulting angel name, but I've got nothing."

"Christine Temetri," hissed Cravutius, "the Mundane Apocalypse is part of a much larger plan, one that would boggle your mind with its far-reaching consequences. It is not given to a lone mortal such as yourself to understand the—"

"Yeah, I get it," said Christine. "You are the great and powerful wizard, and I'm not in Kansas anymore. Look, you people need to get your heads out of your asses and recognize that your vaunted plan isn't worth the lambskin it's written on. I know this is going to come as a big shock to you, but Lucifer is not cool with your plan. See, he evidently read the whole thing, down to the part where he gets thrown in a pit to rot for a thousand years, and he's decided to pursue other options."

"Nonsense," said Uzziel. "The Apocalypse Accord is completely binding on both sides. Heaven's lawyers have been poring over it for centuries, looking for any possible loophole. It's as airtight as contracts get. Hermetically sealed."

"I did no such thing," said Mercury.

Uzziel looked puzzled. "What does that mean? You did no such thing."

"It's a joke," Mercury explained patiently. "'Mercury' is the Roman name for—"

"Silence!" growled Cravutius again. "We are not here to discuss any supposed violation of the Accord. The only threat to the balance at present is the activities of this rogue group of angels with which, I am increasingly beginning to suspect, you are both complicit. If the forces of destruction triumph in the upcoming struggle, it will only be because of the irresponsible actions of these angels."

"Forces of destruction," mused Mercury. "That's an interesting way to characterize your enemy. You know what I was doing before Uzziel here hauled me in front of this court? I was making a snowman."

No one seemed to know quite what to make of this remark.

"A snowman," repeated Mercury. "Do you know who is threatened by a snowman?"

They still stared at Mercury, puzzled.

"No one!" Mercury declared. "A snowman is no threat to anyone. All it does is stand there and make people feel warm inside, with its big trash can nose and bowling ball eyes."

"You're supposed to use a carrot and lumps of coal," said Christine.

"I had to improvise," Mercury said. "Problems of scale. The point is," he said, turning back to the panel, "there is never any reason to wreck a snowman. Wrecking a snowman is just pointless destruction."

"Mercury," said Cravutius, "I've had about enough of this. If you don't start telling me what you know about this rebellion, I may decide that you are of no more use to us."

Mercury went on, unfazed. "That's what I'm telling you," he said. "I've figured it out. I'm the rebellion. I'm the one you want. I realized it when Uzziel wrecked my snowman. I realized what side I'm on."

"And that side is?"

"The one that doesn't wreck snowmen. I'm on the pro-snowman side."

"All right," said Cravutius. "That's enough. Take Mercury away. Perhaps the woman—"

"Listen," said Mercury. "I'll tell you want you want to know. I will. But I want some assurances first."

"Assurances of what?"

"Assurances that you won't harm any more snowmen."

Even Christine was now ready to desert him. "Mercury, are you sure that's the condition that you want to make?"

"Absolutely," said Mercury. "There's no reason to destroy a snowman. I want assurance that you won't hurt any more snowmen."

"Fine," said Cravutius impatiently. "Now tell us…"

"Nor, through inaction, will you cause any snowmen to be harmed."

"I can't possibly make such assurances. The Apocalypse is nigh. Some snowmen are inevitably going to be harmed."

"I'm afraid I can't accept that," said Mercury.

"Mercury," said Uzziel, "enough of this silliness. Get a grip on yourself. This is a real conflict, with real consequences. Are you really willing to allow your fellow angels to come to harm in order to protect *fake people made out of snow*?"

Mercury replied without hesitation, "An angel may protect himself, as long as doing so does not conflict with the first or second laws of snowman protection."

"Look," said Christine. "Let's be reasonable. I'm sure Mercury is willing to make some concessions regarding the protection of snowmen if you seraphim will simply listen to us and try to understand where we are coming from."

Mercury shrugged.

The angels glanced at one another. Finally Cravutius sighed resignedly. "We will listen to what you have to say," he said.

"Here's the thing," Christine said. "I understand that you believe you are acting in the interest of the Divine Plan. But what if we're misinterpreting the Divine Plan? If God had needed a bunch of unquestioning robots—"

"Or snowmen," Mercury added.

"Right," Christine went on, "if God had wanted a bunch of unquestioning snowmen to execute his plan, He could have created them. But He created us. Human beings and angels who have minds, who question things. He gave us the ability to question this so-called 'Divine Plan.' Why? Maybe because it needs to be questioned sometimes. Maybe, in fact, it's not the Divine Plan after all. Maybe this is all some sort of test."

"Blasphemy!" shouted Uzziel. "Don't you see what you're saying? If you start questioning the Plan and saying, 'Well, maybe there's another plan above this one,' what's to stop you from saying maybe that's not the real plan either? Maybe there's another plan above that, and another above that. Where does it stop?"

"It stops," said Christine, "*here*. It stops with us, right now. We stop following orders for the sake of following orders. We stop going along with arbitrary rules just because someone told us that it's God's will. We stop this plot to destroy this world. *My* world."

"Yeah!" exclaimed Mercury. "Let's stop it! How are we going to stop it?"

"The Apocalypse is not simply a plan to destroy the world," Cravutius said. "I understand that is how it must appear to you..."

"No," Christine said. "I mean, yes, it does appear that way. But that's not the plan I'm talking about. This is what we've been trying to tell you. Lucifer is reneging on the Apocalypse deal."

"The Antichrist!" bellowed Mercury. "That's it! We have to stop them from killing Karl!"

"The renegades?" said Cravutius.

"There are no renegades," said Christine. "Izbazel and Gamaliel are working for Lucifer. They're going to kill Karl and blame it on Michael. They'll withdraw from the Apocalypse Accord and attack the Mundane Plane on their own terms. They've used the Attaché Case of Death to start targeted earthquakes that have reconfigured the energy channels, allowing them to open a portal in my condo. They're going to send a horde of demons with anti-bombs through to wipe out Earth."

"Nice summary," observed Mercury.

"Thanks," said Christine. "It's taken until now for me to put it all together."

The panel of seraphim sat in stunned silence. After some time, Cravutius spoke.

"Where is the Antichrist now?"

Uzziel answered. "He's with Harold Giddings, the owner of the *Banner*. We expect Harold to officially denounce Karl as the Antichrist this evening at the Covenant Holders conference in Anaheim."

Now Christine was confused. "I thought Harry was giving a speech about religious media or something," she said. "What's this about him denouncing Karl?"

"Harry believes he's on a divine mission to herald the arrival of the Antichrist," said Uzziel. "Our understanding is that he was selected by Prophecy Division to receive certain information about the Apocalypse via Angel Band. We haven't been able to get any details, of course. You know how it is trying to get any information out of Prophecy. We think something may have gone wrong, though. We've recently learned that he has had contact with one or more fallen angels for some time now. Possibly years."

"Harry has been talking to angels?" Christine asked incredulously. "*Fallen* angels?"

"Listening to them, at least," said Uzziel. "The MOC has apparently known for some time that he has had contact with one of the Fallen, but the information has only just made it to our division. And it's still not clear to whom he's been listening or for how long."

"How is it possible," interjected Cravutius, "that this Harold Giddings has been able to receive transmissions from fallen angels without us knowing?" He turned to Uzziel. "Don't you people track these sorts of interplanar communications?"

"Of course, Your Holiness," said Uzziel. "But that's just the thing: it doesn't appear that the angel, or angels, have been using interplanar frequencies."

"So…angels have been visiting him in person? And somehow you failed to notice that?"

"No, Your Holiness. They are communicating via Angel Band. The transmissions seem to have originated on the Mundane Plane."

"So there's an angel, or angels, on the Mundane Plane somewhere, who has been talking to Harold Giddings over Angel Band, possibly for years, but you have no idea who they are, where they are, why they are talking to Harold Giddings, or what they are telling him?"

"Er, yes, Your Holiness," acknowledged Uzziel sheepishly. "You see, we're not set up to track intraplanar Angel Band communications. Normally one would expect the angel's superiors to keep tabs on what that angel is doing, but since we have no idea who these angels are, we have no idea who they report to. Clearly someone has gone off the reservation, but it's impossible at this point to know who. Harold Giddings has, of course, been under surveillance since being classified as a Person of Apocalyptic Interest, but it's very difficult to intercept these sorts of intraplanar communications.

"In any case, what we do know is that Harold believes that he has been chosen to proclaim the beginning of the Apocalypse. And he is now convinced that his whole life has been leading up to his public denunciation of the Antichrist at this Covenant Holders conference."

"That's where they'll kill him," said Mercury. "It's their best opportunity. Karl will be on stage, in front of forty thousand people. And once Harry denounces him, there will be no question as to Karl's legal status as the Antichrist. They'll kill Karl, and Lucifer will blame it on Heaven and cancel his plans for a war in the Middle East—which he was never going to follow through on anyway, because his focus is on Southern California."

"If this were true," Cravutius said, "we would be powerless to do anything about it. That is, we can convene a hearing into initiating an investigation into the alleged violation of the Accord…"

"Yes," said Christine. "Be sure to look me up on my molten slag heap of a planet and let me know what you find out."

"It's true," said Mercury. "There's nothing they can do. If agents of Heaven are seen interfering with the denunciation of the Antichrist, it will have the same effect as killing him. Lucifer will cry foul, and the rest of his plan falls nicely into place."

"So…what?" Christine demanded. "We do nothing?"

"No," said Mercury. "*They* do nothing." He motioned toward the panel. "*We* can still stop this."

"Out of the question," said Uzziel. "The two of you cannot be allowed to run rampant on Earth. You will both be quarantined indefinitely until we can verify your claims."

"There's no time for that!" Christine said. "The Covenant Holders conference is happening right now. Harry could take the stage at any minute. And you know we're telling the truth. Everything fits. Get your noses out of the SPAM and use your own judgment for once. Even if we're lying, how much damage can the two of us possibly do? Mercury was busy building a snowman when Uzziel picked us up. What are you worried about, that he's going to raise up an army of giant snowmen to wage war on Heaven?"

"More importantly," Mercury said, "Christine is a Person of Apocalyptic Interest. You can't quarantine her without calling a special meeting of the Committee on Persons of Apocalyptic Interest."

"Fine," said Cravutius. "We will hold you until the Committee on Persons of Apocalyptic Interest can be convened."

"Do you have a Writ of Deferment?" asked Mercury.

"A writ of what?" Cravutius replied.

"A Writ of Deferment. You need one if you want to hold Christine until the committee meets. And of course, to hold me, you'll have to charge me with violations of the SPAM. But if you do that, then you have to give me unfettered access to my judicial representation."

"And who might that be?"

"Christine here," said Mercury. "I think she could be an excellent lawyer. Of course, she'll be in Los Angeles..."

Uzziel protested, "Christine can't be your lawyer. She's a mortal. And she's not an attorney."

Cravutius, however, seemed less certain. He could see where this was going: the bureaucratic barriers that had been erected around Christine, as a Person of Apocalyptic Interest, made it virtually impossible to hold her without running afoul of some agency or other. An informal detention such as Uzziel had arranged at the planeport was one thing, but now that the Arbitration Panel of the Subcommittee for Adjudication of Matters of Alleged Violations of the Apocalypse Accord was involved, it could take weeks just to figure out what branch of the bureaucracy was empowered to detain her, and under what circumstances. And Mercury, with a knowledge of red tape that came from skirting it for centuries on end, was doing his darnedest to hitch his wagon to Christine's, so that they couldn't touch him without first touching her.

"Enough," said Cravutius wearily. "I recommend that we name a committee to investigate the alleged violations of the Apocalyptic Accord. This panel is not empowered to do anything else about this matter at present."

Christine was about to protest when the angel continued:

"We find that neither of these witnesses has anything further to offer, and that they should therefore be returned to the Mundane Plane, to be released on their own recognizance. Uzziel, prepare a temporary portal. This panel is adjourned."

TWENTY-EIGHT

How Harry Giddings came to believe that he was chosen to proclaim the end of the world is a strange and fantastically unlikely story revolving around an angel named Eddie Pratt. Eddie Pratt was the closest thing to a demon living in Cork, Ireland.

There is, of course, a lot of disagreement on Earth about whether demons actually exist, what they want, and how much of the tax code they are responsible for. Technically speaking, a demon is simply a fallen angel, which is to say an angel who is in rebellion against Heaven. Many times this rebellion is quite overt and intentional, while in other cases—as in that of Eddie Pratt— it's more a matter of bad timing.

Those who knew him would never have guessed he was a demon, mostly because to the extent that the residents of Cork thought about demons at all, they tended to imagine that they were somewhat more frightening, not to mention motivated, than Eddie Pratt.

Eddie, who adopted that name after tiring of the funny looks he was getting when he introduced himself, was a cherub who was assigned by the Mundane Observation Corps in 1973, as a result of an impressive series of clerical errors, to observe southern Ireland for signs that the Ottoman Empire was weakening. Eddie's protests that the Ottoman Empire had collapsed a half century earlier and that its influence had never, in fact, touched the shores of Ireland, fell on deaf ears.

For several years Eddie did as he had been instructed, filing weekly reports via the interplanar energy frequencies, commonly referred to as "Angel Band."

"Ottoman Empire Still Collapsed," a typical report would read. After a while he started to get more creative, with entries such as "Ottoman Empire: Has Its Time Come at Last?" He was particularly proud of "Ottomans: No Longer under Foot?"

After several years of this, he had become convinced that no one was actually reading his reports. He grew desperately bored and depressed, the upside of which was that the neighbors stopped calling him "that frightfully cheerful bloke." His other eccentricities were chalked up to him being an American, which he was not, but he spoke strangely and had excellent teeth, so there was no blaming them.

He might have been able to cope were it not for certain particularly cruel aspects of the MOC code, which explicitly forbade (1) drinking, (2) leaving one's post, and (3) playing more than nine rounds of golf on a single day. His reports became desperate cries for help, with titles like "South American Locusts Decimate Irish Tobacco Crop: Ottomans to Blame?" But still there was no word from his superiors.

Finally, one damp Saturday evening some twelve years after his assignment began, when he simply could not play one more round of *I think it's going to rain no perhaps not although on the other hand maybe yes but it's hard to say*, he snapped and downed six pints of beer at the local pub.

As fate would have it, that very evening, while he was spending an untroubled night passed out on a rubbish heap in a dank alley smelling of cat urine, his superiors chose at last to make contact. Unable to raise him on Angel Band, they assumed that he had abandoned his post. When he missed his next two report deadlines, they looked up his past several reports only to find incoherent gibberish about Moorish jellyfish attacking Belfast, immediately classified him as AWOL, and revoked his interplanar communication privileges. A thorough review of Eddie's assignment was conducted, which concluded after twenty minutes with the consensus that perhaps it would be better all around if nobody brought it up again. Eddie was sent a terse communiqué which read in its entirety:

Your services are no longer required. Good luck!!!

He spent the next three years falling off barstools in pubs in and around Cork, ranting to the locals about the unfairness of it all, on which point they tended to agree with him, as long as he avoided the specifics of his situation, which tended to confuse and frighten them.

It is difficult for someone not in Eddie's position to appreciate his situation. What one must remember is that the one thing that unites all angels regardless of their position in the Heavenly hierarchy is the overwhelming desire to meddle in the affairs of lesser creatures. More than a simple desire, in fact, this urge borders on biological compulsion. Angels *need* to meddle. This need, in fact, is what separates angels from lower beings.

Angels have no business of their own. Angels don't tend gardens, build cities, or invent hydrogen bombs. Whereas humans are taught at a very young age to use the natural beauty around them to make dismally ugly creations out of macaroni, construction paper, and pipe cleaners, angels instinctively recognize the futility of such tasks and are content merely to intervene in the creative activities of others.

In a sense, lower creatures are to angels what pipe cleaners and macaroni are to human beings. An angel would never paint the ceiling of the Sistine Chapel, but he would be more than happy to drive Michelangelo crazy with constant admonishments that it "needs more green over here."

Most angels take for granted the opportunities they are afforded to meddle in the affairs of lesser beings. Eddie, however, had subsisted on Earth for several decades in the absence of any viable prospects with whom to meddle. He was afraid to reveal himself to the locals for fear that he would be completely ostracized, and he was convinced, despite his superiors' obvious and total lack of interest in him, that something horrible would happen to him if he ever left southern Ireland. So Eddie sat and stewed in pubs, yammering on about angels and demons, events real and imaginary, oblivious to the fact that no one was really listening. And when he ran out of people to talk to, he would broadcast drunken and increasingly apocalyptic missives over Angel Band, forgetting that no one could hear him.

Until the day that someone did.

One dreary, drunken night, at the tail end of roughly 1,347 other dreary, drunken nights, Eddie came across a human who seemed to be able to receive Angel Band transmissions. Eddie, you see, had been prevented from broadcasting to other planes but was still perfectly capable of communicating via Angel Band within the confines of the Mundane. Ordinarily, this would be a little bit like having a perfectly good cell phone on Venus, as there are so few creatures on the Mundane Plane capable of receiving

Angel Band transmissions that the odds of raising one at random are virtually nil.

Ecstatic to have found a being capable of receiving his transmissions, Eddie blathered drunkenly for several hours. He couldn't determine much about the person, other than the fact that she was a young female living somewhere in the southwest United States. She was unable to consciously transmit to him, but she was clearly capable of receiving much of what he sent her way.

Eddie was saddened to find, however, that as he began to sober up, he lost his connection to the girl. This, coupled with his burgeoning hangover, put him in a truly dismal mood. And it was at this point that he discovered *another* human being capable of receiving his transmissions—this one a young male, not geographically distant from the girl. Confused with this turn of events, irritated with the apparent capriciousness of the situation, and now in the throes of a real humdinger of a hangover, Eddie vented all of his frustrations of the past several hundred years on the poor lad.

When he awoke the next morning, unable to raise either of the two, Eddie resigned himself to the idea that his experience had been a one-time fluke and began once again to get exceedingly drunk. As the alcohol kicked in and his mood improved, he once again found himself able to communicate with the girl. Having realized the connection between his insobriety and his ability to connect with her, he resolved to remain drunk for as long as possible. Eventually, however, his angelic constitution rebelled, forcing him to sober up. As he did, Eddie again found himself in contact with the other human, and he spent the next several hours grumbling about the unfairness of it all.

Eddie eventually settled into a pattern of drinking binges followed by painful periods of sobriety, spending roughly equivalent periods of time yammering to each of his new acquaintances. Much of what he told them was true, and a healthy portion of it was false, but all of it was colored by the mood he was in at the time.

So it was that the boy—who was during the initial contact only a fetus—and his mother both became recipients of angelic missives, such as they were. The mother, who joyfully pondered the not-always-coherent communications in her heart, became convinced that her son was to be a great prophet, the very herald of the Apocalypse, and named him accordingly.

The young boy, who became so sober and fatalistic in his outlook that he had to work hard to live down the nickname "Apocalyptic Harold," clearly got the worse end of the deal.

TWENTY-NINE

"All of these people are going to see Harry speak?" asked Mercury incredulously. "Is he that good?"

Christine shrugged. "Don't underestimate the appeal of unwarranted moral certainty."

They were sitting at the back of a city bus, surrounded by overly cheerful people who were on their way to the Covenant Holders conference. They had just transported through a temporary portal, appearing about a mile from Anaheim Stadium. Evidently that was as close as Uzziel could get them without raising suspicion that the Hosts of Heaven were violating the Accord. Having been handed a program by one of their fellow conference-goers, they were relieved to see that they had a good twenty minutes before Harry was scheduled to take the stage. Still, they were anxious to get to Karl before that happened.

"You're a stubborn bunch," said Mercury to a gaggle of folks wearing bright yellow T-shirts emblazoned with a giant *CH* logo. "Hard to shake, as it were."

A middle-aged woman in the center smiled back at him. "I'm sorry?" she said.

"The earthquakes," he said. "They'd have scared a lot of people away."

"Not us," said a teenage boy. "It would take Armageddon to keep me away."

"That's an interesting coincidence," said Mercury. "It took Armageddon to get me here."

The Covenant Holders nodded and smiled, their mood not dimmed by their obvious confusion at Mercury's comments.

Mercury turned to Christine. "Most people would think twice about holding a conference like this only a few hours after two relatively major earthquakes," he said.

"It takes more than a couple of earthquakes to derail an event like this," said Christine. "Especially in Los Angeles."

The Covenant Holders nodded and smiled.

"I hear it might rain later," said Christine.

Their faces paled.

Mercury looked quizzically at Christine. She shrugged and rolled her eyes. "Los Angeles."

Mercury nodded understandingly.

"Speaking of earthquakes," said Christine, "there's one thing I still don't get."

"Only one?" said Mercury. "Are you sure this is your first Apocalypse?"

"Well," said Christine, "I've frankly given up trying to understand most of what's going on. A lot of this stuff is over my head. I've decided it's pointless to try to understand the angelic bureaucracy with its panels and committees and bureaus. And I've come to the conclusion that in the end, none of you really understands where this SPAM, or the so-called Divine Plan, is coming from. You all just sort of assume that someone else understands the details."

"True enough," said Mercury. "You're starting to see why I decided to sit out the whole business."

"But there is one specific thing that has been bugging me. The Four Attaché Cases of the Apocalypse. What's the story there?"

"What do you mean?"

"Who created them? And why?"

"Ah," said Mercury. "The creation of the cases was a joint effort, the result of complex negotiations between Heaven and Hell. You see, as long as human conflict is conducted with human weapons, the chances of things getting truly out of hand are rather small. It was hoped that the creation of nuclear and biochemical weapons in the twentieth century would help Armageddon along, but there are some problems inherent in weapons of such destructive power."

"Because there are no winners in a full-on nuclear war, you mean."

"That's MAD."

"Of course it is."

"No, I mean Mutual Assured Destruction. MAD. And that's only part of it. As you imply, the problem with MAD, from the standpoint of one trying to bring about Armageddon, is that there is no rational motivation on either side that would prompt a first strike. And if no one strikes first, there's no war. That's the first problem."

"And the second?"

"MAD only applies when there is approximate parity between two nuclear powers," Mercury explained. "If you have disparity, such as at the end of the Second World War, when the United States had nuclear weapons but no one else did, the side with nuclear weapons is so much stronger than its competitors that there's no need to use them. I mean, after the initial demonstration. It didn't matter that the United States had only two bombs, because they never had to use another one. For that matter, they probably didn't need to use the second one."

"So in either case, whether there is parity or disparity, there's no incentive to use nuclear weapons."

"No *rational* incentive," corrected Mercury. "A crazy person might still use them, but it takes more than a single crazy person to start Armageddon. Armageddon requires escalation, and the only escalation you're going to get with a lunatic launching a nuclear missile strike is every other nation on earth uniting to wipe the lunatic off the map. It's not pretty, but it's not Armageddon either."

"What if the lunatic has control over a vast nuclear arsenal, like Russia's?"

"Well, first of all, that's harder to bring about than you might expect. Truly crazy people—not just paranoid like Richard Nixon or sociopathic like Pol Pot, but truly batshit crazy—have a hard time working their way up the ladder of political power, even with supernatural assistance. And again, even if he did manage to get control of such an arsenal and launch a first strike, you'd have every other nation in the world retaliating instantaneously. There'd be massive casualties but no war to speak of. It would be over in hours."

"And that's not good enough for the psychotic bastards who are planning this thing?"

"It's not Armageddon. Armageddon is a battle. A struggle between good and evil. The point is to put human society in the crucible and see what happens. To do that, you need to provoke a conflict that involves everyone in the entire world. More than a conflict, in fact. A global crisis. Something that threatens to turn brother against brother. Something that strikes at the core of humanity itself, thereby revealing the true nature of humanity."

"So Armageddon is a test?" asked Christine.

"Something like that, yes. That's my understanding, anyway. Personally, I've never seen the point of deliberately bringing about suffering just to see what happens. There's quite enough suffering on this plane to satisfy one's curiosity."

"OK, so how do the attaché cases fit into this?"

"Ah. The deal with the cases is that they give the user what appears to be the power to change the balance of the problem in his or her favor. But the cases also create collateral damage, as you've seen. They all have some deliberate design flaw built into them so that they are reliable only two-thirds of the time. That thirty-three point three percent chance of error ends up creating just enough side effects that you end up with slightly more problems than you started out with. I mean, you might solve the problem you were trying to solve, but more problems will crop up its place. So you use the case to solve *those* problems, and still more problems arise. It's deceptive because you feel like you're making progress, and sometimes you really are, but in the end it's like playing roulette. The house always wins."

"And the house, in this case, is the angels who are trying to bring about Armageddon."

"Correct."

"So Izzy was right. There really are only two sides: pro-Apocalypse and anti-Apocalypse."

"Izzy's a liar," said Mercury. "He's working for Lucifer."

"But if he weren't, if he really believed what he said...that would be the right side, wouldn't it?"

"The side that wanted to put a bullet in Karl's head, you mean?"

"Oh," said Christine. She had forgotten about that.

"There aren't any good guys here, I'm afraid," Mercury said.

"Just you and me," said Christine.

"Yeah," said Mercury. Then, after a moment's pause, he went on. "You know, about that…"

"Don't you dare abandon me now, Mercury!" snapped Christine, more afraid than angry. The situation seemed hopeless even with Mercury on her side, and without him…

"Oh, I'm not going anywhere," said Mercury. "You're stuck with me. I'm just not sure you want to count me as one of the good guys. I haven't always been very helpful in the past."

"Forget about it," said Christine. "I mean, I'll admit I don't understand what would possess one to play ping-pong at the brink of the Apocalypse, but then I don't understand half of what you angels do. The important thing is that you're on the right side now."

"Yeah," said Mercury. "I guess I feel like I should tell you, in case something goes wrong or whatever…that is, I wouldn't want you to hear from Uzziel or somebody…"

"What? What are you talking about?"

"Well," said Mercury. "Uh, you know how I said that I wasn't sure what my assignment was in the Apocalypse?"

"Yes," said Christine coldly. "You said you had missed some meetings. Of course, you also said you gave the Attaché Case of War to General Isaacson, so I assume that you weren't quite so much out of the loop as you led me to believe."

"I did miss some meetings," said Mercury. "That is, I stopped attending after…"

"After what, Mercury?"

Mercury bit his lower lip, betraying…what? Embarrassment? Guilt?

"After the last round of assignments were handed out."

"So you did get your assignment?"

"Well, not the details, you know…I missed the tactical meetings…"

"The *what*?"

"Yeah, that's what they called them. It was a bit silly because I have very little military training, just the minimum, you know, Flaming Sword 101 stuff. Nothing that would have come in handy for this assignment, but I guess they figured I was personable enough to get in close…"

"Mercury, what in hell are you talking about?"

Mercury sighed with resignation. "My assignment. What I was supposed to do, before I went AWOL. The reason I was in Northern California in the first place. Keep in mind that when I checked Lodi for Karl's whereabouts, it was really out of curiosity. I don't want you to get the impression that I was doing reconnaissance, or that I had any intention at that point of…"

"Of *what*, Mercury?"

Mercury took a deep breath. He said, "Killing the Antichrist. Killing Karl Grissom. That was my assignment, Christine. Heaven assigned me to take out Karl."

Christine was incredulous. "But you didn't. You saved his life."

"Yes," said Mercury. "Of course, it was too early at that point, legally speaking. It wouldn't do Heaven any good to assassinate Karl before he was formally denounced. Technically, in fact, they need to wait three days after his denunciation. There's a sort of a grace period during which Karl is the official Antichrist but can't legally be harmed by the agents of Heaven. After that, though…"

"So," said Christine icily, "your plan was to get close to Karl, earn his trust, maybe save his life from an apparent assassination attempt by a couple of bungling demons…"

"No," said Mercury firmly. "I swear, I didn't know anything about Izbazel's plot. That part was just…"

"What? A lucky break? You get to be the big hero, saving Karl's life, and then when he's not expecting it, you snap his neck with one of your little miracles? Sounds like a pretty good plan. Maybe this whole thing—" she waved her hands to indicate the busload of excited Covenant Holders "—is part of your plan, too. You save Karl's life again, and he'll be like putty in your hands. In fact, as you say, if you were working for Heaven, you'd *have* to save his life, wouldn't you? You can't afford to have it look like Heaven broke the rules by assassinating Karl early."

Mercury was getting desperate. "Christine, please," he implored. "You can't really believe I orchestrated this whole conference, complete with another assassination attempt, just to solidify Karl's trust. I mean, that would take months of planning. And I don't know if you've noticed, but Karl isn't that difficult to sway. Getting forty thousand people into a stadium to fool Karl Grissom is like trying to kill a mouse with an F-15."

"Fine," Christine said. "You didn't orchestrate this whole thing. But how do I know that if we save Karl's life, you're not just going to kill him in three days to get back into Uzziel's good graces?"

"You don't," agreed Mercury. "You just have to trust me. I have no intention of harming Karl. Come on, the whole reason I'm here is to save his life."

"Because it fits your agenda."

"The agenda of preventing people from being killed for no good reason, yes," countered Mercury.

"And you promise me that you haven't once considered taking advantage of this situation to kill Karl."

Mercury paused just long enough for Christine to be certain that he had.

A look of disgust and defeat washed over Christine's face. Once again she felt completely alone in her struggle against the incomprehensible forces threatening to tear her world apart.

"Oh, like you've never thought of killing Karl," said Mercury defensively. "The important thing, like you said, is that I'm on the right side now."

Christine took a deep breath and looked out the window of the bus.

They had reached the stadium.

THIRTY

"So," said Gamaliel. "You told him?"

"I told him," said Eddie, barely audible, his head resting on the counter of the pub.

"And he seemed…receptive?"

Eddie groaned. "He's always receptive."

"So he'll denounce Karl tonight." Gamaliel glanced at his watch. "Er, this morning. Damn time change."

Eddie groaned again.

"Excellent. Then I need to get back to California. It's time to wrap up this business."

Eddie's head lifted slightly off the bar. "And then I can leave?"

"And then you can leave. I'll make an anonymous call to the MOC tomorrow."

"And tell them what exactly?"

"That you're still here."

"I think they know that. They don't care."

"They don't care because it's convenient for them not to care."

"And you're going to make it convenient for them to care?"

"I'm going to make it more inconvenient for them not to care. I'll let the director of the MOC know that if they don't extract you,

I'm going to tell somebody higher up the food chain that they misplaced a cherub several decades ago. It will become inconvenient for them not to extract you."

"Whatever," groaned Eddie. "As long as I get out."

"You're just lucky we found you."

"Sounds like *you're* lucky you found me."

"In the end," said Gamaliel, "it will be the best thing for everyone—even the pathetic souls that occupy this plane. This place is in desperate need of a regime change, and you've been instrumental in making that happen."

"Great," said Eddie weakly. He didn't like the idea of being an errand boy for Gamaliel—or whomever it was that Gamaliel was really working for. But what choice did he have? Another decade stuck on this plane and he would go stark raving mad. Even the prospect of divine wrath began to pale in comparison to a century in Cork. Still, divine wrath was something to be avoided if at all possible.

"You're absolutely certain I won't get in trouble for this?" he asked, knowing full well that Gamaliel was a peerless liar.

"One hundred percent," said Gamaliel reassuringly. "There is no way anyone in Heaven can connect you to any of this. You're thousands of miles away from the action, and nobody at the MOC has any incentive to bring up the timing of your extraction. They'll give you a cushy desk job and hope nobody ever mentions your unintentional incarceration on this plane again. Nobody in my organization has any reason to make an issue of it either. Even if we fail, we have nothing to gain by turning you in. Interfering with an agent of the MOC is a serious offense, so we'd be crazy to admit that we even talked to you. In any case—and you understand that I mean no offense—we're not going to score a lot of points with Heaven by turning in a cherub of your rank anyway."

"I suppose not," admitted Eddie. Sometimes it was beneficial to be a little fish. Not when one has been forgotten for half a century on another plane, of course, but sometimes.

"Look at it this way," said Gamaliel, sensing that Eddie was still not entirely convinced. "If Heaven cared about this place, they wouldn't treat it like some kind of backwater province where they can exile angels that they'd rather forget about. For that matter, they wouldn't permit all the war, disease, and general stupidity that go on here. This plane clearly needs more hands-on management.

"In fact," Gamaliel went on, "now that I think about it, it's almost like they left you down here on purpose so that you could help us whip this place into shape. I mean, we considered other ways to get a leader of the faithful to denounce Karl, but it's difficult to do without raising any red flags upstairs. So when we found out about your relationship with Harry…it was just too perfect. Who knows, maybe on some level it was meant to be."

Eddie grunted.

THIRTY-ONE

The Apocalypse, Harry thought as he stood behind the temporary stage that had been assembled on one side of Anaheim Stadium. This was it. His moment of glory. Karl stood next to him, oblivious to what was going to happen in mere moments on that stage.

For that matter, none of the forty thousand Covenant Holders assembled to hear messages of spiritual encouragement had any idea what was about to go down either. Probably they would think Harry was insane, denouncing a schlub like Karl. But such was the fate of prophets.

At present, some black Baptist preacher—the Covenant Holders' nod to racial inclusiveness—was wrapping up a speech about the power of redemption. When he was finished, it was Harry's turn. Harry had planned to speak on the role of religious media in shaping the emerging world, but he had scrapped his notes in light of recent events. Now he planned to open with a retrospective on his life, climaxing with his life's mission: the heralding of the coming Apocalypse and the denunciation of the Antichrist.

Harry noticed in the front row a jittery, angular man who seemed to be immune to the reverend's impassioned pleas. The man looked as if he were waiting for something. Waiting, perhaps, for Harry? That seemed improbable, as Harry was a competent but hardly invigorating speaker. Unless maybe the man knew what Harry was about to do?

Nonsense, thought Harry. He chalked his baseless suspicions up to stage fright and paranoia stemming from his recent un-nerving trip to the planeport. He pushed the thoughts out of his mind and tried to concentrate on what he was going to say. It was nearly time for him to go on.

"Ready?" he asked Karl.

"I guess," grumbled Karl. "I'd feel better if I had my helmet, though."

"You won't need it," said Harry. "Trust me."

THIRTY-TWO

Christine was dismayed to find that the conference was running ahead of schedule. Harry was already on stage by the time they got through the gate.

"What now?" Christine asked.

"Look!" cried Mercury. "That's Izzy, down in the front row. That scheming bastard is just waiting for his chance to pounce."

Harry was winding up to the climax of his speech. He was talking about the Divine Plan and events that he had experienced recently that only confirmed his belief that God intended great things for him. Karl, looking bored and confused, was standing almost out of sight by the side of the stage.

"I can't get near Karl," said Mercury. "At the first sign of coercion, Lucifer will cry foul and put his plan into motion. You have to convince Karl to get out of here. And it has to be of his own free will. You can't touch him or use any kind of coercion."

"So what are you going to do?" asked Christine.

"I," Mercury announced, "am going to go knock Izbazel's teeth out." With that, he began to walk purposefully toward the front row.

Christine moved briskly to the side of the stage. It seemed to take forever, and not just because she was listening to Harry blather on about God's plan for his life. When she finally got there, she flashed her *Banner* credentials to the security personnel and found herself standing backstage next to Karl.

"Hey," said Karl. "What are you doing here?"

"Hi, Karl," said Christine, still somewhat out of breath. It occurred to her that Karl still thought she was...what was it? Secret Service? If she just told him that there was a threat to his life, he'd most likely believe her. She'd be telling the truth, although her credibility was itself based on a lie. Was that considered coercion? Damn the legalistic Seraphim and their petty Accord.

"Harry says you're not really Secret Service," said Karl.

So much for her credibility.

Meanwhile, Harry had segued into an announcement that the End Times had arrived.

Christine said, "You're in danger, Karl. Izzy, that guy we ran away from at Charlie's Grill, he's going to try to kill you again."

Karl snorted. "Harry says you're just jealous. Because he gets to herald the Apoc...Apoc...the end of the world."

"Jealous!" Christine spat. "Harry's a spineless windbag. Lucifer's just using him for his own ends. And Harry's using you. You realize that as soon as you get on that stage, he's going to denounce you."

Karl stared vacantly at her.

"He's going to..." Christine struggled for a synonym for *denounce*. "He's going to say that you're...a bad guy."

Karl shrugged.

Harry's voice suddenly became louder. "And so I give you... the Antichrist, Karl Grissom!"

Karl bounded eagerly onto the stage. The crowd, uncertain how to react, began to applaud and boo simultaneously. Eventually both died out, leaving only a confused silence.

"You may know Karl as the so-called 'winner' of a little contest orchestrated by the people responsible for the Charlie Nyx books…"

The crowd erupted in boos.

"…and chain of family restaurants…"

Boos mixed with clapping.

"Continuing their pattern of ridiculing the Christian faith, they have proclaimed Karl to be the Antichrist," said Harry. "Little did they know that there are powers at work beyond their understanding. I have recently learned that Karl truly is the Antichrist, handpicked by Lucifer himself!"

Confused muttering mixed with boos.

"Karl," said Harry, turning to face him, "I denounce—"

A commotion suddenly broke out in the front row. Mercury seemed to have gotten into a fistfight with two stadium security guards on the way to Izbazel. Izbazel, holding something round in his hand, was distancing himself from the scuffle and creeping closer to the stage.

Christine, finding it hard to believe that Mercury had nothing better than a right cross up his sleeve, took a deep breath and ran onto the stage.

"Karl!" she said. "We've got to go. Izzy's right there, and he's got a bomb."

Karl waved to Izzy. Izzy waved back. Harry stood open-mouthed, having lost his train of thought.

Having bowled over one guard, Mercury decked the second with an uppercut and advanced toward Izbazel, who flipped open the lid of the glass apple with his thumb.

Christine, realizing that there was no way she could get Karl out of the range of the anti-bomb if Izbazel really intended to use it, considered diving off the stage and attempting to wrest it from his grip. She envisioned this going very badly. Having run out of options, she closed her eyes and said the shortest, most sincere prayer she had ever said. It consisted solely of the word *help!*

When she opened her eyes, a familiar but unexpected figure had joined them on the stage: Gamaliel.

"Come with me!" Gamaliel barked. "Izzy's going to implode this whole place!"

Christine had no time to assess Gamaliel's motivations. She had to get Karl out of here.

"Karl!" she snapped. "This is our only chance. You've got to get out of here."

Karl eyed her and Gamaliel skeptically.

"Karl Grissom," said Harry, having regained his composure, "I denounce—"

"Wait!" said Christine, an idea flashing into her head. "Karl wants to repent."

Karl looked puzzled.

"He what?" said Harry.

"He wants to repent and accept Jesus Christ as his savior."

"He can't...he's the Antichrist! He can't repent."

"I'm sorry," said Christine. "I'm a little rusty on my theology. Can you tell me where in the Bible it says that certain people aren't eligible for forgiveness?"

Harry's face turned red. He turned to the crowd for support, but it was clear that the crowd had finally—they thought—figured out what Harry was up to. He was going to show up the scoffers by baptizing their supposed Antichrist right here in front of forty thousand believers. Cheers and shouts of "Amen!" filled the stadium.

Harry, seeing that he was losing control of the audience, put his hand over the microphone. "It's not true, is it, Karl?"

Karl, more puzzled than ever, looked out at the expectant faces hoping to welcome him into the fold. He looked like he wanted to hide.

"I…" he started.

At this moment, Mercury tackled Izbazel. Izbazel held the anti-bomb out of Mercury's reach, his thumb on the trigger. They were causing quite a commotion in the front rows, but most of the crowd remained transfixed on the surprisingly well-acted drama unfolding on the stage.

"Karl," said Christine as patiently as she could, "you've got to trust me. I'm trying to save your life. And the lives of a lot of other people. We've got to get out of here."

Karl looked at Christine, looked back out at the fervent faces of the crowed, shrugged, and then ran toward Gamaliel. Christine was right behind him.

"This way!" yelled Gamaliel, leading them down a dark hallway behind the stairs.

"Dammit, Christine!" Harry growled, suddenly angry. He removed his hand from the microphone and spoke into it loudly and clearly. "Karl, I denounce you as the Antichrist and a servant of Lucifer, in the name of Jesus Christ! I denounce both of you!"

The crowd gasped and muttered among themselves. This wasn't how it was supposed to end, was it?

Mercury and Izbazel were now rolling around in front of the stage, their gangly limbs intertwined. Mercury had managed to jam his thumb between Izbazel's thumb and the button on top of the apple that served as a trigger. The security guards, having recovered from their pummeling and not realizing the fantastically high stakes of this angelic thumb war, were doing their best to separate the two.

"No!" exclaimed Mercury. "He's got a bomb! Don't let him press that button!"

The security guards paused for a moment, taking note of the fact that Izbazel was, in fact, holding a small, round object in his hand. Then, noticing that the object resembled not so much a bomb as something you might buy on clearance at Macy's for your daughter to give to her fourth grade teacher, they resumed their struggle.

"No!" cried Mercury again. "He's going to…"

But it was too late. Izbazel had gotten his hand free.

Izbazel grinned and said, "No Antichrist, no Apocalypse."

His thumb pressed the button.

THIRTY-THREE

Gamaliel led Christine and Karl to a steel door at the end of a dark, concrete tunnel. The door was marked "PERMITTED USE ONLY."

"No one knows what that means," said Gamaliel, unlocking the door with a key from his pocket. "So they leave it alone."

The door opened to reveal a tiny, featureless room with a flickering fluorescent bulb in the ceiling.

"Get in," said Gamaliel.

They stepped inside, and he closed the door. Gamaliel pulled closed a folding steel curtain on the inside of the door and pressed a button on the wall. "Hold on," he said, despite the fact that there was nothing to hold on to.

The floor fell out from underneath them.

The walls and ceiling fell, too, but it was the floor that really got Christine's interest. A scream stuck in her throat.

They fell long enough for Christine to realize that she had stopped breathing and to wonder whether she might in fact die of asphyxiation before being crushed on impact with the eventual bottom of the elevator shaft.

When at long last the elevator began to decelerate, it did so with such abruptness that Christine's knees buckled and she nearly collapsed. Finally they stopped. There was a *ding!* and Gamaliel slid open the folding door.

"That's what elevators are like when you don't have to worry about OSHA," said Gamaliel.

He led them down another long, dimly lit corridor.

"Hopefully," Gamaliel said, "we're deep enough that if Izbazel does manage to detonate the anti-bomb…"

There was a deafening *BOOM!* followed by a low rumbling and falling chunks of concrete. The three of them instinctively shielded their heads as Gamaliel picked up the pace. "We'll be safe down here," he said. "I think."

"Was that…?" Christine started.

"The anti-bomb," Gamaliel said.

"I'm tired," Karl complained. "Where are we going?"

"Somewhere safe," said Gamaliel.

"Why are you doing this?" Christine asked.

"I guess you've figured out Izzy is in league with Lucifer," Gamaliel said, ducking down another corridor. "I, however, am not. That idiot thought he had me totally snowed, but I was always three steps ahead of him. I really am part of a renegade faction that is trying to foil Lucifer's plans. This way, please."

"By killing Karl?" said Christine.

"Of course not," said Gamaliel. "In fact, keeping Karl safe is critical to our plan. Karl, this way please. We need to get out of here before Los Angeles erupts in chaos."

Karl had balked at the entrance to a particularly dark and narrow tunnel.

"I'm not going in there," he said.

"We have to, Karl. It's the way out."

Karl shook his head. "No chance," he said.

"What's the matter, Karl?" Christine asked. "What are you afraid of?"

Karl dug in his heels. "Trolls," he said ominously.

"There are no trolls down here," said Gamaliel.

"It's just like the books," said Karl.

"The books?" asked Christine. "Oh. *Those* books."

"Well," said Gamaliel, "it's true that there is a secret network of tunnels under Anaheim Stadium, just like in the Charlie Nyx books. This used to be a sort of secret hideout."

Christine turned to stare at Gamaliel. "A hideout for whom?"

"It's complicated," Gamaliel said. "The faction of angels that I'm working with constructed them a while back. Lucifer made Katie Midford put them in the books as sort of a joke. I can explain more later. In any case, I can assure you that there are no trolls down here. This place is completely deserted."

Karl reluctantly followed Gamaliel through the tunnel, which ended at another elevator. They rode it up for what seemed like miles before it deposited them in a remote corner of a parking garage. Sirens wailed in the air as Gamaliel led them to a dusty green Ford Explorer parked by itself on the bottom level of the garage.

"Get in," he said, and they did.

"Gotta get out of LA," said Gamaliel, peeling out of the garage. "This place is going to be like a war zone." They headed east.

Behind them, a massive column of smoke arose where the stadium had once stood.

"They're going to have a hard time blaming that on a natural gas explosion," Gamaliel said. "It's going be terrorism this time around."

"All those people…" said Christine. "There must have been forty thousand people in that stadium."

"Not to mention those in the vicinity," said Gamaliel. "Our best estimate is around a hundred and forty, maybe a hundred and fifty thousand people."

"A hundred and fifty thousand…" Christine murmured, trying to imagine the devastation. Then her eyes narrowed at Gamaliel. "Wait, what estimate? How did you have time to estimate the damage caused by that thing…unless you knew it was going to happen. Unless you…you actually planned for this to happen!"

Gamaliel winced, realizing he had said too much. "Hang on, Christine. It's true that we knew what Lucifer was planning. But we didn't cause that implosion. I would have stopped Izbazel, but it was better that we waited until after—"

"Enough!" Christine exclaimed. "I'm so damn tired of you angels and your grand plans! Don't any of you do anything just because you think it's the right thing to do? Does every single action you ever take have to be part of some convoluted plan?"

The Explorer was now hurtling down the freeway to the east of Los Angeles. Ambulances and fire trucks were speeding the other direction.

"Every side in this conflict has its plans," said Gamaliel. "The only ones who are bouncing around freely, without a thought in their little heads, are you humans. And you'll see where *that's* going to get you."

Christine said, "But I thought you said you were going to put a stop to this. You're saying the Apocalypse is still going to happen?"

"The Apocalypse or something like it," said Gamaliel. "That's not really my concern."

"What is your concern exactly?" said Christine. "What is this faction you're working for?"

Gamaliel laughed. "You actually have no idea, do you?"

Christine sighed. "Are we really going to play this game?"

"I work," said Gamaliel, "for the Great Mother. The author of human ingenuity."

"Uh huh," said Christine. "And does this author of human ingenuity have a name?"

"She goes by many names," Gamaliel said.

"Like Puff Daddy," said Karl.

Gamaliel fixed his eyes in the distance and recited:

"And there came one of the seven angels which had the seven vials, and talked with me, saying unto me, Come hither; I will shew unto thee the judgment of the great whore that sitteth upon many waters: With whom the kings of the earth have committed fornication, and the inhabitants of the earth have been made drunk with the wine of her fornication. So he carried me away in the spirit into the wilderness: and I saw a woman sit upon a scarlet coloured beast, full of names of blasphemy, having seven heads and ten horns. And the woman was arrayed in purple and scarlet colour, and decked with gold and precious stones and pearls, having a golden cup in her hand full of abominations and filthiness of her fornication: And upon her forehead was a name written, MYSTERY, BABYLON THE GREAT, THE MOTHER OF HARLOTS AND ABOMINATIONS OF THE EARTH."

"Wow," said Christine caustically. "Somebody's been taking adult ed classes."

"Scoff not," said Gamaliel. "It is she who shall inherit this plane when Lucifer's schemes fail and Heaven abandons you. You shall tremble before her name!"

"Which is…?"

Gamaliel smiled. "That will be revealed to you in due time."

THIRTY-FOUR

Mercury cradled his head in his hands and moaned.

He and Izbazel sat on a series of gray boulders that littered an otherwise featureless dull brown plain. The dim light of a twilight sun was dulled further by a brown haze that hung in the sky. Occasionally, snowflake-sized chunks of debris would drift delicately to the ground. Mercury was vaguely aware that the dusty haze was all that remained of Anaheim Stadium and its occupants. The anti-bomb had torn a massive hole in the Mundane Plane, instantaneously sucking everything in range through a portal to this place—whatever this place was.

The material forms of the two angels had also been torn asunder, but their bodies had, within a few minutes, reconstituted themselves, and they had found themselves in the vacuum of space, falling toward the gloomy landscape below. Neither of them was in a condition to summon interplanar energies to break their fall, so they had taken the full brunt of the impact. Reconstitution is excruciatingly painful in itself, and to have it followed up with a fall of several hundred miles to a rocky plain just seems excessive, in any teleological framework.

They had more or less pulled themselves together—Izbazel quite literally, as he had been torn in half by a particularly unforgiving rock formation—and now were doing their best to assess their current situation.

"I don't get it," Izbazel said. "Why would Gamaliel help Karl to escape? Is he secretly working for Heaven behind my back?"

"Not Heaven," said Mercury.

"It has to be," said Izbazel. "Who else would want to stop me from killing him?"

"Not Heaven. Not Hell. Turns out I was wrong after all," Mercury said. "There is a third faction."

"Don't be naïve, Mercury. Those Heavenly seraphim aren't as pious as you make them out to be. Maybe they're pretending that Gamaliel is on his own, but I have no doubt they would intervene if they thought they could get away with it."

Mercury groaned. "*If* they thought they could get away with it. But they couldn't. They knew everybody would be watching. It wouldn't have been in their interest to intervene."

"OK, so then who?"

"Look, he's your sidekick, not mine," grumbled Mercury. "You're the one who's supposed to know what he's up to. OK, let me think this through…

"One possibility is that Gamaliel is acting on his own. If that's the case, though, I can't imagine what his motivation would be for tagging along with you. Nobody would put himself through that unless it was for some greater purpose."

"Listen, Mercury, I've had about enough of your—"

"Another possibility is that he really *was* on your side but had a change of heart at the last minute. But if *that* were the case, you would expect him to try to stop you from setting off the bomb and save all those people in the stadium. Why save just one person when you can save tens of thousands? Especially when the one person is Karl Grissom, Dickweed Extraordinaire.

"So let's assume that Gamaliel has some ulterior motivation, that he's been scamming you all along. That presumably means that either Gamaliel is far smarter than I thought, or..."

"Or what?"

"Or you are *even dumber* than I thought," said Mercury. "Wow, I need a moment to recalibrate here."

"Dammit, Mercury. If you're not going to—"

"Either way, Gamaliel could presumably have grabbed Karl right out from under your idiot nose anytime he wanted to. So he intentionally allowed your plan to proceed, right up to the denunciation. He wanted Karl to be officially denounced as the Antichrist. But he didn't want Karl dead. So the question is, who wants a live Antichrist?"

"I'm telling you, it's those Heavenly bastards. They'll do anything to—"

"Holy crap, Izzy, it's *her*!"

"Her who?"

"Lucifer's chief rival on the Mundane Plane, that's who. She double-crossed the king of double-crossers."

"You mean...?"

"Tiamat. That conniving bitch. She's going to kidnap Karl and use him to blackmail Lucifer!"

"Blackmail Lucifer..." repeated Izbazel, trying to make the words mean something.

"Man, you really need to get a job as a middle school librarian or something," said Mercury. "You're really not cut out for diabolical scheming. Lucifer's got a horde of demons hanging out on the Floor, just waiting for his signal so they can wreak havoc on the Mundane Plane. But before he can give them the go-ahead, he's got to withdraw from the Apocalypse Accord..."

"Well I know *that* part..."

"All Lucifer is waiting for is confirmation from you that Karl is dead. Presumably the plan was for you to send a message over Angel Band as soon as you had reconstituted. But now you don't know what to do because you can't be sure Karl is dead. In fact, assuming that Gamaliel knows about Tiamat's old hiding place under the stadium—"

"Her what?"

"Her secret lair. Sorry, I assumed you knew. I guess Lucifer doesn't tell you much. You know that Tiamat and Lucifer are enemies, right?"

"I thought that Tiamat worked for Lucifer."

"Technically, yes. But she's never been a true believer. You remember her little coup attempt in the first century AD? When she tried to seize power from him on the Mundane Plane?"

Izbazel's brow furrowed. "I thought they made up."

Mercury sighed. "Again, for a diabolical schemer, you're not very good with the subtle nuances of intrigue. I should get you some flash cards or something. Lucifer and Tiamat didn't 'make up.' Yes, technically Tiamat works for Lucifer. But she's more like a slave than an employee. They hate each other. And I mean *hate*. He's had her doing his grunt work down there for the past two thousand years. Spreading plague, burning witches, breaking up Van Halen...there's no telling what he's got her working on now."

"So what's this about some kind of hideout under Anaheim Stadium?"

"Lucifer won't let her leave the Mundane Plane. He's got a tracer on her, so he can check up on her anytime he wants. If she removes the tracer, he gets alerted. But it doesn't work perfectly, particularly underground. If she gets more than fifty feet or so underground, there's enough interference that it becomes difficult for Lucifer to pinpoint her location. So she got it in her head to create a secret network of tunnels under Los Angeles, starting under Anaheim Stadium. She and her minions were plotting another rebellion against him. She got pretty far before he figured it out and closed her hideout."

"How do you know so much about Tiamat?"

Mercury shrugged. "I still know some people in her organization. I thought this stuff was pretty much common knowledge at this point. Hell, even the Charlie Nyx books have a reference to those tunnels. Somebody at the publishing company is obviously in touch with Lucifer. It must drive Tiamat crazy to know that every fourteen-year-old in the country knows about her secret hideout."

"You think Gamaliel helped Karl and Christine escape through these tunnels?"

"It's a reasonable assumption. If Gamaliel really is working for Tiamat, he must have known about them. And if he got them down there in time, there's a pretty good chance Karl is alive."

Izbazel did not look happy to hear this.

"So," Mercury observed, "now you're sitting here hoping that I'll tell you what to do next. Do you lie and tell Lucifer that you saw Karl die—risking the chance that Karl will reappear at some point—or do you tell him that you screwed up and bear the price for being a scheming dumbass who is completely out of his league?"

"That implosion must have taken out some of the tunnels," said Izbazel hopefully. "I really don't think it's very likely that Karl survived. In any case, I'm sure Lucifer will take into account…"

"Oh yes, Lucifer is a very understanding chap, as I recall. Maybe you'll get some kind of runner-up medal for getting *really close* to killing the Antichrist. The answer, in case you're wondering, is that you tell him the truth."

"Tell him that Karl might be alive? That's suicide!"

"Well, you can't lie because I can guarantee you that if Karl is alive, Lucifer is going to find out about it."

"How?"

"She's going to tell him," Mercury said. "Tiamat. That's the whole point of this double-cross. She's going to use Karl as leverage, threatening to expose Lucifer's plan. This is her way back to power."

"So what do I do?"

"You tell Lucifer the truth."

"He'll crucify me."

"Not if he thinks you're his only chance to get Karl back."

"But I have no idea where Karl even is!"

"That's OK," said Mercury. "I do. Call your boss."

THIRTY-FIVE

Mundane scientists have never found any evidence of the existence of interplanar energy channels. Furthermore, if they *were* ever to come across evidence of the existence of such channels, the scientists would, of course, insist that the channels are simply another natural phenomenon that has not yet been fully explained. They would patiently explain that the existing model of the Universe simply needed to be updated with this new information and that the rules governing the channels would eventually be discovered.

They would be wrong. There are no rules governing the interplanar energy channels.

This can't be proven, of course, because to insist that a phenomenon follows no rules is to define a rule for that phenomenon. In other words, proving that a phenomenon follows no rules is to prove that it does follow a rule, thereby disproving the statement that it follows no rules. The interplanar energy channels seem to obey only one rule—and that one only intermittently. The rule is known as Balderhaz's Tendency, after the angel who discovered it. Balderhaz, the rare angel with an interest in scientific pursuits, posited that the interplanar energy channels act in a way to deliberately avoid scientific analysis.

This was, after all, the only way to explain the fact that Mundane science has never found any evidence to support the belief in the existence of the channels, despite the fact that they clearly do exist. Balderhaz theorized that the channels essentially hide from scientists. Balderhaz's Tendency can also be phrased thus: "The more likely a miracle is to be subjected to scientific analysis, the less likely it is that the miracle will occur in the first place."

Balderhaz tried to prove this rule—which he had originally planned to call Balderhaz's Law—by observing scientists trying to replicate miraculous phenomena on the Mundane Plane, but he fell victim to his own hypothesis. The channels, while under observation, refused to consistently follow the rule of following no rules. In addition to the discovery of Balderhaz's Tendency, this chain of events had two other notable consequences:

First, Balderhaz gave up science to become a well-respected tennis instructor.

Second, a phenomenon known as the Mundanity Enhancement Field was discovered.

Balderhaz, before abandoning his research, discovered that by assembling certain Mundane minerals into a cubical form, one could create a mysterious field that would interfere with interplanar energy channels on the Mundane Plane within a limited area. The Balderhaz Cube, as it was called, essentially brought into being a "no miracles zone." In violation of the rule that the interplanar energy channels refuse to follow any rules, the channels warp themselves around the field created by the Cube. In essence, the Cube ensures that the physical laws governing the Mundane Plane act predictably, without any extraplanar interference. For this reason, the affected area is known as a Mundanity Enhancement Field.[10]

Now, angels are notorious for relying on their ability to manipulate interplanar energy to bend reality to their respective wills—particularly on the Mundane Plane, where the laws of physics are unusually restrictive. Occasions do arise, however, when it is useful to level the playing field by preventing unwanted extraplanar interference. One such occasion would be if there happened to be a renegade demon who was attempting to subvert the plans of both Heaven and Hell so that she could become the unquestioned despot of the Mundane Plane.

It was due to the scheming of just such a demon that Christine and Karl found themselves inside a one-hundred-yard diameter sphere where miracles were even less likely to occur than usual, just when a miracle might have come in handy.

Gamaliel had driven the Explorer a good hour east of Anaheim, well into the San Bernardino National Forest. He had navigated down increasingly narrow and primitive roads until finally they followed only the faintest hint of tire tracks through the hilly woods. Eventually they reached a chained gate bearing a forbidding sign that read "PERMITTED USE ONLY." Gamaliel got out and unlocked the padlock.

Christine thought about making a run for it, mainly because she thought that thinking about making a run for it was the thing to do under the circumstances. The truth was, she had nowhere to go and no hope of getting there. Having some idea what

---

10   Keen observers will note that if the Balderhaz Cube worked reliably 100% of the time, then the channels could be said to be obeying a definite rule. This fact gave rise to the Balderhaz Constant, which states that the Balderhaz Cube in fact only works 99.45% of the time. It was later discovered that this percentage could vary by as much as .00374389%, a number which became known as Balderhaz's Correction. Variances in Balderhaz's Correction eventually gave rise to Balderhaz's Second Correction. When Balderhaz's Second Correction proved unreliable in certain circumstances, Balderhaz began to spend more of his time perfecting his backhand.

cherubim were capable of, she knew better than to try to get away from Gamaliel.

Gamaliel got back in the Explorer and drove it another half mile to a small clearing. In the middle of the clearing was an oddly well-kept cottage. Guards wearing camouflage gear and bearing assault rifles kept watch outside.

At Gamaliel's command, Christine and Karl got out of the Explorer and walked to the door of the cottage, with Gamaliel following closely behind. The guards nodded respectfully as he passed.

Gamaliel directed them toward the main room of the cottage, where a bookish but not unattractive middle-aged woman sat in a leather easy chair. Across from her was a matching leather couch, and in between was a rustic pine coffee table, on which lay a stack of several hardcover Charlie Nyx books. What caught Christine's attention, though, was something that resembled a cube-shaped bowling ball sitting on the mantle above the stone fireplace. It was featureless and black, and it seemed to Christine to have been formed of some sort of otherworldly material. It was too large and plain to be any kind of decoration. It presumably had some sort of practical purpose, but what?

The woman smiled at them.

"I suppose I'll be released from that damned contract *now*," she said.

Christine was dumbfounded. "What…where…who…?"

"Please, have a seat," the woman said. "I'm Katie Midford. This is my little mountain retreat. Nice, huh? My home in Beverly Hills is much more spacious, but as you know, it's not a great time to be in Los Angeles."

Not feeling like they had much of a choice, Christine and Karl sat on the couch opposite her. Looking out the window, all

Christine could see were massive redwoods—and several armed guards patrolling the perimeter of the cottage.

"You're *the* Katie Midford?" said Karl.

"Indeed," said Katie.

"The author of the Charlie Nyx books?" Christine said.

"I'm afraid so," said Katie. "I'm sorry they aren't very good. Trying to appeal to the lowest common denominator, you know. And those god-awful movies, with the warlocks and the trolls…"

Any number of questions screamed to be let out of Christine's head. She opened her mouth and one of them spilled out at random. "You don't like your own books?" Christine asked.

Katie shrugged. "A necessary evil," she said. "Would you care for some tea?"

Neither of them particularly wanted tea.

"In any case, it's done now. No more Charlie Nyx books."

"But the series…" gasped Karl. "It's not finished!"

"No," said Katie. "And it won't be. For one thing, the setting for the books is now just a gaping hole in the ground. And for another, when Lucifer finds out that the Antichrist is alive and well and sequestered in my mountain getaway, he'll release me from my contract."

"So that's what all this was about?" Christine said, flabbergasted. "You scheming to get out of a book contract?"

"Don't judge me," said Katie. "You haven't seen the contract. And if it weren't for me sending Gamaliel to rescue you, you two would be in a million pieces."

"This makes no sense at all," said Christine. "You sent Gamaliel to rescue us from Izbazel's anti-bomb at the stadium?"

"I did."

"So that you can get out of a book contract?"

"That's oversimplifying things a bit, but yes."

"And how is it that a waitress from Los Angeles has the power to command demons?"

"Ah," said Katie. "That's going to take some explaining. Are you sure you don't want some tea?"

"I'll take a Dr Pepper," said Karl.

"I have Mr. Pibb," said Katie.

"Nah," said Karl. "I've got a reputation and stuff. I don't think the Antichrist would drink Mr. Pibb."

Katie nodded understandingly. "It's good that you're finally embracing your identity," she said. "Now, where to start…

"First off, my real name is Tiamat. I'm a demon—a fallen angel, if you prefer. I rebelled against Heaven shortly after Lucifer did, several thousand years back. The Almighty took issue with the size of the ziggurats I was building. Anyway, Lucifer was convinced that the best way to keep Heaven at bay was to plague the Hebrews at every opportunity. They were supposedly God's chosen people, so he reasoned that if he could keep them down, Heaven's influence on Earth would be minimized. After a while, they started calling him 'the adversary,' or Satan. Frankly, I thought he was wasting his time. I didn't think Abraham's little flock was ever going to amount to anything, so I focused on the Babylonians. I did my best to build Babylon into a sophisticated modern society—as well as a powerful military entity, of course. Hell, we nearly wiped out the Hebrews entirely. If I hadn't gotten cocky and kept them as slaves rather than finishing them off like I should have…

"Anyway, I eventually lost my grip on the Hebrews, and things went downhill from there. Meanwhile, Lucifer was growing ever more powerful, and I ended up working for him. The situation for the Hebrews looked hopeless. After a while only two of the twelve tribes were left, stubbornly resisting Roman rule. Prophets hardly ever appeared anymore, and when they did, they'd be executed pretty quickly. Lucifer was especially proud of how he handled John the Baptist. Then this Jesus of Nazareth appeared, and Lucifer decided to make a public display of his execution, to let the Hebrews know once and for all who was in charge. Well, as you know, *that* went horribly wrong.

"After that debacle, there was a big shakeup of the bureaucracy in Hell. I seized what I thought was my opportunity to take control of all the Fallen, but Lucifer was more stubborn and resourceful than I gave him credit for. He assembled a coalition of demons against me, and I was defeated. Lucifer cast me down to the Mundane Plane, where he's had me doing petty errands for him ever since. So when Lucifer needed someone to assume the identity of Katie Midford, Los Angeles waitress turned bestselling author, he came to me. Of course, he didn't tell me that I'd have to actually work as a waitress for twelve years before he even put the Charlie Nyx part of the plan into motion. And even after the first book was published, he made me wait tables for three more years, just out of spite, the insolent bastard."

Christine's head was reeling. Karl sat in confused silence.

"So," Christine said, "Lucifer put you up to writing a series of children's books?"

"Young adult fantasy," corrected Katie.

"For what purpose?"

"Well, to promote Satanism, for one thing," said Katie. "Although its effectiveness in that regard has been limited. But that was just one motivation behind the Charlie Nyx books. Lucifer also needed a distraction from what was going on in the Middle East. Or, should I say, a distraction from the distraction, because the Olive Branch War was a feint as well. He wanted people thinking that the Olive Branch War was the beginning of the

Apocalypse, and to do that, he had to frame it as part of a larger context. A skirmish in the Middle East is hardly news anymore, but Lucifer saw his opportunity with that Olive Branch incident. He used his agents to manipulate the news media into imparting that little scuffle with symbolic significance. And to cement the illusion, we played our ace in the hole. First, you get the religious folks worked up about the relatively minor threat posed by Charlie Nyx, and then, while you have their attention, you introduce Karl Grissom, the Antichrist."

Karl smiled, evidently pleased with himself.

Christine said, "So you get the fundamentalists up in arms about Armageddon in the Middle East and the Antichrist appearing in California…"

"Not just the fundamentalists. Anyone who spends their time looking for such signs and wonders. That includes most of the angelic bureaucracy. The idea was to convince everyone that things were going according to plan, like clockwork. So the Council releases the Four Attaché Cases, and things predictably escalate."

Christine interjected, "And then Lucifer knocks off Karl, blames it on Michael, and withdraws from the Accord. While Heaven is still trying to get its boots on, he attacks without warning from his portal in Los Angeles. Humanity is basically wiped out." Christine thought for a moment. "But why?"

"Why? Why does Lucifer want to destroy humanity? Beats me. He's a sore loser, I guess. You'd have to ask him."

"So you don't want to wipe out humanity?"

"Not at all," said Katie. "I want to subjugate humanity with an iron fist."

"Ah," said Christine. "That's actually not, from my point of view, a huge improvement."

Katie shrugged. "Your race was destined to exist at the whims of higher beings. The amount of attention that Heaven lavishes on you is absurd. Eventually they will realize that you're not worth the trouble. And then this whole plane will be mine."

"And how does Harry figure into this?"

"Harry is plugged into Angel Band. At least to some degree. Most prophets are. That's where he's been getting his information. He is able to receive fragments of communications between angels. His rather fatalistic outlook seems to have arisen from his contact with this Eddie Pratt, a rather morose cherub." She added, "All sentient beings have some sensitivity to Angel Band, of course. That's how demonic corruption works. Lucifer has a whole plane dedicated to demons planting ideas in the minds of other sentient beings."

"I've been there," said Christine. "Not a pleasant place."

"I would think not," said Katie. "We took advantage of this same channel of communication to deliver certain information to Harry. Specifically, we used Eddie to convince him that Karl is the Antichrist and that it was Harry's destiny to denounce him. The risk with Lucifer's plan was that people would see Karl and realize that he couldn't possibly be the actual Antichrist. Because, you know…"

She gestured at Karl, who smiled again.

"Lucifer needed someone easy to control and easy to dispose of when the time came, but we also needed him to be officially denounced by a prominent leader of the faithful. Heaven and Hell keep a rolling list of ten leaders who are eligible to denounce the Antichrist, and most of the ten wouldn't have lowered themselves to denouncing someone like Karl. The pope, for example. You can't interest the pope in something like that. It's beneath him."

"Not Harry, though."

"No, not Harry. If anybody was going to be taken in by our plan, it was going to have to be Harry. And it had to happen quickly because Lucifer needed things to progress to the point of no return before Heaven got wind of what he was up to. So we whispered in Eddie's ear, and Eddie whispered in Harry's ear. You find, after a few thousand years of corrupting mortals, that people with the most rigid religious viewpoints are the most predictable and therefore easiest to manipulate. They'll do something completely against their better judgment if you can convince them that their doing it fits into some Divine Plan that they can't understand. Humans are easy. The hardest part of this whole plan was dealing with Lucifer's incompetent minions. Like that idiot Izbazel. If it were up to him, Karl would have been dead before he was ever officially denounced. I don't know what Lucifer sees in that knucklehead."

"OK," said Christine. "But so far it sounds like you and Lucifer are on the same side. Where does your brilliant scheming fit in?"

Katie said, "Well, you may have noticed that Karl is not, in fact, dead. Izbazel is probably reconstituting right now..."

"Reconstituting?"

"Everyone within five hundred yards of that anti-bomb was torn to pieces," Katie said, "including Mercury and Izbazel. Yes, in case you were wondering, I know all about Mercury's involvement."

Christine couldn't help feeling relieved. "So Mercury isn't dead?"

"Angels don't die," said Katie. "He's unincorporated."

"Unincorporated?" asked Christine. "Like the Mulholland Corridor?"

"Lacking a corporeal form. As I said, Mercury and Izbazel will be reconstituting shortly on whatever plane the anti-bomb sucked them into. Izbazel will be called home by Lucifer, who will be hoping for confirmation that Karl has been killed. He's going to be disappointed. And you do not want to be around Lucifer when he's been disappointed. Izbazel will be lucky not to spend the next ten thousand years as a crustacean.

"My plan was originally to contact Heaven and let them know that I have some valuable information about a certain planned sneak attack, and that I might be willing to share it in exchange for certain concessions. I've been informed by my contact at the Arbitration Panel of the Subcommittee for Adjudication of Matters of Alleged Violations of the Apocalypse Accord, however, that someone has already tipped them off. I don't suppose you know anything about that, Christine?"

Christine said nothing. Inwardly, she was thrilled to realize that not absolutely everything she had done over the past several days had been scripted. She had been able to throw one wrench in the machinery at least.

"It's of no importance," said Katie, waving her hand. "The important thing is that I have Karl. If Lucifer goes ahead with his attack now, he needs my cooperation. Otherwise I can go public with Lucifer's plans and the fact that Karl is still alive. I'm free! I'm finally free!"

"So you're not going to let Lucifer wipe out humanity?" Christine asked.

"A burnt-out shell of a planet is no use to me," said Katie. "Although a few well-placed anti-bombs could go a long way toward making the human race into an army of thralls."

"OK, well, we're glad everything worked out for you," said Christine, getting to her feet. "Karl, I think it's time for us to go."

"Oh, you're not going anywhere," said Katie. "Those men outside with the guns? My own personal cherubim guard. They're out there to keep you two from leaving just as much as to keep anyone else from getting in. Of course, Christine, I don't particularly need *you*, except insofar as you help me manage...my other asset."

"Yeah, I got it," Christine said, sitting back down on the couch. "You know, you can pretty much just speak English. It's not like he's going to understand you anyway."

"Who's not going to understand what?" asked Karl.

THIRTY-SIX

"So what did you tell Bright Eyes?"

"Bright Eyes?"

"It's my new nickname for Lucifer," said Mercury. "I'm hoping it catches on."

The two angels had materialized in the Temporary Portal Arrivals area of the planeport and were making their way down the concourse.

Izbazel grunted. "I told him what you said. That there were some complications with the assassination, and that I needed to speak with him in private."

"How'd that go over?"

"About as well as you'd expect. He threatened to turn me into a newt."

"No worries," Mercury said. "I think I've figured out a way for everyone to live happily ever after."

"Everybody?"

"Well, almost everybody. And not so much happy as only mildly disgruntled."

"And the 'ever after' part?"

"Actually," said Mercury thoughtfully, "it's more like 'for the very short-term future.' So, to modify my original statement slightly, I've probably found a way to keep almost everyone from becoming more than mildly disgruntled for the very near future."

"That's fantastically reassuring," said Izbazel. "I don't suppose you're going to let me in on your plan."

"Better not," said Mercury. "Plans on which you've been fully briefed have a poor track record. Plans that you're completely in the dark on, on the other hand, seem to work out pretty well. Your ignorance seems to be a key element of any successful plan."

Izbazel asked, "Does this plan end with me being turned into a newt, by any chance?"

"With any plan, there's always a small chance of someone being turned into a newt. I can't make any assurances. The only thing I can tell you is that you have slightly better odds with my plan than with your last one."

"Fine. I get it. I have no choice but to go along with whatever it is you're planning. But you can at least tell me the next step in your plan for near-universal mild disgruntledness."

"Sure," said Mercury. "Go grab that cherub."

"What?"

"That's the next step in my plan. I need you to go grab that cherub over there. The one that looks like he fell off the cover of Van Halen's *1984*."

"Van what?"

"Just go get him. Tell him Mercury needs a witness. Hurry up, he's getting away."

Izbazel *hmph*ed and set off after Perpetiel, who was buzzing away toward the baggage carousel. After a brief exchange, Izbazel returned with Perpetiel behind him.

"Mercury, you old salt!" said Perp. "Have I ever told you how to get red wine out of cashmere?"

"Minor miracle," said Mercury. "It's the only way."

"I know, it's a bitch, isn't it? Poor benighted mortals. Who's this guy? He looks like somebody just threatened to turn him into a newt."

"This is Izbazel," said Mercury. "He works for Lucifer."

Perp cocked his head at Izbazel. "How's that working out for you?"

"Not so great," said Izbazel.

"He suckered you in with stock options, didn't he? I've seen it a thousand times."

Mercury said, "How've you been, Perp? Anything interesting happening in the world of Transport and Communications?"

"Same old," said Perp. "Shoulda seen the pack of noobs here earlier. I swear, these tourists get more tiresome every year."

"I'm sure you made out well in tips."

"You have no idea. So what's this about you needing my services?"

"Got a contract for you to witness," said Mercury. "Your paperwork is in order, I assume?"

"Of course," replied Perp. "As an agent of the Bureau of Transport and Communications, it is my duty to retain the proper certifications. My Witnessing License is in good order, sir."

"Good. Give me an hour of your time, and I'll let you tell me all about how to make mock hollandaise sauce some time."

"Sure. Who's the contract with?"

"Lucifer."

"Ha! Always the kidder, eh, Merc? Seriously, I need to know who the contract is with."

"Seriously, Perp. It's Lucifer. I need his help to unkidnap a friend of mine."

"A mortal, I can only assume."

"You assume correctly."

Perp snorted. "These mortals. They are mere prawns, being shoved about by—"

"Pawns," Mercury said.

"What's that?"

"The mortals are *pawns*. I actually thought it was *prawns*, too, but it turns out that it's *pawns*."

"Are you sure? I've been saying 'prawns' for…must be seven hundred years now."

"Yeah, I've got a friend who knows this kind of stuff. Trust me, it's *pawns*."

"Pawns," said Perp, trying out the word. "You're absolutely certain it's not *prawns*?"

"Quite," said Mercury. "My friend is a writer. I have total faith in her judgment."

"Well then," said Perp. "*Pawns*. Such a strange word. I suppose I'll get used to it though. As I was saying, these mortals are mere pawns in a vast ocean, being shoved about by currents beyond the meager understanding of their tiny crustacean brains."

"Indeed," said Mercury. "So will you help me out?"

"You know what happened to the last guy to make a pact with Lucifer, right?"

"I thought he was still hosting *American Idol*."

"Exactly," said Perp. "A fate worse than death. Between you and me, I'd rather be a pawn, scuttling about on my tiny crustacean legs. An unkidnapping, eh? Not sure I have a standard contract for that."

"We'll draw something up. Nothing fancy. You ready to go?"

"I'm ready if you are," said Perp. "Fresh air is the best remedy for clothes that smell like smoke."

"Good to know," said Mercury. "That one may actually come in handy where we're going."

THIRTY-SEVEN

Other than the fact that there exists no physical plane known as "Hell," the Mundane conception of Lucifer as presiding over an infernal realm of smoke and magma is largely accurate, if somewhat outdated.

When Lucifer fell from Heaven, his original intention was to stay on the Mundane Plane, but the meddling of the angels, not to mention the ever-present irritant that was humanity, forced him to establish his primary base of operations on another plane. Lucifer, who is well known for his pride, could not bear to share a plane with any demonic entities other than his own minions, however. As empty planes are difficult to come by as well as ridiculously expensive, Lucifer found himself with few desirable real estate options. Thus it was that nearly three thousand years ago he put a nonrefundable deposit down on a plane that was previously thought to be uninhabitable, even by demons. Plane 3774d was renamed the "Infernal Plane," and Lucifer set about to make it marginally habitable.

At first he attempted to capitalize on the forbidding nature of the plane, building a city of jagged rock palaces surrounded by a moat of magma. The problem was that cable TV and central air notwithstanding, Diabolopolis was so uninviting—not to mention difficult to pronounce—that not even demons particularly wanted to live there. For many centuries, Lucifer's iron grip on his minions ensured that they would remain on the Infernal Plane if they wanted to remain employed, but the proliferation of a dynamic interplanar economy in the late twentieth century made it increasingly difficult to keep Diabolopolis populated. And even Lucifer had to admit that living in a mile-high monstrosity of magmite had its downsides. For one thing, he kept getting lost down passageways that the contractors had been instructed to make as frightening as possible—an instruction which, he later realized, negated the possibility of helpful maps with arrows labeled "YOU ARE HERE." For another, upkeep was a bitch.

Lucifer decided to scrap Diabolopolis and construct a massive new complex using the latest principles in Mundane domestic engineering. To entice other demons to move into the new complex, Lucifer himself took occupancy in one of its more prominent dwellings.

So it happened that Lucifer, the Light-Bearer, the First of the Fallen, the Father of Lies, lived in a substantial but surprisingly unassuming pink stucco house nestled within a housing development called Hidden Oakes, which backed up against the Hidden Oakes Country Club and Golf Course.

Mercury, who was strolling down Lucifer Lane with Izbazel and Perpetiel, noted that there seemed to be no oakes—nor even oaks—in the vicinity. In fact, there were very few trees of any kind. Of the few there were, most were dead or dying, and the rest were plastic. Even the hills were apparently artificial, as they were covered in Astroturf and surrounded by a seemingly endless and unforgiving desert landscape, broken only by razor-sharp rocks and the occasional stream of lava. If there was a sun, it was blocked out by a foreboding mass of reddish-brown clouds hanging low in the sky. The air was hot and oppressive.

"Nice, huh?" said Izbazel as they strolled toward 666 Lucifer Lane.

"The oak-ees are evidently well hidden," said Perpetiel, tagging along behind.

"Still, you have to admit he's improved it."

"I don't know," said Mercury. "Why bother to live on the Infernal Plane if you're going to spoil its natural charm?"

"It's centrally located," said Izbazel. "Easy planeport access. And you can't beat the price."

A fork-tailed demon standing in his front yard with hedge clippers eyed them suspiciously.

Perp waved at the demon. "Soapy water will deter aphids on rosebushes," he offered.

"Most of Lucifer's lieutenants live here," Izbazel said. "He promised me that faux Tudor over there for killing Karl."

"Nice," said Mercury. "Of course, they'll nail you on the property taxes."

They were stopped at the gate to Lucifer's house by a massive horned demon.

"It's OK, Azrael," said Izbazel. "He's expecting us."

Azrael patted them down and then escorted them inside.

The oversized living room of the house was taken up mostly by a semicircle of flat panel monitors that stretched across the far wall. Sitting in a wheeled leather office chair in the middle of the monitor bank was a tall man wearing a light blue jumpsuit with flared cuffs and trimmed with rhinestones. His unnaturally thick, blond hair stood at least six inches off his head in an impressive pompadour.

Each monitor was itself split into four screens, each of which was displaying some sort of activity. The screens were too small and distant for them to make out the subjects clearly, but Mercury surmised that they allowed Lucifer to keep up with his machinations across several different planes. Many of them showed settings from Earth—shopping malls, bus stations, and the like, and that one…was that the New York Stock Exchange? It was an overwhelming amount of input; Mercury wondered how Lucifer could possibly keep up with it all.

The tall, blond demon spun in his chair to face his visitors. He did not look happy. To be fair, though, it was clear that he had not been truly happy for quite some time. To say that he was disgruntled would have been misleading, as it implied that there was a time within memory that he had been fully gruntled. He had the look of someone who had let what had originally seemed like a really good idea get well out of hand.

Lucifer appeared to take no notice of Mercury or Perpetiel, focusing all of his rage on Izbazel. "I charged you with one simple task," he fumed. "Kill the Antichrist. Karl Grissom. He's a thirty-seven-year-old man with the brain of a squirrel and the constitution of a seventy-year-old. This is a man who was handpicked from tens of thousands of people for the precise reason that he would be the *easiest to kill*. The man's resting heart rate is a hundred and twenty. You could probably give him a heart attack by telling him that professional wrestling isn't real. And yet you couldn't kill him with an implosion that wiped out half of Anaheim. How is that even *possible*?"

"My partner, Gamaliel—"

"The one that you handpicked. The one that you assured me was completely under control. That Gamaliel, correct? Do go on."

"If I may, Your Luminosity," interjected Mercury, "it's clear that Izbazel here is a moron. I don't think there's any reason to tap-dance around that issue any longer."

Lucifer turned his icy glare to Mercury. "Who the hell are you? Some friend of this fool, I take it."

"My name's Mercury. I'm going to help you get your Antichrist back."

"Mercury, eh? You have some gall showing up here with only Mr. Ingrown Horns here to vouch for you. What do you know of the Antichrist?"

"I know where he is, for starters," said Mercury. "Which fact, I believe, gives me a leg up on *you*."

Lucifer was not amused. "Listen, Mercury, is it? Tell me, why should I not turn you into a newt, right here and now?"

Perp chimed in, "Newts lay their eggs one at a time, unlike frogs."

Lucifer turned his hateful gaze to the fluttering cherub, and Perp shrank into a corner.

"Because I'm the only one who knows where the Antichrist is," explained Mercury. "On the other hand, maybe you have a backup plan I don't know about. Like putting up signs around town: 'Have you seen this Antichrist?' That sort of thing. 'Five foot eight, two hundred ten pounds, brown hair, brown eyes, enjoys fries with ketchup, and answers to the name *Karl*.'"

Lucifer's eyes narrowed. "Who do you work for, Mercury?"

"I don't exactly work for anyone," said Mercury. "But I do represent the Antichrist."

"You *represent* him?"

"Correct," said Mercury. "I'm his agent."

"The Antichrist doesn't get an agent," Lucifer said. "That's not part of the—"

"Yes, yes," said Mercury. "The important thing is that we all work together to find a resolution to our current impasse that is, at worst, only mildly disgruntling to all involved parties. And that's something that I believe I'm in a position to arrange."

"I tire of this," said Lucifer. "I'm inclined to turn the three of you into newts. Mercury, you have thirty seconds to offer me something of value."

"I can get you your Antichrist. He's being held against his will by the agents of another faction in this conflict."

"What faction?"

"Please," chided Mercury, "you're cutting into my thirty seconds." He went on, "I believe that you're planning to withdraw from the Apocalypse Accord on the grounds that agents of Heaven unfairly assassinated the Antichrist. Karl being alive and in the hands of a faction outside of your control throws a wrench into your plans. If you cry foul, and then Karl shows up alive and well...or even worse, if this other faction is prepared to produce evidence that you were behind the attempted assassination... well, that could get embarrassing for you. An interplanar commission is appointed to investigate your misdeeds, sanctions are imposed... Feel free to correct me if you feel like I've misrepresented the situation."

Lucifer glared at Mercury. "Go on."

"I want to get Karl free from his captors. You want to be able to ensure that Karl isn't going to pop up at some point and ruin your plans. I suggest a compromise. Izzy and I will spring Karl and return him to you. For your part, you'll let Karl live. You can sequester him comfortably somewhere on one of your less dismal planes, where no one will ever find him. I'm happy because Karl is safe. You're happy because as far as anyone knows, Karl is dead. Izbazel and I will be sworn to secrecy, and you will guarantee our safety. We'll write up a contract. Perpetiel, as an official Angelic Witness, will notarize it."

"How do I know you can actually deliver Karl?"

"You don't. On the other hand, if I couldn't, I'd have no reason to be here, taking a chance at spending eternity as a newt."

"And what is preventing me from just torturing you until you tell me where the Antichrist is?"

"The constraints of time," said Mercury. "Heaven is going to start looking into that implosion in Anaheim. The longer you wait to withdraw from the Accord, the more time they have to figure out what really happened. I haven't told Izbazel where Karl is, so that means you'll have to torture me to get the information you want. And I once sat through a back-to-back showing of *Star Wars* episodes one through three. Give it your best shot."

"I don't suppose you are, in fact, an agent of this third faction yourself?"

"I'm not," said Mercury. "Not that it matters. You're too smart to risk losing Karl to make an example of me. I hope."

"I think," said Lucifer, "that you should tell me who the leader of this faction is, as a gesture of good faith."

Mercury shook his head. "You're free to investigate after the fact, but for now the details remain confidential."

"I don't take kindly to being toyed with, Mercury."

"No toying here," said Mercury. "Just a simple business transaction. Do we have a deal?"

Lucifer studied him for a long time. Mercury could only hope that Lucifer didn't know about Christine's discovery of the portal in her condo. If he did, then he would know that his plan had already been compromised, which left Mercury with no leverage. It also gave Lucifer a pretty good incentive to turn him into a newt—and kill Christine, if he ever got the chance. This last eventuality bothered him more than he would have cared to admit.

Trying not to think about it, Mercury scanned the monitor bank, his eyes darting from one scene to the next. By chance they alighted on a fish-eye view of a small room that was empty except for a small kitchen table and four chairs. As he watched, the image of a young woman flickered into view in the center of the screen. A sickening sensation came over him as he realized that he knew the identity of the woman: he was witnessing Christine's arrival through the linoleum portal earlier that day. Evidently this was either a recording or there was a delay getting video from the Mundane Plane.

Still Lucifer stared at him. Did he have any idea what Mercury was seeing? Neither Izbazel nor Perp made any sign of having noticed. Mercury tried to retain his cool façade, but he was unable to tear his eyes away from Christine standing bewildered in her breakfast nook. Finally she left the screen, and Mercury exhaled a barely perceptible sigh of relief.

Lucifer continued to stare.

Christine reentered the frame, holding what looked like a crystal duck. She slammed the duck-thing down on the floor once, twice, three times. On the last attempt, the duck shattered, and Christine sat there in the middle of the frame, looking like she was trying to figure out if she had another duck somewhere.

Still Lucifer said nothing.

"Oh, for the love of all that's holy," Mercury finally exclaimed in exasperation, "it's going to take more than a crystal duck!"

Lucifer was momentarily taken aback, but this non sequitur evidently had the effect of pushing him toward a decision.

"Fine," said Lucifer. "Write it up. But if you fail, I will turn you into a newt. Perhaps something even worse. Maybe a prawn."

Perp spoke up. "Actually, it's—"

"And Izbazel is getting turned into some sort of insignificant aquatic animal either way. I cannot tolerate this sort of failure."

"No," said Mercury. "I need Izzy's help to spring Karl. You can turn us both into newts if we fail."

Lucifer sighed. "My hopes for your plan are not aided by your insistence on his involvement. But let it be as you say. Do not fail me." He waved his hand and turned back to the wall of monitors.

THIRTY-EIGHT

"Lodi?" said Izbazel. "The Antichrist is in Lodi?"

"No," said Mercury. "Well, he could be. I doubt it, though."

"So why are we here? Hey, isn't this…?"

"Yes," said Mercury. "This is where you managed to lose a tubby, thirty-seven-year-old man wearing a black polyester cape and got taken in by a three-dollar trick spoon."

"I figured it was a trick spoon," grumbled Izbazel. "But you know how gullible Gamaliel is."

Having returned to the planeport, Mercury and Izbazel had charged a temporary portal to Lucifer's account and were now back on the Mundane Plane. They walked around to the back of Charlie's Grill.

"After you and Gamaliel left, Uzziel found me. I had to leave without the Case of War."

"You left the Case of War *here*?"

"Had to. I stashed it before I started the snowman."

"The snowman?" asked Izbazel, confused.

"I didn't tell you? I made a snowman! Well, I made the parts of a snowman. I even managed to find a big, round trash can and two bowling balls. You know, for the nose and eyes. Uzziel interrupted me before I could put it together."

"You really are like a child, aren't you, Mercury? The rest of us are plotting Armageddon, and you're busy making snowmen. You could be making snowmen now if you wanted to. Why do you care so much about Karl?"

"About Karl? I don't. I mean, assassination still seems unsportsmanlike to me, but he got himself into this business. I feel a little more responsible for Christine, though. You noticed that I wrote into the contract that Lucifer would not be allowed to harm anyone else we free from captivity along with Karl, right?"

"So the untouchable, unflappable Mercury has a soft spot— for a mortal, no less," said Izbazel, relishing the moment. "I thought you had turned into a cynic like me, but it turns out that you're a romantic."

"I wouldn't expect you to understand," said Mercury. "You like to think that you're in charge of your destiny, but you're just a typical angel, being pulled about by abstract forces you don't understand. Sometimes I think these mortals have an advantage over us. The eternal perspective can skew your vision, make you think you see things more clearly than you do. I think being mortal, knowing that you only have a few scant years to figure everything out, helps to crystallize things. Someone like Christine, who really understands what's at stake…she takes good and evil seriously in a way that I'm not sure you and I can understand."

"So after everything you've been through," said Izbazel, "you're back on the side of Heaven."

Mercury laughed, a long, loud laugh that made Izbazel feel queasy inside. "Izzy," Mercury said, "you just got schooled by that sap Gamaliel, and yet you persist in the illusion that you've got the whole Universe figured out. You spent a few hundred years schlepping about for the Mundane Maintenance Corps, tuning interplanar energy receptors or whatever, and you think you've earned the right to look down on Heaven. Izzy, do you know what my biggest accomplishment was, in four thousand years on this plane?"

Izzy said nothing.

"It was in 1814, at the Battle of Plattsburg, in New York State. The Americans were still at war with the British, despite the fact that some overly optimistic fool had named it the War of 1812. I was assigned to protect a certain Captain Miller, an American. My superiors never told me what was so special about this guy, but I watched over him day and night. The Brits shot so many shells and rockets at that fort, it should have been just a hole in the ground. But miraculously—thanks to me—most of the rockets didn't explode, and none of the thousands of bullets managed to find Captain Miller. After a while, even with interplanar energy at my disposal, I had a hard time keeping up with it all. At one point a bomb got past me and exploded two feet from Miller. I had just enough time to arc the shrapnel around him. Three other men were wounded and one was killed, but Miller was miraculously unscathed. Miller would have been dead five times over in that battle if it weren't for me."

"OK, so you saved this Captain Miller's life. What's your point?"

"The point is, Miller figured it out. He knew he couldn't have survived that battle without divine assistance. Up to that point, he had been a Deist—a believer in a distant God who didn't get involved in human affairs. But after his miraculous survival at the Battle of Plattsburg, he became a die-hard believer. A real Bible-thumper. So far, so good. A job well done, right?

"But then Miller gets it into his head that the Second Coming is going to happen in 1843, and he starts spreading the word. It doesn't happen, of course, so he revises the date. Still nothing. So he stops trying to predict The End, but by now the movement's got a life of its own. One of his followers declares that the Second Coming will happen on October 22, 1844. Do you know what happened on October 22, 1844, Izzy?"

Izbazel had to admit that he did not.

"*Nothing,*" said Mercury bitterly. "Nothing happened. Thousands of people gathered to experience Christ's return, thanks to Captain William Miller, and nothing happened. The crowning achievement of my angelic career is what is commonly known as the Great Disappointment. I saved William Miller's life so that he could spread disillusion and hopelessness to tens of thousands of people. That's my legacy. So don't you presume to lecture me about which side I should or shouldn't join."

"Yes, well," said Izbazel, suddenly uncomfortable with this turn in the conversation. "In any case, it's nice to see that you actually do care about something. I wanted to tell you, by the way…" Izbazel drifted off.

"What?"

"Well, I wanted you to know that I realize that you didn't have to stand up for me back there, with Lucifer. I mean, if you hadn't insisted that you needed me, I'd be a newt right now."

"Oh, but I do need you," said Mercury.

"For what?"

"Well, somebody's got to dig through all the garbage in that dumpster to get to the attaché case at the bottom."

Izbazel regarded the pile of restaurant detritus and grimaced. "Whatever. It's better than being a newt."

"Or a pawn," added Mercury.

After several minutes of digging through paper wrappers and partial cheeseburgers in various states of decomposition, Izbazel extracted the silvery case, now smeared in mayonnaise and mustard as well as the blood of a recently deceased Israeli general. He handed it to Mercury. "What's the plan? You're going to find them with the case?"

"If Tiamat is the one behind this," Mercury said, "then Karl is most likely still on the Mundane Plane, since she's stuck here, thanks to Lucifer. And their means of escape suggests that they didn't plan on using a portal to extract him. They would have planned to get out of the area of the stadium quickly."

"Maybe an airplane? Or a helicopter?"

"Too high-profile, especially considering that all eyes are on LA right now. They must have escaped by car."

"They might still be on the road then."

"Maybe. Probably not, though. They'd want to get off the road and hide out somewhere safe as soon as they were outside the chaos caused by that implosion. So I'd say we look on the main roads out of the city, twenty to a hundred miles outside of LA, somewhere relatively secluded. Tiamat is known for her personal phalanx of combat-trained demons, so they shouldn't be too hard to find."

Mercury scanned the rocky coast of Malibu and the sparsely populated areas off I-5 before finding a red patch in the middle of the San Bernardino forest.

"There they are," he said. "Sitting ducks."

"Yes," said Izbazel. "Looks like about thirty sitting ducks. With automatic weapons."

"It'll be OK," said Mercury. "I've got an idea. Just give me a minute to call Uzziel and let him know what we're up to."

THIRTY-NINE

After Mercury had briefed Uzziel—leaving out certain details to avoid breaking his contract with Lucifer—he and Izbazel headed south to the location indicated by the case. Being cherubim, they were capable of a top airspeed of nearly three hundred miles per hour, and they managed the journey from Lodi to the San Bernardino Forest in just over forty-five minutes. When they got within a mile of Tiamat's stronghold, they landed and crept to the top of a ridge overlooking the cottage. The sun hung just above the horizon in the west.

"You feel that?" asked Mercury.

"Some kind of disturbance in the Angel Band?" guessed Izbazel.

"It's a Mundanity Enhancement Field, centered on that cottage," replied Mercury. "Seems to be about a hundred yards in diameter. She probably set it up to keep Lucifer from finding her. We'll have to be careful. We won't be able to pull off any miracles within that sphere."

"But neither will they."

"True, but you don't need as many miracles when you have a Kevlar vest and an M4 carbine."

Neither angel had been involved in a hostage extraction previously, but they had both watched enough Mundane television to know that their best bet was for one of them to create a diversion that would lure the bulk of the guards away from the cottage while the other released the captives. They had seen this work dozens of times, although generally the odds were not quite so lopsided, and it tended to involve more diving sideways in slow motion while firing two large-caliber handguns simultaneously than either of them was comfortable with. Mercury persuaded Izbazel to accept the task of extracting Christine and Karl mainly by reminding him that it was the diversion creator who usually ended up gasping something in his dying breath about going on without him.

"Just remember," said Mercury, "you won't be able to use transplanar energy inside that sphere. If you get caught outside of it, though, you've got the advantage. They'll avoid using miracles to keep from drawing attention to Tiamat's stronghold, so they'll stick with their assault rifles. Once you get Karl and Christine out of that bubble, use miracles to protect them from the bullets. The bullets won't kill you, of course, but they'll slow you down and hurt like hell, so protect yourself as well."

"Hang on, Merc," said Izbazel. "You forget, I'm a wanted angel. I can't afford to draw too much attention to myself either. If I start moving bullets around by harnessing interplanar energy, Heaven will be able to get a lock on me. They'll hit me with a Class Five as soon as they catch wind of me."

"Don't worry," said Mercury. "I've apprised Uzziel of what's going on. There won't be any unwanted interference." This was true, from a certain point of view.

"Meanwhile, you'll be doing what exactly?"

"Diversion," said Mercury.

"Right, but what kind of diversion, exactly, are we talking about?"

"The diverting kind. The kind that makes you go, 'Hey, what's *that*? I think we should maybe take a better look at *that*.'"

"I'm going to be a newt, aren't I?"

"Don't worry about it. I got your diversion covered. You just get as close as you can to that cottage and wait for the diversion."

"Which will be…"

"You'll know it when you see it. It will be very diverting."

"Yeah," Izbazel said. "I'm sure."

The two of them split up and headed toward the cottage from different angles.

Izbazel might have felt better about the plan if he knew that Mercury really did have one hell of a diversion in mind. He probably would not have been too keen, however, on the exact nature of the diversion.

FORTY

Izbazel crept as stealthily as he could toward the rear of the cottage. He was roughly three hundred yards away, moving gingerly from tree to tree.

"Bloody hell," muttered Izbazel, an exclamation that could have applied equally to any of the countless annoyances that were currently plaguing him.

First and foremost, he was annoyed that his attempt to assassinate Karl had gone sideways. He had given up a cushy job in the angelic bureaucracy to work for Lucifer, and he needed badly to ingratiate himself to the Evil One. He was annoyed that no matter how this ended, he would not be moving into a cozy faux Tudor in Hidden Oakes with a view of Hidden Oakes Golf Course and Country Club. He was annoyed that he probably would not need a house in any case, as this little adventure would most likely end in him being turned into a newt. He was annoyed that he didn't actually know what a newt was.

He had been annoyed for some time now with the fact that he had been outsmarted by that nitwit Gamaliel, but that annoyance was overshadowed by his annoyance with being led around by the nose by Mercury, an angel for whom he had nothing but disdain.

He was annoyed that he couldn't quite convince himself that there wasn't something else, perhaps grudging respect, hiding out among his overwhelming disdain for Mercury. He had long thought of Mercury as sort of a rabid dog: unpredictable and potentially dangerous, to be sure, but relatively easy to contain. Somehow, though, Mercury had been able to remain one step ahead of the various plotters. This, too, annoyed him.

He was further annoyed that Mercury, for whom he was on the verge of admitting he might have a very slight amount of grudging respect along with truckloads of disdain, hadn't been able to come up with anything better than "I'll make a diversion, and you rescue the hostages."

Finally, he was annoyed that Mercury had instructed him to approach from the east just as the sun was setting, making it nearly impossible for him to see. Even with his angelic vision, he found himself squinting in an effort to distinguish trees from guards. What was Mercury thinking?

One thing was certain: Izbazel had no intention of rescuing anybody. If he actually managed to get inside the cottage, he was going to kill Karl with his bare hands. Probably that meddler Christine, too. Then he would ditch Mercury and make a beeline back to the Infernal Plane, where he would inform Lucifer that he had completed his mission. Mercury, having failed to deliver the Antichrist, would then be fair game. He relished the thought of Lucifer turning Mercury into a newt. He imagined Mercury in the form of a sort of winged oyster, flapping around helplessly.

He crept closer to the cottage.

It was to Izbazel's credit that when he was about two hundred yards from the cottage, it occurred to him that maybe Mercury had anticipated what Izbazel was planning to do with Karl. But that made no sense. Why would Mercury want Karl dead?

Izbazel, his eyes on a pair of guards about halfway between him and the cottage, tiptoed to the next large tree.

A new burst of annoyance washed over him as he recalled how Mercury had denigrated his diabolical competency. What had he said? That Izbazel should be a "middle school librarian." Whatever *that* meant. Well, we'll see what he thinks when *he's* been outsmarted by *me*. How could have been so careless as to put *me* in charge of the rescue?

Hang on, he thought. How *could* he have been so careless? He had to have known. So…Mercury wants Karl and Christine dead? That didn't seem right.

The guards were now facing away from him, so Izbazel seized his opportunity to move forward another twenty feet.

He wondered how long it would be before Mercury's diversion started. He was hoping for an explosion. An explosion would be really neat. But how would Mercury cause an explosion?

It dawned on Izbazel that Mercury wasn't going to be able to cause an explosion. In fact, Izbazel didn't see how he was going to create a diversion of any kind. Which meant that he had sent Izbazel on a fool's errand. He had planned on Izbazel to fail. But why?

Izbazel noticed movement out of the corner of his eye. What the hell? Another guard to his right? And still another coming out of hiding on his left. They had seen him coming. They were trying to encircle him!

Izbazel ran. Automatic weapon fire rang out in the woods.

Forget this! he thought. Nothing to do now but get the hell out. They had failed.

He took to the air, reaching out to the interplanar energy channels to envelop himself in a protective bubble of supernatural power. In the back of his mind he hoped he could trust

Mercury's assurances that Heaven wouldn't interfere. The way he was pulling in interplanar energy, he'd be a sitting duck if Heaven decided this was a good time to take out a renegade cherub.

Hundreds of bullets whizzed past him, miraculously altering their trajectories at the last split second. The bullets didn't bother him nearly as much as the possibility of being hit with a Class Five pillar of fire at any moment.

Now *that* would be a diversion, he thought to himself as he soared toward the treetops. But Mercury had promised there would be no unwanted interference from Heaven. It occurred to him, though, that under the circumstances he and Mercury might disagree on the definition of "unwanted." Maybe, it further occurred to him, Izbazel being incinerated in a Class Five was precisely what Mercury wanted. In fact, maybe Mercury had offered Izbazel to Heaven in exchange for providing a diversion so that Mercury could free Christine and Karl. All Uzziel would need to pinpoint his location would be for Izbazel to draw attention to himself by manipulating interplanar energy—which is exactly what Mercury had told him to do to avoid being shot.

Middle school librarian indeed, he thought to himself. I'm starting to get the hang of this sort of intrigue.

For once, he was right.

FORTY-ONE

"What the hell?" exclaimed Katie Midford, also known as Tiamat, the Whore of Babylon.

"Not Hell," said Christine. "Heaven."

The cottage shook from the blast. They had to shield their eyes from the blinding light pouring in through the windows.

"This must be what it's like to be inside a Thomas Kinkade painting," said Christine.

"What's going on?" said Karl, terrified.

"That, if I'm not mistaken," said Christine, "was a Class Five pillar of fire. Someone in Heaven has evidently taken an interest in our host's little hideaway."

"We need to get out of here," said Gamaliel. "If Heaven knows about this place, we don't stand a chance here."

"They have no right!" hissed Tiamat. "They don't know what they are doing! If I fail, Lucifer's plan will proceed! He'll make this whole plane into a wasteland!"

Christine, having a sudden notion, said, "Why don't you turn yourselves in? If you spill the beans on what Lucifer is planning, I'm sure they'll go easy on you."

"Silence!" snapped Tiamat. "We're not finished yet. Let's get out of here."

Gamaliel led them to the Ford Explorer parked behind the cottage. Two other cherubim, who had been standing guard outside, ushered the captives to the vehicle.

"I call shotgun!" yelled Karl, and one of the guards smacked him in the back of the head with the butt of his rifle. Karl fell forward, dazed. He and Christine were shoved into the middle seat.

"Careful!" warned Gamaliel. "We need him alive." He had to admit that unconscious was, however, an improvement.

The Explorer peeled out of the dirt driveway and headed down the bumpy track that served as a road. Behind them, the towering redwoods were engulfed in flame.

"Heads up," said Gamaliel. "We're leaving the Mundanity Enhancement Field. Ah, hell, now what?"

A tall, lean figure was standing in the middle of the makeshift road. He was holding an assault rifle.

"Mercury!" growled Gamaliel, gunning the engine.

"Wait!" yelled Tiamat as the Explorer bounced crazily along the bumpy ground. "He's going to—"

Mercury steadied his aim at the vehicle, trying to follow its erratic movements. The gun was set to manual fire because he couldn't risk a stray bullet hitting Karl or Christine. He had only one chance. He couldn't rely on being able to manipulate interplanar energy to take out the Explorer, standing so close to the Mundanity Enhancement Field. He hoped he had better aim with an M4 assault rifle than he did with a ping-pong paddle. Or snowball. He was not, now that he thought about it, terribly good with projectiles in general.

When the vehicle was only a few yards away, he fired.

The Explorer's left front tire exploded just as it landed in a particularly deep recess in the track. The vehicle veered to the left, its right tires leaving the ground. Mercury, still immobile, was showered with dirt as the tires whizzed past, inches from his face. With the interference the MEF was causing, he needed all of his concentration to harness the small amount of interplanar energy that was available.

The Explorer veered off the track and rolled into the ravine below. The vehicle turned over and over, countless times, shedding pieces of itself as it went, finally coming to an abrupt stop against a large redwood.

Mercury clambered down the ravine, his attention still on the two mortals ensconced in the wreckage. He could only hope that he had been able to channel enough supernatural energy to keep them from being killed. Jumping atop the overturned vehicle, he ripped the passenger door off its hinges. Inside he found four dazed demons and two miraculously unscathed mortals.

He helped Christine and Karl out of the Explorer. "Get to the road," he said. "I'll take care of these guys."

While Christine and Karl made their way up the ravine, Mercury stood a few yards from the downed Explorer, waiting for the demons to emerge. Slowly they began to pull themselves out of the wreckage. As they did, Mercury fired at them repeatedly with the assault rifle.

Still too dazed and too close to the Mundanity Enhancement Field to force the bullets to miraculously miss them, the demons took round after round in the chest, howling in pain and staggering backwards. Eventually, though, Mercury ran out of bullets, and still the demons came at him. He pulled a Bowie knife that he had pilfered from the same unlucky guard who had provided the rifle.

"Seize the Antichrist!" barked Tiamat to her minions. "I'll deal with this one."

Gamaliel and the other two demons set off after Karl and Christine, who had just reached the track at the top of the ravine.

It was getting dark, and smoke from the growing blaze on the other side of the cottage was making it difficult for them to breathe.

Tiamat turned to Mercury.

"You're causing me a fair amount of trouble," she said, trying to retain a semblance of calm.

"Nothing personal," said Mercury, still holding the knife pointed at Tiamat. "I have a contract to deliver the Antichrist to Lucifer."

"You? Working for Lucifer?" said Tiamat. "I didn't think you had it in you."

"I'm more of a free agent," explained Mercury.

"That sounds more like it," she said. "Always looking out for yourself."

Mercury shrugged. "So," he said, "how have you been? Still building ziggurats?"

Tiamat shook her head dismissively. "I had some problems with outsourcing. Language barriers, you know. These days I'm dabbling in adolescent fiction."

"So I hear," said Mercury. "I've read some of your work. Not bad. I didn't realize you were a writer."

"It's not Shakespeare," admitted Tiamat. "But it pays the bills. Anyway, I can't let you have Karl."

"Well," said Mercury, "I can't let you keep him. So there you go."

The crackle of the forest fire was getting louder. A breeze was picking up, pushing the blaze their way.

"I don't think you have much of a choice," she said, motioning toward Christine and Karl, who were being escorted back down the ravine by Gamaliel and her other two minions. "You're outnumbered and outgunned."

"Won't be the first time," said Mercury.

Tiamat smiled. "Whatever happened between us?" she asked him.

Mercury looked pensively at her. "Well," he said, "there was the status difference. Cherub-seraph romances rarely work."

"True," she said. "That was a problem."

"Also," Mercury went on, "there was that whole 'Whore of Babylon' thing. If I had to pinpoint a moment when our relationship went sour, I think I'd have to go with the first time I heard you referred to as 'the Whore of Babylon.' I mean, that makes an impression on a guy, you know? There were a *lot* of whores in Babylon."

"Oh come on, Mercury. You're not still angry about *that*. It was the ninth century BC. It was a different time."

"Yeah, I get that," said Mercury. "But *the* Whore of Babylon? That's impressive. That's like being *the* hippie at Woodstock. Or *the* drunk at Caligula's place."

Karl and Christine stumbled toward them, prodded by the butts of the demons' rifles.

"Watch it," Karl snapped. He was clearly getting tired of being pushed, pulled, and prodded around.

"Can't we put the past behind us?" said Tiamat. "As you say, this isn't personal. I have some business with Karl here. I don't know how you're involved in all this exactly, but I can assure you that Karl is worth more to me than he is to you. If you're afraid of retribution from Lucifer, join my crew. I'll protect you. And you'll be in good company. I expect a lot of defections from Lucifer over the next few days."

"Yeah," said Mercury. "I know all about your plan. You're blackmailing Lucifer. He needs everyone to think that the Antichrist was killed by agents of Heaven so that he can withdraw from the Apocalypse Accord and launch a sneak attack. So you threaten to go public with the fact that Karl is still alive if he doesn't release you from this plane and give you authority over the invasion."

"Nice deduction," said Tiamat, nodding with approval.

Mercury said, "It was actually Christine here who figured most of it out."

Tiamat cocked her head at Christine, who remained in defiant silence. "A mortal? Deciphering the plans of demons? You always were a joker, Mercury."

"Not this time," said Mercury. "This time I'm dead serious. I can't let you take Karl alive." He tightened his grip on the Bowie knife.

Tiamat laughed. "What are you going to do, kill him?"

In a flash, Mercury moved behind Karl, putting the blade of the knife to his neck.

"What the hell?" gasped Karl.

Christine's face contorted in horror. "Mercury, what are you—"

"No choice, Christine," said Mercury. "I have to kill him. He's no use to Tiamat dead."

"Mercury," said Tiamat angrily, "drop this charade. You don't actually expect me to believe you're going to kill Karl."

Karl was terrified. "Don't kill Karl!" was all he could think to say.

"Believe it, babe," Mercury said. "I can't let you take him alive."

Tiamat's minions were creeping toward him, their guns at the ready. Gamaliel remained still, waiting for Mercury to make a move.

"Easy, boys," said Tiamat. "Mercury, let's think about this rationally. If you kill Karl, then Lucifer can go ahead with his plan. He's going to wipe out this entire plane. Is that what you want?"

"Lucifer's plan is doomed to fail," said Mercury. "Uzziel has already been informed of his intentions."

"Uzziel!" laughed Tiamat. "What's Uzziel going to do, send an army of bureaucrats armed with staplers? It would take weeks for Uzziel to get authorization for any kind of military deployment. By then, this plane will be finished. Uzziel is powerless to stop the invasion."

"He doesn't need to *stop* it," said Mercury. "All he has to do is redirect it. I won't bore you with the details, but thanks to a little interplanar jujitsu, the threat from Lucifer has been negated. In fact, the biggest danger right now is that Lucifer will figure out that he's been had and call off his surprise attack. If he does that, his forces will remain intact, and he may still be able to wreak a fair amount of havoc on this plane before Michael can put a stop to it. But if I can deliver Karl—dead or alive—then Lucifer will go forward with his plan, and Uzziel will take care of the rest.

"So you see," Mercury went on, "I can't risk you throwing a wrench into Lucifer's plan. And frankly, you've always been a bigger threat to this plane than Lucifer and his petty schemes. You're the one Heaven should be worried about. If you manage to return to power…well, I can't let that happen. Which is why I have to kill Karl."

"You can't be serious," Christine pleaded. "If you do this, you're just like them. Playing one side against the other, doing something you know is wrong in the interest of some greater plan you don't even fully understand."

"I understand enough," said Mercury grimly. "There's no other way to stop her. And to stop Lucifer. I have to kill him."

"No!" howled Karl. "I'm sorry I ate all the fries!"

"It's going to be OK, Karl," cooed Mercury.

"Please," said Tiamat. "I know you, Mercury. You don't have it in you."

"Karl, you have to trust me," said Mercury quietly. "Sometimes one of the good guys has to die for the greater good. You understand?"

Karl shook his head as vigorously as he could, given the proximity of the Bowie knife.

Christine urged, "Mercury, don't. Please don't."

"It's like book three," said Mercury. "Where the Urlock queen forces Charlie Nyx to kill his friend Simon with the Sword of the Seven Truths."

Karl looked confused for a moment. "But Charlie used his—"

"That's right, Karl," said Mercury. "Charlie used his sword to kill Simon. You understand? Because the evil queen forced him to."

A look of understanding began to penetrate Karl's face. "So I have to—"

"Yes, Karl. You have to die. Just like in the book. Just like in your favorite book."

"Actually I thought book two was more—"

Mercury clutched Karl's collar and spun him around so they were face-to-face.

"I'm sorry, Karl. I have no choice."

"I thought you were my friend!" wailed Karl.

"I am your friend, Karl. I will always be your friend."

"And I...yours," said Karl.

Mercury plunged the knife into Karl's heart. Karl screamed, a terrified, bloodcurdling, wake-the-dead sort of scream.

Mercury stabbed him again and again until Karl crumpled into a ball on the ground. Blood was everywhere.

Mercury sank limply to the ground. The blood-covered knife fell to the ground. He cradled Karl's head in his hands. "It's OK, Karl," he said gently. "You can sleep now."

Karl's body went limp.

Christine regarded this horrific scene in disbelief. Quite literally—she did not believe what she had just seen. The blood certainly looked real, and she had a hard time imagining that Mercury had been carrying a trick Bowie knife up his sleeve. But she also didn't believe Mercury had killed Karl. Partly because she didn't think he had it in him, but mostly because Karl had used the phrase "And I…yours." Something was *off*.

The demonic minions certainly looked convinced, but Tiamat was skeptical. "Is this one of your tricks, Mercury?"

"Does it *look* like a trick?" he demanded, still cradling Karl in his arms. Vast quantities of what looked very much like real blood continued to pour onto the ground beneath Karl. Christine still didn't believe it, but she had to admit that Mercury was a better actor than she would have expected. He looked like he was in real anguish, and his face was as white as chalk.

"No fluctuations in the energy channels," said Gamaliel. "He's not using miracles."

"A trick knife then," said Tiamat, sounding almost desperate to believe that Mercury hadn't had it in him to kill Karl.

"It's a real knife," said Christine, bending over to pick it up.

"Take it easy," warned a minion, gripping his rifle.

"Would you like me to demonstrate?" Christine said bitterly. "I happen to know a pretty good test to determine whether a knife is real. I just cut the head off a demon. If the demon screams like hell, it's a real knife."

Neither demon volunteered for the test. Karl's body remained limp. He did not appear to be breathing.

Tiamat approached Christine, holding out her hand. Christine handed her the knife. She regarded it suspiciously, running her thumb along the edge. A gasp escaped her lips. Blood dripped from her thumb, joining the growing puddle on the ground. The knife, it seemed, was quite real. She let it fall to the ground.

The fire had by this time enveloped the cottage and was moving briskly toward them. The smoke was getting thicker, and the heat pouring off it was getting uncomfortable.

"We should get out of here," said one of the minions. "Not just anybody can send a Class Five. Whoever sent that pillar is probably working on opening a portal to this plane right now, and we do not want to be around when they get here."

Tiamat knelt down next to Karl.

"No!" gasped Mercury weakly. "I won't allow you to desecrate his body. It's bad enough that you made me…" But he didn't have the energy to resist.

Tiamat felt Karl's neck for a pulse. After a few seconds, she stood up.

"No pulse," she said, sounding like someone who had just finished a jigsaw puzzle only to find she had one piece left over.

Christine didn't know whether to be relieved or appalled. Karl really was dead?

Tiamat, however, still seemed unconvinced. Incontrovertible evidence to the contrary, something wasn't right, and she knew it. She turned to squint into the oncoming inferno, weighing her options.

"Please," begged the minion who had spoken earlier. "If we don't leave now…"

"I'm well aware of the nuances of the situation!" snapped Tiamat. She turned to Mercury. "You realize the kind of trouble you're in, don't you? You can't just kill the Antichrist. They'll exile you for all eternity."

Mercury shrugged. "Extenuating circumstances," he said. "I'll argue that Lucifer selected Karl in bad faith. Once I get him posthumously disqualified as the Antichrist, he's just another unlucky mortal who got caught in the crossfire. And we both know that Heaven doesn't give a damn about the death of one mortal in the scheme of things."

Christine was suddenly overcome with rage. Mercury, it seemed, was no different from all the other callous, bureaucratic angels. "You bastard!" she screamed, leaping upon Mercury and pummeling him with her fists. "You killed him! You really killed him!"

Tiamat turned away in disgust. "Let's go," she said to her minions.

She fled through the woods, away from the quickly advancing forest fire, with Gamaliel and her minions in tow. The valley was enshrouded in darkness save for the orange glow of the burgeoning inferno.

FORTY-TWO

Christine continued to pummel at Mercury for another good minute before collapsing in exhaustion.

Mercury said, in a strained whisper, "That was really good. I think it may have been your performance toward the end there that really sold it."

"Performance!" snapped Christine furiously. "Karl is dead. He's *really* dead!"

"Yes," said Mercury, "that was a lucky turn of events, wasn't it?"

"Lucky? You killed him!"

"Hang on," said Mercury. "That's a bit of a leap, isn't it? Just because he's dead, that doesn't mean *I* killed him. Now drag him over there a ways, would you? I need him further away from the MEF."

"The what?"

"The Mundanity Enhancement Field. It interferes with my ability to do miracles. And Karl needs a miracle, pretty darn quick, if we're going to prevent damage to that unique brain of his."

Bewildered beyond the capacity to resist, she began to drag Karl by his feet further away from the cottage. "Are you going to help?" she said.

Mercury shook his head slowly. "Not feeling so good. Give me a minute." He crawled slowly after them on his hands and knees.

"That's far enough," he finally said.

"Now would you mind telling me what the hell is going on?" Christine demanded. "If you didn't kill him, then who did?"

"Act of God," said Mercury, taking a deep breath. Some of the color was coming back into his face. "Although I'd wager cholesterol had a little something to do with it as well." He put his hand on Karl's blood-soaked chest and closed his eyes.

After several breathless seconds, Karl's eyes opened. He clutched his chest. "Ow," he said. "What the hell?"

"You did great, Karl," said Mercury. "We fooled her, just like in the book."

Karl smiled. "Why does my chest hurt?"

"You had a bit of a heart attack back there, which was a nice touch, by the way. Thank God for all those Charlie's Grill cheeseburgers. I'm repairing some damage to your aorta now. In a few seconds you'll have the circulatory system of a forty-year-old."

"I'm only thirty-seven," Karl said.

"Yeah," replied Mercury. "There is a limit to what I can accomplish with minor miracles. You may want to check out the salad bar next time."

Karl nodded. Charlie's Grill had a *salad bar*?

"Wait," said Christine. "So did you actually stab him or not?"

"Of course not," said Mercury.

"So it was a trick knife?"

"No, it was a very real knife. The trick is to let the knife slide alongside your wrist so that it looks like you're really stabbing him."

"But isn't that dangerous, if you're using a real knife? You could cut your wrist open."

"Yeah," said Mercury. "That's where all the blood comes from."

"So that was *your* blood?"

Mercury nodded. "It's all right, I can make more. Hurts like a son of a bitch, though."

"So you stabbed yourself to make it look like Karl was bleeding?"

"Yes," said Mercury. "Kind of stupid, I know. OK, Karl. Feeling better?"

"Uh huh," said Karl.

"Good. We have a little trip to take. I have a surprise for you."

"Really?" said Karl. "Cool."

"So this was your plan all along?" asked Christine incredulously. "To pretend to kill Karl so that Katie…Tiamat would leave him alone?"

"Certainly not," said Mercury. "My plan went sideways about five minutes in. I didn't really have anything figured out beyond getting Uzziel to incinerate Izbazel. The rest was pure improv. Fortunately, I ran across a stray guard in the woods and managed to tie him up against a tree inside the MEF and appropriate his weapons."

"That sounds more like the Mercury I know," said Christine. "Always planning five minutes ahead."

"Yeah, well, it's still four and a half minutes ahead of just about everyone else, so it works out."

"But if you can bring people back from the dead, why not really stab him? Make it convincing. No offense, Karl."

"I can't bring people back from the dead," Mercury said. "I mean, I can restart someone's heart, but I can't resurrect someone who has bled to death. Tiamat knows that."

Something was still troubling Christine. "Hang on, if you two were acting out a scene from one of the Charlie Nyx books, why didn't Tiamat figure it out? She would have known if Charlie didn't really kill his friend, what's-his-name."

"Simon," said Karl. "Charlie and Simon have been best friends since they met in the lair of the Lizard King in chapter six of book one, *Charlie Nyx and the Flaming Cup*. You see, Simon's parents were—"

"She *would* have known," Mercury said, "if she had ever read any of the books."

"*Read* them?" said Christine. "I thought she *wrote* them."

"No way," said Mercury. "She doesn't have the patience to sit down and write an entire book. Hell, she got bored halfway through the construction of the Tower of Babel. She can blame outsourcing all she wants, but the real problem was the management."

"And you knew the whole time that she didn't write them?"

Mercury shrugged. "I always figured she had a ghostwriter."

"Wow," said Christine. "And you knew all along that Katie Midford and Tiamat were one and the same?"

"I suspected. The parts in the books about the tunnels under Anaheim Stadium were too accurate. I figured that Lucifer had put that part in as sort of a joke. It was meant to remind Katie Midford, best-selling author of the Charlie Nyx books, who was really in charge. She got to take credit for the books, but Lucifer was the one holding the strings."

Christine thought for a moment, trying to process all of this information. "So we did it? We stopped her? And the plan to smuggle the anti-bombs through my condo?"

"Almost," said Mercury. "First we have to pay a quick visit to Lucifer."

FORTY-THREE

Meanwhile, in an unremarkable two-bedroom condominium in Glendale with shiny new linoleum in the breakfast nook, Uzziel the seraph tried to get Christine's DVD player to work.

He was sitting on the couch, randomly pressing buttons with names like PROG and INPUT and quietly cursing whatever demonic entity was behind the creation of this device. He had it in his head to watch something from Christine's impressive Hugh Grant collection but thus far had had little success changing the channel from something called *World's Ugliest Pets*.

Just when his frustration with Christine's audiovisual components—not to mention his horror at a particularly ghastly hairless border collie—was beginning to make him doubt the existence of intelligent design in the cosmos, another angel shimmered into existence in the breakfast nook.

"Hey," said Uzziel. "Do you know how to work this thing?"

"What in the hell?" said the newcomer, a hulking gray figure.

"I'm trying to watch *Two Weeks Notice*, but I can't get it to—good heavens, what is that? Some kind of dwarf albino pig?"

"Uzziel. What are you doing here?"

"I might ask you the same thing, Malphas. I believe we had you assigned to Krakow."

"Ah yes, the hotbed of intrigue and kielbasa," said Malphas. "Can't imagine why anyone would want to leave *that* post."

"You were given that assignment because we thought it was the most we could trust you with. Evidently we overestimated you."

"Or perhaps you short-sighted bureaucratic fools don't recognize real talent when you see it."

"Tell me," Uzziel said, trying to avert his eyes from some sort of malformed flightless bird, "is this your talent on display now? Skulking through a secret portal in some poor woman's condo in Glendale?"

Malphas smiled, an ugly gray smile in the middle of his ugly gray face. "You want talent? Here's your talent." He held a glass apple in his outstretched palm, his thumb on the trigger.

"A housewarming gift?" said Uzziel. "How thoughtful. I brought something for you as well."

Uzziel continued to press buttons on the remote control. "Oh for Heaven's sake, if I could at least get this thing to change the channel…"

"I'm waiting," said Malphas.

"Yes, yes, hold on. Will you look at the teeth on that thing? Oh thank goodness, a commercial. Where was I? Oh yes. Here we are."

Uzziel set down the remote control and pulled a silvery box about the size of a Rubik's Cube from his pocket. Flipping the latch with his finger, he opened the lid to reveal a cubical lump of obsidian.

Malphas's face gray visage shifted a few shades toward white. "Is that…?"

"A Balderhaz Cube. Your anti-bomb won't work within fifty feet of here."

Malphas's eyes darted around, looking for a place to run.

Uzziel brandished a pistol in his other hand. "And this won't let you get more than fifty feet from here."

"A bullet isn't going to stop me."

"No, but I bet if I hit you with several of them at just the right angle, I can knock you back onto the linoleum."

"This is your plan? To send me back to the Floor where I can warn Lucifer to send the first batch through with AK-47s?"

"Look behind you," Uzziel said.

"Please," said Malphas. "Don't embarrass yourself."

"I have to admit that it was actually Mercury's idea, putting a temporary portal on top of your portal. It's not really an original idea, of course, portal-stacking, but it generally has so little practical application that it never occurred to me."

"A portal on top of another portal?" said Malphas, looking back at the breakfast nook to see a second glowing pattern superimposed on the first. "But then..."

"Anyone coming through the linoleum portal gets immediately transported through the temporary portal on top of it. Rather than being loosed on Los Angeles, your demon brigade finds itself on an unexpected layover at the planeport."

"Then we'll just—"

"Take over the planeport and then use the Mundane portal to transport to Megiddo, where Michael's army is waiting for you? Capital idea. Except that the planeport has security systems that prevent unauthorized portal openings—including the sort of rifts created by your anti-bombs. So you'll have a brigade of morons threatening baggage handlers with ornamental glass apples. And even if they somehow managed to cow the planeport security into submission by threatening to upset the aesthetic balance of the baggage claim area, they will still have to deal with Michael's better-trained, better-prepared, better-armed, and in pretty much every other way better force at Megiddo. Give it up, Malphas. You've been outmaneuvered."

Malphas stared weakly at the impotent glass apple in his hand, gradually coming to terms with the hopelessness of his situation.

"If what you say is true, then why am I here?" he asked finally. "Why didn't I transport to the planeport?"

"The temporary portal activated only after you came through. That's why I had to keep the cube shielded until you got here. Now that both portals are open, they are—temporarily at least—part of Mundane reality, so the MEF won't affect them. I assume that Lucifer sent you through to check things out and give him the all clear, correct?"

Malphas remained silent.

"Don't make this difficult, Malphas. You know how this works. We can do things the hard way or the excruciatingly hard way. So what'll it be? Answer quickly, please. The show's about to start back up. I'm finding it has a sort of morbid appeal."

Malphas grunted something barely perceptible.

"I'm sorry?"

"I said, 'the hard way.'"

"Excellent. Now why don't you hand me your little house-warming present and step outside. There are some cherubim in the hallway who will escort you outside the MEF so that you can phone up Lucifer and tell him that the conditions for a surprise attack are sunny with a chance of catastrophic success. Once his demonic horde begins showing up at the planeport, you'll be escorted somewhere comfortable where you can be debriefed on the details of Lucifer's plan."

Malphas, not feeling as if he had much of a choice, complied.

As a result, only seconds later a very surprised horde of demons bearing ornamental glass apples began pouring into the Temporary Portal Arrivals area at the angelic planeport. They were met by two dozen security officers bearing flaming swords and one diminutive cherub who buzzed annoyingly over their heads.

"The sting of a bumblebee will help ease the pain of arthritis for thirty days," offered the cherub.

FORTY-FOUR

Christine, Mercury, and Karl crept as stealthily as they could through the corridors of the planeport. Mercury had managed to convince Uzziel to create one more temporary portal—ostensibly so that Mercury could return to the Courts of the Most High and turn himself in. Mercury, however, had other plans. Amid the chaos surrounding the apprehension of the apple-toting horde, they managed to smuggle Karl unseen to the Infernal Plane.

"So," said Christine as they walked up the steps toward Lucifer's pink stucco house, "you made a deal with Lucifer to return Karl to him?"

"Yeah, but don't worry," replied Mercury. "He'll be perfectly safe. And comfortable. Hey, Karl, that's your house over there."

Karl looked in the direction of the cozy faux Tudor that Mercury was pointing out.

"Looks OK, I guess," said Karl. "My mom won't be there, right?"

"No, Karl. Your mom, along with almost everyone else in the Universe, has absolutely no idea where you are. That was part of the deal."

"And I can work on my music?"

"Absolutely," said Mercury. "I wrote a state-of-the-art sound mixing system into our contract with Lucifer. Plus a T1 Internet connection and full access to Lucifer's library of illegal recordings. That's like eighty million songs. And I'm not just talking about illegally downloaded recordings. I'm talking about *illegal recordings*. He's got a recording of Richard Nixon singing 'Tiny Bubbles' in the shower."

"Huh," said Karl, obviously thrilled to have a place where he could work undisturbed. "That's pretty cool, I guess."

"Yeah," said Mercury. "Also, I think I may have insisted on a crystal duck."

"OK," said Karl, as if he had expected as much.

"And he's not allowed to harass you in any way. I mean, I can't guarantee he's not going to show up at neighborhood barbecues or anything, but he shouldn't give you any trouble."

"Will he do my laundry?"

"Er, you want Lucifer to do your *laundry*? I didn't actually think to ask, but that might have been a deal breaker."

"Whatever. I just don't want to do it."

"I think we can work something out. Just keep in mind that Lucifer might be a little on edge when he finds out that—"

The front door of Lucifer's house swung open. "You!" howled the lanky, blond demon, wearing only a pair of Rocky and Bullwinkle boxer shorts and a navy blue terrycloth bathrobe. "You!"

"It's OK," said Mercury. "I'm no good with names either. It's *MER-kyer-ee*. Like the planet. And you're Lou…Lou…Lou something, am I right?"

"You told Heaven about my plan!"

"True," said Mercury. "Christine here and I told the Arbitration Panel of the Subcommittee for Adjudication of Matters of Alleged Violations of the Apocalypse Accord."

"That's a violation of our contract! Don't you realize what you have done? You will suffer torments unheard of, even on this Infernal Plane!"

"Sadly, no," said Mercury. "We told Heaven about your plan *before* we signed the contract. The contract, as I recall, has no provisions requiring that we go back in time and un-tell people that we had already told. It's your bad luck that we figured out your scheme, like, hours ago. The important thing is, I've told no one about your plan since the contract was signed. And as you can see, I've also delivered Karl Grissom, Antichrist par excellence. No one knows that he's alive except for me and Christine, who is the one who saved his life in the first place. I have held precisely to the letter of our contract. Now I believe Karl has some questions regarding late-night recording sessions. Are you the acting president of the homeowners' association here, or should he address his questions to another demon?"

"The Antichrist is no good to me now," growled Lucifer. "My demonic horde is stranded at the planeport, thanks to your meddling. You knew my plan would fail! You acted in bad faith!"

"Hang on," said Mercury. "I thought it was the good kind of faith that you didn't care for. I was under the impression that bad faith was OK in these parts."

"I will rain down fire upon you!"

"Again, no. Our contract guarantees my safety, as well as that of Karl and anyone else rescued from Tiamat as a part of his extraction."

"Tiamat," hissed Lucifer. "So she's the one behind all of this. She abducted the Antichrist to use him against me. I should have known you were in league with her."

"I'm not 'in league' with her. Well, it's true that I was once in *a* league with her, but it was a bowling league, and in any case, that was years ago. These days I'm a free agent. I work autonomously."

Christine cleared her throat.

"Sorry," said Mercury. "I'm working with Christine. We work together, autonomously. And you can't touch either of us. It's all right there in the contract. If you try raining fire down upon us, you're going to be in a hell storm of trouble yourself."

Lucifer fumed silently.

Mercury turned to Karl. "Karl, it's been fun. Sorry I called you a dickweed. Lucifer here will get you your keys. And, Lucifer, I know you're fond of Karl, but no sneaking out to toss pebbles at Karl's bedroom window. I remember what it was like to be young and in love."

Mercury wheeled about and offered his arm to Christine. "Shall we?"

Christine nodded. "Let's get the hell out of here."

FORTY-FIVE

Christine stood, once again, on the verge of Armageddon.

Having returned to the planeport, she and Mercury had taken the only available portal back to the Mundane Plane—the one that opened to Megiddo.

"So despite all of our efforts," said Christine, "the Apocalypse goes on as planned."

"Presumably," said Mercury. "We can only hope, as you say, that the good guys end up being good guys and don't make things any worse than they need to be. Lucifer bet everything on his sneak attack; he's going to be woefully unprepared when the Heavenly host starts showing up here ready to give him a beat-down. Not only that, but the downside of pulling out of the Apocalypse Accord, from Lucifer's point of view, is that it frees up Heaven to attack him anywhere, anytime. Michael will presumably seize upon the current situation as an opportunity to wipe out Lucifer once and for all."

"And the Four Attaché Cases of the Apocalypse are still out there somewhere?"

"I had to agree to give the Case of War back to Uzziel to get him to go along with my plan without asking too many questions.

Lucifer still has the Case of Death, but he'll probably get rid of it once he starts trying to build a case for plausible deniability of this whole mess. That mutant strain of corn is still wreaking havoc in South Africa, thanks to the Case of Famine, and I think the World Health Organization has the Case of Pestilence."

"That can't be good," said Christine.

"No. I'd expect that to go horribly wrong sometime in the next few days."

"And I assume that the situation in the Middle East has only gotten worse."

"A safe assumption. It usually has."

"So there's really nothing we can do to stop it?"

Mercury shrugged. "These impromptu diabolical schemes are one thing. Stopping the Apocalypse is a whole different deal."

Christine nodded grimly. "So what happened to Izbazel, anyway? You said he got hit by that pillar of fire near Tiamat's hideout. Is he dead?"

"Angels don't die. Izbazel is probably in the hands of the Heavenly authorities. Pillars of fire, in addition to being fantastically destructive and really cool to watch, act as temporary portals. Whatever was left of his corporeal form was sucked back to a special area of the planeport, where he could be collected by agents assigned to apprehending renegade angels."

"What about Tiamat and Gamaliel and the rest of her minions?"

"They're on the run. I wouldn't be surprised if Heaven picks them up, too. They will need to lay low for a while to avoid the wrath of both Heaven and Hell."

"And Harry?"

"Harry's dead."

"Right, but what does that mean? Is he in Heaven?"

"Beats me," said Mercury. "What happens to you mortals when you die is one of the great mysteries of the Universe."

"So we don't go to be with the angels in Heaven?"

"Not that I know of. I hope not, for your sake. Most angels are wankers."

"Yeah, I noticed that. And what's going to happen to you?"

"Well, I did foil Tiamat's plan to subjugate all of humanity and thwart Lucifer's plot to double-cross Heaven and bring about untold destruction, so at the very least I can look forward to spending the next five hundred years filling out paperwork."

Christine nodded, thinking about everything that had happened over the past few days. After some time, she spoke. "Why did you do it?"

"Well," Mercury said, "in all honesty, I was going to just make regular Rice Krispies bars, but I was out of marshmallows. I saw that we had some of those Peeps, and I thought—"

"Seriously, Mercury. I thought you didn't care about anything. Why did you get involved?"

Mercury waved a hand dismissively. "Oh, you know. The whole business with the linoleum portal…and trying to kill Karl. I mean, what did he ever do to anyone? It's like that book, you know…"

"*To Kill a Mockingbird*."

"No, the one with the kids on the island."

"*Lord of the Flies*."

"No, you know. They have a raft, and they're sailing down the river."

"*Huck Finn*."

"And then they get attacked by those flying monkeys."

"Flying monkeys? Are you talking about *The Wizard of Oz*? There was no island in the—"

"*Charlie Nyx and the Terrible Flying Monkeys*! That's it! Book four. It's like that. At the end, where Charlie Nyx has to choose between saving his sweetheart Madeline or killing all the flying monkeys so that they can no longer terrorize the good people of Anaheim."

Christine's eyes narrowed. "How in the hell is this anything like that?"

Mercury thought for a moment. "Well, I suppose it isn't, *exactly*. Still, the whole business seemed unsportsmanlike."

While they talked, a young girl in her early teens was dawdling nearby. She was making a not very convincing show of being interested in a collection of pebbles at her feet.

"Can we help you with something?" Christine said to the girl.

"Uh, sorry, I couldn't help overhearing," she said. "Were you talking about the Apoc...the end of the world?"

"Yeah," Christine said wearily. "We just thwarted two demonic plans for world domination only to have the Apocalypse proceed as planned. It's been one of those kinds of weeks."

"I know what you mean," said the girl. "My dad makes me clean up after my little brothers sometimes. I get so sick of it. It's so unfair. Day after day after day. Sometimes I just want to *end it all*, you know?"

Christine instinctively moved closer to the girl, worried that she might have been planning to throw herself over the railing to the rocky ravine below.

"You're a little young to be so defeated," said Christine.

"Am I?" asked the girl. "How old do you have to be before you're allowed to be defeated?"

Mercury peered curiously at the girl, as if noticing something a little funny about her.

"Well," said Christine, "you know, that's a good point. There's never really a good age to be defeated. I guess we all just have to keep going the best we can."

"Yeah," said the girl, smiling weakly. "I guess. You're kind of a nice person, you know that?"

"Thanks," said Christine. "Unfortunately, that doesn't seem to count for much in the scheme of things."

"You'd be surprised," said the girl. "Hey, can I talk to you for a moment?" She glanced at Mercury. "In private?"

"Um, sure," said Christine. "But I'm not sure what—"

"It's OK, Christine," said Mercury. "I need to get going anyway. Can't stay in one spot too long, you know."

"Wait, you're *leaving*?" said Christine. "Just like that?"

"I can do a little soft-shoe first if you like."

"It's just that…" said Christine. "I was just starting to…not hate you so much."

"Yeah," said Mercury. "You're pretty cool, too. Unfortunately, duty calls."

"Duty? Since when do you care about doing your duty?"

"Oh, not *my* duty," said Mercury. "But if everybody else keeps insisting on doing their duty, somebody's got to clean up the mess."

"Yeah," said Christine. "You're surprisingly good at that."

"Also, I have an allergy to paperwork," said Mercury. "If I stick around much longer, Heaven is going to haul my ass in for debriefing. In fact," he said, glancing at the young girl, "I suspect that the only reason I haven't been apprehended yet is the fact that I have a friend upstairs."

The girl turned to him and smiled an inscrutable smile. Her face was youthful, but that smile had millennia of experience behind it.

"Good-bye, Christine," said Mercury, and he slipped away.

FORTY-SIX

"My name's Christine."

"Yes, I know," said the girl. "I'm Michelle." She was thin and wiry, and her kinky chestnut hair framed a pretty but stern face.

"Nice to meet you, Michelle. Are your parents...?"

"I'm *the* Michelle."

Christine regarded the girl, trying to make sense of this remark.

"Archangel," the girl said. "Commander of the Heavenly army."

"But he's...you're..."

"Mistranslation," said the girl. "You know how male-dominated cultures are. I'd like to think it was an honest mistake, but Gabrielle isn't so charitable. I allow the misunderstanding to persist for security reasons."

"So you...you're the highest ranking angel there is?"

"Well, I command the army. Technically, I answer to the Seraphic Senate. They tend to follow my lead on military matters, though."

"Why are you here?"

"This is where it ends," said Michelle. "This is Megiddo, the site of the final battle between good and evil."

"I know. I've been here before."

"Really? Did you get a T-shirt? There's an excellent selection in the gift shop."

"So I suppose you're here to do some final reconnaissance or something? Make sure everything is in order for the big Apocalypse?"

"Actually," said Michelle, "I'm here to talk to you. I've been watching you with some interest. It's difficult not to empathize with your situation."

"You've been watching me this whole time? Through everything?"

"Not the whole time, but long enough. I was there when Isaakson died."

Christine's eyes widened. "You...you were the one who helped me escape from that house!"

"I was."

"So you're behind all this?" said Christine. "You understand how I got sucked into this whole mess?"

"Actually, no," replied Michelle. "Your involvement is still a bit of a mystery. None of the factions planned on you playing much of a role. Somehow events conspired to place you in the middle of all the action."

"But if I wasn't expected to play some important role in the Apocalypse, why did you save me?"

Michelle smiled grimly. "I felt somewhat responsible for your circumstances."

"Why? Did you have something to do with that rocket?"

Michelle nodded. She said, "Isaakson was supposed to be a known quantity. It had come to our attention that his heart was no longer in the fight. I spoke with him not long before you arrived, under the guise of a Syrian informant. I got the impression that he was on the verge of consolidating his gains and calling off any further offensive action. We needed him to continue escalating the situation."

"So you killed him? Because he had the gall to hesitate on the path to Armageddon? And nearly killed me in the process, I might add."

"I redirected a rocket that was going to hit a civilian dwelling. Rather than seven civilians dying, one elderly general died. A military officer who, I might add, was scheduled to be killed in a few days anyway. All I did was hasten his death to ensure that the conflict would escalate as expected."

"Yeah, well, you could just as easily have turned the rocket into a bowl of petunias," said Christine. "Nobody *had* to die."

"At the time, I was of the opinion that someone did. I'm reassessing that opinion at present."

"So you left me at the hospital with the spelunking note? And the Attaché Case of War?"

"I did. As I was technically not supposed to have any contact with Isaakson, I couldn't risk holding on to the case. I figured it was as safe in your hands as anywhere."

"Then you've been watching me since that rocket strike?"

"No, but I have enough intelligence sources to piece together most of your adventures over the past few days. I have a sense of what you've been through."

"I doubt that."

The girl peered curiously at her. "Can I ask you a question?"

"Sure," said Christine wearily. "Why not."

"What would you do if you were in my position?"

"Hmmm," said Christine. "I'd avoid making any big decisions at this point. I thought I wanted to be a veterinarian when I was your age."

"Lucifer has given me an opening," explained Michelle, "and I'm tempted to take it. To give him the ass-kicking he's been asking for since he first started screwing with the Plan down here. He's off-balance and unprepared for the battle. On the other hand, an operation like this inevitably creates a great deal of collateral damage, and by withdrawing from the Apocalypse Accord, Lucifer has given me a fair amount of flexibility. I could call the whole thing off and just hope for the best. Lucifer's organization would remain intact, but his influence on this plane would be mitigated to some degree."

"Well," said Christine, "the way I see it, God gave us this planet. This plane, whatever. To humanity, I mean. Not the angels. I understand that He's evidently given the angels some authority over certain things, and I won't pretend to understand how all that works. But your organization is clearly too vast and complicated for even you to fully understand or control. And the bigger and more powerful an organization is, the more bureaucratic hoops its members have to go through to get anything done. What I'm trying to say, I guess, is that while I'm sure you run a bang-up organization, it doesn't frankly seem to do us a whole lot of good down here on the ground. You folks are so far removed from the actual events that when you finally do something, it's usually too little, too late. Or far too much, too early. To us down here, your involvement is just another terrifying unknown. Terrifying unknowns tend to create fear, and fear tends to bring out the worst in people."

"So you'd prefer that we pull out of this plane entirely and just leave you to fend for yourselves?"

"I suppose not," admitted Christine. "Granted, if Lucifer is going to keep scheming away, then I suppose some involvement from your side is a necessary evil, if you'll pardon the expression. But maybe you could limit yourselves to preventing Lucifer from wreaking too much havoc down here, so at least humanity has a chance."

"You would have me call off the attack then. Put off the Apocalypse."

"Look, the way I see it, there are plenty of battles between good and evil on this plane already. You might have noticed that we've got a fair amount of war, death, famine, and the other one…"

"Pestilence."

"Right, and pestilence without any help from you. I don't think you need to go out of your way to ratchet up the stakes. Just give us a chance to work things out down here."

"Hmmm," said Michelle. "You understand what you are asking for? You are asking, essentially, that the Apocalypse be left in your hands."

"In the hands of humanity, correct. Don't misunderstand me, I'm not saying you can't help out. All I'm asking is that you don't blindly follow this SPAM, or whatever guidelines you are using. Don't just mechanically follow rules that were written up thousands of years ago, for reasons that you don't understand, in a language nobody speaks anymore. Ask yourself, before you act on the basis of one of these rules, whether you're helping our cause or hurting it."

"A reasonable request. The SPAM is a very powerful document, but between you and me, I find certain parts of it nearly impossible to understand. There is, even among my wisest advisors, a good deal of disagreement regarding the meaning of some sections. Trying to use it to plan a military operation is hopeless."

"This is really all up to you then? Whether the Apocalypse goes forward or not, I mean? You get to make the decision."

"Oh my, no," said Michelle. "I have tactical authority, of course, but all I can do about a decision like this is report to the Senate Committee on Strategic Interplanar Intervention. I do, however, have some pull, and at this point my recommendation could very well make the difference."

"And what are you going to tell them?"

"Well," said Michelle, "as inclined as I am to leap off this precipice, I do find your case compelling. I'm in a difficult position, you see. On one hand, your actions allowed the Apocalypse to proceed according to Plan. I could take that as a sign that it is part of the Divine Will that the Apocalypse go forward. On the other hand, you're only involved in the first place because I violated the SPAM to kill General Isaakson and to spare you."

"So," said Christine, "if you hadn't violated the SPAM, then your Plan—the so-called Divine Plan—would have failed. Your failure to follow the Plan was a critical element in the Plan's success."

"At least as far as I can tell," said Michelle. "That is, perhaps the Divine Plan would have found another way to work itself out, even if I hadn't acted the way I did. Maybe in the end it makes no difference what I do."

"But you're the Archangel Mi—er, Michelle!" Christine sputtered. "If your actions don't matter, then whose do? I have to believe that it makes a difference. I mean, I wouldn't be alive if you hadn't saved me."

"On the other hand, your life wouldn't have been in danger if I hadn't redirected that rocket to kill Isaakson."

Christine groaned in exasperation. "We could play this game forever," she said. "You can't live your life according to far-off consequences you can't possibly foresee. Ultimately, you just have to make the best decision you can."

Michelle sighed. "It's a paradox, to be sure. By violating the Plan, I made it possible for the Plan to succeed. Do I take that to mean that the Plan is meant to succeed, or that I am meant to circumvent it?"

"I'm not sure it means anything," said Christine. "To quote one of the minor prophets: 'You can choose a ready guide in some celestial voice; if you choose not to decide, you still have made a choice.'"

"That's quite profound," Michelle said. "Is that Habakkuk?"

"Rush," said Christine.

"Of course," said Michelle. "I remember when Lucifer lost that bet to Neil Peart."

"So what is your decision?"

Michelle stared over the edge of the valley for a time before answering. "The matter requires further study," she said. "I believe I'll recommend that the Senate appoint an investigative committee and put off taking any further action until the committee has made its findings. Then there will be the interminable hearings regarding the report that the committee generates, the inevitable scapegoating and bureaucratic reshuffling, culminating in a lengthy debate about what course of action, if any, to take."

"How long do you expect this process to take?"

"I wouldn't expect anything this century."

"Wonderful. So humanity gets a second chance."

"Yet again," said Michelle. "I hope you appreciate what this means."

"I do," said Christine. "I will. Absolutely." The Universe, she thought, might not be such a jerk after all. One thought still nagged at her though. "Perhaps it's too much to ask, but I was wondering... Do you think I could be reimbursed for new linoleum in my breakfast nook?"

"Hmmm," said the angelic general. "I'll see what I can do. That's not really my department."

FORTY-SEVEN

In a dingy gray pub on a dingy gray Tuesday afternoon in Cork, Ireland, a demon called Eddie sat, forgotten by the Universe, nursing a pint of Guinness. It had been nearly a year since he had last talked to Gamaliel, and he could only assume that his supposed savior had gotten too busy with his scheming to make the call to the higher-ups at the MOC.

"Figures," he muttered to no one in particular.

The worst part was, he had actually begun to enjoy the visits from Gamaliel. And now, not only had Gamaliel disappeared, he had lost contact with Harry Giddings as well. Eddie was more desperately lonely and bored than he had ever been before. Gamaliel's presence had given him some hope that there was some reason for him being here; now he was once again faced with the prospect that his exile on the Mundane Plane was just a cosmic accident. It was almost too much to bear.

The pub door swung open to let in a blast of cold, damp air, and along with it a pudgy, bespectacled man who appeared to be in his mid-forties. The man carried against his chest a large, brown, accordion-style folder wrapped in a rubber band. He let the folder hit the bar with a thud.

"Bloody paperwork," said the man. He signaled the bartender for a drink.

Eddie grunted his assent. One thing Eddie did not miss about working for the MOC was the interminable paperwork.

The man accepted a pint of beer from the bartender and, after taking a few sips, sighed heavily and removed the rubber band from the folder. Out of the folder slid a massive stack of papers, perhaps seven or eight hundred pages thick.

"Bloody paperwork indeed," said Eddie, with renewed sympathy. "What on earth is all that?"

"Report," said the man, who was now thumbing through the pages, evidently in search of something.

"Did you write it?"

"Did I…goodness, no. It's bad enough I have to read the damned thing."

"And have you?"

"Have I what?"

"Read it."

"Oh. Well, you know, it's not something that you *read*, start to finish. A lot of it is reference, you know, and footnotes. A ghastly number of footnotes. And appendices. Something like thirty-seven appendices. It's not something one, you know, *reads*."

"Why was it written if nobody is going to read it?"

"Well, as I say, it's a sort of reference with, you know, an annotated chronology, cross-referenced glossary, and several hundred pages of recommendations."

"Recommendations for what?"

The man sighed. "The organization I work with has become aware of certain *irregularities*. Violations of protocol, that sort of thing."

"I see," said Eddie, who didn't.

"Yes," said the man. "Rather serious violations. Things not being done by the book. Not entirely on the up and up, as it were."

"Right," said Eddie. "Irregularities, you might say."

"Precisely," said the man. "Irregularities."

"And these irregularities," Eddie went on, "they're a serious problem."

"Well," said the man. "Well. You've got to have, you know, *procedures*. Things have to be done in a certain way."

"Of course," said Eddie. "Because if they're not…"

"Yes, exactly," said the man. "If they're not…"

"Things wouldn't be entirely aboveboard."

"Absolutely," said the man. "Not aboveboard."

"So this is a report on how the appropriate procedures were not followed?"

"Correct."

"With recommendations for additional procedures?"

"Yes, exactly. And footnotes."

"I see. And you think the footnotes will make all the difference this time around?"

The spectacled man's eye moved slowly back and forth between the mountain of papers and the pint of beer several times before eventually settling on the beer. He drank deeply.

"Here's the problem as I see it," said Eddie. "People don't want to read some dry, long-winded report with thousands of footnotes. People hate footnotes."

"What's wrong with footnotes?"

"They're satanic."

"No!"

"Yes. Footnotes were invented by Lucifer in 1598 to prevent anyone from reading the fine print in the Edict of Nantes."[11]

---

11   The veracity of this statement cannot be confirmed.

"Really?"

"Really."

"So what do you suggest?"

"What you need is a narrative."

"A narrative?"

"You know, a story. Are you familiar with the Warren Commission?"

"Should I be?"

"They're the group that investigated the Kennedy assassination."

"Oh, I saw that movie with Kevin Costner. That was the one with the magic bullet that changes course in midair."

"Exactly. You remember the movie because it was a story. Even if it was a contrived and fantastically inaccurate story that completely glosses over Nixon's apprenticeship with the demon Moloch."

"Er..."

"The point is, if you want people to pay attention, you need to give them a compelling story with likable characters and a satisfying resolution."

"So...no recommendations?"

"No. At least nothing explicit. Everything has to arise organically from the story."

"Can I tack a moral on the end at least?"

"Absolutely not. I mean, you can try to wrap things up a bit in the final chapter, and maybe hint at some overarching themes, but no moral."

"But how am I supposed to boil everything in this report down to a single story? There are hundreds of individuals involved. Each one of them has a story of his or her own."

Eddie reached over to the pile of papers, jamming his thumb into the stack about halfway down. He divided the stack in two and slapped the top stack upside down on the counter. Then he ran his finger down the exposed page until he hit a name.

"Here," he said. "This is your main character."

"Mercury?" said the man. "But he's just a minor player. He had almost nothing to do with…"

"Doesn't matter," said Eddie. "Wrap the story around him. He's your hero."

Eddie split the text again, finding another name.

"And this one. Christine. A woman, right? Perfect. Maybe start off with her and introduce her and the reader to Mercury about eight chapters in."

"Wow," said the man. "You're really good at this. Are you a writer?"

"Something like that," said Eddie. "I'm in something of a lull right now, but I've done a fair bit on the Ottoman Empire."

"Ah, so you're familiar with this sort of bureaucracy, then. What with the diwans and viziers and all."

"Oh, well, you know," said Eddie, a bit sheepishly. "My work was mostly conjecture."

"Tell me," the man said, "considering, as you say, that you find yourself in a bit of a lull, would you be interested in helping me out with this report?"

"Er, I'm afraid I'm actually on a sort of retainer… My employers have a very strict policy…"

"Your employers have you assigned to an important lull, do they?"

"The thing is, I'm actually expecting…"

"Expecting what?"

"Well, I've been waiting…"

"For what?"

"Nothing, I suppose. I've actually been let go. I keep thinking that someday they will call, but I suppose I should accept that it's never going to happen."

"So you're free then?"

"I'm free."

"Wonderful. I'll go get the rest of the report from the car."

"The *rest* of the report?"

"Oh yes. This is only the introduction."

Speechless, Eddie turned over the stack to look at the cover page. It read:

An Annotated Accounting of the Irregularities
in Execution of the Apocalypse Accord

Presented by the Independent Seraphic Senate
Commission on Apocalyptic Irregularities in
the Execution of the Apocalypse Accord

"Hold on," said Eddie, his mind reeling. "Are you with the MOC?"

"I'm a little higher up in the bureaucracy."

"The Senate?"

"Higher."

"The archangels?"

"Look, Eddie. I am who I am. Are you going to help me out or not?"

"So this organization…it's…"

"The angelic bureaucracy itself. Heaven. Hell. All of it."

"Does this have something to do with Gamaliel's schemes? The bit about the Apocalypse?"

"That's part of it. I need someone to tell the higher-ups the truth of what happened over the past few days. I need, as you say, a compelling account."

"Why me?"

"You're vaguely familiar with the events, but you're not directly involved. Besides, I like to work with unknowns. It's sort of my thing."

"But I don't really know anything. I've been stuck here in Cork."

"No worries," the man said, patting the ream of paper. "Everything you need to know is right here. And in six boxes in my trunk."

"I see. And if I want to do some investigating of my own, you'll make sure I have access to everybody I need to talk to within the bureaucracy?"

"You're welcome to talk to anyone you like. I'll even make sure you're able to communicate via Angel Band. But I'm afraid I can't vouch for you. My involvement has to be off the record."

"And to whom am I presenting this report, exactly?"

"You should address it to the High Council of the Seraphim, but you can give it to anyone who wants to read it."

"I'm afraid I'm a bit rusty in High Seraphic."

"English should be fine."

"I suppose they will want it in anapestic tetrameter?"

"Whatever you feel comfortable with."

"No footnotes, though. I won't do footnotes."

"Actually," said the man, "I'm rather fond of footnotes. Maybe just a few?"

"How many?"

"I was thinking forty."

"No way," said Eddie. "I'll give you ten."

"How about twelve? I've always liked the number twelve."

"Fine. Twelve footnotes.[12] How will they know I'm telling the truth?"

"They won't. That's why your account has to be compelling."

"Do I have any guarantee that anyone will read it?"

"None."

"This has got to be the worst assignment I've ever heard of."

"Worse than whiling away eternity in a pub in Cork, waiting to hear from a bureaucracy that's forgotten all about you?"

Eddie sighed. "All right," he said. "I'll do it."

"I thought you might," said the man. "Oh, and be sure to use your real name. None of this 'Eddie' business."

"Right."

Eddie pulled a weathered notebook and a pen from his jacket and began to write:

To Your Holiness, the High Council of the Seraphim,

Greetings from your humble servant, Ederatz,
Cherub First Class,
Order of the Mundane Observation Corps

"Perfect," said the spectacled man. "I'll go get the rest from the car."

---

12   Divine providence is a mysterious and wonderful thing.

ABOUT THE AUTHOR

Photo by Julia Kroese, 2006

Robert Kroese's sense of irony was honed growing up in Grand Rapids, Michigan—home of the Amway Corporation and the Gerald R. Ford Museum, and the first city in the United States to fluoridate its water supply. In second grade, he wrote his first novel, the saga of Captain Bill and his spaceship *Thee Eagle*. This turned out to be the high point of his academic career. After barely graduating from Calvin College in 1992 with a philosophy degree, he was fired from a variety of jobs before moving to California, where he stumbled into software development. As this job required neither punctuality nor a sense of direction, he excelled at it. He continued to write in his spare time, and in 2006 he started his blog, www.mattresspolice.com, as an outlet for his absurdist wit. Around the same time, he was appointed to be a deacon in his church, and this juxtaposition of roles prompted him to create the character of Mercury—an acerbic, antiestablishment angel who is well-meaning but not particularly well-behaved. Kroese lives in Ripon, California, with his wife and two children.